Praise for the
Home Repair Is Homicide
mysteries of
Sarah Graves

"Just the right prescription for a post-repair rest."
—*Orlando Sentinel*

"Everything's Jake—until she starts snooping."
—*New York Daily News*

"With an intricate plot, amusing characters and a wry
sense of humor, Sarah Graves spins a fun,
charming mystery that is sure to make you smile and
keep you guessing right up until the end."
—*Booknews* from The Poisoned Pen

"Charming." —*New Orleans Times-Picayune*

"A winning addition . . . A sleuth as tough as the nails
she drives into the walls of her 1823 Federal home
enhances a clever plot. . . . Many will relish the vividly
described Down East setting, but for anyone who's
ever enjoyed making a home repair it's the
accurate details of the restoration of Jake's old house
that will appeal the most."
—*Publishers Weekly*

"Graves gives us a lively look at small-town life in
charming down-east Maine. Her characters, as always,
are captivating examples of Americana and their
relationships with each other are inspired."
—*The Old Book Barn Gazette*

THE
DEAD CAT
BOUNCE

Sarah Graves

BANTAM BOOKS

New York Toronto
London Sydney Auckland

302274921

THE DEAD CAT BOUNCE
A Bantam Crime Line Book

PUBLISHING HISTORY
Bantam mass market edition / September 1998
Bantam reissue / March 2004

Published by
Bantam Dell
A Division of Random House, Inc.
New York, New York

This is a work of fiction. Names, characters, places, and
incidents either are the product of the author's imagination or
are used fictitiously. Any resemblance to actual persons, living or
dead, events, or locales is entirely coincidental.

ISBN 0-553-57857-X

Manufactured in the United States of America
Published simultaneously in Canada

OPM   18   17   16   15   14   13   12   11   10   9

This book is for John Ellerson Squibb.

dead cat bounce *n.* Stock market jargon for a small, temporary rise in a stock's trading price, after a sharp drop.

Thanks to all who helped: John Squibb, David and Kathy Chicoine and *Bullet 'n' Press*, Bob and Ravin Gustafson, Rebecca Robinson, John Foster, Charlie Graham, Judy McGarvey, Sandi Shelton, David Orrell, Kay Kudlinski, Amanda Clay Powers, Kate Miciak, Al Zuckerman, and the friendly folks at the Kissing Fish dive shop in Calais, Maine.

THE
DEAD CAT
BOUNCE

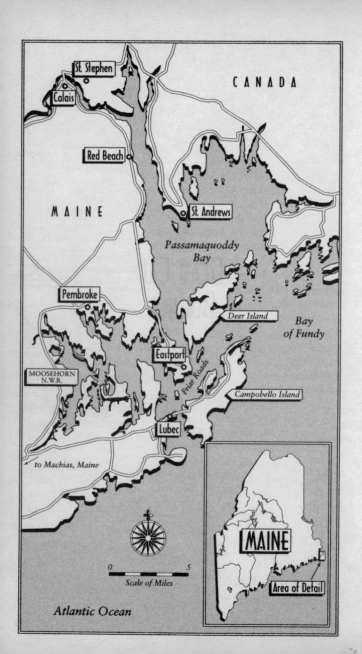

1

My house is old, and rambling, and in some disrepair, and I think that it is faintly haunted: a cold spot forming inexplicably on the stairway, a scuttling in the hall. Then of course there is the matter of the enigmatic portrait, whose mystery I had not yet managed to resolve on that bright April morning when, after living cheerfully and peacefully in the house for over a year, I found a body in the storeroom.

Coming upon a body is an experience, like childbirth or a head-on collision, that takes the breath out of a person. I went back through the passageway between the kitchen and the small, unheated room where in spring I kept dog food and dahlia bulbs, and where apparently I now stored corpses.

"Ellie," I said, "there's a dead man out there on the floor."

Ellie White looked up from the kitchen workbench where she was planting pepper seeds, sprinkling a few into each little soil-filled peat pot, to be set out later in the cold frame. Ellie has coppery hair cut short around a thin, serious face lightly dusted with freckles; her pale blue eyes are so intense that even through her glasses, her gaze makes you feel your X-ray is being taken.

Her index finger paused in the act of tamping soil onto a pepper seed. "Who?" she asked.

Sometimes I think Ellie has formaldehyde in her veins. For instance, when I moved to Maine I thought sill work meant painting them, and if you have ever restored an elderly house you will understand the depths of my innocence; sill work is slightly less radical than tearing the house down and starting over entirely, and almost as expensive, and if you don't do it the old house ends up at the bottom of the cellar-hole.

Ellie, upon hearing that this was what my old house needed, merely remarked how lucky I was that I could pay for it, because she knew of another woman whose house had needed sill work, too, and that woman was now living in the cellar-hole. Ellie's comment shut me up pretty quickly, as she had intended, and I resigned myself to getting the job done in spring, but along about March I'd discovered that sill work was only the beginning. There was also the poignant little problem of the rot-raddled floor joists, and of the support beams holding up the floor joists.

Or rather, not holding them up. "I don't know who. He's lying facedown in the corner where everything sags. I should have had that floor jacked up last autumn."

Ellie was wearing denim coveralls, a bright yellow turtleneck with jade-green turtles satin-stitched onto it, and shiny green gardening clogs over thick, yellow socks. On anyone else the outfit would have been hilarious, but Ellie is so tall and slender that she could wear a painter's drop cloth, possibly with a couple of frayed dishrags belted around it, and still look just like a Paris runway model.

"I don't think the floor is the issue here," she said.

"That's because it's not your floor. The only thing holding that floor up now is habit, and when the homicide detectives and the medical examiner and I don't know who all else start tramping in and out of there, *then* that floor is going to . . ."

She was looking at me as if I'd just arrived from Mars. "Jacobia," she said, "I don't know what kind of law enforcement you got used to, back in the big city where you come from."

She picked up the telephone, dialed George Valentine's number, and let it ring. "But in case you haven't noticed, you're not in New York anymore. You're in Eastport, Maine, three hours from Bangor and a heck of a lot farther from anywhere else, and the only person tramping in and out of that storeroom is going to be George. That is, if he ever answers his phone. He was over at my house earlier, but I don't know where he is now."

Of course it was George's number. In Eastport, George was it: if you had a fire, or a flood, or a skunk in the crawlspace, George was the man you wanted, which was lucky since the rest were out on fishing boats: dragging for scallops, hauling lobster pots, or collecting sea urchins, depending upon the season.

"I'm going out there," Ellie said, after George had picked up at last and promised to be right over.

People in Eastport do not think the telephone grows naturally out of the tympanic membrane, and some of them will actually decide whether to answer it or not based on what sort of news they are expecting. But George always answered his telephone sooner or later on account of being the clam warden, on call to make sure diggers had valid clam licenses, chase poachers out of forbidden clam areas, and spot-check the clams themselves with his two-inch metal claim ring, through which a legally harvestable bivalve must not be able to pass.

"I think," Ellie added, "we should make sure the man is really dead."

This struck me as pointless, since an ice pick in the cranium promised little in the way of future prospects. But Ellie was determined; it was part of her downeast

Maine heritage, like being able to navigate in the fog or knowing how to dress out a deer.

"It might be he's only wounded," Ellie said. "It might be we can still do something for him."

Right, and it might be that next we could multiply some loaves and fishes. When she had gone I ran a glass of water and stood there by the sink, pondering whether to drink it or not. Just breathing in and out suddenly seemed to require a series of massive, separately considered decisions, as if each small action of mine had abruptly become huge compared to all the ones the dead man was not taking.

Outside my kitchen window a flock of cedar waxwings descended on the crabapple tree and began devouring frozen fruit, their short, metallic cries creating a happy clamor. A shower of snow as fine as salt fell around them, whitening the snow already lying on the ground, so their lime-green feathers and candy-corn beaks stood out as brightly as paint drops.

Down at the breakwater, the big ship *Star Verlanger* sounded her massive horn and cast off, loaded with paper pulp, and the dockworkers jumped in their pickup trucks and headed for a well-earned bottle of Narragansett beer, no bottle of which the dead man would be enjoying. I wondered if his absence would be noticed, or if he was from away. Whichever; by tonight, news of his death would be all over town.

That was what I thought when the whole thing began. But back then, I didn't know the half of it.

2

My name is Jacobia Tiptree, and my ex-husband says I am insane. I have proved this, he says, by giving up a perfectly charming little townhouse on the upper east side of Manhattan—complete with doorman, elevator, and building superintendent—for a huge antique structure every centimeter of which needs paint, plaster, or the underpinnings required to hold up both. The roof leaks, the gutters dangle, and the bricks in the chimneys are quietly turning to sand; when the wind blows hard, which it does very often here, the windows rattle as if they are trying to jump out of their frames, and if you put a marble down on the kitchen floor it will probably roll forever.

I found the place on a warm August day when the garden was clotted with raspberries and zinnias, poppies and Michaelmas daisies whose blooms were wide as saucers. I was coming back from Halifax and the kind of contentious stockholders' meeting that sets one to wondering how early man ever found his way out of the cave, and why, considering his natural tendencies, he didn't stay there, when on impulse I drove over the long, curving causeway connecting Moose Island with the U.S. mainland.

I bought my lunch of a sandwich and coffee at the IGA, and walked all over town before sitting down on the green-painted front steps of a big old white house whose bare windows showed a shimmeringly vacant interior. In front of the house I stood on tiptoe and peered in, watching a patch of sunshine move slowly across a pale maple floor that was badly in need of refinishing. Someone had torn the carpeting down from the stairs; the risers looked wormy with old nail holes.

I noted with surprise how certain I felt, how calm. Later I found my way to a tiny storefront real-estate office on Water Street, overlooking Passamaquoddy Bay, and that evening when I drove back to the mainland, the house belonged to me.

What were you thinking of? my ex-husband asked, and so did my relatives and friends. Even my son Sam looked doubtful, although at sixteen he had begun looking doubtful about everything. With a brain surgeon for a father and a money expert for a mother, he was unhappily aware of the problem of living up to all the brilliant genes he had supposedly inherited.

The trouble was, Sam's brains were not of the quick, flashy variety so popular with Ivy League admissions committees. He was the type who could take one look at a broken washing machine, come back from the appliance store with a part that cost five dollars, and a little while later the washing machine would be fixed. He could do the same with an ailing cat, or the gizmo that makes (or doesn't make) a doorbell ring. What he couldn't do was explain how to fix the washing machine, or what sort of attention to give the cat; his perceptions were visceral and immediate, not filtered by words and numbers. They weren't particularly quantifiable, either, unless you happened to have a broken washing machine.

Which is to say that despite every effort of mine, he was flunking out of school, and so angry about it that he had turned to a group of similarly estranged young outlaws, each with a bad attitude and a ready supply of marijuana, and I was worried about him.

"Just come and look at the place," I said. "Will you do that? And if you don't want to, you don't have to stay."

"Yeah, right," he muttered. "Like I can go and live with Dr. Doom."

That was what he had taken to calling his father, on account of the dismal prognosis of most of his father's patients; my ex-husband's operating room is a sort of last-chance hotel for the neurologically demolished.

"Dr. Doom," I told my son, "would be delighted to have you." Over my dead body, I thought but did not say. Sam's father is a charming fellow when he wants to be, but too many years inside other people's heads have convinced him that he is an authority on all that goes on there.

Which he is not. When it comes to the sport of human beingness, my ex-husband knows the rules but not the game, and it is never his blood on the playing field. After six months in the presence of his superachieving father, nothing would be left of Sam but a little pile of bones and hair.

"But that won't be necessary," I told Sam, "because if you don't like Eastport, I'm not going there, either."

Then I held my breath for three days: one while we drove up Route 1 through Bucksport and Bar Harbor and 1A through Milbridge toward Machias, and two more while Sam auditioned Eastport. He explored Wadsworth's hardware store, and pronounced its nuts-and-bolts selection adequate. He stood on the wharves where the cargo ships come in, the massive vessels looking as incongruous as twenty-story buildings plunked down in the midst of the tiny fishing village. He sat on the bluffs overlooking the whirlpool, Old Sow—the largest whirlpool in the Western Hemisphere—and watched the diurnal tide rise its customary twenty-eight feet, which is nine-point-two inches every ten minutes.

During this time I did not smell marijuana, nor did I see the unhappy look I had grown accustomed to back in the city: the look of a boy with a dozen extraordinary talents, none of them valued or even recognized on Madison Avenue, and by extension not in the rest of the world either, because their possessor was unlikely to earn enough money to buy a lot of expensive products.

On the fourth morning I found him sitting at the oilcloth-covered table, in the big old barnlike kitchen with the tall maple wainscoting and the high, brilliant windows. He was drinking a cup of coffee and looking at a set of papers, registration forms for the upcoming year at Shead High School. Carefully, in the labored but rigorously correct block printing that, at age ten, he had finally managed to master, Sam had filled in all the spaces except one.

Parent's signature, the line read. "I think," Sam said, "that you should sign this." So I did.

And that, as they say, has made all the difference.

3

George Valentine came up the back steps, wearing a black cap with Guptill's Excavating lettered on it in orange script. Dark-haired and with the milky-pale skin that downeast Maine people have been passing on for generations, George had the stubborn jaw, diminutive build, and sharp, banty-rooster bearing of a man who, if he did not always have a lot of other people's problems to solve, would chronically be creating a lot of them for himself. As it was, I had been depending on George since practically the day I moved here, and while I was not convinced that he could walk on water, I thought he would probably take two or three steps before he went down.

"Miz Tiptree," George said, slapping his cap against his leg and stomping snow off his boots. Outside the sky had gone grey; to the west, past Carryingplace Cove and the Moosehorn Refuge, loomed a wall of clouds as blue and heavy as lead.

"George," I began, "I can't explain this. I don't even know who that man is. I just found him a few minutes ago and Ellie went out there to make sure he's really dead, but—"

Just then Ellie came back, looking pale and oddly shaken.

"H'lo, Ellie," George mumbled, and if he'd been wearing his cap he'd have tipped it gallantly at her. If he'd been wearing a cape, he'd have spread it across a mud puddle for her, too, and if any dragons had been present he'd have slain them or died trying.

"Hi, George," she said, breezing past him. George said privately that Ellie was still the prettiest woman he'd ever seen, and Ellie said privately that she had survived thirty years unmarried, and thought she could stand another thirty years the same way, but if she did get married it would certainly not be to that tongue-tied, beer-drinking, pickup-driving, gimme-cap-wearing little Eastport clam warden, George Valentine.

I did not point out that George was also a part-time police officer, and thus a very responsible young man in town, since in Ellie's opinion this was only a ploy to get his beer-drinking buddies out of whatever trouble they might, and by Ellie's report habitually did, get their own damn-fool selves into. Somewhere along the line, I thought, George Valentine had said or done something that marked him in Ellie's book as no-account, and that, in Ellie's opinion, was the end of it.

Now his mouth wobbled as in her presence it tried and failed yet again to form a simple English sentence.

"Jacobia," Ellie said, "I'm going home. Mother's got a doctor visit to go to and a hair appointment at Shirley's, and Dad's got his lunch at the Happy Landings."

When she wasn't at my house, Ellie spent much of her time taking care of her aged parents, for while her ferociously independent mother still insisted on driving the car and her father kept in touch with his broker, in other respects both old people depended utterly upon her. Today, Ellie had promised to do driving duty, since her mother could not take her dad to his weekly social group while at the same time getting a blue rinse put into her white hair.

Ellie dropped the pepper-seed packets into her coverall pocket and swept crumbs of potting soil from the kitchen table, dusting her hands over the wastebasket.

"I'll call you later," she said, sounding oddly detached, "and see how things turned out. I couldn't," she added, "do anything for him."

This did not come as a surprise, but the look on Ellie's face did. Everything okay? I telegraphed wordlessly at her, and her gaze back at me was as loaded with meaning as the clouds barreling down out of the mountains at us were full of April snow.

"I'll talk to you," she repeated, "later." Then in a burst of cold air from the back door, she was gone.

"Have a nice day," George managed at last as the door closed, but when he turned back to me he was all business again.

"Now," he said, "about this body."

I don't know why I suddenly wanted to stall him. The dead man felt all at once like a dreadful embarrassment, the sort of thing no good Eastport housewife would ever let happen. Ellie's look bothered me, too; her eyes, ordinarily as clear as spring water, had been full of the old, hard-bitten Yankee secretiveness you still run into now and then in places like this, mingled with what I thought was a plea for help.

George pulled the storeroom door open and our little black Labrador retriever, Monday, made a beeline for the forbidden area, rolling a defiant eye at me.

"Go on, you knucklehead," George said, "get out of here," but she ignored him, flinging herself into the storeroom and locating the scent of the mysterious visitor without delay. Her tail began wagging in the joyous frenzy she reserves for human beings of the unmet persuasion; to this she added the canine version of a buck-and-wing, her nails clicking delightedly on the ancient linoleum.

And then she stopped, her tail curving down like a lowered flag. She stared at the body for a moment as if to make certain of its condition. Finally she turned and walked back out of the storeroom, into the kitchen, and I heard the soft shushing of the sleeping-bag material in her bed as she turned around on it and lay down.

"Well, that's a body, all right," said George. He looked at the door leading outside, which was closed but unlocked, and at the floor, across which someone had tracked snow. The storeroom was too cold for it to melt, so it lay there in the shapes of boot prints.

"Miz Tiptree," said George, "do you have a Polaroid camera?" For while he was indeed a tongue-tied, cap-wearing, beer-drinking, pickup-driving little Eastport clam warden, he was also no fool. I fetched the camera while he called Bob Arnold, the Eastport police chief, and told him what we had found.

"We don't need the ambulance, and we don't need sirens," said George. "And we don't need any hurry. Sand trucks aren't out yet, and it's snowin', and this fella's not goin' anywhere."

I wished he hadn't said not to hurry. Except in emergencies, Bob Arnold had two speeds—slow and reverse—which after being in Eastport a while I'd found I liked a lot. Bob would think it over before letting his heart beat if he could, which meant he tended to make good cop decisions. Under his slow, non-confrontational scrutiny, guys who would otherwise have charged him with their hats flying and their arms windmilling ended by being driven home peaceably in the back of the squad car to sleep it off. The next day they wound up greeting him on Water Street, too, just as cheerfully as you please, once their hangovers had ratcheted down a notch.

But now Bob was going to take his sweet time, and I wanted that body out of there, pronto. For one thing, nothing makes a place look so decrepit as a body. Also, the body in question didn't seem to have an ice pick in its head anymore, and where that had gotten to worried me. The size of Ellie's coverall pockets, for instance, sprang to mind.

"Could be worse," George said. "Could be summer." He said it the Maine way: *summah*. "We'd have to get ice."

"Here's the camera." He took it and, without looking at it, lifted the flash mechanism. It struck me that he had done this sort of thing before, which I suppose should not have surprised me. Not all Maine law enforcement consists of rounding up the good old boys out carousing on a Saturday night. A week earlier, a man in a township so remote that it didn't even have a name had been charged with double murder, for burning a mobile home with his aunt and uncle in it. And when the fire marshall investigated, he found that in addition to cutting the phone wires and dousing the place with kerosene, someone had nailed the door shut.

George aimed the camera at the boot prints. "Too bad Ellie had to go," he said. "I sure like Ellie."

My heart hardly jumped at all in my throat. "I like her, too. She's been a friend since the day I came here. I don't," I added, wondering if my voice sounded as strained to George as it did to me, "know what I would do without her."

The boot print nearest the dead man had finally begun

melting. A trickle ran down the sloping floor into the corner where he lay. An inch above his ear, a small purple hole showed through his hairline; from it ran a thin red track along which the hole had bled, across his forehead and onto the floor.

George took a picture of the hole, and a picture of the blood track, and a picture of the puddle on the linoleum.

"It's good," he said, backing up to frame the whole scene, "that Ellie takes care of her parents the way she does. Otherwise they'd be in a nursing home. 'Course it's her dad, mostly, that she does it for, but still."

"Yes," I said foolishly. "Very good." I was babbling, and I couldn't stop. "Of course, it's good that her parents have money, too. Or Ellie would have to get a job."

George crouched by the body, wrinkling his nose at the pack of cigarettes showing from its shirt pocket; George has asthma, and he hates cigarettes like poison. "Don't happen to know who this is, I guess."

"No," I said. "I don't."

He touched the man's sparse strands of silvery hair with his fingertip. Someone, I decided, had come in and taken the ice pick, and gone out the back door. As I thought this, George got up and opened the door, aiming the camera at the single set of footprints leading to it. The footprints were filling up with snow.

So much for that idea. The problem was, I couldn't think of any good reason for Ellie to have taken that ice pick, but obviously she had, and saying so could get her in trouble. On the other hand, no one else had seen it but me.

"I wonder," George said, "where the ice pick went."

I just stared at him.

"Head wounds bleed," he explained, "but a puncture wound won't till you take the weapon out. That's why you never pull the knife out of a stabbing victim, if it's in. Ice pick," he added, "makes a little round hole like that. Or a tanner's awl."

He pointed. "See that gash?"

It was a long, jagged cut in the dead man's scalp, half an inch from the less dramatic but more deadly little puncture.

"That bled straight down his head; he was upright when he got it. Somewhere else, or there'd be more blood right here. But see, you can tell by the way this other trickle ran, he was down when the weapon got pulled from the main wound. Or he'd have bled toward his neck, the way the scrape did, not to the side."

George turned the body over. The dead man was in his sixties, with light green, half-open eyes and white, bushy eyebrows. His nose, which was pushed to the side from pressing against the floor, was large and had been handsomely shaped. At his throat was a blue-and-red-striped silk tie with a bit of dreadfully familiar gold jewelry glittering in it.

He looked like old money of the kind I used to meet regularly with back in my previous career, trying to persuade it to snuggle down safely in blue-chip securities wrapped up in charitable remainder trusts, and it hit me all at once who this guy must be; Eastport is lovely, but the fabulously rich were not yet flocking here, or at least not in great numbers.

Only one was doing much flocking here, in fact. "Threnody McIlwaine," I said.

George nodded glumly. "You knew him?"

"No. I just know he's a friend of Ellie's father, and I've seen him from a distance. But that's who wears a tie pin shaped like an infinity symbol with a dollar sign crossed over it." It had been in *Fortune* magazine.

I wanted to sit down, but there weren't any chairs in the storeroom. "George," I said, "when I found him, there was an ice pick in his head, and I'm afraid Ellie took it with her."

Threnody McIlwaine was one of the fifty wealthiest men in the world, a corporate raider so aggressive that it was said, only half jokingly, that his limousines ought to fly the Jolly Roger. It was all in the *Fortune* piece I'd recently read about him, along with his shameless tie pin.

No way were we going to have a nice, quiet little Eastport police investigation. By tonight, the news of McIlwaine's murder wouldn't only be all over town; it would be all over the globe.

Which meant Ellie needed help. "Oh, hell," George said, "I thought you two looked a little hinky. Guess I'd best get on the horn to Arnold again."

He made a careful, experimental jumping motion on the floor; it sprang up and down vigorously. "Better call Tim Guptill, too," he said, "see if he can get over and put a few jacks in, brace these boards up. Going to be a lot of people tramping in and out of here."

And so much for Ellie's prediction; on the other hand, Maine weather has a way of establishing its own priorities. "Um, maybe not," I said, glancing out the window.

Snow on Moose Island is not as common or plentiful as it is on the mainland. But when we get a blizzard, it is the kind that awakens human genetic memories of snow: fat white flakes falling thickly and determinedly straight down, piling up in driveways and dooryards, deepening in drifts and closing the roads so swiftly that the plows may become trapped in the public works barns before the operators can slog their way over from homes and businesses, to get them running.

An ominous creaking sounded from the century-and-a-half-old rafters. "You know, George," I said, thinking about the weight of a couple of feet of snow on the roof, "maybe you'd better call Tim Guptill, first."

The winter had been freakishly dry, allowing me to think that I might really squeak by until spring, but now the snow was coming down fast. I had the clear mental image of a dump truck, unloading a ton of white.

"Tell Tim," I added, "maybe he should hurry."

4

Back in the eighties, I was a money trader for one of New York's largest financial institutions. Unlike most traders, I made versatility my strong suit: betting dollars against Deutschmarks, selling pesos against pounds sterling, squeezing the last fraction of a percentage of profit out of a momentary spread between rubles and drachmas, and playing chicken against the legendary yen masters, faceless syndicates who moved blocks of Japanese currency across the trading wires with what some said was inhuman, even supernatural skill.

I earned a lot of money at that job, and nearly ruined my digestion. By eleven each morning the office corridors were filled with currency traders rushing to the lavatories to upchuck their breakfasts; when I caught myself thinking about buying Maalox in large, institutional-size bottles, I decided to pack it in before I, too, became what was known on the street as gut-busted.

Next I became a financial advisor to the wealthy, which some might say is also an anxiety-provoking line of work. Rich people get rich and stay rich by caring about money, and the richest ones care about it a lot. I once met a dowager who dressed like a queen and whose face resembled your sweet old grandmother's, who was later arrested for beating her husband with a stick, injuring him quite severely, because she thought he had cheated her out of the return deposits on a case of Hire's Root Beer bottles.

But the super-rich are as little lambs when placed up against an ex-Wall Street money hustler, equipped with a take-no-prisoners mentality and fully accustomed to the piquant sensation of having half a billion of the bank's favorite dollars burning a hole in her trading account. I found that advising the well-fixed set suited me fine, especially after I got married and had Sam and the bottom dropped out of the money business.

Well, you couldn't expect the world's governments to

sit quietly while packs of hyenas savaged their currencies, could you? So by the late eighties they began building in safeguards to make money's value reflect more closely what went on—productivity, national revenue, other real, at least putatively measurable factors—and this went directly against the whole underlying idea of money trading in the first place, which was to make it reflect whether or not somebody felt lucky.

I certainly did. My clients paid huge fees, in return for which I kept them from having to pay the IRS even more. Meanwhile, currency reform sent thousands of my ex-colleagues trudging back to graduate school, or worse, out into the imploded job market (the swishing sound they all heard was their employment prospects circling the drain), and I was happy not to be among them.

Or at least I was happy until I learned that besides being a brain surgeon and the father of my ten-year-old son, my husband was a lying, cheating, son of a bitch with a stone where his heart belonged.

Fortunately, I had not spent all that time on the currency desk for nothing, or in the confidence of flinty-eyed tycoons with smiles on their faces and larceny in their hearts, either. By the time I discovered the obligatory bit of black lingerie stuffed into my husband's coat pocket, I was an expert not only at getting blood from a stone, but at making it spurt bright green cash.

5

I couldn't very well not tell Sam about the dead body, which I was reluctantly coming to think of as *our* dead body on account of its having been in the house for hours and hours, but I didn't want to upset him or worry him, either. So when he got home from school that afternoon, I sat him down calmly and explained to him that there was a deceased person in the storeroom. I said that the care of a human being's physical remains was a very special duty, and the two of us should try to think positive thoughts about the departed, and maybe even pray for him, and that the presence of the body was also an opportunity for Sam to consider the immense preciousness of life.

"Wow," he breathed happily when I was done, "a stiff!"

"Do not," I commanded him in my best I-am-your-mother-and-I-control-your-allowance voice, "touch that telephone."

But it was too late; Sam's ten best friends were programmed into the speed dialer, and for the next hour and a half I could hear his excited murmurings, interrupted by periods of silence during which he did his homework, and by tiptoeing trips to the storeroom door so he could observe and report the latest details of what was happening out there.

Which, I am sorry to say, was not very much. Some men from Guptill's had come over with jacks and crawled down into the space beneath the storeroom, set the jacks up, and began hauling on them, which was when I discovered that jacking a floor up is not at all the same as changing a car tire. When you jack up a floor, you are allowed to raise the jack a scant quarter-inch per day; otherwise you end up with nice, high floor jacks around which the house has collapsed. Also, no one had told me about the sounds an old house makes while it is being lifted. An antique house, as it turned out, sags because it wants to, and the unholy creaks and groans of agonized protest that I endured all afternoon made a dead man's presence seem not only natural, but positively required.

Sam hung up the telephone, and I heard him rummaging in the closet under the stairs. A moment later he appeared in the living room doorway with his cross-country skis over his shoulder.

"Hey, Mom, the guys say it's gonna snow three feet! And all my homework is done, so can I go out in it before it gets dark?"

Sure, I wanted to say, and take the stiff with you. Special duty or not, I was feeling less reverent by the minute.

Sam took my silence as assent; it was a trick of his, lately. First he hit me with some thoroughly mind-boggling request, like could he drive to Caribou to go ice-fishing? The other guys' moms had already all said okay so could he please, *please* go, and he would only need the car for two days? And then while I was still struck dumb by the outrageousness of it, he went ahead and did it.

Only this time he didn't. "Unless," he ventured, "you want me to stay with you. While he's out there, I mean. The dead guy."

Occasionally, and by that I mean very rarely, a teen-aged boy will happen upon a perception so accurate, and react to it so sweetly and manfully, that it takes all the strength a mother has not to throw her arms around that boy and weep. George had gone down to the office on Water Street to file a police report, and after that he had traffic duty, because in the snow a few cars would be certain to slide off the causeway. In weather like this, his habit was to sit in a squad car at the causeway's end until the tide went out, so that any drivers who did slide off the road would not compound their bad luck by drowning.

"No," I told Sam, "if you've finished your homework and left it out for me to look at, then you go on and ski."

For a sixteen-year-old, it was a very conservative request, and I was saving my ammunition; next time he'd be demanding to know if he could row to Deer Island, or go bear hunting. "Bob Arnold's coming," I added.

I let my hand rest on his arm for the instant of contact allowed to mothers of teenaged boys. He was taller than I was, and solid muscle on account of all the outdoor exercise he got, and I remembered with a burst of nostalgia when he was a skinny little twerp. "Besides," I said, "I think your dad's going to call, and I want to be able to tell him you're out."

Sam nodded. He'd been putting off discussing his college plans with his father, whose wish list included Harvard and Yale.

"Thanks. Mom, do you think Dad will ever understand?"

No, I thought. "Yes," I said, "of course he will."

Sam's own plan was for the local technical college, and a course in the fundamentals of boat building. He was looking forward to a two-day visit to the school, but had not yet informed his father of his intentions.

"Go on, now. And be careful," I called after him as he went out into a rumble of young male voices.

"Be *care*-ful, Tiptree," rose a mocking falsetto as they glided away in a mob down the snowy street. I recognized the voice as that of Sam's closest pal, Tommy Daigle. "Don't get *hurr*-urt."

He would, though, and probably soon; to my ex-husband, the technical school was about as real an education option as one of those earn-your-veterinary-assistant-certificate-at-home schemes they pitch on cable TV. In his view, Sam just didn't try hard enough; never mind that Sam would have sat down in front of a freight train if he thought it would please his father.

And then I was alone. All around me, the big old house seemed to hunker down against the coming blizzard; what we'd had so far was only the teaser. Reports out of Bangor and Augusta said Routes 9 and 1A were closed, which meant that about a trillion reporters were holed up in Holiday Inns and Ramadas, waiting to descend. I went around checking windows for drafts and plugging them when I found them, trying not to remember that what I saved in heating oil I was probably spending on rope caulk.

Trying not to think, too, of a certain harbor pilot of my acquaintance, who if memory served was right now out on the icy water, guiding a freighter into port. It ain't the fog that'll do you, he'd said of his job, nor tides, nor the ledges, neither. It's the wind. When the wind comes, look sharp.

Another gust rattled the windowpanes. As real weather came on, the wind was rising and swinging around out of the northeast. By the time Wade Sorenson got the good ship *Amaryllis* within sight of the harbor beacons, it would be blowing a gale.

I caulked the last window and started on the drafty doorways: tacks and felt weather stripping. One of the pleasures of fixing up an old house is knowing that you can never be finished; there is always another small task, a creaky floorboard or a leaky radiator valve, to keep your hands occupied and your mind from becoming the devil's playground.

A creaky floorboard, for instance, like the one on the other side of the storeroom door.

Which was ridiculous; there was nobody out there but the dead man. Probably the jacks were making the floorboards creak.

Only, not to the rhythm of stealthy footsteps.

Steeling my nerves, stiffening my spine, and praying hard for whoever it was to go away, just go away and leave me alone, I yanked open the storeroom door. This, in retrospect, was probably the stupidest thing I could have done, but at the time I'd had it to the eyes.

"What's going on out here?" I bellowed, loud enough to bring Monday barking to defend home and dog chow. Seeing who it was, she gave me a look and ambled back to her fort beneath the dining room table, where she had been dismembering a rawhide bone.

The bare lightbulb hanging in the storeroom swung wildly in the gusts from outside, hurling Ellie's shadow against the walls and snatching it back before the door leading to the yard slammed shut. "Jacobia," she said weakly, jumping up, and her tone broke my heart; Ellie never sounded weak.

For an instant I thought of asking her why she had come in by the storeroom door. Then I saw the ice pick, glinting from beneath the body where she had been trying to hide it. The idea, I supposed, was that while McIlwaine was still alive the weapon had fallen from the wound, or he had taken it out, and then he had rolled onto it. The theory might have flown—maybe he really wasn't quite dead when I found him—if George hadn't turned the body over, then turned it back. But now Ellie might as well have left the police a little note: Weapon Not Here Earlier.

She might as well have signed it, also, because there would be fingerprints, and because I had already told George the truth.

She saw it in my face. "It's okay," she said. "I'd have told him, too."

I went to the outside door, opened it, and peered out. The wind had dropped off, gathering its gumption for another blast. In the moment of stillness before I pulled the door closed again, I glanced across the yard to the pale lighted windows of the Whalen house, ghostly in the snow, and the arrowhead shapes of the pines forming a windbreak along its white clapboards. To the side, a low palisade fence separated my driveway from Victor Sawtelle's trim, empty bungalow; Bath Iron Works was hiring, and Victor was bunking over there for the duration.

The foghorn at West Quoddy Light honked in the dusk. It was only four-thirty, but the snow had pulled around us like a thick curtain, smelling of salt and woodsmoke. The red glow of the sanctuary lamp in Christ Church spread bloodily through the plastic-sheeted windows, diffusing onto the white lawn.

One street over, Sam and his friends were having a snowball fight, their shouts muffled by the falling flakes. I latched the door, and the silence in the icy room was huge. "At least you've got the money to hire a lawyer."

"Not anymore." She broke off staring at McIlwaine and looked up at me, and I thought that if it came to a choice between the truth about the ice pick and the truth about the expression on her face, I'd take the ice pick.

"Not after what he did. Threnody McIlwaine," she spat, "the big-deal expert. I wish I'd slit his throat for him, that's what I wish."

Which was when I got the message, finally, or thought I did. "You know, Ellie," I told her, taking her arm and guiding her through the passageway, sitting her down at the kitchen table, "you need to shut up."

I filled the kettle and smacked it onto the stove. "Because," I went on, determinedly filling air time since if I did not she was only going to talk some more, which in her situation was about as helpful as washing cyanide down her throat, "you and I may be good and dear friends, and we are, but what we aren't is married."

I slapped mugs onto the table. "And *that* means," I said as she opened her mouth and I gestured sharply to make her shut it again, "*that* means I can be required to testify against you. Which naturally I would be loath to do, and I would go to jail to avoid it, except of course that if I did get put in jail, Sam would have to go and live with his father and I don't know what might happen to Monday."

I flung tea bags into the mugs. "So don't put me in that position any more than I am already."

Back in the old days, Ellie's ancestors had made a living off the blockades intended to keep Americans from trading with the British, many of whom lived within sight of Eastport just across Passamaquoddy Bay. After a few skirmishes, both sides figured out what a silly waste of ammunition this was, what with the War of 1812 going on and all. Thereafter, the American traders began quietly allowing the seizure of meat, grain, and other delicious items much hungered after by their British neighbors—cargoes they just happened to have taken out for a sail, of course, just to give them a breath of fresh air—and the British traders in ports like St. George and St. Andrews bought the seized cargoes. Finally, the payments made their way back to the American traders, who promptly ransomed their boats and went home to start the process over again.

All of which was of course very strictly forbidden, and subject to punishments including fines, confiscation of boats, and in the worst cases, being hung for the crime of treason, and this, if you ask me, is among the many historical reasons why downeast Mainers are such silent types: like navigating in the fog or knowing how to dress out a deer, it runs in their blood.

Ellie watched me pour boiling water onto the tea bags, and waited for me to set out the sugar and cream, then dosed her mug liberally with each. Putting her face over the rising steam, she inhaled it gratefully, then lifted her mug and took a sip.

"There," she said, seeming to accept my warning. "That's much better."

And then we said nothing, sitting companionably together while the windows rattled and the clock ticked and the woman in the portrait propped on the kitchen mantelpiece watched over us, her eyes luminous and intelligent. In the portrait she was wearing a white linen shift, shirred at the smooth, round neckline, and a strand of pearls. Her dark hair was beautifully cut to take advantage of its wave, and sidelit so that it shone like sun on water; her complexion was smooth and apparently without makeup, her expression serene but not dramatically so.

There was nothing of theatricality about her, and nothing of impatience. She neither smiled nor frowned. She simply was, in that long-ago moment when the shutter snapped and the image of her became captured, to be passed down through who knew how many years and generations until one day, while sorting through a pile of age-stiffened draperies in a forgotten cupboard, I came upon her.

No one knew her: not her name, or whose wife or mother or sister or cousin she was, or if my house had once been hers. She might have lived twenty years ago or two hundred, so timeless was her unspoiled serenity. I was about to ask Ellie again if she could think of anyone else in town who might remember, when footsteps clomped up the steps.

Sam, I thought hopefully, or Wade Sorenson, back early from the boat. But of course it wasn't, and now here was Ellie at the scene of the crime.

"Jacobia," said Bob Arnold, his round face ruddy with cold. Snow crusted his hat brim and the furry rims of his earflaps. "Hey, Ellie. Wicked bad out. Cars all over the side of the road."

He looked hopefully around for coffee as two more men came in. The insignias on their jackets said they were from the Washington County Sheriff's Department and the Maine State Police. I shot Ellie a look to tell her to keep quiet; if she had anything on her conscience she could unburden herself later, preferably to an attorney, should unburdening prove necessary.

But it was no use. Ellie looked at Arnold and smiled, her silence not bred in deep enough, or perhaps it was, but some long-ago pirate's briny lies were bred in stronger and deeper. Cargoes are not only for trading, after all, but for heisting, and this is especially so for illegal shipments, and that was how Ellie's forebears had made their bloody livings: by the hissing of steel cutlasses, at the dark of the moon, on nights so cold that rags of sea smoke trailed over the water like remnants of tattered sails.

"I did it," she announced. "I killed Threnody McIlwaine with an ice pick, after he swindled my father out of a fortune."

The men looked wonderingly at her.

"And," she added in bold, ringing tones that I thought owed plenty to her rascal ancestors, damn their eyes, "I would do it again."

6

"So they let her go home," said Wade Sorenson. "That's good. Makes good sense."

It was two in the morning, and the *Amaryllis* stood

safe at harbor. From the dining room window I could see her glowing through the gale-driven snow like a beacon somebody has thrown a sheet over, her decks floodlit for the line-haulers laboring to make her fast.

Waking from an uneasy half-sleep, I'd come downstairs to see whether Wade had returned from the water and found him at the dining room table, cleaning an antique Smith & Wesson revolver. The room smelled sweetly of gun oil but not, I noticed gratefully, of Hoppe's No. 9 Bore-Cleaning Solvent, which is so awful I sometimes wonder why people bother shooting actual bullets; the stink alone could kill you at twenty paces.

"Hi," Wade said, reaching up to put an arm around me, and for a moment I just leaned against him. He had his own little bungalow down at the water's edge, on Liberty Street, but in his quiet way he had recently installed a spare shaving kit at my house. Coming from Wade, it was a gesture akin to a gift of diamonds.

I let my arm rest on his shoulder, and my head on his wiry hair. He smelled of soap, shaving cream, and the bay balm he used to keep his hands from cracking in cold weather; his body, squarish and solidly muscled from years of activity on and around the water, had nothing to do with workouts and everything to do with work.

"Glad you're back," I said.

"Glad to be back. Didn't mean to wake you." He squeezed hard around my waist once, then gazed up assessingly at me as if checking the status of some complex machinery that he very much wanted to make sure was operating properly.

"You didn't wake me." I gestured at the table, unsurprised that he was still busy at this hour. A harbor pilot in the act of guiding a thirty-six-thousand-ton commercial vessel up to a cargo dock is one of the more wide-awake persons you will ever meet, and he will stay that way for hours after a job. "What's the project?"

He grinned like a kid with a new Christmas present. "A six-shooter. Cowboy gun. 1876. Smith & Wesson made a zillion of them for the Russians, but it turned out a lot of guys here liked 'em, too. See, it's a top-break, the barrel's on hinges, opens down." He broke open the most recent addition to his antique weapons collection and handed it to me, and I took it unhesitatingly.

Which right there was pretty remarkable. When I first came to Maine I believed that if I even touched a gun, my right hand would shrivel up and fall off. Guns were for guys who drove old pickup trucks riddled with body rot, who took their girlfriends line-dancing on Saturday nights and beat them bloody-faced afterwards, who drank Lone Star and spat plugs of chewing tobacco and said things like, "Ma'am, you look vurry, vurry purty tonight," while the jukebox played Johnny Cash singing "Ring of Fire."

And mostly, guns were for guys. But then I got to Eastport, and the first thing that happened was this: a skunk settled in under the porch. Every night at ten o'clock, that skunk would come home and direct an aerosol of the most astonishingly penetrating poison fumes I have ever smelled in my life, straight up through the floorboards of the house.

Well, we just about died. You couldn't think, you couldn't sleep, the reek drilled into your sinuses and poured out through your tear ducts. It got so bad that Monday would run up two steep flights of stairs into the attic, which was as far as you could get from the skunk's residence, and hide in a closet and howl.

That was what I felt like doing, too. We tried blocking the skunk's entry-hole with chicken wire, and after he chewed through that we tried filling it with bricks, which the skunk most definitely did not like, and his protest nearly gassed us to death. We bought one of those catch-and-release traps and were all ready to use it, only neither Sam nor I could figure out what to do once we captured the skunk, since neither of us owned a chemical warfare suit and the release portion of the program seemed likely to be fatal without one. We even thought of putting out a bowl of delicious (to skunks) antifreeze, so that he would drink it, stagger away, and die, but then

Sam had a bad thought: what if he didn't stagger away? What if he crawled up under the porch, into the wall, and *decomposed* there?

So it was a skunk stalemate. He wanted to get rid of us so he could live in the whole house, and we wanted to get rid of him so that we could live in any portion of it at all; by now even the orange juice in the refrigerator tasted like wild animals, and people were beginning to look oddly at us when we went into the library or the grocery store, on account of the aroma we had begun radiating.

And then one day a fellow came to the door, who said that his name was Homer—only of course he pronounced it the Maine way: *Homah*—and that he had heard we had a skunk problem.

I didn't quite fall down and kiss Homer's feet, but I did bring him into the kitchen. I poured him a cup of coffee and gave him a sweet roll and begged him, positively implored him, to tell me how to get rid of the skunk.

"Oh, that's easy," Homer said, chewing appreciatively on the sweet roll. He swallowed. "I come ovah, late one night, and blow 'im to nevah moah. You can keep the cahcass if you want, or I can take it with me."

I told Homer he could keep the cahcass, and any others he happened to find on the property, at which he brightened. "There is," he confided, "a nest of squirrels in your shed roof, fouling your attic ventilation."

But there wasn't for long. One night soon after I met Homer, our whole neighborhood sounded like a battle between the Hatfields and the McCoys, and the next night we did not get fumigated by a skunk. It wasn't a solution any animal-welfare advocate would have appreciated, but we enjoyed being able to go to bed without having to wear gas masks; soon even Monday would come downstairs without whining, and my eyes stopped resembling peeled grapes.

So I had to rethink my attitudes about firearms, and without getting too deeply into the murky area of my

childhood history—deeper, that is, than my knowing all
the words to "Ring of Fire" must inevitably, I imagine,
suggest—may I simply say right here that for one thing,
the whole idea of shooting a varmint without having to
pick the birdshot pellets out of it and eat it afterwards
came as a revelation to me. Then in my fast-paced city-
dwelling adulthood—before I came to Eastport to work
on the house, relax, and just breathe in and out for a
while—the word "shoot" got itself linked with such
tabloid phrases as "convenience-store clerk," "domestic
dispute," and "postal worker," not to mention the ever-
popular "gang-style execution" and the ubiquitous
"romance gone tragically awry."

But here in Maine, I was learning very quickly, things
were different. People had shotguns, rifles, and handguns
of all descriptions, and mostly they didn't shoot their
neighbors, their co-workers, or their kids. Women didn't
blow their husbands' heads off, men didn't romp around
the household threatening to add extra apertures to their
wives, and generally if somebody wanted to use a weapon on someone, they bonked them with a telephone or
smacked them with a two-by-eight, or in the tougher
cases ran over them with their cars. Maine could be
violent, especially in winter when people drank more—
witness the trailer-home fire up there in the numbered
township—but it was low-tech violence; for one thing,
ammunition was so expensive. Guns, I decided, especially rifles, weren't so bad, particularly during deer
season when they put venison on the tables of people
who otherwise couldn't afford to eat meat.

And that was where I had gotten to on the topic of
firearms, on the morning—about six months before
McIlwaine died—when a big, burly fellow named Wade
Sorenson waltzed into my life, carrying a six-shooter the
size of a cannon and enough cartridges to re-enact the
gunfight at the OK Corral. He was going, he said, target
shooting.

And at the confident look in his pale grey eyes, the
soothing, unhurried sound of his big, deep voice, and the

easy, no-problem expression weathered into his rugged face, I'd felt a bull's-eye forming in bright, iridescent circles around my heart.

Now Wade took the revolver back and closed the barrel up. "So how'd that happen? Them letting Ellie go home, I mean."

"Well, the state guys didn't want to, at first," I replied. "There was too much wind to drive anywhere by then, but they were all for putting her on a fishing boat to Lubec, and having someone from Machias pick her up there. Or calling in a helicopter, if you can imagine that. I don't know who they expected would fly it, in this weather."

Ordinarily, Bob Arnold would have had to drive Ellie thirty miles to Machias, where they had modern conveniences like fast-food restaurants and jail cells, but because the sheriff's deputy and the state guy were already here, Arnold said that one of them would probably end up doing it after the snow stopped.

"Arnold could have put her in the lock-up at the Coast Guard station," I said, "but that would have meant putting a seaman on duty there, and in an emergency he couldn't stay with her."

Once they realized the tabloid nature of the situation—murdered billionaire; remote, snow-choked town; beautiful young suspect—neither the deputy nor the state officer had wanted to take custody of Ellie without first receiving further instructions from his superiors. A case with national publicity could kill you or cure you, career-wise, Arnold had explained, and in the event one of their agencies decided later to punt, they didn't want to have created a tar-baby.

"And since they couldn't get a lawyer over here in the storm, anyway—"

The district attorney in Calais had been notified, and had promptly passed off to the attorney general and his crack team of prosecutors and investigators in Augusta. The state police out of the barracks in East Machias would still begin the investigation, and a local assistant

DA would file a complaint in district court, but all of that, Arnold had said, was just the opening act. In Maine's two-tiered judicial system, district courts handle mostly misdemeanors, sending serious offenses up to superior court.

"They read her rights to her, but they didn't want to take her statement until she'd had legal advice," I added to Wade. "So the way it ended up was, Ellie promised to surrender into custody tomorrow morning, and then she went home and the state cops went down to the Bay-watch, had dinner with Arnold, and went to Motel East for the night."

Which to me had been absolutely astonishing, but when you came right down to it, what else were they going to do? The town's only attorney had made it off the island ahead of the blizzard, which made him about as accessible as the moon; snow alone probably wouldn't have stopped anyone, but the wind was now truly ghastly.

Meanwhile the phones in Eastport worked perfectly well—we are nothing here if not self-sufficient—but the mainland phones went out soon after Arnold had his chat with the district attorney, and Bangor and Augusta were both shut down for the night anyway—on the mainland, the storm was what old-timers called a gully-whumper, massive and paralyzing—so that even via radio the officers couldn't get fresh orders immediately.

"Not to mention what would have happened to her parents," I went on, "if she'd had to go so suddenly, without any warning. The upset alone would have been awful for them."

And as Arnold pointed out, if Ellie didn't mean to turn herself in tomorrow, why confess? It wasn't as if she had a big city to vanish into, or even any way to get out of town. Besides, he'd told the state and county men stoutly, he'd known Ellie all her life and she'd never broken a promise yet that he knew of; he doubted she would start now.

"So Arnold talked the deputy and the state cop into waiting," I finished. "No one's going anywhere tonight."

Actually, Arnold hadn't precisely talked them into anything, but he can move block granite with his voice box when he's motivated. Discovering that neither of the officers knew what their next move should be, he'd simply told them what to do, and they had done it as if by reflex.

Wade popped the cylinder back into the revolver and tightened the catch-screw. "Nothing more to be done about it, then, for now. Things'll start straightening out in daylight, I expect."

Wade's idea of trouble was no land, no lifeboats, and a bilge pump operating as ballast. Boarding a big vessel preparatory to bringing it into port, he would step from the pilot boat's open deck to a gangway up the vessel's side. Sometimes the gang led to a hatchway and an enclosed stair. Sometimes it didn't, and Wade scrambled up over a rolling sea.

"I hope so," I said. Upstairs, Sam had turned off his stereo and gone to bed hours earlier, tired out from skiing and exhausted from a long conversation with his father, which I had not after all been quick-witted enough to prevent, nor had the phones gone down early enough to do it for me. And then there was Ellie, who was clearly in terrible trouble, and I didn't know what to do about it.

Wade looked up questioningly at me, seeing something in my face, then got up and put his arms around me. "Cat got your tongue all of a sudden?" he asked softly, and I nodded against him.

He chuckled. "They'll do that, sometimes. But they let loose when they're ready." He put his face against my hair. "Anyway," he said in tones of quiet amusement, "the spoken word can be a highly overrated item."

I smiled in spite of myself. "A lot of times," he went on, "words don't even make sense."

He lifted his hand and moved it in a flying-away

gesture. I could feel his muscles, as powerful as heavy-duty springs, through his flannel shirt.

"You don't," he assured me, "have to bother with 'em anymore, tonight."

Whereupon a little clamp, tight and sharp-edged as steel, unpinched itself somewhere in my chest.

Later, after he had cleaned up the newspapers and put away his gun things, we went upstairs, and for a while we said nothing that made sense to anyone but us.

To whom it made perfect sense, indeed.

7

Just before dawn I got up and stood at the hall window, and watched the snow as it swirled on down through the streetlight.

At this hour, when the house shoulders into a storm and the windows are rattling like snare drums, it is possible to remember how exposed we are, here on our little bit of rock out in the Atlantic. For that is where we sit; only the Canadian islands and Nova Scotia are farther out in the chilly ocean than we are. The Vikings even made it here in wooden boats, leaving runic artifacts not two miles off as the crow flies, in what is now Lubec.

The Vikings were newcomers to Maine, of course, as are we. Before them were the Abnaki and the Etchimin, People of the Dawn and People of the Sea, and before them the mysterious Red Paint People. No one knows where they came from or what they believed, only that they buried their dead with red ochre and that their remains predate five-thousand-year-old shell heaps—remnants of much later native shore picnics—still found along the Maine coast. In all, it is believed that people have been living on Moose Island—one and a half miles wide, four and a half miles long, with an elevation of two hundred feet at its highest point—for perhaps ten thousand years.

Which tends to put my little problems into perspective, but it didn't this time.

Downstairs, I found the issue of *Fortune* magazine that contained the McIlwaine profile and settled on the sofa with it. McIlwaine had originally been an Eastport boy, which explained at least in part why he made a habit of returning to the tiny town on the island just off the northeast seacoast. As a young man, the article said, he had gone to New York immediately after high school, swiftly displaying a cutthroat talent for business as well as the ferocity and drive for acquisition that, over the years, had become legend.

He'd started out in the trucking game, short-haul transport and trash collection, mostly, but by the age of thirty he'd diversified so much, you couldn't really tell what business he was in, only that it was all profitable. Now the McIlwaine empire spanned the globe, with emphasis on mining, shipping, timber, and resort properties, although he would snap up anything if it looked the least bit vulnerable.

Or if he could make it vulnerable. Skirting the libel laws, the *Fortune* writer managed to note that unions had a habit of getting out of the tycoon's way; that house fires, car crashes, and sundry other instances of bad luck had a tendency to afflict his more stubborn opponents; and that his string of ex-wives, in particular, routinely refused comment about him. The exception, a fiery Bolivian beauty who had agreed to be the primary source for a book about him, had actually been on the point of traveling to New York to work with the author on the project when, on the eve of her departure, she was struck by a violent gastrointestinal illness and died, apparently after eating a bad oyster.

The rest of the article had to do with the nuts and bolts of the business magnate's major interests: board feet of lumber, rates of occupancy, short tons shipped, and outlooks for tourism in the various exotic places where McIlwaine had put his luxurious resort destinations. The photograph showed him gazing out through the French doors of his Chicago mansion, across a slate terrace onto what looked like approximately ten acres of lawn manicured to the fineness of a putting green.

On the terrace were two large Irish wolfhounds, relaxed and smiling with the illusory good humor of a couple of well-trained hit men. The wolfhounds' grins, wide and predatory, were very much like McIlwaine's own as he posed for the photographer.

McIlwaine, the article said, had only two children: Patricia, the product of his marriage to his first wife, and Janet, whom he had adopted from a New York orphanage when she was an infant. His current wife—his sixth or his seventh, depending upon whom you believed; the Bolivian's status, since her death, had apparently come into question—was "a young foreign-born beauty who manages the family's social and charitable activities."

In other words, she went to parties. I had met Nina McIlwaine briefly around town. About a year before the article was written, she had taken a fancy to Eastport and now spent most of her time here. McIlwaine's two daughters, Patty and Janet, had come with her, and Patty had even married a local fellow.

But parties here were mostly of the church-supper variety, and I had no idea what Nina did with her time these days. McIlwaine himself flew in and out on a regular basis, his Learjet cutting through the sky with a racket that rattled the dishes in every cupboard in town before settling on the island's airstrip, which he'd had lengthened to accommodate the aircraft. Soon after Nina had indicated her liking for the place, he had built a house for her, putting up in record time a dwelling that in Eastport was the equivalent of the Taj Mahal, out at Mackerel Cove.

I put the magazine down thoughtfully. In his career, a guy like McIlwaine would have made enemies: bitter, even murderous enemies. Ironic, then, that he should have been done in by a woman with all the killing potential of an embroidered handkerchief.

If she had, which despite her unfortunate remarks I did not believe for a minute.

Wade had switched on a lamp when I got back into bed, and shadows gathered in the stamped tin ceiling's wreathed acorns-and-oak-leaves pattern. A fleck of rust showed in one corner, hinting at a leak above; the third floor of my old house is still piped for gas lamps and chimney-flued for wood stoves, but it is not yet equipped with storm windows.

Prybar, I thought automatically; a scraper and a sander.

"Masking tape," Wade added to my mental list as he followed my gaze. "And paint. Putty, and a putty knife. And glazier's points, of course."

Of course. I closed my eyes.

"You know," Wade said after a while, "I'm thinking about what Ellie said. Making such a production of saying she killed the guy. And it reminds me how, in the old days, there were sardine canneries up and down the wharf. Big old buildings, with hundreds of people working in 'em."

I nodded against his shoulder, not making the connection but remembering the sepia-tinted photographs of long wooden structures jutting out over the tidal waters, supported by forty-foot pilings too thick to put your arms around.

Wade's voice was like the sound of an outboard engine idling, steady and slow. "People worked their whole lives in those canneries, cutting and packing, sealing cans, putting the labels on. Tin, you know. Soldered seams. A fellow could make a career of sealin' the leaky ones, he had a mind to."

He got up, and I settled into the warm spot where he had been. "Gradually, though," he said, "sardines went by. Catch fell off, and people didn't eat them anymore, or not so much. Canneries closed until there was just the one left, and that one had a steam whistle my great-grandfather used to tell me about."

He began pulling on his pants. "Whistle used to call people to work, sound the break, send 'em home at the end of the day."

I wondered if the woman in the portrait had lived here then. She looked too fine to be a cannery worker. As if replying to my thought, the open bedroom door swung smoothly closed and latched itself shut with a crisp, interesting little click.

Wade tipped his head, smiling curiously. One day when he had been hammering on the attic hatchway, blocking off the drafts to the rafters that warmed up the roof and made ferocious ice dams of the melting snow, he had reached out for the nails and instead put his hand on a ribbon: pink, with tiny seed pearls sewn onto it. He'd put the ribbon in his toolbox to show me, he'd said, but when he looked for it again, it wasn't there.

"Anyway," he went on after a moment, "my great-grandfather said that at the end of the last day, the foreman sounded that steam whistle for the final time, a great big mother of a blast. And as the sound faded, the boiler ran dry and the machinery went dead. And that was the end of the cannery."

There was a restaurant now where the cannery had been, out on the dock. Polished floors, and a grand piano with a fellow playing cocktail music, weekends.

Wade finished dressing, and fastened his wristwatch.

"A loud noise," I said.

Wade nodded. "Sound and fury."

"But nothing behind. You don't think she did it, either."

He paused, adjusting the slide on his string tie. The first time I met him, he told me sincerely that if you touch the two metal ends of a string tie together, they will make a spark.

"Ellie and George were engaged to be married, once. Neither of 'em 'll talk much about it now," he said, "but they were. Story around town was, Ellie's mother put the brakes on it."

The revelation didn't surprise me as much as it might have. I'd always thought Ellie's disparagement of George as a romantic prospect was a case of protesting too much—although I wouldn't have told Ellie so. She could be prickly about her privacy.

Wade sat down and bent to tie the black leather, rubber-soled utility shoes that he wore for work. "Ellie," he said, "should have got shut of that old woman a long time ago."

Wishing Ellie's mother would take a sudden notion to walk east until her hat floated was not a new idea to me, either, or to anyone who knew Ellie. I looked at the door, which had opened again a fascinating quarter-inch. "You think Ellie is protecting George?"

The idea of George as a killer was almost as bad as the idea of Ellie as one, and more plausible from the upper-body-strength point of view. George performed hard physical work all day, and never mind that he didn't have any motive, since as far as I was concerned, Ellie didn't, either, despite what she'd said about a swindle. I made a mental note to find out more about this, if only to discount it, since the notion of Ellie killing over money was, to me, outlandish.

"No," Wade said, "I don't. But it might be I just don't want to. Because if Ellie didn't do it, and she's confessing, it stands to reason she's protecting someone, doesn't it?"

Over on my dresser, McIlwaine's tie pin glittered spitefully. Bob Arnold had given it to me for safekeeping the evening before, asking me to return it to McIlwaine's widow, Nina, when I could, as he imagined that he would be on the job all night and who knew where he or it might get to by morning. As if to prove this, the radio on his belt had begun sputtering, so I'd taken the thing reluctantly, McIlwaine's body itself having at last been removed to Flagg's Funeral Home at my absolute insistence.

"Paintbrush," Wade said. "Silicone caulk."

The bedroom door sneaked open another inch.

8

"I'm not going," Sam insisted a couple of hours later, his face set into the hard-jawed, mulish expression that reminded me so much of his father. "I'm not, and you can't make me."

I dropped two bagel halves into the toaster and poured myself a glass of V8. Sam made a face; he regards vegetables as garnish, mere obstacles between himself and the meat and potatoes.

"Dad said I shouldn't go." Sam sank into a kitchen chair. "He says boat building is for losers. He says I'm getting to be a local yokel, all I want is a dog, a shotgun, and a pickup truck."

At the word "dog," Monday got up and put her head in his lap, and gazed up at him adoringly. He smoothed her ears.

"Dad says," Sam went on, "I'm wasting my life. He says you're making me waste my life, up here."

I did not look at Sam, just kept buttering the toasted bagel halves, while in my head the coffeepot smashed against the wall and the knives all flew out of the kitchen drawers, gnashing their blades together and impaling themselves in the countertops.

"Is Wade wasting his life here? Or George?" I asked. "Or," I went on, my voice rising despite my resolve, "the men who go out on fishing boats, and risk their lives trying to support their families? Do you think," I demanded, "those two guys who drowned trying to bring the scallop dragger over from Lûbec in the storm, that those guys were *yokels*?"

The bad news had come in a call for Wade, just before he left for the Federated Marine office. The previous evening in Lubec, the next town down the coast from Eastport, four men had set out in a sixteen-foot wooden skiff, trying to reach a dragger that one of them had left moored offshore. Their plan was to get the big boat into the boat basin, where it would be safer from the weather.

Instead, a wave swamped the skiff. Two of the men had clung to mooring balls, and two drowned, their bodies swept out by the tide. Wade was part of the recovery team.

Sam looked momentarily shamefaced, but where his father's advice was concerned he was like an alcoholic: knowing it was bad for him, hoping this time it would come out differently.

"I know I'm not doing so good in school, but I'm going to get a tutor, and work harder," he insisted. "Dad says if I do, he can still get me into Yale." He frowned at his clenched fists.

"And I know what you think," he went on. "That I'll fail. But you want me to fail, you want me not to be anything like Dad."

His tone was growing frantic; this, in a nutshell, was the trouble with calls from Sam's father. His vindictive, grandiose notions seeped through the phone lines like poison gas.

"Look," I said, mustering a smile that felt nailed on, "it's no big deal. I'll just call the school and have them take you off the tour list."

Twelve hours earlier, Sam had been enthused about a plan that I thought was just perfect for him. But in only a few minutes his father had convinced him that learning to build ships, a skill that would make Sam employable anywhere in the world, was about as worthwhile as learning to carve tugboats out of bathtub soap.

"Okay," Sam relented. "I'm sorry. I know you don't want me to fail, and I don't think those guys are yokels. It's just . . ."

He spread his hands helplessly. "Why can't I be *smart*, like you and Dad?"

I looked at my son, with whom I had always tried to be honest. "Because," I said, "you have to be smart like yourself."

"Yeah," he snorted dismissively, "me and Bozo the Clown."

Which was when I decided that what Sam needed was

lies: the sort of low trickery and shameless, silver-tongued deceit that only a seasoned financial professional can properly deliver.

"You know," I ventured, "in a way, your father is right. If you visited the boat school, you'd probably find out you didn't like it, anyway. So in that sense, it would be a waste of time."

Sam looked up, his expression doubtful. But he was listening, and all I'd ever needed was to keep them listening.

"Still," I said slowly, as if just now thinking it through, "I'll bet they could hook you up with a good tutor. Some of their students must want extra help, too, wouldn't you think?"

Sam brightened. "Yeah, I bet they could," he allowed.

"And," I said, moving in to close the sale, "it would be too bad to make Tommy Daigle go alone, when he's been counting on you all this time."

Sam looked vexed as he remembered his commitment to his friend. "Daigle," he moaned, clapping his hand to his forehead. "Oh, man, he'll kill me if I wimp out on him."

"Besides," I continued smoothly, "I've heard that some of the students over at the school have some pretty cool tattoos. Not," I added, "that I am going to allow you to get any such thing."

The tattoo question had been bouncing around the house for weeks, with Wade saying I ought to just let Sam do it, and me quailing at the idea of some coarse Hell's Angel type sticking a dirty needle into my baby boy.

Sam eyed me speculatively. He really wanted to go on the boat school tour. "A tattoo would make Dad bonkers."

"Indeed," I agreed, "it would. If you had one, which you won't, and if he saw it, which he wouldn't. Would he?"

"No, of course not." He got up. "You know, Mom, maybe you'd better hold off canceling me out. Just, you know, let me think it over a little while longer."

My throat opened, allowing a morsel of bagel to pass

through. "Good. That's all I want you to do. Think it over, maybe talk it over with Wade."

After the first night Wade had stayed with me, Sam met him coming out of my bedroom in the morning. The two men eyed one another cautiously, then went on about their business: Sam to eat breakfast and head on off to school, and Wade to go down to the Federated Marine office on Water Street.

Later that day, though, I spotted them together on the fish pier, Sam with a Coke in his hands and Wade with a bottle of Narragansett. Neither of them ever told me what they talked about that day, and I have never asked. But I had noticed Sam beginning to ask Wade for bits of advice, and Wade thinking carefully before providing any.

"I don't suppose we even need to worry your dad about it, at this stage. Do we?"

Sam paused, and I thought I might have gone too far.

"No," he said at last. "We don't. At this stage."

And with that it was, as they say, a done deal.

Or so I thought. Moments later Sam was gone in a whirl of books and athletic gear. So many high school teachers lived on the island, and so many high school students had serious summer jobs, that a snow day was out of the question even though it continued snowing hard, with the forecast of a foot or more still to come.

What I ought to do, I knew, was call Sam's father, but what I wanted to do was kill Sam's father, and this desire would surely lend an unhelpful note to the tenor of our conversation. So in the end I settled for cursing Sam's father, fervently and colorfully, while doing up the dishes that always got heaped in the sink somehow between midnight and seven A.M. And gradually, under the influence of a sinkful of hot soapsuds and the hushed, marooned feeling of a major snowstorm, I grew more cheerful.

I had lost the tattoo battle, but this was a concession I would willingly make in order to save Sam from a type of schooling that I thought was about as suitable for him as an ax-murderers' academy. And even Ellie's problems, I felt, could be resolved; surely no one would believe she killed McIlwaine, or that George had. There was another explanation and it would be revealed, I assured myself confidently.

Thinking this, I hung up the dish towel—smiling at the polka music oompah-ing out of the Canadian radio station, enjoying my solitude in the big old house—and contemplated taking a bath.

Which was of course when the telephone should have rung, but instead the back door opened without warning and Can Man strolled into my freshly neatened kitchen as if he owned the place.

"Keep your chin up," he advised cheerfully, shedding snow down onto my newly mopped floor and dropping his burlap bag full of bottles and soda cans onto my clean kitchen table. "Look on the bright side. Don't," he counseled, "take any wooden nickels."

Can Man was in his forties, tall and slender, with thinning blond hair and long, spidery fingers that were always in motion, plucking up the returnable aluminum and glass beverage containers he found on his tramps all over the island.

"You should knock," I said, but I couldn't be angry. Can Man's pale face was so simply, guilelessly sweet and his manner so harmlessly friendly that even though I had asked him not to a dozen times and he still kept walking right on in anyway, I kept saving all our bottles and cans for him; everyone did.

"A rolling stone gathers no moss," he observed. "Could I have a glass of milk?"

"Of course. Wash your hands," I added. "Do you think that if I gave you a pair of gloves, you would remember to wear them?"

His answering smile was beatific. "Uh-huh." Then without washing his hands or accepting the gloves I offered him, he drank his glass of milk standing up.

He wasn't ever going to remember to knock, either. What Can Man remembered was every old proverb ever minted, every bright color he had ever seen, and three other unchanging facts: where he lived (with his mother, in a house on High Street), what he did (pick up bottles and cans), and where to take returnables for the deposit (Sawtelle's Redemption, which when I first came to Maine I thought had something to do with born-again Christians).

"When interest rates rise, liquidity dries," I said, taking the emptied milk glass from him, and he looked at me, delighted.

"If the currency's weak, inflation will peak," he replied, stunning me in return; it was one I'd told him months earlier.

"How do you find cans when it snows?" I asked, handing over the clanking sack of containers I had saved for him. "Don't they all get covered up?"

Can Man emptied my paper bag into his burlap one. "It's not easy," he replied. "It's not easy at all."

He slung the burlap bag over his shoulder. "But," he added with another of his purely happy smiles, "hope springs eternal."

A thought struck me. "You didn't happen to be out yesterday, I suppose?"

He nodded. "Oh, sure. Work," he confided seriously, "expands to fill the time allowed."

"But not here on Key Street? Seeing," I added, "since you're here today. Yesterday, you probably went somewhere else."

"I was here." He gestured at his bag. "First come, first serve. The early bird gets the worm."

Something occurred to him, and he looked alarmed. "Fish and visitors. Two days. Yesterday, today." He counted on his fingers. "Two days."

"No," I assured him. "That's all right. You can come here as often as you like. I just wondered if maybe you saw anyone at the Whites' house, yesterday."

Because if Ellie didn't do it, and George didn't do it, who did? But Can Man wouldn't remember. He never remembered anything outside of his categories.

"Red," he blurted, startling me. "I saw George's red truck. I saw Ellie's green shoes. I saw a gold thing, like a bottle cap, on a man's front." He pointed to his chest. "Right here."

McIlwaine, I realized, and his tie pin.

"And . . . blue!" Can Man exulted.

McIlwaine drove a blue Lincoln, I remembered, but it hadn't been anywhere around when his body turned up. And when he was on the island, he didn't have a chauffeur. I wondered if maybe Nina had driven him in from Mackerel Cove, and dropped him off.

"Blue," Can Man murmured, and looked frightened. Then he seemed to give himself a brisk mental shake, like a dog coming out of the water.

"I have to go now. My mother says don't stay unless you're invited. She says, never ask for anything but bottles and cans."

He looked strickenly at the milk glass on the table. "White," he whispered.

"Tell your mother I said it's fine. About the milk. Tell her I said don't worry."

His face cleared; he hoisted the burlap bag. "Have a nice day," he said, heading for the door, and at that point I still believed I might.

Can Man stepped out onto the porch, where his footprints and Sam's had already filled completely with new snow. Just then McIlwaine's big blue Lincoln went by, toiling in the wake of the orange town snowplow.

"Blue!" Can Man said, and it seemed to me that the Lincoln slowed slightly, as if the driver had spotted him, then drove on.

"Don't count your chickens before they're hatched," Can Man advised as he went away down the sidewalk, his face lifted bravely into the whirling snow, and I should have listened to him.

Instead I wiped the burlap shreds off the table and washed out Can Man's milk glass. Through the kitchen window I spotted a dozen bobolinks, each appearing to wear a black-and-white tuxedo scarved with butter-yellow, sheltering in the raspberry thicket at the rear of the lawn and eating (I hoped) plenty of weed seeds.

The radio stopped playing polkas and began playing show tunes. Monday sighed and stretched, smiling in her sleep. The coffeemaker burbled and fell silent, and I poured myself a cup.

That bath, I thought hopefully.

Which of course was when the telephone did ring.

9

"Girl! Where's my tea?" Hedda White thumped her cane on the Oriental rug, in the Whites' back parlor.

"It's not ready yet, Mother," Ellie called patiently from the kitchen. "You know you don't like it too weak."

Hedda rolled her eyes, which were heavily outlined in black, fringed with thick, dark mascara; her wig, elaborately arranged in a coiffure that would have been appropriate for a costume ball, was the metallic color of a new penny. Apparently she hadn't cared for the rinse put into her own hair at the beauty shop the day before, but then not much ever pleased Hedda.

"Oh, come off it," she bellowed back at Ellie. "Too strong, too weak, who cares? I'm a helpless old lady, nobody worries about what I like anymore."

Au contraire, I thought, determinedly saying nothing. Hedda was as helpless as a scorpion, and nearly as pleasant, her moods ranging from manipulatively charming through irascible to the one she had chosen to inhabit today: hell on wheels. For her morning at home, she wore a gold brocade dressing gown belted with a gold tasseled cord, along with more jewelry than she should have been able to lift, given the severity of her arthritis.

"Just hurry it up," she ordered, banging the cane again, "and never mind your excuses."

"Yes, Mother," Ellie called from the kitchen, exhibiting more forbearance than I could have summoned to save my life.

Hedda let out a heavy sigh of impatience. Ranged around her in the Whites' large, overfurnished parlor, perched on the mantel and massed against the gold-patterned wallpaper, were photographs of her in her heyday, the thought of which I found terrifying: Hedda with even more malignant energy than she possessed now.

"Everyone cared what I liked back then," she said, seeing me examining the photos. With Hedda, I never knew where else to look; if I stared straight at her I wouldn't be able to keep my opinion of her out of my face, and that would spell disaster.

At any rate, there she was, out nightclubbing with the fast set she'd been part of in New York, thirty years ago: politicians, movie stars, rock idols, gangsters, and their retinues. Other photos showed her on stage in a spangled leotard, fishnet tights, and the sort of precipitously high-heeled pumps that showed just how immortal she must have felt back then. Like McIlwaine, she had left Eastport in her dust when she was young, and like him she had returned.

"And do you know why they cared?" she demanded, her gnarled fingers gripping the head of her cane. "I had great legs."

She did, too, although in the photos it was mostly her face, heavily caked with stage makeup, that you noticed—that, and her massively teased, bleached-blonde hair. For one brief, glorious season she had been a dancer in a chorus line patterned after the Rockettes. Some of the photos caught her in action, high-kicking, her smile vivacious and her eyes as wide as the ones you see when a deer appears suddenly in your headlights at night, only not a bit scared. That face, so painted as to look barely human, shone with manic energy and the thrill of being in the spotlight, smack at the center of attention. The world had been her oyster in those days and she'd gulped it down alive, just as she now devoured anyone unlucky enough to get near her.

"But I came back. To my home and my family. I knew where I belonged," she said to me, who so patently did not.

In Hedda's view, anyone who sold an old Eastport house to somebody from away, like me, might as well burn it down. Worse, the house I had bought once belonged to some of Hedda's relatives, and from the way she carried on about it when I first came here, you'd think I was desecrating their graves.

For my part, I thought there was more to the story behind her return to Eastport than she let on. Still, she had come back, married Alvin White, and produced Ellie, all in a single year, with the swift efficiency of a sharpshooter knocking down clay pigeons. For whatever reason, Hedda had known what she wanted.

As she did now. Stomping her foot, which was encased in one of the flat, hard-soled slippers she insisted on wearing in order she said, to keep her step from getting sloppy, she yelled again to demand refreshment.

"Coming, Mother," Ellie called. "Jacobia, why don't you come in here and help me?"

I got up gratefully, Hedda's querulous tones rising at my back. "Sure. Leave the old lady by herself. That's typical of you young girls, today. No consideration."

Ellie shut the kitchen door on her mother's voice and leaned against it. "Jacobia, what am I going to do about her?"

There were no photographs of Hedda before New York in the house. Hedda had burned them, Ellie said, before Ellie was born. *This* is who I am, Hedda seemed to feel about her New York memorabilia, and god help anyone—or anything—daring to suggest otherwise.

"Well," I told Ellie, "I suppose you could have her stuffed and mounted. She'd have to be shot, first, but I don't see that as a problem."

On one of the kitchen countertops, a radio scanner

sputtered static and occasional bits of dispatchers' voices. It was a common diversion here in town, listening to the radio traffic, and with the storm there was plenty of it.

I went over and turned the volume all the way down. The Whites' kitchen was the *after* picture to my old house's *before*: smooth white cabinet fronts, Corian countertops, state-of-the-art appliances, all installed at the behest of Ellie's father, Alvin, who from the day of his marriage to Hedda had decreed that Hedda should have the best.

Not that Hedda cooked, washed dishes, or performed any of the other tasks essential to running a household. Hedda's contribution consisted of emptying her highball glass. The icemaking machine in the pantry was big enough to supply a hotel bar, and from little hints Ellie had dropped here and there, I gathered that Hedda had kept it running steadily until her doctor delivered an ultimatum: one single cocktail, its size monitored by Ellie, per evening. Personally, I'd have doped her to the eyes and let her liver go hang. "Have you told her about last night?" I asked. "About confessing?"

"No, I haven't told her," Ellie said, then sighed. "They both know about the murder, and I told Dad about what I said to the police. He understands, I think, what's going to happen. She's . . ."

"A mean old bat," I supplied, and Ellie shot me a look; the topic of Hedda was a perennial land mine in our friendship, and I insisted, perhaps too stubbornly, in stepping on it.

"Jake, you know how I feel," Ellie began.

"I know." Her patience made me even more rebellious. "But if she were *my* mother . . ."

"Lucky for both of you, she's not. Besides, I promised Dad a long time ago I'd never do anything to . . ."

Her voice trailed off, but I knew. To get back at Hedda for her miserableness, Ellie meant, for her constant complaining and criticizing and demanding. And Ellie's record of keeping promises, as Arnold had told the mainland cops, was sterling.

"Anyway, that's not why I called you." Ellie got the spoons out, setting each one on the tray with a meaningful *clink!*

"Well, why did you, then?" I asked, but she didn't reply.

According to Ellie, Hedda's vicious temperament dated from a mugging in Manhattan, thirty years earlier. A pair of young thugs, a robbery and beating, her ankles broken. Hedda never danced again.

Ellie used the story to explain why she made such allowances, but I was not nearly so inclined to forgive Hedda's chronic abuse of my friend, which was almost as wearing to witness as it must have been to endure. In fact, if her hands hadn't been too arthritic to wield an ice pick, I might have wondered whether Hedda killed McIlwaine herself. She was mean enough, and with her, no obvious motive for wickedness was required.

In the pantry, the ice machine hummed quietly. Hanging beside it was a metal scoop for getting ice out. No ice pick was anywhere in evidence; probably one of the officers from away had taken it.

"Jacobia," Ellie began again; the silences between us never lasted. "The thing is, I'll be going to jail."

"Don't be silly. Of course you won't." I filled the creamer. "You'll say you didn't mean it, you were in a state of shock. Or something." I tried to think of what.

"Jake." Her voice was gently amused, probably at the idea of her ever being in shock. Despite her ethereal looks, Ellie was as tough as an old boot.

And stubborn. Dear god, but she was stubborn. "Listen, could you keep an eye on my folks while I'm gone? You won't have to stay here or anything," she hurried on, "they're fine at night and I've got someone to come in, daytimes. Just . . . watch out for them."

I set the sugar bowl on the tea tray. "So you're sticking to your story. I can't believe this. Ellie, *why?*"

"You told me not to talk to you about it. That was good advice." She lifted the top of the teapot, sniffed the

contents, and set the teapot on the tray with the rest of
the things.

"Anyway, I will be going. Bob Arnold's coming over
in a little while to tell me what to expect. But he thinks
it's pretty certain I'll be charged with murder."

She made it sound like a parking ticket. "So what
I want to know is, can I count on you?" She lifted the
tea tray.

"Ellie, I . . . yes." I faced her helplessly. "Of course.
With Hedda. Keeping an eye out, and so forth."

She turned to me and for a moment I had the feeling
she was about to ask something more. But all she said
was, "Good. I knew I could. Do you think I should
pack?"

Already I felt bereft. "What? No. I'm sure they supply
your clothes."

Prison greens, I thought, the memory of Can Man
flickering and vanishing, or blues; dear god. But Ellie's
composure bolstered me, as it was meant to do.

"You'd better bring change for the pay phone,
though. Soap, shampoo. And your toothbrush. Personal
items," I added sorrowfully. "I don't know how much
they'll let you keep."

A lump rose in my throat at the thought of Ellie's
dressing table upstairs, its silver-backed mirror and hair-
brush, her jars of scented creams. She was clean as a
cat, and as particular about her things. "Ellie, *why* are
you—"

Her look stopped me: clear-eyed, resolute. "I'm
depending on you, Jake," she said, and I thought she
meant with Hedda.

Which of course in a way she did. When Hedda could
get around better, she got a ladder and put rat poison
into the bird feeders Alvin had hung in the yard, so
pigeons wouldn't mess up the lawn.

When Hedda first met me she was sweet and amusing
to my face, then told anyone who would listen that Sam
was not really my son at all, but a teenaged lover whom I
had kidnapped out of a reform school.

When Ellie began spending time at my house, Hedda summoned me one day to inform me that Ellie was a seriously disturbed young woman who had been known to become violent without provocation.

I thought that if I had a provocation like Hedda, I might get violent, too, possibly even enough to start murdering old ladies in their beds. And that, I supposed, would be my main challenge while Ellie was gone: not killing Hedda.

"Anyway," Ellie said, "Janet Fox will be coming to help out during the day. I've been having her in a few mornings a week, and it seems to be working all right. Mother treats her badly, but Janet doesn't seem to mind. I suppose she got used to it with her father. I spoke with her early this morning."

I nearly dropped the plate of toast I was holding. Janet Fox was a terminally shy young woman with chewed fingernails, a tragic manner, and almost as much long-suffering patience as Ellie.

She was also, as the *Fortune* magazine piece had reminded me, Threnody McIlwaine's adopted daughter.

I stared at Ellie in disbelief. "Would you care to hazard a guess as to why the daughter of a murder victim wants to help out with the mother of his confessed killer?" I asked.

"I'm sure I don't know, but I didn't feel I was in a position to quibble. Mother's temper is pretty famous, so there weren't a lot of candidates for the job."

"You could have asked me. I'd have done it."

A horrible thought, but still; she'd have done it for me, had our circumstances been reversed.

Ellie managed a smile. "Thank you. But Janet gets along with my mother, and you don't. Besides," she added in a thoughtful tone that produced a quiver of apprehension in me, "I've got another chore in mind for you, Jacobia."

I was about to ask what, but just then Hedda's voice rose from the parlor, accompanied by the thump of her cane. I wondered if the cane could be fitted with a hand buzzer, of the kind available from catalogs also offering whoopee cushions and exploding cigars, so that Hedda would receive a corrective little shock each time she thumped it.

Ellie picked up the tray, then stopped me with a look as I moved past her to open the door.

"Jacobia," she said. "I need you to find out what happened."

At first I wasn't sure I had heard her correctly. Feeling dazed, I gazed out the back windows of the kitchen at the little frame shed filled with Ellie's gardening supplies—bags of peat moss, bark chips for edging, and sacks of lime—and at her neat rows of herbs and perennials covered for the winter with compost. In the summer, Ellie's garden was a paradise.

"What?" I asked, coming back to myself with an effort.

"I need you," she repeated patiently, "to find out. The way you've found out things for me, before."

"Ellie, I don't understand—"

"Tea! Tea! Tea!" A crash stopped my questions and sent us both running to the parlor, where the old woman sat smugly amidst the ruins of a lamp.

"So, I got your attention, did I? That'll teach you to leave your mother out of the conversation."

Greedily, she eyed the tea tray. "Give that here."

"Oh, Mother," Ellie scolded sorrowfully, and went to get a dust pan.

Setting that tray down and backing away from it took every ounce of self-control I had. "You should be ashamed of yourself," I told her angrily, "the way you behave."

Unfazed, she lifted her cup with both half-crippled hands and slurped from it. "You girls are the ones who had better behave," she retorted, "or I'll shoot you with my pearl-handled revolver."

Ah, the famous pearl-handled revolver, yet another charming conversational gambit of Hedda's, much threatened, never produced. "You ever pull a gun on me and I'll brain you with it."

"Ellie wouldn't let you," she snapped back at me. "I want more toast."

"Do I look like I'm wearing the maid's uniform?"

She shot me a poisonous glare and got to her feet, then decided she didn't need further nourishment after all and sank down again. That was the worst thing—when she wanted to, Hedda could do for herself. An ice pick or a fountain pen were too slender for her bent hands to grasp, but she had no trouble with a steering wheel, after wrapping it with layers of tape and gauze to make it thicker; driving the Whites' Buick she was slow but no less safe than most people. She wasn't even really old; I calculated sixty or so at the outside and probably much younger.

Only her hair, which had whitened early—probably on account of systemic meanness—truly aged Hedda's looks, and it was typical of her that she took endless trouble with it, keeping it rinsed to a really rather shocking shade of blue, then covering it with turbans and wigs suitable for a much older woman. An appearance of aging infirmity suited her purpose, which was to keep Ellie hopping.

The telephone rang just as Ellie got the room set to rights. Hedda's eyes snapped open.

"Who's that?" she demanded. "I want to talk. I've got to let someone know about the shabby way I'm being treated."

"Never mind, Mother, I'll get it." Ellie slid open one of the pocket doors between the parlor and the front room that served as her father's office. But he had already answered.

"Hey? Who's there?" he shouted into the phone. "Damned fool won't speak up."

In the doorway, Ellie turned. "I know what you think of me, Jacobia. It's what this whole town thinks—that I've been brave and strong."

She glanced at Hedda. "And very foolish."

Hedda bridled at Ellie's tone. "Why, what do you mean?" she demanded. But she knew, and for an instant she looked ashamed.

"Only they're wrong," Ellie said, "and so are you. I've been a coward, and a foolish one at that. But I'm not," she finished softly, "going to be a coward, anymore."

Turning, she took the telephone from her father, whose growing deafness made it a frustrating instrument. At the same time she placed her hand gently on his shoulder, and if a lifetime of devotion could be conveyed in a single gesture, that one did it.

But it didn't comfort Alvin, who glimpsed me through the narrowing gap of the pocket doors as Ellie closed them. I caught his look of appeal in the instant before they slid shut.

"You're the cause of it all," Hedda told me sourly. "Before you came, everything was hunky-dory around here."

"I'm sure it was," I said, knowing she would hate this. Hedda adored a battle.

"You know, though," I said, "if I were you I'd watch my step. Because," I went on, hearing Ellie still murmuring into the phone, "you're on thin ice."

She opened her mouth in outrage, ready to blast me.

"Quiet," I told her sharply, and she blinked in surprise. "That lamp, now, for instance. That's a perfect example. Smashing things, violence toward caretakers." I'd seen her swing at Ellie often enough, and suspected that sometimes she connected.

"That's not normal, Hedda. It's the sort of thing health care professionals look at when they're wondering whether a person can go on living at home, or whether they might be better off in some other setting. A more controlled," I emphasized, "setting."

Her lip curled. "Ellie wouldn't let them." It was her mantra whenever unpleasantness threatened, and it always made me want to throttle her.

But now was my chance to put her on notice that

her reign of terror might be ending, and if it was, she had better watch out for me. "Ellie might not be able to stop it."

A flicker of alarm showed in Hedda's malevolent eye. Just then the pocket door slid open again and Ellie reappeared.

"You took long enough," Hedda snarled, then glanced warily at me. "And I hope," she modulated, "it was a fine conversation."

Mission accomplished, I thought.

"Not exactly," Ellie said. "Jake, that was Mrs. McIlwaine, and she says . . ."

The tie pin; I'd forgotten it completely.

"Bob Arnold told her you might be here," Ellie went on, "and she's worried about where her husband's pin has gone. I guess," she added uncomfortably, "she thought I'd be gone by now, too."

Of course the news about Ellie's confession was already all over town. Arnold wouldn't have talked about it, but the deputy and the state cop would, and in Eastport news travels fast. And although the weather had given us a brief reprieve, very soon now the story would be all over the country.

"Gone where?" Hedda demanded. She was going to go ballistic when she found out. I felt torn between hoping not to be around when it happened, and wanting to be, for Ellie's sake.

"Who's that?" Hedda's look of anxiety ratcheted up to alarm as footsteps sounded on the porch, a man's shape moved across the frosted glass of the panes at either side of the front door, and the brass knocker rattled as Bob Arnold let himself in.

"Hello? Anybody home?"

"Oh, the police!" Hedda struggled up theatrically. "Why is he here?"

Ellie took three swift steps, put her hands on her mother's shoulders, and replaced her in her chair.

"Now, you sit there," she said, in a low, fierce tone I had never heard from Ellie before.

Hedda's eyes filled with tears; her lip began trembling. It was a wonderful act, but this time Ellie was having none of it.

"No shouting," she instructed. "No getting up. And if you hit anything with that cane, I'll take it away from you and burn it."

She turned to me, visibly composing herself. "Jake, will you please stay here with my mother for a little while? I need to talk to Arnold before the rest of them get here."

"The rest of who?" Hedda asked tensely, cranking up the drama—but without, I noticed, budging from her chair.

"But . . . the tie pin." All at once I badly wanted it out of my possession; it seemed such an evil little icon of everything that was happening.

Ellie's calm fled. "Oh, the hell with the damn tie pin. Can't anyone just do what I want, for once?"

It was the most refreshing thing I'd heard from her since the whole unpleasant business began. "Why, Ellie," I said, "I believe you may be growing a spinal cord."

She made a face at me—there had never been any doubt about the existence of Ellie's spinal cord, only its activity in Hedda's presence—and went to have her chat with Arnold out in the dining room, while Hedda sat trembling furiously but so far obediently.

"Hedda," I said, "I think I'd better tell you—"

"I know what I need to know," she spat, her eyelids lowered balefully, but I noticed that from beneath them her gaze kept returning to the door of the dining room.

There was something repulsively stagy about her distress—her frightened outrage, expertly mingled with a touch of frailty; heartrending, if you didn't know her—as if the whole point of a man with an ice pick in his head was to illustrate something about her.

"And it's all your fault," she complained, "you're a very bad influence, and I don't mind saying I think you should pack up your things and go back to wherever it was you—"

With any luck, I thought, she would just drop dead.

"You know Threnody McIlwaine has been murdered," I told her flatly, "but what you don't know is that Ellie has confessed to the crime. She'll be charged with it soon, and you need to be prepared for considerable uproar. The house will be examined, of course. There'll be an investigation."

Hedda's face smoothed as if it were made of wet plaster and someone had gone over it with a skimming trowel. I'd seen the same shocked reaction before, in other contexts; informing people that their financial lives have fallen into ruin, for example, that they have come to me too late and must now sell the racehorses, the jewels, the paintings, and the speedboats has a similar effect.

"Ellie," Hedda repeated slowly, "charged with his murder."

She got up, seeming to look past me into the distance, but when I turned, it was one of the old photographs she was staring at: Hedda, all made up like a movie star, and a famous gangster, now deceased.

"The snow has given us time," I said, still waiting for the explosion; I have seen Hedda apoplectic at the discovery of a dry-cleaning error. "If it weren't for that, they'd have been all over the place by now. But they will come, and soon."

"Ellie," Hedda murmured. She tottered, and nearly fell. Fortunately I caught her—she timed her collapse to put me conveniently within reach; *she shall have drama wherever she goes,* I thought—and it didn't take long to revive her. We propped her on the sofa with a pillow under her feet, and her eyelids began fluttering almost immediately. Tucking the gold brocade dressing gown in around her legs, I noticed the old scars marring her ankles. But I didn't stop to think much about them, too worried about what might happen next to give thought to what must, after all, be ancient history now.

Alvin hovered on the periphery, frowning and clasping his pale hands together, shooting anxious, communicative glances at me. Clearly he was torn between his concern for Hedda and a desire to get me away from her as quickly as possible, and into the privacy of his office; we ex-hotshot financial disaster-management specialists can just sense these things.

Meanwhile I remained readied for the blast: it was a favorite trick of Hedda's, collapsing in distress to draw people near, then erupting when everyone was conveniently within killing range.

But the explosion never came. Hedda's first words when she could speak again were so out of character that I thought she must have suffered a stroke.

"'Ellie," she said, in mild tones that I had never heard out of Hedda before, and I was willing to bet Ellie hadn't, either. "My dear, I support you completely."

She did, too, only not in the way I thought, until the end.

Or almost the end.

10

Once we got Hedda settled and the terrible wig had been straightened once more over her hair, I followed Alvin into his office and closed the pocket doors behind me. He had a story to tell, I could see by the way he had set out his financial records on a long oaken table, the ledgers and folders with covers laid open in the soul-bearing, confessional way desperate people arrange when they have decided to fling themselves on the mercy of somebody like me.

Alvin was older than Hedda, well into his seventies: a stoop-shouldered man with bushy grey eyebrows, pink cheeks, and a bald, freckled head. Wearing a white shirt, bow tie, and blue knitted cardigan, he resembled a retired attorney or college professor, neither of which he was. Instead he had run the town lumberyard for half a century, inheriting it from his father and operating it until it closed, a victim of superstores and a dwindling regional economy.

I found his frankness touching, and after a moment's thought, frightening. Alvin's reserve was ordinarily implacable, a wall of quiet dignity and privacy behind his courtly manners.

But not today. I thought about the previous evening's sequence of events: first we found McIlwaine; then Ellie went home and told Hedda and Alvin that McIlwaine was dead. But she'd told only Alvin about confessing to the crime herself, perhaps for fear of Hedda's reaction.

"Thren and I were arguing yesterday," Alvin said. "About this, and I'm afraid Ellie must have overheard us."

Then he sat in silence while I turned the pages of his books. The records spanned decades, but absorbing them didn't take long; they were impeccably kept and he had opened them to all the right sections, so the important parts jumped out at me. When I was finished, I had two clear thoughts:

First, the charming little fishing village of Eastport was nowhere near as isolated from the world and its sordid workings as I had imagined. The tale Alvin's books told was connected to one I knew well from *The Wall Street Journal,* and from ex-colleagues with whom I still kept in touch. And second, Ellie was in more trouble than I'd thought, because the story went like this:

Once upon a time, in a country far away—but not so far that it didn't have extradition treaties—an enterprising fellow named Charlie Finnegan discovered some platinum.

Well, actually, it wasn't just Charlie; it was his American mining company, and it wasn't just some platinum. It was a huge deposit, and rich as Croesus according to the core samples analyzed by the geologist Charlie had hired.

Somewhat later, the geologist jumped off a tall building, or fell, or was pushed; details of the event remain murky. At which point, people began asking why a geologist hired by Charlie, paid by Charlie, and in essence held captive in the middle of a jungle by Charlie (that was where the platinum was, in a jungle in Surinam) would report anything but what Charlie wanted him to.

Which was that the platinum in the core samples had been drilled from the exploration site. But that, as I say, was later.

At the time, when the core sample results came in, Charlie's company immediately went public: people could buy shares in it, for money that Charlie would then use to go back and dig up the platinum. (The geologist, at that point, had not yet fallen, or jumped, or been pushed, off the building.)

Which was where I entered the tale, peripherally but decisively enough to keep its plot points fresh in my mind: one morning soon after I arrived in Maine, I'd gotten a call from one of my old clients, talking about a new offering of platinum stock he'd heard of and wanting my opinion of the issue.

I'd never paid much attention to initial public offerings, other than the ones I privately called BFGs: buy, fly, and goodbye. These I chose by asking myself one question: how cool?

The common stocks of Reebok, Snapple, and Netscape, for example, passed the test; people liked those products in a big, special way: they were popular, yet they felt somehow exclusive. You had to have a certain tuned-in awareness of the culture, an awareness you believed not available to everyone—although of course it was; the culture was saturated in these products— to know you were *supposed* to like them: that they were cool.

Until they weren't anymore. One day Sam came home wearing Nikes, drinking Fruitopia, and talking about logging onto AOL (not all on the same day, naturally, but you get the idea). I sold each of my BFGs a quarter before it plunged, and since that era in my financial life there hasn't been another BFG worth talking about, although I will admit I've got my eye peeled for the next Amazon.com.

But back to Charlie and the platinum stock: Platinum was not cool. Furthermore, I'd known Charlie in the old days when he was finding other platinum, along with silver and gold and the gemstones set into them, inside the jewelry boxes of ladies whose houses he entered by crashing parties to which he had not been invited. Charlie was always a persuasive, dashing-looking fellow, a fact that helped him get into the houses in the first place, and one that assisted him also at his sentencing hearing—no mention of which appeared in the prospectus of his new company.

I advised my ex-client to avoid the stock; if what he wanted was to lose his money, I said, he could do it by visiting the racetrack. But this was a decidedly contrarian opinion at the time; Charlie had enlisted one of the best underwriters in New York to assist him in his capital-amassing project. Pretty soon everybody who was anybody was on board: investment companies, pension funds, all the big opinion writers in the financial newspapers, here and abroad.

Nobody seemed to care that there was no independent assay of the core samples, or that a mysterious gang of thugs had destroyed Charlie's office trailers, or that the government of the country where the site was located had jacked up its permit fees. The point was, the platinum was there and they were going to get rich.

Until the geologist took his fall, and they weren't getting anything. It was a debacle of massive proportions, one all the big names on Wall Street claimed they had gotten safely out of before the crash came.

They hadn't. Charlie had hoodwinked them all. Many individual investors got badly burned, too. One was my ex-client, who ignored me. Another, according to his books, turned out to be Alvin. But that wasn't the most remarkable thing in Alvin's financial records.

"These are all your brokerage statements?"

He nodded, and I paged back through them: listings of

stocks he'd bought and sold over the years, the prices he'd paid and what he'd gotten. Twice, he'd taken enormous fliers on small companies, selling everything to acquire huge holdings in unpromising-looking little businesses no one had ever heard of.

It was most emphatically not what I would have advised. Sailing out onto the perilous sea of a single holding—instead of a well-managed, well-diversified set of investments—may be fine for young men with whole lifetimes ahead in which to recover from their errors. But it is not recommended for fellows like Alvin, who by their forties should be constructing deep, tranquil ponds of financial security upon which to float their golden years.

Contrary to this wisdom, Alvin had sold everything in his portfolio—mutual funds, T-bills, municipal bonds with coupons so generous they were to die for—to amass his risky positions.

And he had done it twice. What happened after that had me squinting at the statements in disbelief:

Each time, the shares had begun their plunge soon after Alvin bought them. He had ridden them stubbornly into the cellar. His losses had been huge, and not all on paper, either. He'd sold big blocks, probably to keep his cash flow going; some of the things he'd held earlier were income producers, utility companies with interest-bearing nuclear exposures, and pharmaceutical blue chips.

But then, just when his buys started edging into free-fall, the stocks began rising. And the reason it was all so amazing to me was this:

Stocks do not generally crash without warning, all at once. Instead the collapse comes in stages: first the insiders sell, then guys who are watching the insiders, then people who are primed to get out at certain levels or who have entered stop-losses, and finally the general public. This results in predictable waves of selling: not a single plunge but a series of definitive drops.

Now, if you look at the chart of a stock that has suf-

fered a collapse, you will see that at the bottom of each
drop there is a small uptick, a rise in the price. This
uptick, representing the smart money getting out because
it knows what is coming, and fools getting in because
they don't, is known as the dead cat bounce, so-called
because if you drop a dead cat off a skyscraper the cat
will bounce, too, but the movement doesn't mean the
cat is alive.

Alvin had done the impossible: he had bought dead
cats and survived them, not once but twice. In each case
the market for the stock had revived with a vengeance,
and Alvin had made a killing.

But then came the third time: Finnegan's platinum
company.

On that one, Alvin had gotten killed, and it was McIlwaine's fault.

I turned back to the beginning of the books. There
were small mysteries in them and I wanted Alvin to
explain them to me. But Alvin had come to the end of his
patience, waiting for me to decode his financial doings—
and, as it turned out, Threnody McIlwaine's deep
involvement in them. Now Alvin wanted to talk about
Ellie and the events on the morning of McIlwaine's
murder.

I sat and listened to Alvin for a long time.

"So, can you help me hide this?" he wanted to know
when he was done, meaning the information in his
ledgers. "Because," he finished, "it's all going to look so
bad for her."

Alvin was a sweetheart, but nobody was going to mistake him for Mr. Wizard. Gently, I explained to him that
mocking up a whole new financial history was beyond
even my considerable ability, and advised him to keep
quiet unless someone asked a direct question. It was the
best I could do for him under the circumstances, but I
could tell he didn't think it was good enough. I didn't,
either.

As I was leaving, I met Bob Arnold in the hall, looking

like a mile of bad road. From his red-rimmed eyes and unshaven face, it was obvious he'd been up all night. He was leaving, too.

"Alvin say anything pertinent?" he asked.

"I don't know," I lied. "He's pretty shaken up."

Arnold nodded, undeceived. I was sure he could tell from my face that Alvin had said plenty. But Arnold was patient.

"Well, it'll all come out in the wash, I guess. Anyway it's out of my hands now. State people are on the way." He glanced at the window. "Storm's layin' off a tad."

"Did she tell you anything," I asked, meaning Ellie, "about how she did it, or where?"

In other words, could she substantiate her story?

I already had a *why*. It had been in the tale Alvin had told me, and it was a beauty: that Threnody McIlwaine had ruined Alvin White as surely as if he'd taken a hatchet to him, because Alvin's disastrous investing had been on McIlwaine's advice. But I wasn't going to volunteer it, which Arnold understood; let someone who questioned Alvin on an official basis get the *why* out of him.

He shook his head. "Won't. She did say it happened here, which if I'd known, I'd have had to seal the place off. I guess she didn't want that. Wanted a last night, here, what I figure.'

Sighing, he added, "Too late now. Scene's all contaminated. Plenty of people're gonna be mad about that, but hell, it's water under the bridge. I know Janet Fox was here with Hedda, they were upstairs together, and McIlwaine was down here in the office with Alvin. As for the rest, Ellie says she'll tell it all at one time, not string it out in dribs and drabs."

Arnold looked miserable. "What a mess. And on top of the Lubec thing, too."

"They find them?" The drowned men from the dragger, I meant.

"Yeah. One of 'em." He added a few details. "I saw Wade coming off the boat. Said it was bad. Tide and waves, knocked the body around some, before they spotted it."

"But why did those guys go out last night in the first place? They must have known the weather had gotten too bad."

"Well, a boat's a big investment. Fellow wanted to save it. Other fellows, I supposed they'd promised to help. That's the way of it, sometimes, on the water. You do what you say you'll do. Plenty of times, you squeak through. Skin of your teeth."

And other times not. Arnold shrugged his parka on, pulled his earflaps down over his ears. "Bad day all around," he said, going out the front door.

When he was gone I stood in the hall, thinking it over. Alvin was still in his office, and Ellie and Hedda were upstairs in Hedda's room; I could hear their footsteps over my head.

Outside the snow had stopped falling in honest, steady bucketsful; instead, it sneaked down. One minute a few sly flakes floated from the sky, and in the next another inch had accumulated, everything coated in white again.

Until I talked with Arnold I hadn't been sure what to do next, but now I was. Helping Ellie was going to require some thought before I could take action. And that tie pin, I decided, could wait.

Instead I went home and got my own gun from the lockbox Wade had built in the corner of my cellar, zipped it along with some other things into my backpack, and walked downtown through the shrouding, deceitful snow to the Federated Marine building.

11

Federated Marine was a no-frills, white-painted frame structure on the north end of the waterfront, overlooking Deer Island. Outside, it seemed to blend into the snow falling in bursts from a squall that had whipped up over the water. Inside, its walls were plastered with navigation charts.

"Want to go shooting?"

Wade looked up from his battered, grey metal desk. His face, ordinarily so good-humored, was drawn and disconsolate.

"Yeah." He pulled on his heavy parka and strode out of the building ahead of me without another word.

We got into his pickup, a rusting Toyota with a cherry beacon on the dash and a marine-band radio mounted on the console. The squall of a moment earlier had dissolved as suddenly as it came, and now the background snow had begun slacking off as well, the wind gusting up only to settle again into a damp, steady blow that was moving the storm's first blast out to sea.

Wade cast an eye up, unfooled. "Not over by a long shot."

"No. Just enough for the flatlanders to get in." It was what downeast Maine natives called inland folk, who retaliated by calling the vicinity a backwater. I supposed it was, too, if you thought of it only in economic terms: so thinly populated as not to be worth ruining with the commercial graffiti of billboards, neon signs, and strip malls. When I came here, it stunned me at first to realize how much of what I had thought of as civilization was really just advertising and marketing, incessant urgings to *buy,* BUY, *BUY.*

At any rate, the storm's second punch was holding off long enough to let them onto the island: more deputies, state cops, crime scene investigators, and of course the newspeople. By nightfall they would all be holed up in Eastport's bed-and-breakfasts or at the Motel East, gawking at the locals—who would not deign to gawk back—and wondering how in the world they would get out again.

"What did you bring?" Wade downshifted, and we made our way up Washington Street past the U.S. Customs building, whose massive granite shape hunkered squarely over the harbor.

"The Bisley, and a box."

Of ammunition, I meant. We rode in silence on 191 out of town, across Carlow Island and onto the two-lane causeway. Close on either side of the narrow, curving strip of road, the heaving waves were black, bannered with grey foam.

When we got to Route 1, there was a fender-bender sitting crosswise in the intersection. The first vehicle was a white Econoline van with a Bangor TV station's call letters on the side, its driver wearing a blue suit and tasseled loafers but no hat or gloves, stomping around in the slush. The van had tangled with a scummy-looking green Ford sedan with a bumper sticker that read: Don't Like Loggers? Try Plastic Toilet Paper.

"Damn fools," Wade said grimly, not meaning the drivers. The body of one of the fellows drowned at Lubec had fetched up in some rocks out beyond the Narrows. I could see the icy water reflecting in Wade's eyes, hear raw sorrow in his voice. He would talk about it when he was ready, if he ever was, and that was fine with me. For some things, a decent downeast silence was the only good response, at least in the immediate aftermath.

South on Route 1, the pines reared up blackish-green on both sides of the highway, their boughs bending low under heavy loads of white as if shielding the red fruits of the savagely thorned barberry brush beneath, but the pavement itself was mostly clear beneath an iron-grey sky. A couple of miles beyond Pembroke Center the snow stopped entirely, and Wade turned off onto an unmarked road that wound between tiny, picket-fenced cemeteries with small American flags poking up through the snow and widely separated mobile homes set on cleared quarter-acres of brushlot.

Bud Abrams' place was a neat, double-wide prefab with a wide, pristine blacktop driveway, perfectly cleared. Nobody was around but Bud's dogs, a couple of shaggy tan mongrels who charged us, teeth bared and sounding like the hounds of hell, until they caught our familiar scent. After that they trotted back up onto Bud's deck, satisfied that they had performed their canine duty, and flopped inside the plywood lean-to he had built for them.

We carried our weapons and ammunition out to the picnic table behind Bud's shed. Wade unlocked the shed with the key Bud had given him and got out the paper targets and steel fall plates, while I carried the Bisley and cartridges to the clearing behind.

"Ready?" Wade managed a smile, grateful to be active and outdoors. It was the only medicine that ever worked on him.

"Ready," I replied, putting a hand on his arm for a fleeting instant.

A small laugh escaped him; he knew what I was doing—not cheering him up, exactly, just getting him out here.

"Think you're pretty smart," he said.

"Sometimes," I replied, and then we got back to business.

In the thicket of mixed hardwood and stunted pine that bordered the granite outcropping where Bud had placed his shooting range, a bluejay screamed into the silence as if protesting our disturbance of his peace. I cleared the table of snow, spread a tarp on it, and opened the locked weapon box and the boxes of ammunition. Wade set up the fall plates and thumbtacked the paper targets, tramping a path fifty feet through the snow to the target butt that Bud had built out of two-by-fours and a steel backdrop.

A few flakes were drifting from the sky as we got everything set up. When we were ready, Wade watched as I pulled the hammer back two clicks to the loading position, slotted the cartridges into the Bisley's cylinder chambers, and took my stance: at a forty-five degree angle, resisting the temptation to turn my body.

As I pulled the hammer back a third click to the firing

position, I took a deep breath and let it out, slowly, getting my sight line, squeezing with my whole hand, as Wade had instructed me to do when I first began shooting the revolver.

The Bisley's polished walnut grip felt warm and alive, even in the cold, and through the earmuff-like hearing protector I wore, its report was a distant *smack!* The gun jumped sharply but not crazily, and I did not attempt to prevent this, but tried not to anticipate it. Then I took another deep breath and stopped trying altogether, just looked and fired, and things went better for the next five shots.

When I had gotten off all six, I opened the loading gate, dropping the spent cartridges, and lay the Bisley open on the tarp while we went to examine the target.

"Nice group," Wade said, sounding less dismal than before, and it was, for me. Five holes bunched in the lower left sighting-in target, two or three inches between them. The first hole was high and wide, almost into the black silhouette of the man-head centered on the target paper.

"You could work on your sight picture, still," Wade said.

The trick isn't in seeing it. The trick is to keep on seeing it, right through the moment of the event.

"Dry-fire it if you want, at home. Keep the seeing and firing as one thing, unified."

He said this quietly, without any special, heavy import. He was a good teacher, and we'd been coming here once a week for months, since I found out he collected the old Wild West replica handguns. The Bisley was a .45, Italian-made, not as fast as a modern .38 semi- but with a load that would, as Wade said, sit 'em down if you ever had a call to shoot somebody with it.

Not that I expected to do any such thing. "Again?" he asked.

I shook my head. "After you."

Then I stood back and let him go to it, watching the smooth routine of handling the Bisley, loading and looking and firing, resetting the fall plates, and walking back under a silent sky, wipe the horror of the morning from his mind.

"It was just a goddamned boat," he burst out abruptly, reloading for the third time. "It wasn't worth dying for."

"No. It wasn't. I wish they hadn't gone out, too."

He looked at the fall plates, grimaced, and shot them down.

"But they did. There wasn't a thing I could do about it," he argued.

Arguing with himself. "No," I said quietly. "You couldn't."

He lifted his chin, raised his hands, and gripped the weapon stubbornly, sighting over the fall plates. On a deadfall beyond the targets, silhouetted against the snow, the bluejay had settled stupidly, accustomed I imagined to the sound of the firing range.

Wade's eyes narrowed purposefully at it. A long moment passed.

Then he lowered the gun. "But they did," he repeated, his shoulders dropping. "They did go out, and now it's over and done with. And damn, but that water was wicked cold."

The bluejay flew off. "You got one body recovered," I assured him. "So his family can have a funeral. You did that."

He thought about it. "Yeah," he said at last, accepting it reluctantly. "And the other one might still show up. At least we know where it didn't go, so the searchers can rule out some areas. It doesn't undrown them, but yeah, I guess that's something."

"Under," I agreed, "the circumstances."

Wade is ordinarily so stoic that the only way you'll know he has smacked his thumb is by spying his blackened thumbnail. This time, though, it was what he needed: not comfort, but company, and a little talk. Under the circumstances.

"Thanks," he said quietly, and went back to shooting.

By the time he finished and I'd had a few more turns, the box of cartridges was emptied and the air was peppery with the smell of nitrocellulose powder. And when Bud's shed was locked securely once more and we were headed back through Pembroke, Wade was himself again.

"So Alvin spent more on the bad stocks he bought than he got for the good ones he sold," he said. I felt better, too. Before I came to Maine I'd spent most of my adulthood in competition as cutthroat as any shoot-out. The principles, clear sight and pure, purposeful action, were exactly the same, and nowadays I was content with paper targets.

Almost. "He spent a lot more," I said. "A hundred and fifty thousand each time, that didn't show on any of his 1040s." A deer stepped delicately from the thicket alongside the road.

Wade whistled. "Undeclared. So where'd he get it? And what's it got to do with what's going on now?"

"Well, it was a little bit difficult, getting that part out of him."

The deer bounded across the road in front of us, through the snow that had begun sifting down heavily again, and vanished into the brush on the other side.

"I asked him where the hundred and fifty grand came from. Bottom line, he says McIlwaine gave it to him, along with stock tips. But he's vague on why. All he would tell me was that it was for old times' sake, which I don't understand, and he was in no mood to enlighten me. He's frantic about what might happen to Ellie."

I explained what Alvin had wanted: for me to kick dirt over the fact that McIlwaine had as good as ruined him.

"He thought if I did that, it might help get rid of Ellie's motive, that she was angry over what McIlwaine had done, that somehow she thought it was deliberate."

"Was it? McIlwaine ruining Alvin, I mean?"

"I don't know. Alvin says not. But Alvin's not making a marvelous amount of sense, right now. Besides wanting me to clear what he thinks could have been Ellie's motive for killing McIlwaine out of the picture, he also seems to think I can kick a clear, ongoing scheme of insider trading under the rug.

"All those tips from McIlwaine," I explained, "over all those years—that's big-time illegal. The SEC should have been onto it, bells and whistles should have gone off—the second time for sure, if not right from the start. I have no idea how Alvin and McIlwaine could have managed to pull it off. But there's got to be a reason the authorities didn't nail them. Nobody gets away with being so blatant as that."

I frowned at the memory of Alvin trying to persuade me. "As if I could do magic," I finished, annoyed at Alvin's simplistic expectation. "As if I could just make it go away."

Wade shrugged. "Alvin's not the sharpest knife in the drawer, that's for sure. But he did raise Ellie pretty much single-handed. That's got to count for something."

"Oh, it does. Of course it does." Ellie had told me how he'd been there every step of the way: sitting with her every night while she finished her homework, helping her with her spelling. Listening, year after year, to her hopes and dreams, and trying to explain why Hedda was the way she was, letting Ellie know Hedda's meanness was not Ellie's fault, that it was just something neither of them—not Alvin, and certainly not Ellie—could help.

Alvin had made Hedda not so terrible as she might have been, and this in the end was perhaps his greatest accomplishment: that Ellie was not an emotional cripple— far from it—on account of her mother.

"He did a fine job," I said. "It's just when people dump their money troubles in my lap, I always wish they'd done it back when they first started making them, instead of now when it's too late."

"Uh-huh," Wade agreed. He took the long turn out of Pembroke without slowing, then eased back for the straight stretch, which ices up suddenly and treacherously.

"As for old times' sake," Wade went on, "that's easy. Everyone around here knows they grew up together. Alvin stayed home; he was the steady one. McIlwaine went off to make his fortune, and people said he was the crazy one of the pair. Now he's built that big, ugly house out on the point, lawn looks like a damned landing strip, to show the home folks they were wrong. Rub their noses in it, you might say."

"Oh," I said inadequately, struggling to absorb yet another thing that everyone knew around here: that McIlwaine was not only an Eastport native but Alvin White's old pal. Sometimes I felt as if life in this state consisted mostly of discovering facts that everyone else had known since the day they were born.

Or earlier. Soon after I came to Maine, for instance, I'd learned that fresh scallops could be had by the gallon or half-gallon from the Dockside Cafe, so I'd gone in one day and asked about them.

The decor in the Dockside consisted of red-checked plastic tablecloths, a round-shouldered old Frigidaire, and a galvanized sink crowded in by the smoking grill and the Fryolator. At the tables by the windows overlooking the waterfront, men in boots and overalls hunched over coffee as black as crankcase oil, platters heaped with french fries and onion rings, and haddock sandwiches dripping with tartar sauce.

"Ayuh," said Greta Holabird, her muscular arm making sweeping motions as she wiped down the counter. "Wrap 'em in butchah papah, lay 'em in the freezah. Sell you the butchah papah, if you want."

She named a price and I allowed as how it seemed reasonable, her downeast Maine twang still sounding exotic to my ears. "When can I have them?"

"Well," Greta replied, "it depends. Y'see, some days the men go out scallopin'. And other days, they go out whorin'."

Taken aback, I was about to agree that this too sounded eminently reasonable, when a rumble of men's laughter began rising behind me, and after a moment even dour Greta cracked a smile.

"That's what they call the sea urchins," she explained. "Whore's eggs."

A sea urchin is a creature about the size of a baby's fist, round and covered with green spines; a less edible looking item could not be imagined, but there is a market for them in Asia and when there is a market, a downeast fisherman knows what to do.

"You come along when the season opens," Greta said, "bring a bucket, take your scallops home in. For a pretty girl like you, I expect even these boys can leave the whores be, day or so."

I'd felt the men's eyes following me out into the bright, salt-washed morning. Across the street, Henry Wadsworth had been unrolling the green-striped awning in front of the hardware store his ancestors had founded, back around the time their cousin was writing *Hiawatha*. Margaret Smythe was setting chrysanthemums in the bent-twig planters on the sidewalk outside Fountain Books, where you could buy the latest issue of *Wired* magazine or a copy of Sarah Orne Jewett's *Country of the Pointed Firs*, depending on what you were feeling short of that day.

On the dock, yellow forklifts beetled between the Rustoleum-red quonset warehouses and the dangling, many-hooked grappling cranes of a Swedish container vessel, the *Selander*, her cargo holds gaping and her flags snapping in an onshore breeze. Half a mile off, the lighthouse on Deer Island twinkled in the sunshine, under a cloudless sky.

I walked home slowly, feeling a realization form and storing it away for future use, like a scallop on ice. Over the months since then I had told the sea urchin story many times, always with pleasure and amusement.

But I'd never confessed the rest of my downeast tale, the verdict in the laughter at the Dockside. For while I was accepted pleasantly enough when I came here, and everyone was friendly and helpful in the extreme, the undeniable fact was that I was from away, and could not ever be expected to understand some things.

"The first two times," I went on to Wade as the low frame building of the Wabnaki store with its ocean sunrise mural came into view, signaling the turn to East-port, "McIlwaine's stock tips panned out and Alvin made a bundle on takeover rumors that ended up being true: McIlwaine bought the companies, and the stocks rocketed."

Wade slowed for the turn. The fender-bender was cleared, with only a sprinkle of orange taillight glass to show where it had been.

"Alvin never changed his way of living," he said. "That's standard in this neck of the woods, not lettin' your neighbors know you've got money. Bet he never spent a dime of it, or even told Ellie or Hedda."

"Right. They were comfortable anyway, on account of the lumberyard—Alvin closed the business early enough so that ending it didn't bankrupt him, not by a long shot. And he said he kept thinking the money he made by following McIlwaine's advice would disappear, that it was all too easy. Which it did, because the last time," I went on, "McIlwaine changed his mind, found out the company was a loser before anyone else did and canceled his takeover plans. Trouble was, he didn't tell Alvin about it, and Alvin took a bath. That was about six months ago."

Wade raised his eyebrows. "And Ellie found out about it, thought McIlwaine double-crossed her father."

Out over Moose Island, clouds bunched together like dark fists mounded one on top of the other, ready to hammer down.

"Nearly half a million is a lot of money for old times' sake," I said, "no matter what good buddies they used to be; that part still doesn't make sense, and that's how much McIlwaine gave Alvin. But what I do know is, Alvin didn't invest only McIlwaine's contribution. He bet his whole stake, all three times—including this last one."

"So now he's in trouble."

"Right. Serious financial trouble. I'm going to have to take another look at his situation, but at a glance I'd say he'll be lucky to hang onto his house."

Wade digested this as we came back into town, past

Shead High School and the ruins of Fort Sullivan where the War of 1812 was lost—at least for Eastport—without a shot fired, the British having simply engulfed the strategically crucial location with a massive armed fleet. After that, the town languished under British rule for six years, the only piece of post-colonial–era U.S. soil that has ever been occupied by a foreign power.

"Well." Wade finally spoke as we continued down Washington Street toward a row of nineteenth-century red brick storefronts and the pea green water churning beyond them. "That's a motive, all right. Ellie thinks the sun rises and sets on old Alvin. I can see her getting mad about it."

"I wish," I said, "it was only that."

He pulled the Toyota to a stop on the street outside my house, glanced in the rearview to make sure the snowplow wasn't coming, and looked inquisitively at me.

"Alvin also says McIlwaine promised to leave him some money," I said. "A lot of money."

Wade closed his eyes momentarily at this further piece of bad news. "Ellie believed it?"

"Alvin says she did. He only told her about it recently. But he says George Valentine also knew that when McIlwaine died, there would be something set aside for Alvin. Something big. Seems Ellie and George have been seeing each other again, recently, on the quiet. Or," I added, "as quiet as you can be here."

At the end of my driveway loomed a huge pile of burlap bags, each filled with construction gravel, that the truck from Eastern Building Supply had unloaded while I was out shooting. I made a mental note to let George know they had arrived, as they were for a project he was working on in my cellar.

Meanwhile Wade and I went on sitting in unhappy silence, watching an unmarked state cop car pull up in front of the Whites' house. Three men and a woman got out, one officer in uniform, the others wearing sober business attire.

"Money solves problems for people," Wade allowed

regretfully. "Or they think it does." His tone expressed his own opinion: that money might raise a sunken boat, but it wouldn't bring back the guys who'd drowned on it.

"Uh-huh." The state people went up to the White's front door, knocked, and were let in by someone I couldn't see.

"If Alvin could afford to hire full-time people to help with Hedda, maybe Ellie would feel she could get free of Hedda. Maybe," he added, "even take up serious with George again."

"The thought crossed my mind."

There had been, Alvin said, an argument between himself and Threnody McIlwaine, yesterday. It degenerated to shouting; Ellie couldn't have helped but overhear. Then McIlwaine went out to the pantry, where the ice maker was, for another drink; he liked his eye-openers in the morning, though Alvin had stuck to coffee.

When McIlwaine didn't come back, Alvin thought he'd changed his mind and gone away angry. Alvin had wanted McIlwaine to make good on Alvin's loss, seeing as he felt McIlwaine was responsible for it, but McIlwaine had refused.

"George was working there yesterday," I added unhappily. "He could have overheard the argument, too."

The uniformed officer came back out of the Whites' house, unholstering his radio and speaking into it, then waiting by his car for a second squad car to pull up.

"If he did overhear, he'd have realized," Wade agreed, "that the little boat he was maybe hoping for was sinking."

He rested his hands on the steering wheel, thinking aloud. "Ellie turned her back on him, hard, when they broke up. No sense wanting what you can't have, I guess she thought. But if her folks were taken care of, that might change, he could've figured."

"And the only way to refloat that particular boat, now that Alvin had lost his financial holdings, was over McIlwaine's dead body, with the money he was supposedly leaving Alvin. Either one, Ellie or George, might have worked that out. And so will the police," I added.

From the second squad car emerged a young Asian man with thick, dark-rimmed glasses. A blonde woman, clearly his assistant, carried a large, crush-proof metal equipment case and looked deferentially to him as they went up the sidewalk, another uniformed officer following. All three newcomers accompanied the first uniform into the house and closed the door behind them.

As they did so, the Bangor TV van we'd seen earlier pulled up, follow by another van and three late-model sedans with sun-faded, weather-buckled "Press" placards on the dashboards. Some of the men and women in the vehicles got out and gazed around at the sweetly silent, snow-filled neighborhood of venerable old Federals and white clapboard Colonial houses. The rest began unloading sound and video equipment from the vans, scouting places to set it up.

"But Ellie," I finished, "is the one who's confessed."

"Yeah, that's the hell of it, all right," Wade agreed grimly, watching the TV technicians train their camera-eyes on the Whites' front door. With their bright winter outerwear flashing against the snow, the news crews looked as exotic as tropical birds, and as misplaced.

"Is there anything else I ought to know about Ellie?" I ventured. "Any trouble she's in, anything she's got going on that she might not want to say right out? Something she needs done?"

I couldn't shake the renewed awareness that there was still a great deal I didn't know about Eastport, and even about Ellie. Nor did I know what to make of her request. If she was confessing to keep the truth from coming out—or, god forbid, because she really had killed McIlwaine—why ask me to try to figure it out?

"Ellie has her head on straight," Wade asserted stoutly, reinforcing my own belief. "I've known her a long time, and if that's the feeling you got, it's the one she meant to give. But I sure don't know what she's got in mind now," he finished a little helplessly. "I wish I did."

One of the reporters began staring at the Toyota. I could see the idea of interviewing the neighbors forming in his brain.

"How about driving me around to the back and letting me out there?" I asked Wade, and in reply he dropped the Toyota into four-wheel, energetically attacking the snow-choked alley. But the back door to my house, as it turned out, presented its own problem.

12

Hedda White didn't like any adults but she did like naughty children, which was lucky for little Sadie Peltier. The youngster visited Hedda whenever Ellie was away or otherwise occupied, to load up on the sweets and soft drinks that Sadie was forbidden to accept and Hedda was forbidden to give, but of course Hedda did it anyway.

Now as I slogged in from the alley through my side yard, I found Sadie swinging around the lamppost at the end of my back walk, licking a lollipop that she clutched in her grimy mittened hand and singing, I thought, a rhyming song to herself.

From a distance, Sadie was charming: long, black ringlets, snapping dark eyes, a blue quilted jacket over a flowered dress, leggings, and loose galoshes, her urchin face smeary with lollipop juice. As I neared, though, I could hear the words that she was singing:

"Dead, dead, smash her head, put dead bugs into her bed . . ."

She glanced up brightly as she caught sight of me. "Do you know if Mrs. White's still home?"

"Well, yes, I think she is," I replied. "But I don't think she's taking visitors right now. Besides," I added, gesturing at the candy, "I can see you've already been there once today."

Sadie's parents never gave her candy, in the hope (so

far unfulfilled) that restricting processed sugars might put a damper on the little girl's destructive energy. No cats or dogs had gone missing from the neighborhood yet, but people kept watch on them; Sadie was a terror.

"I can go back," Sadie informed me freshly, "anytime I want." She took a tentative poke at me with the lollipop. "So there."

Her small nostrils flared in defiance, and it crossed my mind that I would be seeing that face on a wanted poster someday. Sadie's parents were really very lovely people, and by all accounts at the end of their rope with the tiny sociopath they had produced, but that didn't keep Sadie from tormenting the neighbors. Pulled flowers, broken fences, and smashed windows trailed in her wake like the path of destruction after a small tornado.

"Because," Sadie added, "I'm her helper. Anyway, I'm guarding this sidewalk. So *you* better get out of my way."

She let go of the lamppost, pretending to fall so she could swipe the sugary-red, dripping lollipop at me.

I stepped aside quickly as a smile of satisfaction lit her face. Then I feinted past her and hurried up the steps to the back door before she could strike again. There was no use arguing with Sadie, or trying to scold her. But if I ignored her, she would get tired of me and leave—eventually.

The trouble was that with Sadie, eventually was never soon enough. If you chased her off, she found a method of getting back at you: a broken window, a tipped-over trash can, a scratch on your car. And no way, of course, to connect it to Sadie, except that for the next week or so the child would hang around you, sweet as cream but with those bright points of triumph dancing in her dark eyes. All I wanted was for her to forget about me.

But Sadie's attention, once captured, was as focused as a laser beam, and she had sensed my annoyance. For the next half-hour, as I laid the Bisley open on the kitchen table and got out the soft cloths and gun oil and began cleaning the weapon, and later when I came up from the cellar after locking the gun away, I could hear her stomping up and down my back porch.

When I glanced out, impatiently and in spite of myself, I could see her, too: swinging the lollipop, kicking my steps, and singing the bug song at the top of her horrid little lungs.

So that eventually, and even though I knew I ought not to, I went out and shooed her away.

13

An episode of family psychodrama was not what I was after later that afternoon when I finally headed out to the McIlwaine house, a huge faux-Victorian eyesore too top-heavy with turrets, towers, gables, and other items of conspicuous architectural consumption, perched on the bluff at Mackerel Cove.

But that was what I got, along with a creeping sense of unease that began when Nina McIlwaine opened the door herself, greeting me like a long-lost pal.

"Darling," she exclaimed, enveloping me in a cloud of Joy perfume.

Nina was a determinedly well maintained thirty or so, with dark, straight hair, gold-flecked brown eyes, and the kind of lean body that always reminds me of a switch-blade, the product of careful diet and a long line of skinny ancestors. A white silk tunic, black trousers, and espadrilles completed her elegant appearance.

"You are truly a courageous person to come out in the storm," she said, welcoming me in.

"It wasn't so bad," I replied, stomping snow onto the mat. I'd followed the town plow out County Road, squinting past the snow and the flapping of my wind-shield wipers to spot the turnoff for the cove road. A sudden downhill swoop led me along an inlet whose stony beach glistened wetly, with little waves slopping up to nibble the edges of the melting snow.

Finally I'd reached the ornate iron gates that stood open at either side of the narrow private lane leading to the McIlwaine compound: twenty acres of professional landscaping with tennis courts, a domed indoor pool, guest quarters, and a putting green. McIlwaine's own plow and truck kept the lane clear, so driving the quarter-mile to the house had been no problem. Still, coming from the deliberately plain style of Eastport, where gratuitous displays of wealth were about as welcome as a plate of bad clams, the grandeur of the compound made me feel like I ought to have a visa to get in.

I wasn't the only one hoping for entry papers. Around the gates huddled little groups of bundled-up reporters, squinting between the bars and hunching ineffectually against the wind, which must have felt razorish out here without any protection from the weather. They moved in on me as I pulled between the gateposts, pressed the small black button on the intercom, and announced myself, whereupon a fellow in an enormous hooded down jacket appeared from a gate hut just the other side of the iron fence, and waved me in, the reporters gazing hungrily after me.

"Is kind you made this trip only for me," said Nina in her heavy Eastern European accent, her face revealing nothing but eager avarice.

The tie pin Nina wanted was in my pocket, but once I got into the tiled foyer I resisted handing it over at once.

Aside from getting the pin out of my possession, this was perhaps my only chance to snoop further into the topic of McIlwaine's money, specifically why he had handed so much of it over to Alvin. So I did the only thing any reasonable, forward-thinking person would do under the circumstances—I barged in.

"I'm very sorry for your loss," I murmured, pulling off my parka and handing it out for her to take.

"Oh," Nina answered, nonplussed, but then a quick recalculation occurred in her dark eyes. Moving to hang the parka on a coat tree among a rich-looking collection of minks and curly lamb, she hesitated at its damp aroma of dog; when Monday could get at the parka, it was her favorite bed.

"Let's just dangle it here for a while," Nina said, finally dropping it on a doorknob. "That way, it be drying quicker. Now, what can I get you?"

Having adjusted at once to my intention to stay, she made it seem she'd thought up the idea herself. "I can't thank you so much for coming, you know," she added.

Despite my having met Nina a few times around town, her accent and word choices were still jarring to me, a weird mixture of central Europe and old Hollywood movies: Katharine Hepburn, I thought. McIlwaine, I remembered hearing somewhere, had met and married Nina in one of those tragic, impoverished little countries whose precise borders and ethnic/religious identities the inhabitants are always killing one another about, apparently on account of having so little else left to fight over. That these wars have been engineered specifically to enrich strongman dictators and arms-dealers does not occur to them, mostly because—again deliberately—they are all too hungry, cold, and tired to be able to worry about it.

Biting back the anger that assaulted me whenever I thought of this, I followed Nina past a hall table covered with silver-framed photographs into the living room, where a broad expanse of windows looked out over Prince's Cove and across the bay to Campobello.

"Everyone," she announced a bit too enthusiastically, "look who's there."

Beyond the windows, an elaborate wooden deck hung over the precipitous cliff atop which the house was built, jutting out into the emptiness as if thumbing its nose at the sheer drop. The latest snow squall was drifting down the cove toward the Narrows, looking like salt being steadily poured out in a stream.

"Jacobia, you know Patty and Gerry," Nina said, "my husband's daughter and son-in-law." She waved me into the sleek, modern room: white walls, wool carpeting, plushly upholstered furniture. There had been an attempt to make it look homey with expensive bric-a-brac, but there wasn't a green plant in sight, or a pet, or a magazine, except for the six issues of *Architectural Digest* fanned out on the cherry coffee table.

"Hello, Jacobia," Patty Porter mumbled, her voice dull and her eyes puffy-red with weeping. A handsome, athletic-looking woman with big, all-American-girl features, a rangy build, and masses of wavy yellow hair held back by a covered elastic, she was wearing a navy warm-up suit and running shoes.

"Gerry," Patty ordered, "get me a new drink. This is watery."

Gerry Porter sprang alertly to obey, nodding a nervous greeting to me as he crossed to the drinks cabinet. Unlike Patty, he was an Eastport native, owner and operator of a gas station over on Route 1. He was also a fine mechanic and a good-hearted soul. It made me wince to see him jump at Patty's command.

"Hi, Jake," said Bobby Taylor, grinning at me. He had a Coke in his hand. "Patty, you shouldn't drink so much. It'll make you feel worse."

Bobby was local, too, a painter and sometime carpenter, tall and sandy-haired like Gerry—probably some relation; there were more cousins on Moose Island than you could shake a stick at.

"Oh, shut up, Bobby," Patty retorted, grabbing the drink that Gerry had gone to pour for her. "What do you care? Everyone knows you're happy Daddy's dead." She took a deep, consoling swallow.

Bob shrugged and sent an amused, what-can-you-do? look at me, while Nina looked on but did nothing to halt the hostilities. Beside him, Janet Fox sat looking uncomfortable, staring at her hands and picking steadily at a cuticle, which had begun to bleed.

"And here is Janet, of course," Nina said at last, not quite able to disguise the dislike in her voice. Not that Janet was particularly likable.

'That's not true, Patty," she uttered just loudly enough

to be audible. "You know it isn't. You say those things to be mean."

Janet was small and dark-haired, with a delicately pretty face that was spoiled as usual by a woe-is-me expression, wearing her standard drab outfit of jeans and flannel shirt, as if she wanted to disappear. I knew her story as well as I did that of all the others in the room; in Eastport, gossip is the equivalent of a national sport, and no one needed a *Fortune* magazine article to know about McIlwaine's adoption of Janet when the girl was an infant—the magazine had called it, rather meanly, his only recorded act of charitable whimsy—or that her glum, obstinate search for her birth mother was the central preoccupation of her life.

"I say it," Patty retorted, "to be accurate. Someone might as well be honest around here," she added, with a poisonous glance at Nina McIlwaine.

I crossed to the sideboard, examined the ranks of bottles, and selected the Laphroaig, whose smoky flavor I thought would go nicely with fumes of brimstone. At that point I still wasn't quite sure how knowing more about McIlwaine and Alvin would help Ellie, only that I found the combination of murder and half a million dollars very intriguing.

"I'm trying," Patty went on sloppily, "to keep you from making the same stupid mistake I did. He's a drunk," she said, jerking her head at Bobby Taylor, "and he only wants your money. That's why Daddy didn't want you marrying him. Daddy did care about you, even if you were only his adopted daughter. Not," she added with another hate-filled glance at Nina, "that it'll do you any good, now."

She had already had a lot to drink, and either didn't notice or didn't care how many people she wounded.

"I mean," she went on after another long swallow, "it's not your face or your body Bob's after, or the mystery of your missing mother who you're never going to find, is it?"

"All right," Bobby Taylor said evenly, "that's enough. You should keep a civil tongue, Patty, and not go blathering on about money when your dad's not even in the ground yet."

He got up. "And for your information, I was a drunk until I gave up booze, which I advise you to consider doing, too. Unless," he added with a good-tempered twinkle in his eye, "you want to end up going along with me to meetings."

He drew Janet up from the sofa. "Come on, kiddo. Your sister didn't mean what she said. Let's go watch ourselves a ball game on that great big satellite TV your dad put in the rec room."

Wanly, she followed him out, looking as limp and passive as it is possible for a woman to be without actually dissolving into a spot on the carpet. As she went, she fingered a bright, beaded Passamaquoddy pendant that hung on a narrow leather thong around her neck. She'd bought it, I supposed, at the Quoddy Crafts shop where she put in a couple of hours, one afternoon each week. On anyone else the pendant would have been pretty, but on her it only emphasized her sparrow-drab appearance.

Watching her go, I took a sip of my Laphroaig, allowing its smoky burnt-peat taste to rinse away the sourness gathering at the back of my throat.

"I did mean it," Patty spat when the two had left the room. "You'll notice he already knows where all the good toys are. Got his eyes on that big TV, I'll bet. How long d'you think it'll take him to ask for it? Janet," she finished, "is a fool."

"Honey," Gerry murmured in embarrassment, glancing at me.

"Oh, get away from me. You're just as bad." Then, as I'd known she would eventually, she turned her pie-eyed gaze on me. "What're you doing here, anyway?" she inquired owlishly, waving her drink for emphasis. Her voice turned uglier. "You're *her* friend, the one who killed him, aren't you? What," she demanded injuredly to no one in particular, "is *she* doing here?"

"Jacobia is my guest," Nina answered in sharp, warning tones, and Patty subsided sullenly.

But not completely. "Oh, sure. Janet plays nursemaid to the mother, and you invite the friend," she muttered thickly, not quite to herself. And then, "Why is she taking care of that old bitch, anyway?"

Have another drink, I urged her silently, and pass out. But aloud I answered as politely as I could. "Well, Janet's been caring for Mrs. White all along, when Ellie couldn't. Perhaps Janet feels that now is the time she's needed most. Maybe," I finished into the sudden silence in the room, "Janet is like all of us, and wants to feel that somebody needs her."

As soon as I said it, I felt that it was at least partly true. Janet wasn't sticking with Hedda for no good cause; she was doing it for a reason. But Patty made a rude noise, incredulously.

"Yeah, needs her. Like I need typhoid." She took another gulp, to express her opinion of this theory. "I say," she asserted thickly, "someone oughta burn that house down, with *her* in it."

Ellie, she meant, and I folded my hands as to avoid wrapping them, firmly and fatally, around this poor soused idiot's throat. But just then a funny expression spread across Patty's face: one part sudden unhappy realization, one part pure green-gilled misery.

"Oh, damn it." Putting a hand across her mouth, she bolted unsteadily from the room, with Gerry following behind.

Which left me and Nina. "My family," she commented in tones that, if she had been a poisoner, would not have reassured me—whereupon a small light bulb went on in my head: why had *that* particular thought occurred to me?

She waved a graceful hand. "Sit down, please. I think it's safe to do that, now. The piranha are left. I mean gone."

She sank onto the tan suede sofa that Janet and Bobby had vacated, and I sat on a matching chair across from her, placing my glass on a low table whose surface was made from a gleaming slice of polished onyx.

The room smelled of lemon oil and Windex, and had the staged, spotless look that you can only really get in houses where there are plenty of servants: wiping fingerprints, plumping pillows, sweeping crumbs by hand from the carpets with brush and dustpan. I hadn't seen them, but I felt them—a not-quite-silent presence, like squirrels in the walls.

"I really am sorry about your husband," I began.

She nodded. "Thank you. He was kind to me."

An interesting way of expressing wifely grief. It emboldened me to cut to the chase. "But I wonder if I could ask a question." Hey, all she could do was toss me out.

"Sure. Any you like." She was dry-eyed and calm, and I thought—again—that her composure was not artificial. McIlwaine was dead and Nina didn't give a damn.

"I was going over Mr. White's books this morning, at his request. From them, I learned that your husband and Mr. White were financially . . . entangled."

She eyed me acutely, her gaze narrowing at the mention of money. "Maybe. They were old friends. My husband told me that when Mrs. White was in New York, he spied an eye on her. Kept her out of troubles."

Then she smiled. "I was not even born, then. Did you know he had six wives before me?" Now that Patty and the others were gone, she was relaxing a bit, dropping the lady-of-the-manor act, and her accent was more audible.

Bosnia, I thought, or some other difficult place. Somewhere hard and dangerous. For all her china-doll prettiness, she wasn't fragile; you could see it in the determined lift of her chin, the firmness of her carefully painted lip. And despite her casual manner, I could see that her brains were fully operational, thoughts clicking back and forth in that sleek head like beads on an abacus.

She hadn't, I noticed, tossed me out, or told me that none of this was any of my business. Instead, while denying she knew the answer to my question, she'd elaborated in another direction, diverting me from the topic without making a point of it.

The topic being money, and when people divert me from it, it alerts me. But for the moment, I let her steer me into less tricky territory. "That must have been complicated for you, sometimes. How did you meet him?"

Her smile twisted wryly. "Complicated, yes. I lived in a tiny village. Lots of war, fighting, getting worse. Everything broken."

Another diversion, as she mentioned a place name I didn't recognize and couldn't have pronounced without practice. "We had a cow, and chickens. So we were rich. My father would have given a good dowry for me, but I did not want the men who wanted me."

"You wanted to come to America," I guessed. A beautiful girl in the midst of a civil war that was simmering, rising to a boil; of course she would want that.

"Oh, yes. I saw magazine pictures, and at the hotel there was a television." She smiled at the memory. "Everything on TV was so beautiful and clean. People were eating delicious foods, driving around in shiny cars."

She looked at me. "Do you want something else to drink, or to eat? A sandwich? The cook will fix. Have something, please."

All her brittle manner of earlier had vanished, replaced by the simple hospitality of a girl taking pleasure in the ability to offer food. The golden flecks in her eyes still gleamed with avarice, though, undiluted by grief. I asked for coffee, and moments later a carafe and cups arrived, confirming my squirrels-in-the-walls theory.

"I don't quite see what your late husband was doing in your village, though. Was he on business?"

Nina waved a dismissive hand. "One of his companies. There was a river, and they thought they would put a dam and a factory. But it didn't work out. Too much fighting. Not like here."

"So all he got out of it was you."

Her eyes crinkled but the effect did not charm, for the accompanying smile was coldly calculating. "And my mother, my father, two sisters, brother. All in America, now. Only my . . ."

She paused, searching for a word, and a shadow of caution muted her voice. "My cousin," she seemed to decide finally. "He is still there, somewhere."

She fell silent, gazing past me out the windows at the storm, which was again struggling to revive itself. The bouts of snow just kept coming, dying away only to resume when you were sure they were finished, like a mean fit of coughing.

"Fighting," she said at last. "I wanted to keep searching for him, but my husband said he was a . . . a killed issue."

I thought about the strength it must have taken to keep her father from handing over that dowry, to learn her English from television and old magazines, to spy her chance in the visit of an aging industrialist—Threnody McIlwaine—and snatch accurately at it.

Accurately and, I thought, mercilessly; if it had suited her purposes, I felt sure as I sat there across from her, she'd have had his liver for her lunch.

Nina blinked, seeming to come back to herself. "What else have you wanted to ask me?"

Either she really didn't know why McIlwaine had given Alvin all that money, or she wasn't saying. I ran at it from another angle.

"Well, it's a bit awkward, actually. I don't mean to pry, and I know this is a bad time. But I wonder about your husband's will. Whether his death might benefit the Whites, or they might think it would."

"Maybe. I don't know," she replied again. "The policemen say they will come back and ask me more things about it, too."

Then she laughed, a startlingly merry sound in a house so recently visited by death.

"Forgive me. You will think I am terrible. But it is just

the idea of knowing about my husband's money, where it all is or where it will go."

I sipped my coffee. "I'm afraid I don't understand."

Her eyes remained mirthful; she had decided to level with me a little.

But only a little. "In New York," she said, "my husband showed me once a man on a street, playing a game. He was moving some cups around very fast. One had money underneath it, and the people watching, they are trying to guess which cup. To make the bet on it."

She tipped her head at me. "You know about this game, yes? You could not see which cup it was, with the money under."

I knew about this game, yes. On a larger scale, it was called Hide the Assets, and in my heyday I had played it against some of the meanest divorce lawyers in town. Just as with the shell game, there were two tricks to winning, the first being to keep the cups moving faster than the human eye could track.

A thought struck me. "You do," I probed delicately, "know what your own arrangement will be? Financially, that is. To cover your living expenses, and so on."

The other trick to winning the game, of course, was that by the time it was over, none of the cups had any money under it. I felt certain that McIlwaine had known that, too.

"Yes," she replied with a brilliant, confident smile. I had again the sense of a ravening ego no longer forced to hide behind feminine wiles. "My husband explained my part," she went on, "and I have seen the papers about this money he leaves to me. Nothing else, but I saw that."

She sat up straight, like a child reciting. "The other wives, he didn't take care of them anymore if they got married again, and they all did. Except," she added, "the one who died. A sorrow about her, yes? But I was more careful, so his dying makes me become, how do you say it? Filthy rich."

That was how you said it, all right.

"He shouldn't," she ended with unconcealed satisfaction, "have showed to me that cup game. Although I do not see," her slim shoulders moved under the silk as she glanced around the sumptuous room, "how that is making any difference, now."

Nicely done again, separating the topic of her inheritance from that of her husband's death, and she had a point; she'd been filthy rich when he was alive, too.

She looked up openly at me. "You are wondering how I fooled him," she said. "The big, smart businessman. But I didn't fool him. He made a deal. And I," she finished—coldly, terrifyingly—"made a deal, too."

Part of the deal being that now she could stay rich, even if she remarried. In the financial world McIlwaine inhabited—not to mention that of the police—it was a point that would swiftly become public, and she'd gotten it out right up front.

She'd seen the question in my face, of course. My estimation of her went up another notch. What I didn't yet understand was why she'd answered it; after all, I wasn't the police, and I hardly thought she cared about public opinion.

But in this—as in so much about Nina—I turned out to be wrong.

"What about his children?" I asked. "Did he also tell Janet and Patty what they would inherit?"

She looked at me acutely. "Mr. Arnold said that Mr. White's daughter Ellie had confessed to killing my husband."

"So she did," I agreed. "I didn't mean to imply otherwise. I only wondered . . ."

"I know what you wondered," she said, her eyes unfooled.

She went to the window. Through the snow, the bridge at Lubec was etched in charcoal against a grey sky, while the island of Campobello lay blanketed in white, clouds still hanging behind its long, low rise of land as the weather moved off toward Halifax.

"My husband kept his money matters under his vest,"

Nina said. "But I told him that I must know before I married him what I would have, I must see the papers to be sure. Otherwise I would not marry him. I think," she finished, "that maybe his daughters were not so particular."

An ultimatum to the wicked old pirate of Wall Street; the idea was hilarious, or terrifying, depending on how much you knew about McIlwaine. He must have wanted her very much.

Underestimated her, too, I thought, which was possibly the funniest thing of all—although you had to know just how heartless he'd been in his own business dealings to appreciate the humor of it. Now his widow turned, having told me precisely what she wished me to know, and no more: that she herself was going to make out like a bandit, while Patty and Janet got nothing.

The question was, what did she want me to do about it? For I no longer believed she had welcomed me in as an antidote to the always unpleasant company of the disinherited. She had a use for me.

"I brought your husband's tie pin," I said. "It's in my coat; I'll give it to her on my way out."

In the hall I handed it over at last, and made one more try at my own agenda. "Why was your husband at the Whites' house, do you suppose?"

She shrugged. "Visiting, maybe. I told you, the two old men were friends." Then her voice grew somber. "You think badly of me, now. Everyone will."

I turned. "Not exactly." Hey, two can play the honesty game, and there are worse things than merry widows. Unless, of course, they've made themselves widows on purpose.

She followed me to the door. "In my old country, a woman like me is weeping, tearing her clothes. No one can console her, because her husband is dead."

She looked out onto the grounds, an artificial park created amidst the harshness of the Maine seacoast, the clipped hedges and topiary shrubberies standing out sharply against the fresh snow.

"You wonder," she continued after a moment, "why I am not doing those things. Why I don't behave like a proper widow."

Because you've been waiting for him to kick off since you married him, I thought. And if I could figure out how, I might even believe you'd killed him. But all I said was, "You are in America, now."

"You are kind," she responded. But her smile did not reach her eyes.

"My husband," she went on slowly, "was not always a nice man. If you went against him, he was . . ." She shook her head.

There was a story on the street about McIlwaine, around the time I got out of the money business: that whenever he went after a new company, union leaders in the factories he had targeted sent their wives and children on vacations and bought life insurance, double indemnity if they could get it. Union guys were not high on his favorite persons list, and when push came to shove as it often did when he was around, they had a tendency to suffer accidents.

"Look," I said, "why don't you just tell me what you want me to do for you?" It had to be something; nobody dances you around like that for no reason.

She looked down at the vulgar tie pin in her hand. "I decided I want to live here. Not in the mansion in Chicago, or the place in New York. I want to stay where I can see the bay, and watch the little boats."

"You don't need me to help you do that."

"Oh, but I do." Her voice was childishly eager. "I do not want my neighbors to turn away in the street because I am a bad widow. I want you to tell the people in town I am sad my husband is dead. Tell them I am weeping, no one can make me stop to weep."

Little boats, my great-aunt Fanny; she could buy every little boat in town with a day's worth of her spending money. It occurred to me suddenly that she might have other reasons to want to stay here, out of the public eye—reasons she was keeping the media away, too. But I didn't know what they were. Yet.

"Tell them," Nina begged, dry-eyed, "I am tearing my clothes."

"Excuse me." Patty Porter had come up silently behind us. "Nina, Bob Arnold is on the phone for you."

Nina gave me her smooth, cool hand very briefly and hurried away, leaving me to zip my parka under Patty's flat gaze.

"So, has she given you the helpless-peasant-girl act? It's what she used to get out of that rat-hole of a country she came from. Worked pretty well, wouldn't you say?"

Pausing by the table with its gallery of photographs, she laughed contemptuously. I could smell the alcohol on her breath.

"What a crew," she observed scathingly of the pictures. "You know what they were eating when he found them? Potatoes and acorn coffee. The dental work alone must have cost my father a fortune."

I bent to inspect the photographs. Nina had her father's high cheekbones, her mother's wide smile. They all looked ragged and vitamin deficient: gaunt necks, bony wrists. All had Nina's dark hair and dark, thick-lashed eyes.

"And then there's this guy," Patty went on, picking up the smallest of the frames. It contained a shot of a grinning young man with intelligent eyes, curly hair, and a wolfish expression. "He's the real interesting one of the bunch, don't you think?"

She thrust the photograph at me. Unlike the other frames, this one was made of some cheap metal, dinged and scratched as if from being carried for a long time at the bottom of a handbag.

I set the photo back where it had been on the table. The battered item looked out of place amidst the silver and platinum frames, yet had been given the place of honor: center stage, up front. The pallor of the rest of

Nina's people contrasted sharply with the healthy complexion of this handsome fellow.

Patty seemed to read my thought. "Cousin," she snorted. "She just put that picture out this morning. Until my father died, we only had to put up with looking at the rest of the motley clan."

"Patty?" Gerry Porter's voice rose from the service part of the house. "Where . . . oh, there you are."

He looked discomfited at finding his wife with me. "Honey, I hope you haven't been saying anything too awful to Mrs. Tiptree. I know you're feeling blue, but you gotta believe things are going to look better, tomorrow."

Patty blinked at her husband in boozy wonder. "You think," she pronounced carefully, "it will be better tomorrow. My father's dead and that Transylvanian bimbo is going to get everything, but I should look on the bright side?"

Her voice rose hysterically as she turned to me, her 90-proof breath gusting sickeningly into my face. "Is that what you think? I should look on the goddamn bright side?"

"Now, honey," Gerry began placatingly, but it was no use.

"What should I do now, Gerry, huh? I thought I'd be able to get out of here, that once he was dead I'd finally have some real money of my own, but now it looks like there isn't going to be any money. Should I hang out at the gas station, listen to the goddamn police scanner all day long?"

"Patty . . ." Gerry tried again, but she was unstoppable by now. In a minute she would be passed out.

"You know, my father was pretty smart about some things. But in other things, Gerry? He was almost as dumb as you."

She snatched up the cheap frame, grimaced at it, and flung it down. Its machined metal corner dug a gash in the gleaming surface of the table.

"Cousin," she pronounced, "my ass."

14

Other than the prospect of being hanged, nothing concentrates the mind so wonderfully well as a session of scraping paint.

When I got home I set up the stepladder in the bathroom, fitting its legs between the pedestal sink and the clawfooted tub. I had already pried the crown moldings away from the ceiling; under the moldings lurked layer upon layer of antique wallpaper, and finally the original horsehair plaster.

The ceiling was a textbook project: some of the sagging plaster could be screwed back up again, using drywall screws and pierced washers called plaster buttons. With an electric drill you run screws into the lath, predrilling the holes and using a plow bit to sink circular depressions for the plaster buttons. Once they are in, you float the whole surface with a coat of patching material mixed to the texture of oatmeal.

The result, especially if you practice on holes in the attic until you have got your plastering chops together, is a pristine surface that looks even better by contrast with the rest of the house, which of course is still crumbling around you.

Repairing almost anything in an old house, however, involves scraping paint as a sort of soul-testing prologue. Each swipe of the scraper should have brought down an avalanche of paint chips, but this was lead paint, the most infuriatingly adherent material ever invented. Perched atop the ladder with a dust mask strapped to my face—I'd have used a respirator, but these were *big* chips—I concentrated on removing the stuff, one too-loose-to-leave, too-tight-to-fall-off bit at a time.

Item: Nina McIlwaine had called all over town that morning looking for me, supposedly to retrieve her late husband's tie pin. But when she did get it back, she barely glanced at it.

Theory: What Nina really wanted was for me to put a

story around town, the theme of which was to be how devastated she was by her husband's death.

Item: Patty Porter, supposedly weeping her heart out over her late father, apparently knew enough about the terms of his will to be enraged by them, so much so as to make a drunken scene in front of me. But something about her performance felt false, as if what she really wanted was to get some information across.

Theory: The real point of Patty's outburst was the fellow in the photograph. Patty had arrived in the foyer when she knew I was there, and had deliberately drawn my attention to him.

Conclusion: Like the rock-hard little refugee survivor she was, Nina had taken my measure and decided to try enlisting my sympathy by seeming to speak frankly with me. But the appearance of grief she wanted me to help maintain had nothing to do with keeping her reputation. Instead, she wanted a smoke screen for an ongoing relationship with the supposed, and supposedly lost, cousin. Patty, on the other hand, wanted me to comprehend the truth about Nina's ruse . . . why?

Simple mischief, perhaps, and anger over a lost inheritance; there was clearly enough malice there to float a barge. I even found myself sympathizing with Patty and Janet. Having a father who married young girls, divorced them, and went on to marry new ones had likely made their family life feel about as secure as something built out of Tinkertoys.

The money questions, though, were what really interested me. How, for instance, had McIlwaine gotten that much money into Alvin White's hands without setting off IRS alarm bells? Alvin had paid capital gains taxes when he took profits, which should have raised questions about the money he used to buy the stocks, since it was more than he could account for with declared income.

Then there were the SEC questions. One lucky pick on the order that Alvin had made was plenty to set the hounds howling; two was indictment time, and three was when you got the tailor working on your wardrobe of prison stripes.

And these, at least, were questions to which I could find answers. Between modern banking regulations and electronic methods of tracking any fund transfer short of handing over a wad of bills, there are only a few good places left to hide money nowadays. And while I couldn't poke into each of them, I had friends who could: tax attorneys, IRS investigators, even guys skilled in tracing cash to its former, unsavory associations—girls, guns, gambling, and so on, right down to the last load of sub-standard concrete. These were guys who, as they themselves put it, could find a penny in a privy-hole, and one of them just happened to live right here in Eastport. I made a mental note to call my old buddy, Jemmy Wechsler, as soon as I got down off the ladder.

As for why McIlwaine would give money to White at all, the answer felt tantalizingly at my fingertips.

Item: Over a period of thirty years, White receives money and stock tips from McIlwaine, amassing a fortune. Over the same time, he's led to expect big benefits in the event of McIlwaine's death.

But then an about-face: McIlwaine puts his old friend, whom he's known since childhood, into a stock that takes a cataclysmic dive, wiping out not only McIlwaine's contributions and the profits on them, but everything White owns.

I slipped the scraper under a paint chip and flipped the chip off the ceiling. McIlwaine hadn't become a world-class financial power by committing many foolish errors, and certainly not ones of that magnitude. In his fifty years of financial swashbuckling, in fact, he had hardly made any missteps, financial or otherwise; at least, not any that anyone could prove.

Except maybe his old friend Alvin.

Theory: McIlwaine had engineered Alvin's disaster on purpose. The money he'd paid over the years to Alvin was blackmail, and the crash was McIlwaine's revenge.

15

He lied, he cheated, he threatened me with mayhem, but if you want a really straight answer, go ask a neurosurgeon. They are accustomed to telling the most awful truths, as long as the truths are not about themselves.

"Arterial spasm?" my ex-husband mused over the telephone. "Maybe an intracranial bleed? How far in did you say that weapon was? And where?"

Of course the police would also be pursuing all of this. But their agenda was entirely different from mine: they thought Ellie was guilty. Meanwhile, my ex-husband knew all about the connections inside people's heads. It was his job to reconnect them, or if that was not possible, then to core them out like a rotten spot at the center of a piece of fruit.

Outside, helicopters were arriving in town thick and fast, whap-whapping over my house toward the airport, and the vans with radio and TV stations' logos had multiplied in the couple of hours since Wade and I had seen the Bangor station's Econoline, out at the Route 1 intersection. Key Street was lined on both sides with recreational vehicles fitted out with rooftop transmitters; crews of goosedown-jacketed broadcast technicians swarmed importantly on the sidewalks; and smart-suited, sleekly-coiffed reporters of both sexes jostled for good camera angles, their expressions under their full on-air makeup grimly avid.

It was turning into a no-holds-barred feeding frenzy, with everyone from the Calais *Advertiser* to the *National Enquirer* represented: the major U.S. networks, Maine Public Radio, and the Canadian Broadcasting Company out of Halifax were there, someone had set up a coffee wagon on the church lawn, and at the corner of Key and Middle streets a flatbed was unloading Port-a-Potties.

"Jacobia?" my ex-husband demanded. "Are you there?"

"Yes," I replied distractedly, wishing I weren't. Across

the street, the Whites' house had taken on the appearance of a building under siege, and it occurred to me that I had better get over there to check on Ellie and her parents, before the milling crowds of story-hungry reporters started throwing flaming torches and actually tearing people limb from limb.

"What I'm trying to do," I told my ex-husband, "is figure out exactly what could have happened."

I described the wound McIlwaine had suffered. "They'll be taking him to Bangor for the autopsy, I think, but I don't know which hospital." My ex-husband hadn't asked about Sam and I prayed he wouldn't; I wanted this conversation to remain friendly.

"Probably a bleed," he theorized. "Slowly diminishing function, irreversible when the intracranial pressure rises too high. Enough blood leaks into the skull," he translated for me, "it squeezes the brain to death."

That might account for the single set of footprints out in my yard. With his awareness level dropping, McIlwaine could have made it into my shed and collapsed there. My train of thought, though, kept traveling straight back to the money: why, specifically, had McIlwaine been paying Alvin, and why had he suddenly stopped?

"We had a guy last year, got shot through the skull with a crossbow," my ex-husband went on. "Same kind of injury as the one you're describing, but through and through. The guy looked like he was wearing one of those trick hats with the fake arrow through it, only this one wasn't a trick."

Just then Same came home, slamming the back door and dropping his books in the hall, thundering in to find me.

"Hey, Mom—" He looked agitated.

I shushed him violently with my hand. If his father knew he was here, he would insist on talking with Sam, and the first thing he would want to know was about the boat school tour. Had Sam stuck with his decision not to go? Or had Sam's mother undone all his father's good work?

Which of course Sam's mother had.

"But *Mom* . . ."

Not many years ago, in New York, I got a call from a trader friend of mine in Hong Kong. In a badly concealed panic, he said he needed to sell off a certain position; could I help him out?

Translated, this meant my friend's account was being audited, and the auditors were going to come up with a row of zeros where a pile of glowingly reported profits were supposed to be. Nothing else could account for such a naked appeal for help.

I said I was sorry, but I was fully bought up; if only he had called a day earlier I'd have been in all cash.

Right, he'd replied, undeceived, and later I watched him being marched through an airport on the evening news, on his way to a Belgian jail. But even then I didn't regret my decision; he'd bought that trip.

And that was how I felt about Sam and my program of defusing his father's influence over him: sorry and cold.

Sam was hopping with urgency; I waved him off, giving him my worst I'll-kill-you-if-you-don't-stop-it look, at which he rolled his eyes in the time-honored way that smart teenagers have been inflicting on their hopelessly stupid parents for generations, and stalked out.

"So what happened?" I asked my ex-husband, keeping my voice light and unconcerned, as if I had not just deprived him of another chance to run his son's life off the rails. "Did the guy die?"

"Oh, no," my ex-husband said. "Once we got the shaft out of his skull and cleaned up the damage, he healed up fine. Well," he amended with a little laugh, "he's sure not going to be a nuclear physicist. But he's alive."

And that, in a nutshell, was my ex-husband: the little laugh while the guy with the arrow through his skull tries to pick up the shattered pieces, tries to fit them into the pattern that once was his life.

"So why," I said, "did he live and the guy up here died?"

"Two things," my ex-husband responded swiftly, like the gold-star, head-of-the-class student he was. "First, it could've been a freak thing, kind of thing no one's ever going to be able to say for sure, even after the autopsy."

He was enjoying this. "But you said the guy was older. What was he, mid-seventies?"

I allowed as how that sounded right. Even in death, McIlwaine had looked well taken care of, plump and glossy as a prize pig, but if he was a contemporary of Alvin White, he'd been older than he looked.

"So maybe he was on some kind of a blood-thinning drug, like Coumadin," said Sam's father. "They stop clots when you don't want them, after coronary artery bypass, for instance, or if you're on an anti-stroke regimen. But they also stop them when you do."

When, for example, you have an ice pick in your head. I asked my ex-husband to find out if McIlwaine had been taking Coumadin or any other blood thinner. I asked him also to learn what he could about the autopsy results—this, for a New York neurosurgeon who is well known both here and abroad, is not as difficult as you might think—and let me know.

This exhausted the number of favors I would request from him, since I knew he would use them as an excuse to call me. That I had asked at all he would regard as a major breakthrough; it is amazing how desirable I have become, now that I reside in a separate state and would prefer, actually, a separate planet.

Once again I assured him that Sam was not home, that I really had no idea when Sam would be home, and that when Sam did get home I would be certain to have him call his father.

Then I hung up and went to Sam's room, meaning to tell him that he could stay the night at Tommy Daigle's house after all, and watch the prize fights there on Tommy's satellite TV. Sam has no skills at lying or disguising his voice, so I thought it might be better if he didn't answer the telephone at all for a while.

But when I knocked and went in I found him kneeling

on his bed, peeking out through the edge of the window shade.

"What's going on?" I moved up alongside him. Reporters were clustering excitedly in the street below; something was happening.

"That's what I tried to tell you. Man, look at those people. They practically attacked me when I got home."

"Did you talk to them?"

"Yeah, I blabbed my head off. *Not.*" He pressed his face to the crack between shade and sill. "Uh-oh. Here she comes."

"Who?" I squeezed in beside him, noticing that among the mobile news vans was a blue-and-white from the Washington County Sheriff's Department.

Then I saw Ellie, her coppery hair swinging against her face, shielding it, shoulders hunched tightly against the forest of microphones thrust at her, flanked by two sheriff's deputies who were guiding her toward the squad car.

"That's what I was trying to tell you, Mom," Sam said. "The reporters were all saying it. Any minute now, they were saying."

The deputies helped Ellie into the back seat and shut the door, and made their way through the reporters to the front seats. The long black microphones bristled like a mass of waving insect legs as the squad car moved from the curb, the reporters breaking ranks to let it pass, the cameras swinging around to record its progress down Key Street.

Under a brightening sky, the bay was the color of tarnished nickels lightly scratched with silver. Ellie would be looking at it, memorizing it. On account of the blizzard it had taken them about twenty hours after Ellie's confession to get out here and get themselves organized.

But now they were taking her away.

As soon as Ellie had gone, I hurried across the street to see about Alvin and Hedda, shouldering my way through a gang of journalists whose rudeness would have shocked all their mothers permanently speechless. One of

them shoved himself in front of me, his face thrust vehe-
mently up into mine, and poked his microphone roughly
at me.

"Do you know her?" he demanded excitedly. "What
was she like? Was she ever violent? And how do you feel
about a brutal stabbing right here in your neighborhood?
What can you tell our viewers?"

"That they should mind their own damned business,"
I snarled, and pushed him aside to hammer on the
Whites' door.

"Alvin," I shouted, "Alvin, it's me! Open up!"

The door opened and he yanked me inside before
slamming it shut again on a babble of shouted questions.
From this angle the camera lenses looked like alien
feeding apparatus.

"My god," Alvin panted, his eyes huge and his bow tie
hanging askew. He peered out the window. "My god, my
god."

He seemed to be in shock. "They've taken Ellie. Did
you see them?" he demanded insistently. "Did you?"

This was not a good sign. "Alvin, look at me." I seized
his shoulder. "Look at me, Alvin. It's me, Jacobia. Hey,
buddy, get a grip, now. Ellie needs you to be all right."

It was the last bit that did the trick. He stopped suddenly and a shudder went through him, as if he were
shaking off some awful fever. "Yes," he murmured.
"Ellie needs me. I've got to be strong."

"Right. Now let's get you settled down a little.
Where's Hedda?"

"I'm right in here," came the furious blast of her voice
from the parlor, "and I can tell you that I have *never*
been so *insulted* in my—"

Well, at least Hedda was all right. "Okay, Alvin,
here's the deal. You need to get Janet over here, see if she
can stay the night. Have you got everything you're going
to need—food, any medicines you or Hedda are taking,
all that kind of thing?"

He nodded resolutely—feeling better, clearly, now
that someone was helping him. "I think we're fine on

that score," he said, his voice steadying. But then a thought struck him.

"What about Ellie? What'll they do with her?" he inquired plaintively.

"She'll be fine," Hedda boomed from the parlor. "She's young, she can take anything."

I felt like punching her, but Hedda's reply seemed to cheer Alvin. "It's true, you know," he allowed fondly. "Ellie is a tough little nut, always has been. I made sure she could handle herself no matter what happened."

"All the more reason, then, to take care of yourself. That's your job, now, to make sure you and Hedda come through without any damage. Can you do that for Ellie?"

"Ayuh." He squared his shoulders. "I guess I can, for her."

"Good." I gripped his arms. "We'll get through this, Alvin. One foot in front of the other."

His lip trembled, but he stiffened it bravely. "One foot," he repeated, "in front of the other."

But he didn't say that he was sure it would all turn out all right, and I didn't either; neither of us could have stood it. He went to his office to call Janet Fox and I stayed over there—checking the pantry, the freezer, and the refrigerator, making sure there was fuel oil in the furnace tank and propane gas for the cookstove—until she arrived.

From the window I watched as she made her way through the hordes of reporters. She kept her head bowed, eyes down, her shoulders hunched, and her mouth shut—which for Janet was no particular feat; dull silence was her usual condition. Only her eyes, glittering darkly with dislike once she got inside, showed how intense an ordeal the trip up the front walk had been for her.

"Fine," she said, surveying the downstairs rooms as I went through them with her, listing things I thought the Whites either wanted or needed: some conversation, a little distraction—but not the TV, which was packed with news of the murder and Ellie's arrest—and of course decent nourishment.

"I'll be right across the street, so call me if you need anything, and good luck. And Janet, thanks a lot for this."

She eyed me curiously. "I said I would do it. I told Ellie," she replied in a flat, affectless voice.

"Yes, well. I appreciate it anyway." I went to the door; if her odd expression struck the tiniest of sour notes with me, I managed to rationalize it. After all, it was her father who had just been murdered.

Then I let myself out, steeling myself for the reporters' gauntlet, and ran it successfully—a good, sharp elbow, properly placed and accompanied by an obviously insincere apology, can do wonders—reaching my own door in record time and flattening myself in immense relief against it, once I was inside.

Duty, I thought gratefully, *discharged.*

For now.

16

The rest of the early evening was taken up with chores: dinner, dishes, Sam's homework, several loads of his laundry—the doing of which I had traded for a couple of hours of his work on that bathroom ceiling—and a walk for Monday, who had been getting rather short shrift in the fresh-air-and-exercise department.

Meanwhile the state police investigators had been in the storeroom, taking photographs and measuring distances and doing whatever else they do in locations where dead bodies have been discovered. They had also questioned me, but without, I thought, any particular urgency. Having a confession, they seemed to feel (although of course they would have denied this fervently), made the rest of their activities merely *pro forma.*

Also, as it turned out, the prize fights had been put off

on account of some difficulty with the referee. An out-
standing warrant for arrest on racketeering charges was,
I gathered, an impediment to his employment. So now, at
midnight, Sam was in his room working on a model of
the warship *Calypso*, a coal supplier to a World War II
gun flotilla that stood in Eastport harbor on July 23,
1916—two years later, the *Calypso* vanished in the
Bermuda Triangle—and Wade was in the living room in
front of the television, asleep.

It was a talent I admired, his ability to sleep while life
went on without him in the rest of the house. My ex-
husband couldn't sleep if a single unrinsed cup stood
lonesomely in the kitchen sink. He wouldn't even lie
down until every light in the apartment was switched off
and every appliance double-checked. His eyes would
snap open alertly if, two rooms down the hall from our
bedroom, Sam turned over in his crib.

For a while I had tried reading in bed, using one of
those clip-on book lights angled away from his head, but
he complained that he could hear the hum of the electrical circuit, that I might forget and leave it on, setting
the bedclothes afire, that even after he turned away from
me on his side, he could feel the light particles seeping
into his skull.

Now, sitting alone in the kitchen while Wade slept in
the recliner two rooms away, I thought about a short
conversation I'd had with Ellie at this same table, the
night before. It was right after she'd confessed to McIlwaine's murder, and before they had let her go home.

"Jacobia," she'd said, while the state and county cops
tried to get hold of their superiors by radio or telephone,
"do you remember last fall right after you first came to
Eastport? Hedda needed to have her hip replaced, and I
was so awful spleeny about it?"

Spleeny: nervous, upset, unnecessarily anxious. It was
among my favorite bits of downeast dialect.

"I remember," I'd told her. "You came over for coffee
one afternoon and you ended up telling me the whole
story."

She nodded. "It was the first I'd even met you, but by the next day you'd called all over the country, finding out whether the surgeon in Bangor was good, or if there was someone else we should go to."

Being the ex-wife of a famous neurosurgeon has its perks: The surgeon in Bangor, as it turned out, was board-certified and so expert that patients came from New York and Philadelphia. The day after Hedda's successful surgery, Ellie and I drank champagne at lunch and went to the Bangor Garden Show.

On the way home the next afternoon, the sun shone slantwise on the blueberry barrens: high, Alpine-feeling hills with granite boulders the size of Volkswagens pushing up out of them, blanketed with the ankle-high shrubs. Winter had come early and the remains of last year's growth were the color of raspberry syrup spilled out across the snow.

Now I thought of her reminding me about it: that I had found things out for her before. As for why I might trouble to do so again, I needed no reminding.

Once, when my ex-husband telephoned in a fury, demanding to speak to me for some reason that I cannot now recall—I had bought Sam an air rifle, perhaps, or allowed him to go fishing; my ex-husband thought hunting and fishing were marks of impending degeneracy— Ellie answered the phone and told him I wasn't home, and that by the way, she had heard a lot about him and wanted to congratulate him on being so flexible.

Flexible? my ex-husband asked, puzzled.

Yes, she had told him, she was sure he must be very flexible. Otherwise, how could his head have gotten up there where it was?

I could hear his reply boiling out of the receiver like an eruption of lava. This was just shortly after Ellie and I had gone together to Bangor; the lunchtime champagne had made me talkative, and I may have mentioned one or two things about him.

Calmly, Ellie had hung up. "Excitable, isn't he?" she'd said, turning back to the rhubarb pies we had been making, and I was so astonished and terrified by her action that it wasn't until much later that I realized what she had done for me.

The thing was this: after I left New York, my ex-husband had begun threatening me. It sounds unbelievable now, but at the time it was frightening, and at first it was about Sam: that he would sue for custody, or cut off all contact, or take Sam to Europe on vacation and forget to bring him back.

Later, it became more personal: old houses like mine were notorious firetraps and it wouldn't take much to light one up. I should check my groceries when I bought them; something could have been tampered with. I had better lock my doors and windows when I was home alone, in case someone tried to sneak in with a knife.

It was totally bizarre and unexpected, and it got worse and worse. I consulted my attorney, who said little could be done. The threats were indirect; my ex-husband, while obnoxious, was still within the law. I spoke to a psychiatrist, who advised me to call the police if the remarks grew more explicit, or if my ex-husband did anything overt.

But after Ellie hung up on him that day, I began doing as she had; nervously at first and then with increasing confidence. I would stay on the telephone while he was civil, but if he started threatening me I put the receiver down.

And after a while the threatening went away, like a child's tantrum if you ignore it long enough. Ellie had done exactly the right and proper thing, though at the time I was horrified by it, believing it could only make matters worse.

17

When I opened my eyes the next morning, the first thing I heard was foghorns. From the upstairs hall window, the rooftops of Eastport floated on an ocean of grey; gulls perched sullenly on the rooflines, grounded by the weather, and the few cars moving in the street had their headlights on.

Wade kissed me hard on his way off to work, causing me to linger dreamily in the kitchen for several moments until my nerve endings had settled down again. Sam had gone over early to Tommy Daigle's to see the old Ford jalopy Tommy had bought in hopes of fixing it up by the time he could afford to insure it, so Monday and I were alone. At the back door, she waited impatiently for me to pull on my green rubber rain boots, black oilskin hat, and yellow slicker—one of the pleasures of Maine weather, I have found, is the chance to wear the costume—then bounded into the yard.

Outside, droplets plinked steadily in the downspouts, the cool, drifting fog was tinctured with the smell of woodsmoke, and the snow on the ground was shrinking as if sluiced away; it was what the old-timers called a snow-eating fog.

No activity was evident across the street at the Whites' house—it was 7:30, too early for the reporters, apparently—and Janet's car was marooned behind a foot of icy muck thrown into their driveway by the snow-plows. Then Monday reappeared from the murk and we went back inside, where the telephone was ringing.

"Hey, Jacobia," said Toby Alderman. I pictured Toby in his tiny, neat-as-a-pin law office on Water Street, with its big window looking out on the best view in the world: water and sky.

"Hey, Toby." On a clear day, you could see to St. Andrews from Toby's desk; in a way, it was the opposite of the view you got when you looked at Toby. His eyes, like his office window, were wide and blue, but they gave away nothing.

Nor did his voice. It was a matter of principle with him. "I talked to Ellie this morning," Toby said.

"And?"

"She asked me to let you know that the arraignment's

this afternoon. That's when they'll be reading the formal charge, and she has to plead."

I already knew what an arraignment was. "What time?"

He told me, but then he added, "She doesn't want you to be there."

"What? That's ridiculous, of course I'm going to—"

But he was firm. "Listen, I had to practically break her arm to get her to agree to accept counsel at all. The only reason she did was that the judge won't let her plead without legal advice. If she sees you there, I don't know what's going to happen."

"So she's going through with it." Somehow I'd hoped that when some time went by, she would see reason.

I should have known better. "She's just bound and determined, Jacobia," Toby said, "and you know how she is when her mind's made up."

"Yeah, I do. So what happens next?"

"Well, I think the judge will decide not to accept her guilty plea, send her up to superior court, and wash his hands of her. If that's the case we'll have a little more time, maybe a few months, to try straightening out this nonsense."

"What happens meanwhile?"

"I can try to get her out on bail. She's going to look like a decent bail risk: roots in the community, no prior record, so on. Maine's funny about bail in a murder case, though."

"Which means?"

"State constitution. It says every citizen has a right to bail except in capital cases. Now," he went on, "we don't have the death penalty in the state of Maine, anymore—"

For which I was fervently grateful.

"—but murder is still defined as a capital offense."

"Bottom line, Toby. What are the chances?"

There was a silence. While I waited, a picture of Ellie popped into my mind: coppery hair blowing, she perched on the flying deck of Wade's summer runabout, the *Little Dipper*, her eyes alight and her arm joyously outstretched as she pointed to the sleek, arched back of a surfacing minke whale, out on the water almost in sight of Head Harbor.

"One in a thousand," Toby Alderman said. "Boy, criminal law is tough when your clients are your friends. I like real-estate law, where hardly anyone goes to jail."

"I know. If we could get another lawyer in this town, then you could give it up." But it wasn't likely; there was enough defense business here to support one, but not in the style to which most modern attorneys have become accustomed. It's the big crimes of wealthy clients that generate the big bucks.

"Thanks, Toby, for helping her out," I told him. "Anything else?"

"Oh, yeah, nearly forgot. She said to tell you not to give up on that portrait, if that means anything to you. Said you should try again, because it's important."

I had a minute to think that over while he put me on hold to pick up a call on his other line. While I did, the woman on the mantel gazed down at me, inscrutable as ever.

What the hell was Ellie talking about? Finally I decided her remark was only meant to cheer me—as if that were possible—and that Toby, who disliked nuance and implication, had conveyed her tone inaccurately.

When he came back, he said, "Listen, Jacobia, I took this case as a favor. Not to Ellie, she still wants me like gum on her shoe, but for her dad. But I've got to tell you, if she goes on sticking to her guns on this guilty business, I'm not sure how much I can do. And she sounds like she is going to."

If Toby had already talked to Alvin, he knew he was working Ellie's case *pro bono*; I had a sad, momentary picture of Alvin, going hat in hand. Not that Toby expected to be tied up on it for long. The way he was talking, there wasn't even going to be a trial, just a guilty plea followed by a sentencing hearing. He was warning me, in his careful way, not to get my hopes too high.

"I understand, Toby. I appreciate your calling. She didn't say anything else about this portrait business?"

"Nope. Didn't even make that big a deal of it. Just said she'd rather do the arraignment alone, and that you've got plenty to keep you busy right here in town. Anyway, I'll be there with her, and I'll call if things don't go the way I'm expecting."

If the district judge took her guilty plea, Toby meant. If it was all over, right then and there. It wasn't likely— serious crimes, Bob Arnold had pointed out, were supposed to go right up to superior court—but I'd been consultant in enough bankruptcy proceedings to know that in the judicial system, almost any damn fool thing was possible, and judges could be as jealous over their turf rights as anyone else.

"Okay," I said. "If she needs anything, let me know and I'll take care of it. Let me know either way about the plea, will you? And be sure and call me as soon as she can have any visitors."

Another brief silence told me not to hold my breath. "Right," he said then. "Well, I'd better get busy."

Me, too, I thought, hanging up.

18

I do not think money is the root of all evil, but I know it makes an effective fertilizer. And money, I felt sure, was at the root of this mess. Snapping Monday back onto her lead, I tucked my scarf down into the neck of my slicker and set my sou'wester on my head, then waited for one of the mobile broadcast vans to block the reporters' view of me as I started for town. It was time to talk to Jemmy Wechsler.

The fog thickened as I neared the harbor, lending a hushed, ghostly atmosphere to the streets. The antique red brick of the Arts Center building glistened in the mist, and the green silk "open" banner hanging from the upstairs window of Ted Vinson's pottery shop flapped wetly. Passing the Mexican restaurant with its gay strings of Christmas lights twinkling through the salt-smelling murk, I shot a wistful glance at the grey, weathered timbers of the Happy Landings Cafe, where hot coffee and good company—not to mention fine blueberry pancakes—were always on the menu.

But they were pleasures I would have to defer, I thought regretfully, crossing the street toward the fish dock, where the squat, grey tugboat *Ahoskie* rolled at the half-tide, the lights on her bridge faint gleams through the enveloping mist. Beyond her, the *Star Verlanger* loomed up out of the fog like an apparition, her cranes grappling white-wrapped pallets of particleboard and swinging them into her cargo bays.

Past the roar of the trucks lining up to be unloaded and the payloaders scuttling among them, the gangway to the *Hoodathunkit* was a metal stair leading down past a forest of weed-draped dock pilings toward water level, which was dead low tide. I slipped Monday's leash and she scampered fearlessly ahead of me, her toenails clinking on the metal steps, which in addition to being nearly vertical were also moving, on account of being attached to the floating dock.

By the time I made my own way down, she had already leapt from the dock and nosed into the cabin, and Jemmy Wechsler was calling out my permission to board the *Hoodathunkit*.

"So," Jemmy inquired a few minutes later when he had supplied Monday with biscuits and me with a strong hot toddy, "to what do I owe the honor?"

Drinking in the morning is not by any means my habit, but around Jemmy Wechsler almost any action seems permissible; the things he has done and seen are so far beyond the pale that a toddy for breakfast is as nothing. His final act before leaving New York two years earlier was to transfer something approximating a king's ransom to a series of confidential accounts at a large, well-known bank in Zurich; the numbers and ID codes

of these he had committed to memory and also—he
had informed me recently—to the links of the *Hoodathunkit*'s anchor chain.

"To my need for information," I said. Monday glanced
at Jemmy, got a nod of assent, and hopped up to settle
herself on his lower berth, while Jemmy's Irish whiskey
warmed me from within, burning off the fog's penetrating chill.

I'd gotten one phone call from Jemmy, soon after his
hasty departure, and I'd had to do some fast talking—
first in English and then in my few little broken bits
of French, German, and Italian; the only thing I can talk
about in any of these latter languages is, of course,
money—to persuade the Zurich bank to accept him as a
client. The bad publicity the institution had gotten over
its private accounts made it leery of deposits in cash.
Only my threat to take the deposit to nearby Lugano,
some of whose bank managers are equally silent about
the identities of their account holders but less inquisitive
as to the gory details—such as, for instance, the precise
method by which the cash had entered the country in the
first place—had turned the trick.

"I'm following some money around," I revealed cautiously. "Last time it stuck its head up, it belonged to
Threnody McIlwaine."

Lean, brown, and bearded, Jemmy wore a black fisherman's sweater, faded blue jeans, and work boots. To
look at him, you'd think he was just another downeast
lobsterman, but a glance around his living quarters dis-
pelled that notion; from the outside, the *Hoodathunkit*
was a common dragger with a high, nosy prow and the
bare necessity of an operator's shack plopped amidships.
But below decks, she was all gleaming teak and polished
brass, fitted out with enough electronic gear for the flight
deck of a 767. In addition to the usual loran, global satellite positioning, wind speed indicator, and depth finder,
he had built-in racks of other stuff I knew nothing about,
only that it looked complicated.

Jemmy grinned. "Mac was one of the big boys." He raised his mug. "To the undear departed, may his soul get what it deserves."

I felt my eyebrows go up. "Connected?"

"Like the Pope," Jemmy replied, "is Catholic."

And as to that, who should know better than Jemmy? Before he left New York, he was a banker to the mob from Providence to Newport News; if the guys who were looking for him ever found him, Jemmy was fish food.

I told him what I wanted, and asked what it would cost me in return, meanwhile mulling over the idea that McIlwaine was mob-related. It made sense; a lot of the industries McIlwaine had been involved in were traditional organized-crime territory—trash collection, construction, and so on. And the people he'd bullied and terrorized, possibly even murdered, in order to be so successful in those businesses—well, nobody believed that the tycoon had gone out on any leg-breaking expeditions, himself.

Or anyway, not recently. "Send Sam down here when he gets home from school," Jemmy replied. "One of my outboards is turning over funny, I need him to take a listen."

Hearing Sam's name, Monday thumped her tail happily. "You in a hurry?" I asked. My eyes kept returning to the space under the neatly made berth. Last time I'd seen it, it had been packed full of Jemmy's favorite method of filling his time: books.

"Little bit," Jemmy replied, following my gaze.

The space under the berth was now stuffed with diving gear: I recognized a Diver's Unlimited International dry suit, the one-piece kind with latex seals and neoprene hood and mitts. With it I could see a mask, a set of fins, a snorkel, a tank and regulator, and a BCD—a buoyancy compensation device. Stuffed in alongside were what looked like several sets of thermal underwear, the kind local divers wear under dry suits to protect them against the fifty-degree water of the bay.

All these items were similar to ones I'd seen on various trips to Federated Marine—a lot of the guys who work there are divers for the aquaculture outfits, or on boat-repair crews—but with one difference:

The DUI dry suit colors are orange and black, for safety; their brilliance makes a diver visible in the dark water. Jemmy—or somebody—had covered the orange parts with strips of black friction tape.

Jemmy watched me assess the gear without comment. I didn't make one either; I knew better than that. But it looked to me as if he planned to be underwater. And invisible.

Monday descended from the berth and I clipped her back onto her lead. "A little bit of engine repair isn't much of a return favor, especially since I'm not going to be the one doing it. Am I running up a tab?"

Jemmy grinned, his teeth gleaming white behind his beard. Half his mouth was a product of space-age materials and high-tech dental reconstruction, the result of an argument between Jemmy and a fellow with a nail-studded two-by-four. The guy (and I knew this for a fact) had not survived the encounter.

"Have you broadcast my whereabouts yet?" he asked, taking our mugs to the galley where he washed, rinsed, and dried them, then stowed them neatly away. Back in Manhattan, his attention to detail had been legendary.

"Not yet." It was a running joke between us, funnier to me than it was to Jemmy, perhaps. Imagine his surprise when, after absconding with a pile of the mob's ill-gotten gains and going on the lam for almost two years, Jemmy chose Eastport as the bolt-hole where he was least likely to be spotted, only to find me, an old Wall Street chum, already snug in it.

"Then you don't owe me anything," Jemmy said. "Might take a while, though. I can't exactly call those fellows direct, can I? But I left myself a few back doors, and it's time to put an ear to a couple of 'em, anyway. Find out," he added, "what the opposition is up to."

As if he didn't know. I had a feeling his knowledge

might have something to do with all that diving gear, but I wasn't about to ask that, either.

He closed up the galley cabinets. "I find out what you want, I'll give you a holler."

"Fair enough." I sent Monday back up through the hatch, and followed her. Jemmy came topside, too, stretching and breathing the raw, moisture-laden air with pleasure.

Breathing any air at all was a luxury to Jemmy; what he was up to was no joke. But once he got over the shock of running into me in Eastport, he'd said he was glad to see me, to have someone that he could talk to. Running from the mob was a lot of things, he'd said, but mostly it was lonely.

Above our heads, the cargo vessel cut off the sky; beside us, the dock pilings were like a forest of dark, dripping tree trunks. The water in the boat basin was flat calm, the waves slopping softly against the cannery foundation ruins.

On the deck, several boxes lay under a blue tarp. The tarp had come loose at one corner, fluttering in the breeze. Jemmy strolled casually over to it, and tucked it in, but not before I glimpsed what was printed on one side of the exposed crate.

"I hear your friend Ellie was the one stuck a sharp thing in McIlwaine," Jemmy said. "These questions of yours, they wouldn't by any chance be connected to that?"

The roar of truck engines rumbled distantly. "You always were a quick study."

He laughed. "Yeah, that's why I got the hell out of Dodge. Thing is, you're not the only one interested in that money."

"What makes you think that?"

Jemmy shrugged, watching a pallet of particleboard sail up off the bed of an eighteen-wheeler, swing around, and hover over the *Star Verlanger*'s open cargo bay.

"So I'm in the Baywatch the other night," he said, "minding my own business, having a quiet nightcap. My back's to the room, but I could still hear pretty much everything."

Of course; if his hearing weren't good he'd be resting in pieces, surrounded by a forty-gallon drum at the bottom of the East River.

"And I hear these two talking about just what you're talking about," Jemmy went on. "Quiet, but I hear it. So after a while, I look in the mirror behind the bar and there's the two of them with their heads together."

Impatience overcame me. "The two of *who*?"

Monday glanced up, then returned to crunching one of the urchins whose crisp, sea-green shells blow like small tumbleweeds all around the perimeter of the island. I glanced again at the tarp-covered crates on Jemmy's deck, now safely concealed again.

Back in another life, before New York, before what I thought of as my real life even began, I'd seen a lot of those crates. For an unwelcome instant my first sight of them came back to me, along with the unwanted recollection of a smell that had permeated my entire existence back then: the thin, sour reek of poverty.

Once I'd gotten out of it, I never went back, but the scenery stuck, vivid and unerasable, in memory.

Explosives, the legend on the side of the wooden crate had read before Jemmy covered it up; that and the bright yellow danger triangle and health-hazard warning. I remembered them well.

But now all I smelled was salt water, seaweed, and a whiff of diesel from the trucks moving busily above. That old life of impoverishment and of struggling up out of it was in the past, and I would never have to live it again, except in a few unhappy memories.

Money may be the root of all evil to some, but it is better than the alternative; take it from one who knows.

"It was Ellie," said Jemmy, "and George Valentine."

19

When I first came to Eastport, I was optimistic about doing small repair jobs myself, and I thought replacing a toilet seat was within my home fix-up capabilities. So I went to Wadsworth's and bought a new toilet seat, with plastic attachment bolts.

Unfortunately, someone had attached the old seat with metal bolts, securing them with metal nuts, and over the years these items had fused themselves together via the miracle of rust. No turning or twisting had any effect whatsoever on them.

Undeterred, I went back to Wadsworth's and bought myself a hacksaw, sat down on the bathroom floor, and slid the hacksaw's blade between the first rusted bolt head and the ceramic surface of the toilet bowl. Happily, I began sawing back and forth; home repair, I thought, took ingenuity, which I had in spades.

Whereupon the rubber seal between tank and bowl, embrittled over the years and disturbed by the vibrations of my energetic hacksawing, gave way, pouring water into the crawlspace over the basement stair, where it was my understanding that a lot of very important electrical wires were located.

The shut-off valve broke off in my hand; I scrambled to the basement, where pipes crisscrossed along the ceiling. All were draped in thick, greasy-feeling cobwebs, and a confusing number of them seemed to be connected to the hot-water boiler, which I believed would explode if allowed to run dry. Nevertheless I began turning valves, since my homeowner's insurance covered explosions but not floods, and I was certain that it did not cover a basement stairway transformed inadvertently into an electrocution chamber.

When I had turned off all possible water flow, I went back upstairs and opened the telephone book, knowing it was hopeless. It was Sunday afternoon, I knew nobody in

Eastport, and I really needed a plumber right away, which as everyone knows is when you really can't get one.

But there was a number in the book, so I called it, and a nice, elderly-sounding woman answered and said that her nephew was watching football, but she would tell him and he would get over as soon as he could. I was about to give my address, but she said she guessed I must be the lady who bought the big house on Key Street.

Yes, I said, imagining her blue-rinsed hair and flowered apron; no doubt I had called away her from her doughnut-frying, or from the fixing of a traditional downeast casserole dish in which potatoes and salted codfish were important ingredients.

Well, she had to go, now, she said. She and some friends were going to ride their motorcycles out to Meddybemps, and she didn't want to be late.

Bemusedly, I hung up. Probably, I thought as I went around back to open the Bilco doors, it would be days before the plumber got here. Probably he was too busy with football to care about me: new in town, all alone, and in danger of drowning, electrocution, or both.

Just then a bright red panel truck pulled into my driveway, neatly avoiding the raspberry canes on the left and the lilac bushes on the right. A small, wiry fellow of about thirty-five jumped out, carrying a toolbox.

"So," he said cheerfully as he strode toward the Bilco doors, slanting metal hatchway-covers that led to the below-ground cellar entrance. "I guess you must've tried to fix that toilet seat."

He looked down at my hands, which were smeared with rust from those damned bolts.

"Hacksaw," he diagnosed. "That's good. The direct approach. Got its pitfalls, though, old houses like this one. Got what you might call a falling-domino effect. Well, let's have a look."

Swinging his toolbox, he hopped over the Bilco foundation, ducked accurately under the header above the doorway, and vanished into the basement. Moments later

I could hear him whistling down there, and then his bootsteps going up the basement stairs.

"Wow," I heard him say to no one in particular when he got to about the level of the wet electrical wires.

Half an hour later he had sealed the toilet tank, fixed the shut-off valve, dried the electrical wires with my hair dryer, and drawn a diagram of the pipes in the basement so I would know which ones to shut off, next time something happened; we both knew there would be a next time.

Oh, and he had also replaced the toilet seat.

He gazed at the house. "You know, though, your water pipes are old. You want to watch out, if you ever turn off the water main, that you turn it back on slow. Otherwise they could go," he gestured vividly, "kablooie."

He pulled an inhaler from his pocket and drew on it. "Doctor gave me this," he explained at my inquisitive look. "My whole family's got asthma, some worse'n me. But if I take my pills and stay away from cigarette smoke—"

His nose wrinkled just at the mention of the stuff.

"—and keep a couple of these babies on me all the time, I'm all right." He tucked the inhaler back into his pocket.

"Thanks for coming over so fast," I told him, getting out my checkbook. "I appreciate this a lot. How much do I owe you?"

He waved off the check and picked up his toolbox, setting his black gimme cap with Guptill's Excavating lettered on it in orange script atop his small, neat head.

"This one's on me. Welcome to Eastport."

He said it the Maine way: *Eastpawt.*

And that was how I'd met George Valentine.

Now the rumble of media vehicles arriving and departing outside kept up a constant bass counterpoint as I set a plate of scrambled eggs and toast in front of George.

He tipped his head at the sound, sighing heavily, then began devouring the toast and eggs. He wasn't telling me all he knew, but for a born-and bred Eastporter that was standard operating procedure; except for a year or so— out in Colorado, where I gathered from Ellie that he had been working construction, and sowing his wild oats— George had lived here all his life.

"Thanks," he said when he had finished. "I've been feeling too hungry to sleep and too tired to eat. That hit the spot."

He got up and made to set his cap on his head; I'd gotten him over here on the pretext of fixing a faucet, but I wasn't finished with him.

"Not so fast," I said, taking the cap away. "There are a couple of things I want to talk to you about."

I poured more coffee, and he sat down again, looking trapped.

"A little bird told me you knew all about the big money Alvin White had salted away. And that you and Ellie might have been on the front burner again, romance-wise. So what's the deal, George? This doesn't look so good for either one of you, you know."

His face was miserable. "Maybe," he appealed, "we could go down in the cellar. Now that the gravel is here, I want to look at the dry-well hole again, and I talk better when I work."

The dry well was an ongoing project I kept George plugging away at, when no other area of the house was actively engaged in collapsing. "Fine. Get your toolbox, and we'll go."

In the cellar, George examined the Bilco doors that led to the outside, and the wooden steps leading down from them. The damp in the cellar was so persistent that even in the winter with the furnace on, the rough concrete floor was a patchwork of darkened wet spots, so that as a cellar it made a great spot for a mushroom farm but was useless for much of anything else. That, and the fact that I now kept the Bisley locked down here along with the ammunition, had made me determined to solve the dampness problem.

Which, it seemed, George was actually going to fix, and

maybe even soon. "Here," he said, indicating a hole as deep as I was tall, "is where the dry well goes. The boys'll be bringing in the rest of the gravel this afternoon—"

The gravel, he meant, in the burlap bags at the end of my driveway; there was already another stack of bags down here.

"—so leave the Bilco doors unlocked for 'em if you think of it."

"I will," I promised, "think of it." The hole was as wide across as four large oil drums, which he had already brought down and stood on end in the corner where the coal bin used to be.

"But what's the lime for?" Besides the oil drums and the sacks of gravel that he meant to use for filling the hole once the drums were set in, several bags of lime like the ones in Ellie's garden shed were also stacked in the corner.

"Oh. Well," he explained, "the thing is that even after I cut the channels in the concrete—"

He was planning to route all the water that seeped in through the foundation into channels he had cut in the ancient concrete at the foot of the cellar walls.

"—Even after the water gets into the channels, and runs down into the dry well, the hole will be damp. And where there's damp, there's a smell. Lime, see, it helps keep the earth sweet."

"I see." That seemed a sensible answer.

"Then, after I route the water to the barrels that are full of gravel, fill around with gravel and put the lime on top, I cover it over with concrete, or more gravel if you want."

"Gravel would be better," I told George. Given the checkered repair history of my old house, I thought paving over the dry well might be unrealistically optimistic.

He nodded. "Okay, then. Guess I'll get to work." He reached for the first of the oil drums, turning his back as if I might just leave him to it.

"Not so fast. You told me you were going to talk while you worked."

He shrugged, looking caught, and peered around at the dim, ramshackle cellar as if one of the holes in the foundation might be about to let him out. "Well," he began reluctantly when he realized none would, "the thing is, I cornered Ellie at a church supper about a month ago, and told her how I felt."

Sighing, he let his breath out hard. "I told her it was a sin to let that old witch Hedda spoil our lives, that Ellie's promise to Alvin didn't mean she had to be a martyr. I said I loved her and I was always going to, and I knew she felt the same way, and wasn't that worth something, too?"

"She promised what, exactly? Not to hurt Hedda? And marrying you would do that?"

He nodded despairingly. "Hedda smacked Ellie hard, once, when Ellie was fifteen, and Ellie raised a hand to her. Alvin got in the middle of it, got them quieted down, and when Ellie had cooled off he made her promise never to do anything to hurt Hedda. Not in any way at all."

His shoulders sagged under his blue poplin work jacket. "And I can understand that. But Ellie, she takes it too far."

Then he smiled a little, thinking of her again. "I swear, Miz Tiptree, mostly I'm a pretty reasonable guy, but I'd walk on water all the way to Campobello for that woman."

"Right," I said. "I know the feeling. So then what happened?"

He stared at his hands. "Well, Ellie talked to Alvin about us, on the quiet. That's when he told her about the money, how his deal had gone bad but he thought he could get McIlwaine to make good on it, and also that McIlwaine was leaving him some. He said he was going to hire live-in help, either that or move into that brand-new retirement community down in Blue Hill, the fancy one where they do just about everything for you."

George looked up. "Either way, Ellie wouldn't have to take care of Hedda anymore. Which everyone knows she shouldn't have had to anyway, but she felt she did. Because of Alvin, you know."

"What's he got to do with it?" I knew, but I wanted to hear it from George, get his slant on it.

"Well, because he raised her," George said.

He set the last big oil drum in the bottom of the dry-well hole. "Let that lumberyard of his run itself down into the ground, spent all his time on Ellie. Taught her how to throw a fastball, take your head right off," George added admiringly.

Then the knowledge of her present situation overcame him again. "I don't guess Alvin meant to make Ellie feel duty-bound, but she does. She won't leave Alvin alone with Hedda, and she won't marry me and take care of Hedda at the same time. Says it wouldn't be fair to me or Hedda. Ellie," he repeated, "made a promise. And you know Ellie," he finished glumly, "when she's set on something."

"Yes, I do. Although," I added, "it was Ellie's reputation for keeping those promises of hers that kept them from trying to haul her out of here on a helicopter the other night, so I guess that's good for something, too."

"Yeah," he agreed. "I guess. But right now I sure don't know what."

I caught him as he turned away again. "So George, what is it you're not saying? Oh, come on," I added at his denying look. "It might as well be embroidered on your cap, there's something else you're not telling me."

George looked unhappily at the dry-well hole. "Still got to wait for the rest of the gravel," he said. "The bigger stuff, that goes inside the drums. Maybe I'll just run over and ask the boys when they—"

"Oh, no you don't. Come with me." I herded him back up the cellar steps; now that I had him, I wasn't letting go until I got it all out of him.

In the kitchen, I began slapping sardines onto slices of bread and slathering them with Raye's mustard, which is made right here in Eastport and is a blend, as far as I can tell (and I mean this figuratively, of course), of dynamite and cocaine: delicious, energizing, and an excellent sinus remedy to boot.

As for the other ingredient in the sandwiches, it seemed to me that sardines were small, whole fish, and I felt as likely to eat them as I was to swallow a few gold-fish straight out of the bowl. But Wade said sardines were brain food and Sam preferred them to peanut butter, and when Ellie disguised them with fresh herbs and garlic in spaghetti sauce, even I devoured them.

"So what's the rest of it?" I asked. "Come on, George, you might as well tell it all."

George reached out and plucked a sardine from the tin, and put it in his mouth, chewing thoughtfully on it. "Those are good sardines," he said.

"Don't stall me." I wrapped the sandwiches in waxed paper, which Wade says keeps the damp out better than plastic wrap, and put them in his lunch pail with a thermos, two brownies, and an apple, sliced into quarters and cored.

I know; it was awfully old-world domestic, wasn't it, my fixing Wade's lunch. But when people go out on the water, all you can send along with them is food; that, and a vigilant turning-away from your own fear. I would go up on the widow's walk, I suppose, but the house doesn't have one and Wade wouldn't stand for it, anyway. That there's little to earn and many to keep is a fact of downeast life, but the other line of that old sea-chanty—that men must work and women must weep—is not a part of Wade's repertoire.

"You were working over there the day before yes-terday in the morning, weren't you?" I asked.

George's throat tightened; I saw the sardine he was chewing go down in a lump.

"Because Ellie says she killed McIlwaine," I went on, "but I don't believe her, and I don't think you do, either. What I think is that she's protecting somebody. Jemmy Wechsler overheard you two in the Baywatch," I added.

George stared at me, his milky-pale skin gone even

whiter. "We were talking about the money, about how if Alvin got McIlwaine to replace it, we could get married. That's all."

"And," I asked, "about what Alvin might get if McIlwaine died? That would replace the money pretty efficiently, too, wouldn't it?"

George shook his head. "That's crazy. Counting on an inheritance—why, you might as well bet on the weather. I don't believe old McIlwaine did anything of the sort, leave Alvin White any money. And I was there, but even if we'd done what you're thinking—planned it together, I mean—it's a stupid way to do it. The guy," he added, "shouldn't even have have died, in my opinion."

I closed the lunchbox. "Why not?"

"Well, you saw it. Ice pick in the head." George's voice was full of disgust. "Buddy of mine down in Portland is a bouncer in a bar, he got shot in the head. Week later, he's up walking around. I don't know what's inside a person's head, I mean, where the big connections are and so on."

He picked up his cup and swallowed the last of his cold coffee. "But I've seen a lot of things, car wrecks, logging accidents and so on, and I'm telling you, that one shouldn't have been a fatal head wound. Back of the neck, maybe, but not front of the head. I've been wondering about it."

He'd lost all his uncertainty, and I had to admit what he said made some sense. My ex-husband, for instance, dug around inside people's skulls all the time, admittedly with more planning and awareness than your standard ice-pick wielder, but still. And even he had mentioned similar wounds that weren't fatal.

The sound of a helicopter interrupted us. From the window, I could see the craft's shape through the fog—which was dispersing slightly—and the big red M emblazoned on the side of the fuselage, as the 'copter headed for Quoddy Airfield.

"They're taking McIlwaine's body," I guessed. "Take it over to Bangor, I suppose, for the autopsy." To me it seemed like forever since he'd died, but it was really only two days.

"No way." George stood beside me, watching the helicopter dissolve into the low clouds toward the west side of the island. "Arnold says someone pulled strings, got the body released to somewhere in New York."

He sniffed. "Guess Maine Medical Center isn't good enough for him, even when he's dead." He picked up his hat with the air of someone about to make an escape.

"Listen," he went on, "I've got to go talk to Bob Arnold. If the weather's clearing enough for that helicopter to get in here, we're going to have even more people in town pretty soon."

He was right: the influx of yesterday, intense as it had been, represented the bravest reporters, hot to file a story on the Bastard of Wall Street and how he died. Today, the second wave would be coming in: stringers, freelancers, and smaller publications. It would be good business for restaurants and the Motel East, and a mixture of comedy and annoyance for the rest of us who lived here. After a year or so without twenty-four-hour Thai take-out, while-you-wait photo processing, shopping malls complete with international food courts and thirty-screen, Dolbyized surround-sound cineplexes, you tend not to miss these things very much or very often. But the media were about to go cold turkey on the whole latter half of the twentieth century, and the shock was going to make them irritable.

George's mouth curved into a small, anticipatory smile; he was thinking the same thing I was.

"I saw a guy once," George said, "in Leighton's Variety, up there by the counter between the newspapers and the Megabucks tickets. He's got his silver Beemer sitting idling outside, and he's so mad, he's pounding the counter so the little boxes of nail clippers and Red Hots jump. And he's saying, 'What do you *mean*, I can't see a real-time stock market ticker up here? What do you people *do* with your lives in this damned burg?' "

George's imitation was more than passable: chest

puffed and expression terminally affronted, as if he'd been told that the drinking water in Eastport contained cholera germs, and that the local people sort of liked it that way.

"You can get real-time here, now," I said distractedly. "Buy the service, dial it up. On the Internet."

Not, of course, that it is going to do you any good. With a real-time ticker, all you get is the benefit of knowing fifteen minutes sooner what the real players on the Street knew yesterday, or last week.

"Yeah," George said thoughtfully. "You can get anything you want in Eastport, really. It's just you're not having it forced on you all the time. 'S why I came back. One of the reasons. Thanks for the breakfast."

"George."

He stopped at the door, smiling as if I might ask him to pick me up some drywall screws at Wadsworth's, or another giant economy size box of rope caulk.

Wild oats, I remembered, asking myself what he would hate most to have revealed, and why in the worst of all possible worlds he would let Ellie confess to a crime instead of confessing to it himself. Then I took, you should excuse the expression, a stab at it.

"George, have you ever had a felony conviction?"

What little color there was in his face drained away. He pulled out his inhaler and sucked on it unhappily, short of breath at being confronted with a question he'd hoped no one would ask.

Damn, I thought: there was Ellie's reason.

20

Ellie's trip from her front door to the squad car had made breaking-news headlines on all the networks. The papers were full of it, and tonight, Larry King would be making hay on it, on account of McIlwaine being so famously who he was.

"I wish," I said heatedly to Bob Arnold, "the cops hadn't taken her right past all the cameras. In fact, I wish they hadn't taken her at all. You know as well as I do that confession can't be true."

The Eastport Police Department operated out of an old frame storefront on the west side of Water Street. Two plate-glass front windows furnished a view of passing cars and pedestrians, and of the hand-carved Atlantic shorebirds Rollie Bach was displaying in the window of the Eastport Gallery.

Now Arnold put his big hands together on the top of his desk, in full view of the reporters shivering hopefully outside. He had banished them from his office, as firmly and completely as if he were quarantining against plague, but he couldn't order them off the sidewalk. "I can't help the way it worked out," he said. "What was I supposed to say, she confessed but we all just like her too much to let you guys do anything about it?"

He sighed heavily. "I'm sorry, Jacobia. Truth is, we stalled as long as we could, but if there was an arrangement between the cops and the newspeople, I wasn't in on it. What I wish is, she'd kept her mouth shut, let us figure it all out if we were able to and not if we weren't."

In the gallery window, a pair of plump puffins with black-and-white feathers, huge webbed feet, and bulbous beaks as bright as orange slices waddled atop a chunk of salvaged dock piling.

"And why did it have to be somebody like McIlwaine? People from away," he said, "just come here and screw things up." Then he caught himself, mortified.

"I mean, not you, Jacobia. Not ordinary people. Aw, hell," he gave up, "you know what I mean."

"That's okay," I relented, because I did know. Exotic as they looked, the puffins belonged here, and I at least had transplanted myself fairly credibly. But McIlwaine hadn't; he'd grown up here, but only returned to make a display of his success, showing in the end how much he really didn't belong.

"I'm sorry I got all hot at you," I told Arnold, and he accepted this.

"Ellie says she killed him out in that pantry of theirs, on account of some money deal. You know anything about that?" Arnold asked.

"A little," I admitted, and told him about the stock flop Alvin had gotten caught under. It would all come out now, anyway.

Arnold nodded. "Alvin's a sweet old guy, but imagine him thinking he could change McIlwaine's mind."

I was still thinking about the pantry. "So she just left him lying there afterwards? Is that what she says?"

"Well, no." Arnold looked unhappy. "Once she'd lost her temper and done it, she got in a panic about it. Tiptoed into the hall, she says, to make sure Alvin was still in the front room. Janet Fox and Hedda were upstairs. Seeing if the coast was clear, while she tried to figure out what to do. And when she came back . . ."

"He was gone." I could picture it: McIlwaine struggling up, stunned but not yet unconscious, maybe confused. Key Street is quiet in the morning, with people already all off to work or to school; he could have crossed it unnoticed, looking for help.

But the part before that didn't sound right to me: Ellie in a panic, or losing her temper. Ellie wouldn't panic if you set a bomb off under her, and while she was fully capable of skewering you verbally, I couldn't imagine her becoming physically violent.

"Did George come and talk to you?" I asked.

"Yeah," Arnold said, glowering at me again. "Gave me his badge and his weapon. How'd you know about the felony thing?"

"I didn't. I thought about what might make Ellie protect him, and him let her. It would go harder on him than on her if he had a prior. They'd end up being together sooner."

Arnold looked thunderous. "Now wait just a damned minute."

"Well, that's what the state cops will think, if they ever stop fixating on Ellie. Which they probably won't, but Arnold, George was there. Hedda's not physically capable, Janet was with Hedda, and Alvin wouldn't let Ellie go to jail for him, you know that. Believe me, I hate it as much as you do, but tell me: who's left?"

Other, I meant, than Nina McIlwaine. She *felt* so right, I could practically taste the triumph of seeing her led off in handcuffs. But so far there wasn't any point mentioning her to Arnold; I had no real evidence she was even near the house when the killing occurred, much less inside. Nina was cold, calculating, shrewd, and—I was willing to bet—as mean as a snake, but that wouldn't cut it in the arrest-and-prosecution department. Meanwhile, though: (a) Ellie had confessed, (b) I was sure she hadn't done those things, herself, and (c) George—now that he and Ellie were together again—was a fabulous candidate for Person Most Worth Protecting, from Ellie's viewpoint.

Which suggested that he actually had done it, or she thought he had. I didn't much like those ideas, either, especially the first one, and I hoped that there was (d) some other alternative. But good alternatives, ones I liked contemplating at all and could put forward convincingly, were getting as scarce as bargain-priced blue chips, lately.

Watching me, Arnold seemed to follow my line of thinking, and it made him mad.

"Come with me," he growled, heaving himself up out of his chair. "I want to show you something."

21

Dying in winter is a troublesome business in Eastport. Saturated by fog and by squalls blown in from the North Atlantic, overlaid with ice for weeks at a time, the island's soil—and it really is an island, connected to the mainland only by the one narrow causeway—freezes hard as the granite ledge beneath, requiring that the dead be committed not to the earth but to the mausoleum in Hillside Cemetery. From this fact the serviceberry bush received its name, for when the tiny white flowers of the common shrub are in bloom, we may begin holding graveside rituals for those who have passed away from us since autumn.

Waving the reporters off curtly, Arnold backed his squad car out of its angle spot outside the storefront, made a U-turn in front of the fish dock, and headed back up Water Street toward Dog Island. On our way we passed the white clapboard *Quoddy Tides* building, home of the easternmost newspaper in the United States, then climbed the long hill past the entrance to the Deer Island ferry and into North End, where two-story wooden row houses gave way to frame cottages and then to the wide grassy bluffs overlooking Harris Cove.

When we got to the cemetery, Arnold pulled onto the shoulder. Ahead, now invisible in the mist, lay the light-house at Deer Point with Indian Island beyond and the Friar Roads to its south, to our left the Western Passage leading up to the mouth of the St. Croix River and the distant hills of New Brunswick. The fog had gobbled snow at the rate of an inch per hour, so that the yellow meadow grass and the black-cherry canes of *rosa rugosa* had already begun showing through the drifts.

"I'm really sorry about George having to turn in his badge," I began. It was what I'd gone down to talk to Arnold about; George had seemed so horrified by my question that I thought I'd better mend some fences.

"You didn't do anything." Arnold broke his silence angrily. "You didn't go off and do any damn-fool thing, get all liquored up out there in Colorado with your buddies, smoke yourself some pot, get caught with enough of the stuff so possession with intent would stick like stink on a skunk. Dammit, I've known George all his life."

He pulled a cigarette pack from his pocket and rolled the car window down; it was against the rules to smoke in the squad car, and besides, he was in the habit of not leaving smoke smell for George to suffer in.

"It wasn't even his. The pot the cops found in the car, one of his buddies already had a felony pop. George took the weight."

"You knew about it?" It was against the rules to make a cop out of a convicted felon, too.

Arnold was silent a moment. "Yeah, I knew," he admitted. "George told me about it when he applied for the job. I told him I didn't give a rat's ass what they thought about it in Augusta, the job was his, and if we caught flak about it, we'd handle it when we caught it."

He shook his head. "Show you what a damn fool I am. I even went out and talked to McIlwaine one time myself, see if he could maybe use his influence, help George get a pardon. McIlwaine had reach in the state-house, out in Colorado. And in just about every other damn state, I guess."

"What happened?"

Arnold made a face of disgust. "Didn't have any more luck with him than Alvin had. Oh, he talked a good game. Nothing ever come of it, though." He dragged hard on the cigarette.

"What's going to happen now?"

"Nothing," he replied, blowing smoke in a stream. "Somebody asks me a question, I'll give an answer. Otherwise, all of those state guys can go piss up a rope. Bad enough George's lost his badge. And I'll tell you another thing, he didn't kill anybody."

A breeze stirred up, shifting the mist and dropping it, so that the yellow summer cabins on Harris Point materialized for an instant and vanished again, like a magician's trick.

The same thing seemed to be happening inside my brain: a hint of something and then not. Or something that ought to be there but wasn't.

"Aw, hell, Jacobia." Arnold broke the silence. "I'm sorry I got so mad at you. I guess those investigators'll

know about George's trouble, anyway. They get on a
thing like this, they run everyone through the computer."

Right. I had it: how?

"Arnold, do you know the joke about the thermos
bottle?" I asked. "Why it's the most miraculous inven-
tion in history?"

Arnold turned his long-suffering face to me, as if
in light of the foolishness that had gone on so far, this
was just par for the course. "No," he said patiently.
"Why is it?"

"Well, all a thermos bottle does is keep hot things hot
and cold things cold," I said. "The miracle is, how does it
know?"

A grudging smile twitched the corners of Arnold's lips.
Out on the bay the mist had thickened to rain: showers
marching in angled lines toward the shore, greying the
water's surface.

"What if somebody else knew George was in trouble
while he was away? Somebody other than McIlwaine, I
mean."

McIlwaine himself was too canny a wheeler-dealer to
talk George's problem around, here or away. He might
not help if there wasn't enough percentage in it for him,
but he'd keep it under his hat, in case he ever needed
Arnold to keep something quiet in return.

Arnold frowned. "And killed McIlwaine just when
George was around, hoping he would get blamed for it?
Knowing he'd get looked at hard, because he's got a
felony record?"

"Maybe knowing the whole thing, Arnold. The
record, and that McIlwaine's death was going to help
George out. Knowing it would look like George had a
wonderful motive. But not," I added, "knowing what
Ellie would do. Her confession would have been an
unexpected piece of luck for somebody."

He put the cigarette out by holding it into the rain,
then tucked the butt into his cigarette pack. "Awful dicey.
Too many things would have to go just right. Besides—"

"Yeah, but it looks like they all did go just right, doesn't it?" I interrupted. "That is, if we're assuming neither Ellie nor George did it."

Which we were: I could see by his face that Arnold would suspect George of murder when pigs flew, if then.

"Huh," Arnold replied. "I guess that's true enough. If you were patient, you could bide your time, wait for your chance. Some time when George was there to get suspected, *and* when you could do it without being noticed, yourself."

Then he shook his head, as something else seemed to occur to him. "But come on, sneaking in and out of that house while there were people in it. And anyway—"

"Never mind that," I said. "Let's assume for the sake of argument that the chance came along, and somebody grabbed it. Then the question isn't how much somebody planned. The question is, how did somebody know about George?"

Arnold sat considering this, but he still just wasn't going for it. Below us the new section of the cemetery, called Bayside, spread out: marble monuments jutting up through the melting snow. Here and there among the marbles stood stacked bricks of sod, showing the final destination of folks who had died over the winter.

The marbles weren't the only things that were as hard as rocks around here, I thought impatiently, eyeing Arnold's head.

"Look at that cut work," he said in a distant voice, indicating a monument a few yards away. "Not too many stonecutters around can do that anymore."

The monument, in polished black marble, showed the name and dates of a local boy lost when a dragger snagged up and capsized off Grand Manan. Below the stark facts, the stonecutter had created—in perfect, lithographic detail—a dinghy with her oars shipped.

Arnold put his hands atop the steering wheel and looked over them to the water. "You know, after my father died, George buried him here. In February, two years ago this week."

"But you can't dig . . ." I began, but Arnold went on as if he hadn't heard me.

"Dad had an awful horror of the mausoleum, of being shut up in there with all the other bodies. Tried to hold on until the ground thawed, but in the end he couldn't. And George, he'd shot the breeze with my old man enough to know all his stories."

He took out another cigarette and lit it. "He'd been buried alive, my old man, in the war over in Germany. A bunker got blown up. All his dead buddies around him, pressing on him in the dark. And rats, he said. Lots of rats."

Arnold shuddered, shook it off. "Dad made me promise not to winter him over in the mausoleum, and I said I wouldn't. But I didn't know how I was going to keep that promise. I just said it to give the old man some comfort. 'Long as he was alive, I didn't have to keep it. And the old man knew that, of course. Fought for every damned breath."

"But then he died."

Arnold nodded. "Then he died, and jeez, it was cold outside. Worst February a lot of us had ever seen. Next morning George went up to Calais and rented a backhoe, brought it out here. Got down three feet, hit rock ice, dropped some fertilizer and black powder charges in the hole, dug it the rest of the way."

Out on the water, the big ship *Star Verlanger* resembled a toy ship, making way for Head Harbor and the open sea.

"Next day," Arnold went on, "we had the graveside service. Only winter service I ever remember in Eastport, and when it was over George hauled the backhoe to Calais again. Cost him an extra hundred bucks, get it back late, not countin' what he'd paid out to hire it, rent the flatbed."

Arnold shook his head, remembering. "Said he didn't want to miss the old man's last party, and he wouldn't take a dime, not that I had two dimes to rub together, then or now."

He pointed. "That's Dad's stone right over there."

It was a small white granite obelisk: all, I supposed, that Arnold had been able to afford.

"Dad never spent a single night in the mausoleum," he said, "rubbin' shoulders with a bunch of other dead bodies. And I didn't break my promise, on account of George Valentine."

More promises: the island seemed full of them today, and people kept them, here. You couldn't vanish into the anonymity of a mass of people, and pretend you hadn't given your word. In Eastport, there wasn't a mass of people; just you and your neighbors, every one of whom knew your name and where you lived. It was yet another reason I was determined to keep plugging away at this: not only because Ellie was my friend, but because I had given her my word.

Arnold pulled the car around the paved circle at the end of Dog Island and headed it back uphill, toward town. Rain spattered the windshield.

"You know," he said, "when you came to town, people wondered about you. Here's a woman with a kid, buys a big old house. Pays cash, she's got no job and no husband. That's food for thought in a town like Eastport."

For gossip, he meant. Personally I didn't mind my neighbors knowing my business, which was lucky since if you burp at one end of Moose Island, someone will start mixing up a Bromo-Seltzer for you at the other end.

"But you settled in real well," Arnold went on. "And when Wade Sorenson took to you, that was a point in your favor. People around here think a whole lot of Wade."

"I'm glad," I said drily, "I'm getting such a high approval rating."

Arnold smiled. "You're doing okay. The thing is, there's some things people here won't tell you, or at least not right off."

Belatedly, I began sensing what one of those things might be. He nodded, knowing I was getting it.

"Oh," I said, deflated.

"It's a good thought, there maybe being somebody in town who found out George's deep, dark secret, used it in some complicated plot to frame him up for murder. But it depends on George having a deep, dark secret, doesn't it?"

He pulled into his parking spot in front of the police station. "The trouble is, just about everyone in town knows about George's drug bust in Colorado. Everyone who's from here, that is. Just not," he finished gently, "many people from away."

"Oh," I said again. "Well."

"No one talks about it much 'cause they know that if word got off the island, George couldn't be a part-time cop any more."

He shut the ignition off. "Have to take some crap about it now, I suppose. Kinda doubt they're going to send a firing squad all the way from Augusta, though, and if they do, we've probably got 'em outnumbered."

He seemed entirely unperturbed by the prospect. "George was awfully upset about my knowing what happened," I said.

"He likes you. He's worried you'll think less of him. He knows that in bigger places, sometimes people do." Arnold turned his calm, assessing gaze on me. "So do you?"

"No. Of course not. He's George, for heaven's sake."

"Good." His eyes sought the middle distance for a moment, and I guessed he was thinking about that granite obelisk.

"That's how I feel, too. He's George, and he didn't kill anybody. And if you're thinking about shifting suspicion from Ellie to George just to get her out of trouble, think again. I won't stand for it, and she wouldn't, either."

Nor would I; even thinking about going down that road was about as attractive as deciding which kitten to drown. The trouble was, at the moment I couldn't think of any other options.

He pulled the keys from the ignition, then frowned as an official-looking car pulled in alongside of him. "Hell. I bet that's the woman from the attorney general's office, called up earlier. I'd better get ready, hear some big-city nonsense."

We got out. "Anyway," he finished, looking over the hood of the squad car at me, "I'm sorry about the way it happened with Ellie going, the timing of it. I couldn't do anything. And I appreciate you trying to help."

He didn't sound particularly sincere about that last part.

"Right," I said, and then I remembered.

"Arnold. You telling me about that hole George blasted—it reminded me."

I wasn't sure how to put it, then figured there wasn't any good way. "Is anyone around here missing, um, any dynamite?"

He eyed me narrowly. "Yeah. Fundy Construction warehouse called me, couple days ago. Crate and some radio signalers. Why, you know something about it?"

"I'm not sure. Maybe. I just overheard something funny, not sure what it means. I don't," I lied hastily as his expression darkened, "know where it is. I'll tell you about it later, okay?"

I nodded at the dark-haired, blue-suited young woman who had already stepped from her car and was sticking her hand out at him in brisk, no-nonsense fashion.

"Yeah," Arnold said, not letting me off the hook despite the woman's obvious impatience. "Yeah, I think you better."

Then he turned to his visitor, and it wasn't until I was walking home through Peavey Park, picking my way among patches of slush between the bandshell and the red brick library building, that it hit me: Arnold had missed something.

If I didn't know George's Colorado drug bust was common knowledge, maybe somebody else hadn't realized it, either. Someone like me, from away, who hadn't been told.

Someone like Nina. I nearly turned around, but instead I continued uphill toward the now-untenanted VFW Hall. It was a massive, cedar-shingled 1820s mansion on a corner lot, once glorious but now in a sad state of decay. In the rotting eaves beneath its clipped gables, pigeons nested profusely, and the tall windows of its third-floor ballroom resembled blinded eyes.

On moonlight nights, an apparition was said to appear in one of those windows, a spectral figure called the Green Lady who glowed the same otherworldly color, it was said, as the radium dial on an old wristwatch. But now in the dull afternoon the windows were blank and lusterless.

Arnold wouldn't want to hear any more of my theories. He had told me so, as nicely as possible. Still, I kept thinking about who had a way to know—perhaps from talking with her husband—that George Valentine had a troubled past, maybe even that George wanted Alvin to inherit big-time. Someone with her own motive for wanting the victim dead.

Nina McIlwaine, I thought, filled the bill perfectly.

Approaching the corner of Key Street, I turned quickly to avoid being seen by the reporters still hanging around the Whites' house, making my way in by the alley to my back door.

By the time I got there, I was in a hurry to get inside, so I nearly missed the bit of paper caught in the antique mail slot, no longer used officially now that I have put a mailbox on my front porch. Only its pale color against the dark green of the door made me spot it, and pluck it from the slot as I let myself in.

Shutting the door quickly to keep from being spotted by any intrepid newspersons, I unfolded the thing, expecting a request to contribute to a bake sale or an invitation to a potluck supper.

But it wasn't any of those. The note was on lined, colored paper, the kind you can buy in tablets at Leighton's Variety Store, the writing in ballpoint, shaky and obviously disguised; it was the penmanship, I thought, of a right-handed person producing cursive script with the left.

Or vice versa. I blinked at the note several times, unable to believe that I had actually received such a thing, then caught myself glancing around guiltily as if merely touching the hideous little missive were a shameful offense.

Mind your business, it said. *Or you will be the next.*

22

"Got a letter?" demanded little Sadie Peltier. Eastport's youngest and most troublesome juvenile delinquent had pushed open the door without knocking and was suddenly at my elbow.

"Lemme see," she said eagerly, snatching at it.

I pulled it away, in no mood for Sadie and her fresh ways. "Did you see who put this here?" I demanded.

She shrank back. "No," she denied exaggeratedly. "I was over there at Mrs. White's house. Ellie got *arrested* yesterday. The cops came and hauled her away."

Her face clouded; possibly Sadie had been told that the same thing might happen to her someday if she didn't mend her ways.

The confidence returned to her face. "Is it a *love* letter? I bet it's a *love* letter."

Then she dashed outside again and, grabbing up some of the remaining slushy snow, crammed it wetly together in her hands and flung it at me.

It missed, spattering against the outside clapboards, but in my state of mind that was no consolation. "Sadie," I told her, "you're a brat. Get out of my sight or I'll wring your neck."

Just then her mother's voice rose from the next street over, calling Sadie's name in tones of hope and terror: hope that Sadie had not yet done something truly awful, and the realistic terror that any day now, Sadie would.

"I'm going to tell what you said," Sadie informed me. "I'm going to tell my mother you called me a brat."

"Do that," I replied distractedly, looking at the note, about which the first question for me was not *who,* but *why?*

"What an idiot," I said in puzzlement, to myself.

"Idiot!" Sadie shouted at the sky as she ran off, energized by this fresh bit of ammunition. "Idiot, she called me an idiot!"

Once the sound of her voice had faded away, I put the note on the kitchen table and frowned at it. Aside from the melodramatic disguising of the handwriting and the shoddiness of the pastel notepaper, the very presence and message of the thing were silly.

Whether or not I believed in Ellie's confession, the police did; otherwise she would not now be in a courtroom. Trying to discourage my nosing further into the matter would only alert me—and perhaps the police, too, in the event I told them—that further nosing was warranted.

Not only that, but how had anyone known I had been taking any interest at all?

The whole matter was so perplexing that it took me a moment to realize: my eyes were watering, my nose was running, and a haze was filling the room with the smell of roasting chestnuts, if the chestnuts happened to be made of styrofoam. As I thought this, a piercing, intermittent howl of the type ordinarily used to signal nuclear reactor emergencies began blaring, driving all thoughts of notes or disguised handwriting from my mind.

The smoke detector. I grabbed the fire extinguisher from its mount by the kitchen door. In old wooden houses there are few blocks to prevent flames from spreading quickly in the balloon-framed walls, so it pays to have an extinguisher within reach even when you are in the bathtub.

Unfortunately, once I had it in hand I couldn't find anything to shoot the extinguisher at. The air in the kitchen had thickened so fast that it was impossible to see where the fire might be; meanwhile, Monday came romping in from the dining room, expecting a biscuit, and got instead a snootful of smoke.

Just then, luckily, Sam came home from school. "Yikes," he said, and ran to call the fire department, then ran back to grab a coughing Monday and take her outside, while I alternated between flinging open windows and yanking open cabinets, drawers, and cupboard doors, aiming the extinguisher into them, then moving on like a SWAT team member trying to clear a building of terrorists.

Sam ran back in and stopped. "You know," he said, "that smell, it's like . . ."

His voice trailed off as he strode to the oven and opened the door, leaning back as a cloud of ghastly fumes billowed forth.

"Cripes," he said, grabbing a potholder and pulling out the object smoldering inside. It was a package of hot dogs from the deli counter at the IGA, wrapped in melted plastic and sitting on the melted stuff that used to be the hot dogs' molded foam tray.

"I didn't," Sam said, holding up his hands as the men from the volunteer fire department thundered up onto the porch.

"I know you didn't," I assured him as they flung open the door and swarmed in, dressed in rubber coats and boots and their big, yellow fire hats, dragging heavy fire hose behind them.

We looked at Monday, who had come in with the men to see what all the excitement was about, and to find out if firemen carried dog biscuits.

"Nah," Sam said, looking at me. "Couldn't be. She wouldn't cook them. Would she?"

By now the smoke was beginning to clear away, and Sam had turned off the oven and the smoke alarm. I made coffee for the firemen, and offered them doughnuts, and apologized for bringing them out in the truck. They were very nice to me in return—George would have been with them, they said, but he had gone up to Calais; something about a load of gravel—but I knew by tonight it would be all over town that Mrs. Tiptree put meat in the oven without even unwrapping it, and forgot it in there, and jeez did it stink.

Only I hadn't. I hadn't taken any hot dogs out of the freezer because we were having chowder, and I had already cut up the haddock pieces, sliced potatoes and onions, and remembered to buy pilot crackers. I hadn't forgotten to turn off the oven, either, because I had let a casserole bubble over in it the night before, and I remembered turning the oven off the instant I smelled it.

"Maybe it was the ghost," Sam said when the firemen had gone and we were going around opening more windows, letting the breeze off the harbor blow the smoke smell away.

"Maybe," I agreed. But I didn't really think so.

I thought whoever left the note had also been in the house.

23

Back in New York, I used to believe that car phones were handy gadgets that allowed me to conduct essential business while speeding on a highway packed with road-rage-afflicted maniacs. But now that I have become a Maine-iac myself, my car phone has become emergency gear; who knows when I might hit a moose?

"He had," said my ex-husband, "six months to live. Tops."

I was driving north along a curving, narrow stretch of Route 1 through Red Cliff, a bit of shoreline created by rose-colored granite being slowly beaten away by the sea; its nickname, derived from the only known case of stranger-murder in remembered local history, is Dead Lady Beach. To my right in the cove, a couple of fishing boats bobbed at their buoys near the remains of a herring weir, its thin poles sticking up out of the water in a criss-cross pattern, it nets long rotted away.

"Autopsy found an aneurysm as big as a grape," said my ex-husband, "in his brain stem. Inoperable, and ready to blow."

Translation: McIlwaine's head had contained a blood vessel that was about to rupture.

"Would he have known that?"

"Oh, yeah. There's records on him. He had the full workup."

After Red Cliff came a straight stretch of two-lane: hills rolling away on the left, rocky farms and ancient Grange halls crumbling a stone's throw from the pavement, which after the storm was mottled with salt residue like splashes of thin white paint.

"But here's the funny thing," my ex-husband went on. "From the rest of the autopsy results, you'd think he was trying to kill himself. Big-time gastric erosion. The guy was an aspirin eater."

"So?" I was entering Calais, border town on the St. Croix River between the U.S. and Canada. Here fast-food restaurants, new motels, and used-car lots mingle with some of the loveliest old structures still standing anywhere. You'll be driving along wincing at the gritty storefront of a down-and-dirty, no-frills plumbing supply outfit, then get smacked broadside by the sight of a two-hundred-year-old Federal boardinghouse, set on the original bit of sloping, unsidewalked street, its red brick mellowed over the centuries to dusky rose and its trim and foundation stones painted the color of the ivories on an antique piano. Seeing it is like falling suddenly through the viewer of an old stereopticon, and your breath is just taken away.

"What?" I said, over the sound of my ex-husband's voice droning on academically. "Sorry, I was distracted there for a minute."

"I said," he replied with heavy patience, summing it up for me, "aspirin makes you bleed."

After the note and the fire—I'd called Arnold, and he had listened patiently but unenthusiastically—I'd had to get out of town, off the island and away from everything, to sort my thoughts. Thirty miles of two-lane highway through a countryside dotted with saltwater farms, tiny crossroads villages, and the occasional glimpse of a bald eagle soaring overhead—along with a sense that if I wanted to I could drive straight on to Labrador and never be heard from again—didn't quite assuage my restlessness.

But it was a start. In town, I slowed past the old railroad station and the car barn where trolleys used to be housed, back when Calais had trolleys, and looked downriver to the site of the first European settlement in the New World north of St. Augustine, in 1604. More than a third of the settlers died over that first winter; in spring, the survivors moved away.

"So," he went on, "the weapon caused bleeding. In you or me, the bleeding would stop. We'd get a hematoma, probably need some surgery, end up with a droopy eyelid, a little facial paralysis, something minor. But in McIlwaine, the bleeding kept on."

I just loved all the things my ex-husband thought were minor. No matter what might be annoying me at the time, a peek into his world always reminded me to be grateful that I could blink my eyes without assistance, close my mouth well enough to drink through a straw while not supporting my lip with my index finger. Probably if he'd been camped on the St. Croix that first winter, he'd have told the dying settlers that scurvy was a minor nutritional imbalance.

"But wait, there's more," he said, whereupon the cell phone abruptly fritzed out.

"Blast." I smacked the handset down, knowing that it was his connection busted, not mine. Technology in Maine works wonderfully well, for the most part, on account of its not being swamped by so many users that it cannot work at all. Also, when something breaks here, there is somebody to fix it, and generally it is somebody who cares.

I drove, and waited for the handset to beep. My ex-husband always calls again, unfortunately, and better his nickel than mine is the attitude I have developed about it.

It happened as I was driving home, laden with items that can only be purchased in Calais unless you want to drive to Bangor: Eukanuba dog food for Monday, raw sunflower seeds, more than one artichoke at a time, ginseng and tea tree oil from the health food store. I never put much stock in herbs until I met Ellie, but she is gung ho about them, and the tea tree oil has done wonders for Sam's complexion and the ginseng has a kick like a Kentucky mule.

"Okay," said my ex-husband, "the tracks of the weapon."

I blinked at the plural. "What?"

"One entry, two angles. The first as the weapon penetrated, then a second track, shifted anteriorly."

"Translation, please." Approaching the Perry post office, I slowed for a cherry-red Ford pickup with an Irish setter grinning out the passenger window, then made my own turn.

"Somebody stabbed him in the skull," my ex-husband said, "and then gave the weapon a second shove, harder. A lot harder."

"Criminy." More pickups were pulled to the side of the road on Carlow Island, the bent figures of clam-diggers scattered on the glistening flats and the herring gulls wheeling above. Cormorants clustered on the rocks, black cutouts against the tide pools.

"You got that right," he said. "That second track was a monster. You owe me for this," he added, which should have alerted me. "Anyway, is Sam around? I need to talk to him. He sounded kind of uncertain about himself the other evening."

"Mm," I said, refraining from further comment. "I'm on the car phone."

But he was not to be deterred; it was payback time.

"Then maybe I'll come for a visit," he said. "Next weekend. I'm seeing somebody, and I think she might enjoy a little rural charm."

I bit back several very uncharitable comments. "Fine," I lied heartily; if he sensed any reluctance on my part, it would harden his resolve. "Come whenever you want. As long as you understand, I'm seeing someone, too. I wouldn't want you to be surprised."

The silence that ensued while he processed this did my heart good.

"Oh," he said finally. "That's great." He was lying through his teeth. Until I came along, no one had ever dumped him before, and where women were concerned my ex-husband was the original dog in the manger, as well as the original dog.

"What is he," he went on, "some rustic practitioner with a sign hanging off the porch? I know you always went for doctors and lawyers, and there can't be many of those way up in the sticks where you are."

He chuckled, and of course I could not punch his lights out over the phone. "He's a harbor pilot. Drives big boats around dangerous obstacles."

"Oh," said my ex-husband, losing interest. "Picturesque."

Yeah, well, picturesque this, I thought. I could hear people talking in the background.

"Listen, I gotta go," he said hastily. "Tell Sam I'll see him this weekend, get his future straightened out for him."

"Oh, good," I replied, pulling into my driveway, wondering whether it could be moved to the moon by next weekend, or perhaps to Aroostook County. Many of the roads there are one-lane and the logging trucks have right-of-way, and with any luck at all my ex-husband might meet up with one of them.

"Listen, that might not be the best time," I began, suddenly remembering something else going on then, although not precisely what.

But he had broken the connection.

24

In winter, the trail to the overlook clearing on Shackford Head is icy and steep; the woods crowding in around it are filled with snow long after the rain has washed the rest of the island bare. Just below the meadow at the top, the ruins of a Revolutionary War fort run in a broken line between cedar and jack pine, slumping where the old stones have fallen amidst chunks of antique mortar.

"I'd think Sadie did it, if it was only the fire," I said. "Setting fires is the logical next step in her development; indoor fires, I mean. She's already torched a dozen leaf piles. But Sadie couldn't have written the note."

The narrow path opens suddenly onto water and sky; beyond, a scrub thicket ends in a sharp drop. Arnold had decided that I had left the hot dogs in the oven, probably to thaw them out, and that the note was some kid's prank, even if not produced by Sadie.

"So your theory is?" Wade squinted out over the salmon pens, which are rectangular floating docks below which thousands of hatchery-raised fish swim inside huge mesh cages. A small raft of eider ducks floated past the cages on the tide, emitting their moaning calls at regular intervals as if urging one another on.

"I don't know. Can Man said Nina McIlwaine's car was there that morning. Dropping him off, probably, to see Alvin White. But she doesn't strike me as stupid, and this stunt definitely was."

A bright red dragger with black rail and foredeck, the *Becky Jo*, puttered around the point of Estes Head. Despite the decorative care her owner had lavished on her, she looked all business as she motored out to the middle of the cove, then idled.

I took a breath of fresh air. "It's so clean out here. The kitchen still smells like a garbage dump burned in it."

"Yeah. Good breeze." He turned from watching the dragger to look at me. "So what's your plan?"

That was what I'd come here for: more thinking, with Wade along as a sounding board.

"Just keep trying to figure it out, I guess. That's what I think Ellie wants, although I don't know why. Nor," I went on, "do I see why she couldn't just tell me what she wants. Why's she being so annoyingly mysterious?"

"Too bad Hedda didn't do it," Wade remarked. "Half the town'd like to see her run out of Eastport on a rail."

"Right. I thought about that. But her fingers are so crippled up, no way she could have handled that ice pick, even if she did sneak away somehow from Janet Fox."

The *Becky Jo*'s operator was wrestling with a part of her dragging gear, which was several times larger than himself.

"Which reminds me, I've got to get over there again and see how they're doing. Listen," I went on, "maybe Ellie didn't really want me to do anything like this. Maybe I misunderstood."

I could take out an ad in the *Quoddy Tides*, I supposed: I, Jacobia Tiptree, do hereby and as of this date renounce interest in all crimes committed by anyone other than myself.

Wade didn't answer for a while, and when he did, it was in the oblique downeast fashion I had learned to expect from him. Stepping behind me, he slipped his hands into my jacket pockets and wrapped his arms around me.

"See that fellow out there on that little boat?"

At the moment, mostly I saw fireworks behind my eyelids; with Wade there, that beach after a snowstorm was the warmest place I had ever been.

"Yeah, I see him." I did, too, although right then I'd have agreed to just about anything. Whoever coined the phrase "animal attraction" was talking about Wade Sorenson.

The *Becky Jo*'s operator scrambled into the shack; her engine rumbled briefly. Then he ran back, leaning over the stern as the engine sound cut out and was replaced by the thrum of the hauling motor. I couldn't see exactly what he was doing, but it looked difficult, and one false move would have put him in the frigid water, where survival time was a scant few minutes.

"He could've bought a larger vessel, hired along some help. If," Wade said, "he'd wanted to boss anyone but himself. Or if he wanted to do things by committee."

Finally the *Becky Jo* began easing ahead, as whatever had been fouled got freed up. "Okay," I said, "I get the point."

He stepped away from me and shook out the yellow slicker he'd been sitting on, and looked out over the water.

"Place like this, way the hell and gone, it's far enough off the beaten track that if you want something a certain way, you can still make it that way," he said. "Unless you let someone stop you. Or you stop yourself."

By losing my nerve, he meant, or second-guessing myself. Halfway across the bay, the *Becky Jo*'s low wake spread in a fantail.

"Course, there's no shame in being extra careful," he continued. "Putting fresh batteries in the smoke detectors, locking up your doors for a while until this is straightened out."

He nodded toward the retreating dragger. "Just like on a boat: the more alone you are, the more safety gear you want to carry."

The comment popped Jemmy Wechsler's face into my mind; what the hell was he up to? But it was none of my business and I couldn't do anything about it. I put the thought of him away, at least for now. "You're right," I agreed. "I'm just starting to wonder if anything I do is going to do her any good, that's all."

Wade slung the slicker over his shoulder, and we started down to the beach. In the lee of the cliffs, Broad Cove spread ahead of us, dead low, with acres of green rockweed sprawling up from the water's edge. "You might be surprised," he replied at last, "at what you can do."

We came to a stretch of low granite ledges and began traversing them. "Sam ought to go to boat school," Wade said suddenly, stepping smoothly from one chunk of rock to the next. He was too large a man to possess that kind of grace, but he had it, and he didn't even seem to know it.

He turned, balancing easily on one booted foot, and caught me watching him. "What?" he grinned.

"Nothing." I felt a smile spread helplessly across my face. "Go on with what you were saying. Boat school."

He light-footed it deftly to the next rock. "Oh. Sam. Harpwell'd hire him right now, but he won't tell Sam that. He figures Sam ought to get his schooling in, first."

Ron Harpwell was a big, burly fellow who had sailed from Halifax to the Caribbean, built boats from scratch, and ran his marine design-and-repair business in the same shipshape way he kept his vessels. The idea of Harpwell taking Sam on was a gift.

"Only," Wade said, "not the kind of schooling your ex-husband wants. The technical school is big on applied sciences, computer-aided design, high-tech materials, all the real hands-on stuff. And Harpwell needs a hands-on kind of guy."

Fresh water trickled through crevices in the shale looming up out of the beach, flowing in rivulets among the pebbles back to the ocean. You could pluck out slices of the ancient rock, solidified silt from the bottom of a Paleozoic sea, and sometimes discover fossils.

"What I don't get," I said when we had tramped up the beach almost back to the lot above Broad Cove, "is how someone knew that George would be at the Whites'."

We stopped to watch a pair of mallard ducks tipping up in the shallows, only their tailfeathers showing, like a pair of twitchy fishing bobbers.

"I mean, if he was supposed to be the suspect," I went on. "To some degree, it would have to be happenstance, just waiting for your chance and taking it."

The thought of Nina McIlwaine seizing the opportunity to get out of her war-torn homeland recurred to me with some force. I had no doubt that a woman who had accomplished such an escape would also be capable of murder, if she were determined enough.

"But it would be better if you had some warning in advance," I said, "just so you could . . . gear yourself up."

"Well," said Wade as the ducks' heads popped to the surface, "maybe somebody knew where he'd be, because he said where he'd be."

The mallards launched themselves from the water in a flurry of quacks, their wings trailing sparkling droplets.

"I was in the IGA with George, early that morning," Wade continued. "We were getting coffee, and George was talking about what he was doing for the day. Working," he added, "at the Whites'."

He bent to examine an old iron spike. Around the turn of the century, a half-dozen wooden warships had been burnt on this beach, after all the useful fittings had been scavenged from them but before anyone thought of them as interesting. Then, they were just boats nobody wanted anymore, and at low tide their charred timbers are still visible.

"And while he was talking about it," Wade went on, putting the spike in his pocket, "Nina McIlwaine walked by with that cook of theirs, the one that doesn't speak any English. Maybe she heard George say it. Mrs. McIlwaine, I mean."

I looked at him. "You're kidding."

"Nope."

"She *heard* him?"

"I'm pretty sure she did."

So she'd known he was there, and it wasn't much of a leap to think she had also known he would make a great suspect. All Nina would have had to do was make it in and out of the Whites' house unnoticed. At that moment, I stopped wondering *whether* and started wondering *how*.

We made our way carefully over some thick mats of rockweed, dark green and fibrous. The stuff looks like perfectly good footing and is slippery enough to break your leg.

"Anyway," he said after another long pause, "I was thinking. You might want to consider bringing the Bisley upstairs. If," he added, "you're planning on pursuing this."

"Don't you think that's a little extreme? Keeping a handgun ready?"

Among the stones on the beach were red, round-shouldered bricks, smoothed by decades of rolling under the tide, and shards of china, their scraps of blue and white antique glaze still visible from the days when the schooners brought it from the Far East as ballast, when the harbor bristled with wooden masts.

"Extreme," Wade repeated consideringly, seeming to turn the word one way and another in his mind. He picked up a piece of blue beach glass, its edges smoothed and frosted away by sand, and put it in his pocket with the spike. "I'm not sure I would call it extreme."

Broad Cove curved around to where an old pasture rambled bumpily over the uneven fields, down to the shore. We jogged away from the water, up a sandy path between *rugosa* bushes still sagging with rose hips. Sam said that in summer Broad Cove smelled just like Cleopatra, although at low tide in any season, it still smelled like low tide.

"I think," Wade pronounced finally as we made our way through the tall grass to the lot where we had left my car, "an ice pick in the head is extreme."

The parking lot was edged with white boulders, and because Shackford Head was state property both the lot and the road to it were generously furnished with gravel. Even when roads on the rest of the island were ghastly, you could almost always make it out to Shackford Head.

"I didn't," I told Wade, "misunderstand."

"No. I don't believe you did. Find out what happened . . . she meant it. Ellie's depending on you for something, but she won't say what. Or can't."

Emerging from the tall grass, he paused. "That's the way it works around here, though." He waved a hand, indicated the water and the wild-looking landscape.

"We're just far enough from official kinds of help that most times, we end up helping ourselves."

At the trailhead stood a trash barrel and a sign prohibiting guns, alcohol, and dogs not on leash. I had parked directly across from this sign, and the Honda stood where I had left it.

The difference now being that all of its tires were flat.

25

Half an hour later I stood in the tiny, cluttered office of Porter's Garage, peering through the doorway into the spic-and-span work area where Gerry Porter was crow-barring the first tire off its rim.

"You backed out of your driveway. You backed over a nail. You drove to Shackford Head," he said. "Then the air leaked out."

Gerry was a wizard with cars, but he was an airplane mechanic at heart—in his spare time he hung out at Quoddy Airfield; that was how McIlwaine's daughter Patty had met him, when McIlwaine's jet flew in—and as such he tended to think that if you weren't actually planning to take a vehicle up into the air, you would be safe in fixing it with a few lengths of baling wire, maybe a wrap of duct tape, and as an extra-special security measure, a wad of chewing gum thumbed onto the critical spot.

The wonder of it was, Gerry was usually right. Like Sam, he had a talent for the unlikely fix, but what he didn't have was a head for nuance.

Or for malice. "I didn't back over a nail, Gerry. I backed over four nails; one for each tire. *Capisce?*"

But Gerry did not want to *capisce* the implications of that; it wasn't in his sunny nature. "Bad luck. You better start readin' your horoscope. It's all," he said, "in the stars."

Which was a hell of a lot more comforting than what I thought it was in: somebody's cold heart.

In the corner, Gerry's police-band radio sputtered, blurting out another request for a license plate check.

Gerry laughed. "Boy, they got that dispatcher hopping. All the reporters speedin' in over the causeway, gettin' tickets. I guess Arnold's checkin' out every one. He's not happy with 'em."

Undeterred, I began again. "Gerry. They were new nails, poked through cardboard squares so they would stand up straight."

The cardboard squares, of course, had gotten nailed to the tires, proof in case I needed it, which I didn't, that the bad luck I'd had wasn't the kind Gerry insisted on believing it was.

Gerry paused. "Ayuh. Well, I guess you're right about that. Can't really think who would do such a mean thing, though. Don't know as you've been makin' any enemies, not that I've heard."

"Haven't you?" I inquired a little too sharply, and his face closed up the way it did when somebody spoke unpleasantly to him.

"You come back a little later," he said quietly. "I'll have the tires on, good as new."

I swallowed my impatience. "Sorry, Gerry. I'm just on edge, after the fire and all. Thanks for coming out and getting us."

We'd called from my car phone, and Gerry had been there to rescue us in five minutes, driving Wade back down to Federated Marine before bringing me up here.

"Aw, that's okay, Mrs. Tiptree." He wiped his hands on a rag. "Way I figure, if you can't help your neighbors, what's the good of having them?" He glanced outside. "Say, you want a ride home?"

"No, thanks. I think I'll get a little exercise, clear out my head. Maybe it'll put me in a better mood."

"Yeah. A walk'll do that, sometimes. Listen, Mrs. Tiptree, I don't know whether you know this or not."

He looked uncomfortable. "Jeez, Patty'd kill me, she knew I was telling you this. She likes listening, and she says I've got a big mouth. But those scanners pick up cell phones. And so many people in town have got 'em. Scanners."

As I may have mentioned, in Eastport you don't have

to worry about keeping secrets, because for the most part it is impossible. Your bank balance, your medical history, your marital situation, and the pattern of the wallpaper you are thinking of using in your kitchen are all common knowledge the minute they happen, and my strategy from the start has been to relax and enjoy it.

So I hadn't worried at all about the cell phone, and had in fact forgotten its broadcast capabilities, since the broadcast capabilities of the Ultra Low Frequency station down at the U.S. Navy Station in Cutler are the equivalent of a couple of tin cans strung together with twine, when compared to the communications skills of most of my neighbors.

Now, though, it hit me: Plenty of people had undoubtedly been all ears every time I picked up the handset, including the occasions when I'd talked to my ex-husband about clotting times, head wounds, and the surprisingly indirect path a certain ice pick had taken through a certain dead person's bone, blood, and tissue.

It was, aside from the active back-fence network in Eastport, how someone could know I'd taken an interest in McIlwaine's murder.

"So, Gerry," I inquired casually, pausing in the doorway, "how's Nina doing?"

He shrugged. "Well as you'd expect. Thing like that, it comes as an awful surprise. But she's been kept busy. Cops coming out to talk, lawyers from the old man's company, so on. Enough to keep her, you know, from dwelling on it. And then . . ."

Gerry hesitated. "Aw, hell. Patty'd kill me if I told you this, too. But the thing is, you shouldn't expect Nina to be too broken up. Woman gets smacked around, can't expect her to grieve too hard, the old guy kicks the bucket."

"He hit her? You mean McIlwaine?"

"Yuh. Nobody was supposed to know about it. You know how it is, a woman thinks it's shaming, or something. But he was a mean old bastard, and that's the truth. I'd hate to see Nina get a bad name, just 'cause she's not cryin' her eyes out over him."

"You like her?"

He paused again. "Don't know. She's . . . different. All that money, and her coming from another country . . . I don't understand her, is what I guess I'm trying to say."

He thought for a minute. "And then what he did to Patty and Janet, making the one so tough and the other so, well, you know. Janet's got no backbone at all."

He levered the final tire off the rim. "All I know is," he finished slowly, seeming a little embarrassed by his own momentary flash of insight—Gerry, I reflected, probably thought more than anyone gave him credit for—"that old man was a son of a bitch. 'Scuse me for speakin' ill of the dead."

"Don't worry about it," I said. "I won't tell anyone you did. We all have to get things off our chests sometimes. And thanks for reminding me about that scanner business."

He nodded, falling into another of the long silences that are a standard feature of conversation, downeast; I used to find them unsettling, but now I find them peaceful, these absences of verbal obligation.

"I'll be more careful," I told him, going out.

I was, too. Not that it did me a bit of good.

26

"Okay, here's the scoop," said Jemmy Wechsler. "Thirty years ago, McIlwaine paid White a hundred and fifty grand on a handshake deal. There've been two similar payments since."

I'd tossed the cell phone receiver into my bag, and it had beeped again just as I'd been leaving Porter's Garage. Come on down, a familiar voice had said, and that was all. No one had to remind super-cautious Jemmy Wechsler of the broadcast capabilities of cellular instruments.

"Twice they ran it through the lumberyard books. Phony purchase orders," said Jemmy matter-of-factly. This sort of thing was nothing new to him. "Then Alvin 'borrowed' the money out of his own business, on the up-and-up. The last time, it was a straight loan, or that's what they called it, anyway. They worked it so it wasn't income."

Which still wouldn't have put off IRS interest in where the money came from, but that wasn't my big question now. "And you would know that how?" I asked.

I sat in the scoured-clean galley of his boat. He was packing shaving things into his leather kit bag. The *Hood-athunkit*'s decks were cleared, her fuel tanks filled to capacity, and her big anchor hauled. Jemmy was leaving.

And the anchor chain wound around the capstan, I'd noticed as I came aboard, was brand-new.

"Don't worry, Jacobia." He followed my uneasy gaze, then tossed some charts out onto the table in the galley. "You didn't blow my cover."

"I shouldn't have asked you to find out about McIl-waine's money. You asked somebody else, and now someone knows where you are."

He shook his head. "It's not like that."

He finished packing up his gear and began stowing provisions: flour, salt, eggs, tins of meat and fish, boxes of dry milk, two five-pound cans of coffee and a bottle of brandy. Wherever he was going, he expected it to be a long trip.

"Hey." He put his hands on my shoulders steady-ingly. "The guy I asked, he's not with the guys who want me. He's above that. You might say several levels above. Top," he emphasized, "level."

In the organization that wanted to kill him, he meant: an idea that had always seemed somehow reasonable in the abstract. But now, without warning, it was real.

"Hey, when it comes to information," Jemmy told me breezily, "we're like animals in the jungle. All gotta drink at the same watering hole. But the fellow I talked to, well, you could say he's the source of the water."

He slid one of the charts into the chart rack. "Any-way, I knew this was coming. Had to, sooner or later.

Nothing to do with you. You must have noticed I was getting ready for it."

I sat on the lower berth. "I don't get it. I thought Junior was the top level, now." Surely Jemmy hadn't been trafficking with that little hoodlum.

Jemmy grinned. "You and most of the rest of the population. Because," he added, "that's what you're supposed to believe."

He fiddled with a knob on the depth finder, frowned, adjusted it until he was satisfied. "Think about it. Here's a group that controls everything, and I mean everything, in the tri-state area. They buy judges the way little kids buy candy, put the jurors and even the prosecutors in their pockets."

He opened a compartment, pulled out a 9-millimeter Glock semiautomatic pistol, and checked the weapon over, handling it as easily as I'd run portfolio hypotheticals, back when I was a professional.

Which of course Jemmy still was. "Then all of a sudden," he went on, "they're lettin' the fibbies crawl around the ceiling of a social club, buggin' the lady's apartment that lives upstairs."

As he spoke, his speech patterns modulated and his gestures became jerkier, more abrupt. It was as if, having been called back into the old life, he was reassuming the colorations that would allow him to survive in it: the Brooklyn-tinged speech patterns, the bulky-shouldered, faintly threatening stance.

"Gotti goes away for life. *Life*." Jemmy turned on me. "You gonna tell me that's an accident? Sammy the Bull's on television, showin' his face, talkin' about the thing's dead?"

He chuckled. "Jacobia," he laughed softly, "don't tell me you swallowed that. You didn't used to believe everything you heard on the news."

It struck me, what he was telling me: that the crime families had orchestrated a major takedown, and that the FBI had needed a win and had gotten one by mutual agreement.

And that despite what you may hear on the news, things are not always as they seem.

Take my own case, for instance. In the old days the people I worked for, especially toward the end of my career, were not all fine, upstanding citizens. In fact, they tended to lean more toward the felonious, with lapses into the frankly murderous.

You will forgive me, I hope, for not telling you this sooner. But you must have wondered how I came to be acquainted with a guy like Jemmy Wechsler, a fellow who in his salad days did more evil deeds than Vlad the Impaler: back then, Jemmy was a psychopath.

Which, I hasten to add, I did not know when I met him, and by the time I found out, Jemmy was gone, vanished out of New York with all that money. But how did you think he knew how to get it out of the country, into the care of the close-mouthed folks at Le Banque Suisse? The ability to pull a trigger or wield a garrotte not being associated with the knack for financial sleight-of-hand, last time I looked.

My point is that when you are a financial consultant to the dripping-with-dollars bunch, yours is not to reason why. It is to make that money produce—the same as when you were at the currency desk, reeling the exchange rates through your head and facing down those rat bastard yen-masters, whom by the way I have always suspected of being Canadian; it would have been the perfect foil.

Your job, simply, is to win.

"Anyway, something else I heard," Jemmy Wechsler said.

He stowed the Glock. "The old lady, Ellie White's mother? She was some kind of a dancer, back in New York?"

I shook my depression off. He was right: none of what he'd said came as any sort of shock to me, any more than it did to him. "So?" I managed a smile.

"So I heard, and this is a very reliable source here, that the money was payment—Alvin takes a certain blonde bombshell out of the picture. Like a conveyance fee."

I sat up on the berth.

"And I heard," Jemmy went on, "the bombshell didn't exactly want to go. So McIlwaine hired a couple of guys, got the bombshell persuaded."

Those scars, I realized. That legendary, inexplicably vicious mugging, just before Hedda came home to Eastport for good.

"That's right," Jemmy said, seeing my face. "My source tells me McIlwaine got a couple of goons to break her ankles, make sure she didn't have any reason to stick around. No future, anymore, on the stage."

I found my voice. "You're sure of this."

Jemmy looked at me. There was distance growing already in his eyes. That, and the increasing knowledge of what he might have to do with the Glock.

"Guy I talked to," he said quietly, "he happens to be one of the guys did it. That's how he got so high-level, how he got his start, doing the nasty work for McIlwaine. One of the ways," Jemmy corrected himself.

"So couldn't one of those guys have killed McIlwaine?" I kept coming back to it: somebody from away. "Maybe he'd made an enemy out of somebody crime-connected?"

Like you, I thought but did not add.

Jemmy grinned, understanding. "Jacobia, when one of those guys wants you, he does not come along while you are visiting a house, and stick an icepick in your head, then let you wander off so maybe you will recover and testify who he was. One of those guys, he shows up at your own house and goes boom, you are dead. Take my word for this."

He angled his head at the hatch. "C'mon, let's go upstairs."

I followed him up on deck, still thinking about what he had told me. Alvin had gotten money from McIlwaine after McIlwaine had Hedda's legs broken, to make her go home to Alvin.

"One thing about McIlwaine," Jemmy went on. "He never forgot an injury. Or a favor. Speaking of which."

He turned, gazing past me at the waterfront, looking as if he were trying to memorize it, as if he'd forgotten what he'd been talking about moments earlier. "Look at those guys," he said.

Down in the boat basin, men moved on the decks of the working vessels, painting and scraping, fixing engines, tinkering with their gear. They wore old clothes and rubber boots and ratty-looking slickers, and the pickup trucks lined up above them on the docks showed the scars of long service.

"Lot of 'em don't have two dimes to rub together, and when they get 'em, a headgasket blows or it's time to pay the fees or the insurance, or one of their kids gets sick, or their back goes out, or something. But I'm damned if they don't look happy."

They did, too, shouting companionably to one another as they stepped from the rail of one moving, rafted-together vessel to the next, borrowing tools or trading stories, easy as strolling down a city sidewalk.

"Anyway, about that anchor chain."

The old one with account numbers and ID codes etched on it, Jemmy meant. "Oh, no," I said. "I don't want it."

The guys who go boom had never showed an interest in me, a situation I had gone to some trouble to maintain. "I'm not keeping that thing here for you, Jemmy. You want to dump it, go ahead, but you'd better make sure you've got those numbers memorized."

"I wasn't thinking of dumping it. Actually, I was thinking of giving it to you."

I stared at him. "Why?" It was a *lot* of money.

He laughed. "Call it a reward. I've had six months here, not looking over my shoulder. Maybe thinking about some things, for a change. And the reason is, I knew you would keep your mouth shut, because you promised to."

Promises again. They were haunting my existence. For

a minute I wished I was known as a non-keeper of any promise whatsoever, especially the ones I'd made to Ellie.

"I'll never be able to spend that money," he went on. "Crazy to think I could. They're always going to be watching for a guy like me, anywhere I go. If I'm living large, you know they'll find me. But you, you could figure out a way to dribble it back into the country, get some good out of it."

Yeah, I thought, I probably could, at that.

But I wasn't going to. Maybe it's a fine line, but getting paid for giving financial advice is one thing, even if it's to a bunch of crooks. Simply appropriating the proceeds of murder and extortion was, in my book, another.

"Jemmy," I told him honestly, "where that money came from, the only thing I could do with it if I had it would be to give it away."

He nodded. "Funny, but that's kind of what I figured you'd say. So maybe I'll have to find some widows and orphans, dump it on them. All I know is, I don't want it anymore."

He sounded surprised, but certain. We looked at each other.

"Hey, have a good life," he said, and the warmth in his voice was genuine. Then, astonishingly for Jemmy, he reached out and hugged me hard.

The metal gangway swayed with the rising tide. When I looked down from the dock platform above the water, the *Hoodathunkit*'s twin outboards were already idling and Jemmy had gone below.

I didn't think I would ever hear from him again.

27

The stairs to the attic rooms in my house are bare boards that creak whenever you walk on them. At the top, paneled wooden doors lead from a small, shapely entry hall into three tiny chambers whose walls are papered with antique cabbage roses.

These were the servants' rooms in the days when each of the family chambers had a fireplace that had to be supplied with wood and kept burning day and night, whose hearth needed sweeping and whose ashes needed carrying down interminable flights to the ash pit. In those days the kitchen floor was kept shining by a scullery maid who crept back and forth over it on her knees, scrubbing it with sand.

Climbing to the attic I always imagined the dreadfully fatigued young girls going up to it at night, each longing only for the peace of her own narrow bed and the privacy at last of her own thoughts. It was here that I most felt the age of the house, its long, abiding quiet where my own life rarely intruded.

A handful of cut iron nails lay forgotten on a windowsill. Black iron filigree brackets supported a short shelf, creating a makeshift mantel. A fallen strip of wallpaper pulled down a swath of old plaster, exposing the ancient lath.

The plastic that somebody had fastened across a window to keep drafts out moved gently in the puffs of air from a broken windowpane, with a sound like tinfoil being crumpled. I crossed to examine the spot where water had come through, leaking down to my bedroom ceiling.

The repairs wouldn't be as difficult as I'd thought. The long strips of wood holding the window sash in its channels were loose, susceptible to removal without splitting. The putty and paint had long ago flaked away, so not much scraping would be needed. Wade had cut me a square of the expensive restoration glass that I had ordered from Boston—one pane of modern glass in an antique twelve-light is as jarringly wrong as one unground lens in a pair of prescription eyeglasses—and after that I had cut the panes myself, using a T-square and a diamond cutter.

Slowly, I set to work, removing the side trim and

lifting out the heavy old sash, cleaning out the broken pane with a tack hammer and a silent apology; I never know quite what to do with old bits of the house that have served so faithfully for so long, yet are too ruined to stay.

The mundane chore with its simple series of tasks put my thoughts into order. According to Jemmy, McIlwaine had begun paying Alvin White large sums of money soon after Hedda's forced departure from the New York scene.

This implied to me, as it had, apparently, to Jemmy's source, that Alvin had done something McIlwaine wanted him to do, at just about that same time.

But McIlwaine, if Jemmy's source was correct on the rest of the story, was the one who had done something, back in the days before McIlwaine took on the protective coloration of a super-successful businessman. He had been, at that time, just another hoodlum, albeit an obviously up-and-coming one, and he had been behind the attack on Hedda.

Which was fascinating, but not very useful. I hadn't wanted to show Jemmy my disappointment, but all he had reported, intriguing as it was, had happened a long time ago.

What I had wanted was news of some current motivation for McIlwaine's death: a business feud, union dispute, or a cunningly disguised mob-related rubout.

Some news, in other words, to suggest that I ought to be thinking about something besides Nina McIlwaine's new status as a rich, no-longer-abused widow—for her having, in other words, a solid-gold motive for murder.

But if Jemmy was right, there wasn't any such something. Of the capable persons whose potential guilt I could bear contemplating, Nina remained the one with a credible reason to want Threnody McIlwaine dead—the reason being that she was going to get rich *and* get rid of an abusive husband.

A simple divorce, for Nina, wouldn't have been enough. After all, look what happened to the Bolivian beauty. But with McIlwaine dead, Nina was truly free, and very wealthy. All she needed was the nerve, and I knew she had plenty.

She was gutsy, greedy, and—I was increasingly convinced—as guilty as mortal sin.

Turning this over in my mind, I kept working on the window sash. If you coat the old, bare wood with linseed oil before laying in new glass, the wood will not draw the putty's moisture into itself and the putty will not embrittle as it ages. I laid the glass in, tapping in the bright, triangular metal glazier's points, careful to keep them flat to the surface of the glass itself, and drew a bead of putty over the seam with a putty knife.

The putty would need to cure before I could paint it, but the bulk of the job was now complete and the sash had been snug in the channel, so I replaced it, gathered the newspaper full of glass bits, and dropped my tools into my apron pockets. I'd been at it, I thought, about an hour, still pondering the problem of Nina.

In terms of information, she was as remote and well protected as the woman in the mysterious portrait, down in my kitchen. There had to be a way to turn my near-certainty into proof; the difficulty lay in how.

Later, I felt certain that what happened next was linked to my thoughts, but at the time all I knew was that the room filled suddenly with the scent of camellias.

Turning, I saw nothing but the lightbulb hanging from the switch cord over the attic stairway, shining into the corners of the hall and throwing the pattern of the antique cabbage roses into relief.

But I had not switched that lightbulb on. On my way up the stairs I had been carrying a pane of glass, a bottle of linseed oil, some folded newspapers, and a can of putty, plus the tools. Meanwhile, switching on that bulb two hands: one to steady the hanging fixture, which otherwise slips from your fingers as stubbornly as a puddle of mercury, and one to turn the wickedly elusive little knob. Both my hands had been occupied.

The scent of camellias thickened, drowningly sweet. I

had the strong, sudden sense of someone in the room with me, almost inside my head, like the quick, certain awareness you have when you first understand that you are becoming ill or falling in love: as if you are discovering consciously what you knew all along.

That's the thing about living in a haunted house: the subtle, out-of-left-field aspect. People think it must be as constant and obvious as a message written in blood, but it isn't.

It isn't at all.

28

The Eastport Artisans' Guild shop, Quoddy Crafts, is located on Water Street overlooking the harbor, and the best advice I can give you about the place is not to bring more money than you can afford to spend.

There were handmade baskets with sweetgrass woven into the tops, dream-catchers spiderwebbed with silver and turquoise beads, notecards inked with shore scenes so sharply rendered, they might have been sketched with a hypodermic needle. At the display shelves I paused over a linen kitchen calendar embroidered with a flock of chickadees, fingerless gloves made of hand-spun local wool in the same pale mauve as a winter sunset, and deerskin slippers with porcupine-quill motifs worked into the sueded uppers.

Eventually I worked my way around to the counter and to Janet Fox, who was tending it, this being her regular afternoon to work in the craft shop.

"Beautiful, aren't they?" Janet said of my choices, her voice a near-whisper as she put them into a bag for me.

As always, I found her too-soft speech an annoyingly manipulative habit. "Yes, they are." I left the bag where it was.

At the rear of the shop, a fire burned cozily in the ceramic woodstove. On the braided seat cushion of the rocking chair pulled in front of the stove, a cat curled with her paws crossed over her eyes.

"You know," I told Janet, "I'm so glad to see you. I've been wanting to tell you how sorry I am about your father."

"Thank you." Her head lifted bravely, in a studied motion. "No one else seems to think I feel anything about it."

That, I thought clearly, is because you are such a little sad sack, nobody can tell the difference.

"And I wanted to tell you, too," I went on, "how good of you I think it is, your taking on the care of Ellie White's mother the way you have. It must," I probed delicately, "be awfully difficult sometimes."

In a haunting, the one with the most information is the one who cannot be questioned. That doesn't mean, however, that nothing can be learned; only that it cannot be learned directly. And while I was standing in my attic inhaling camellias, it had occurred to me that this fact bore some relevance to my quest.

Carefully, Janet wrote my purchases in the dog-eared spiral notebook that comprises the Artisans' Guild's bookkeeping system. Fortunately, the artisans are not in it for the money; the guild is a fund-raiser for the Maritime Museum, a fact with which I assuage my conscience each time I walk out of the shop laden with packages.

"Oh, it's not so hard," Janet said finally, after a pause during which she seemed to be deciding how best to answer me—if at all. "Mrs. White is an old darling, once you get to know her."

I managed to pretend that something had gotten into my eye; over the time I had known her I had heard Hedda White called many things, but "old darling" was not among them.

"I think," Janet said, still seeming to choose her words carefully, "that Ellie is too hard on her."

"I've been wondering about that myself," I replied, again covering my astonishment. "Of course," I added,

"I hated to say anything to Ellie about it. Still, she just doesn't seem to have the same way with Hedda that you do."

Oh, Ellie, I begged silently; forgive me. But the idea was to get Janet talking, so I went on agreeing with her.

"Tell me," I said, "what's your secret? I swear," I put my hand up as Janet looked anxious, "I'll be as silent as the grave."

Janet eyed me warily. Then, "I let her drink," she admitted. "It keeps her quiet. I figure, what the heck, she's a crippled old lady. Let her have some fun in her life." She glanced at me to see how I took this.

Janet, I thought, you little slyboots. "How do you manage to hide it? The smell—didn't Ellie notice?"

"Peppermints," Janet confessed, "the really strong ones that Ellie makes with the mint she grows in her garden. I pour Hedda a couple of drinks in the morning," she went on, "and that holds her until lunchtime. Sometimes I powder half a Valium in, too. First she gets giddy, then she eats, then she sleeps it off."

"Why, Janet," I said, a faint chill coming over me, "you are more practical than I realized." It was, after all, one thing for me to have imagined doping Hedda into a stupor, quite another for Janet to have gone ahead and done it.

Apparently encouraged by my lack of outrage, Janet preened. "You have to know how to handle people. You can't be having a knock-down, drag-out every day. You have to give them," she finished, "what they want from you." But even as she said this, she kept on glancing at me, ready to change her tack the instant she sensed disapproval. Janet, I thought, was going to come back in her next life as the doormat she already nearly was.

Outside, a couple of sailors pressed their noses to the glass, shielding their eyes with their hands to see the window display of knitted goods, hand-sewn blouses with pin-tucked bodices, and tatted lace collars as delicately perfect as candied violets.

"Janet," I said, leaning in even more confidentially, "what happened over there the other morning? I am," I added in my best you-can-tell-*me*-about-it manner, "just *dying* to know."

Janet paused. She so seldom had any good gossip to tell, it was really a sin to tempt her. I vowed inwardly to make a good Act of Contrition as soon as it was convenient.

Or possible; one of the requirements, I hear, is that you be sorry.

"Well, I shouldn't say," she began, then glanced around with elaborate preliminary caution.

No one was eavesdropping from among the racks of flannel jumpers, soft and comfortable as baby's blankets, or from under the pile of toy stuffed seals, their black whiskers bristling and their shoe-button eyes gleaming bright, that one of the guild's artisans had spent the whole previous winter creating out of the covering from an old Naugahyde recliner.

"But," she added slowly, with a little frown, "if I *don't* say, people will gossip anyway, only the gossip will be wrong."

"That is so true," I agreed, wanting to reach out and shake her. She was being so slow, it was as if she was trying to remember what happened instead of merely getting ready to tell it.

"I was upstairs with Hedda," she began at last, but just then the bell over the shop door jingled as a local woman, Marion Waddell, floated in on a happy cloud, having married a fellow twenty years her junior, two weeks earlier.

Marion favored Janet and me with sweet, sympathetic glances as she bought herbal bath salts, a white voile nightdress luscious with lace and ribbon trim, and a box of note cards.

"Oh, I hate that woman," Janet said when Marion had floated out again. "Her and her silly romance."

I hated her, too; I'd had Janet right on the edge of talking, and Marion had knocked her off the track.

"Come on. What have you got to be jealous about? Bobby Taylor isn't chopped liver."

Janet shrugged sullenly. "Patty's right. He's only after the family money. Not that he's going to get any of it, now, but what else would he want with me?"

"You're being much too hard on yourself," I said. "Now tell me what happened the other morning."

Sometimes a sharp, direct order will get people going; in her case, it worked perfectly. Janet Fox was like a dog who has been trained with a shock collar: so anxious to please that it negates any pleasure you may derive from its efforts.

"Well, I was upstairs," she said. "I heard my father and Mr. White arguing in the study. We both heard it. Hedda and me, I mean."

"Could you hear what they were arguing about?"

She shook her head. "No. Well, only a few words. It was about money. Mr. White wanted some and Dad didn't want to give it to him."

So far this agreed with what Alvin had said. "Was that all?"

"No." She looked uncomfortable. "My dad said that Mr. White owed everything to him. Even . . ."

Janet's voice dropped to a whisper. "Even his wife."

"Really. What did he mean by that, do you suppose?"

"I don't know." She started at her bitten nails. "That's all I heard." For a moment the comfortable crackling of the fire in the woodstove was the only sound in the little shop.

"Dad wasn't a nice man," said Janet softly, and all at once I felt even sorrier for her. She was so passive and pliant that if I'd ordered her to stand on her head, she'd probably have tried.

"He thought it was funny, my wanting to find my mother," she said, biting her lip. "Like it was some big, stupid joke I'd thought up to make myself ridiculous."

She shrugged, her eyes glistening with sudden, resentful tears. "But it wasn't a joke to me."

"No," I replied. "Of course it wasn't. It must have

been hard to put up with him, sometimes. How is that going for you, by the way? Looking for your mother?"

Once, the previous summer, I'd asked Ellie how she put up with Hedda. We'd been driving along the road to Gleeson's Beach, in the sunshine after a brief spring shower, slowing as a grouse made its herky-jerky way out of the scrub trees, breathing in the sliced-apple smell of fresh chamomile mingled with the perfume of rain-slaked pavement.

"Hedda," said Ellie, "is a grim, hateful person. She is an unnatural mother, she is never going to be anything else. I didn't make her that way, and I can't stop her being that way."

She looked at me. I remember she had tied her red hair back with a purple plaid ribbon, and the effect was jauntily harlequin.

"She is never going to love me," Ellie said. "She is never even going to like me."

We'd rounded the last curve, past the ball field that a bunch of the local men had carved out of an abandoned pasture. A skinny old fellow was hauling a brace of chains across the infield. After that the road went to rutted dirt, opening onto a sandy spit over a tide pond where the wreck of a dory sagged against an abandoned pier.

"And the day I figured that out," Ellie had said, "was the day I became able to deal with Hedda."

Ellie had come to an agreement with herself about her mother, but Janet Fox hadn't ever gotten that far with her father, and now she wouldn't. I thought it would make Janet's search for her birth mother more urgent, but Janet surprised me.

"I've decided to forget about that," she answered, busying herself with a needless tidying of the counter. Her gaze darted up to meet mine in a flash of hostility; that and something else, but I wasn't sure what, only that I'd touched a nerve.

"Anyway, a little while later I heard Ellie down there,

with my father," Janet said, resuming her normal plaintive tone. "I'd gone down the back stairs to the kitchen, because Hedda wanted a drink. But Ellie and my father were together in the pantry where the liquor is, so I stopped."

"What were they saying?"

"I don't know." Janet looked anxious and angry. "Ellie sounded upset, but he was laughing. He would always do that, laugh when you were mad at him. Like you were such a fool to disagree with him, you know, because he would always get his way in the end."

She paused, her lips tightening as she remembered this.

"I don't understand," I said. "If you could hear their tone of voice, why couldn't you hear what they were saying? You weren't very far away, were you?"

"No, I was only on the back stairs, where it turns. But one of them"—she frowned, concentrating on getting this part right—"was chopping ice. I heard the ice pick going into a bunch of ice cubes from the bottom of the ice maker. The sound it makes, a sort of chunk, and then ice cubes rattling."

Damn. This was bad for Ellie. "So then what did you do?"

"I had to go back upstairs and tell Hedda she would have to wait."

Making Hedda wait was like shaking nitroglycerine. "That couldn't have been too pleasant."

Janet looked up, surprised. "Oh, no," she said. "It was no trouble. If you just explain things to Hedda, she goes along pretty well."

In other words, Hedda had already been too plastered to make much fuss. "So what happened when you did go down to get Hedda her drink? And when did you?"

Something was wrong, a muddle in the sequence of events, but I couldn't quite put my finger on it.

"Well," Janet said, "it was a while. Maybe half an hour. I'd been doing Hedda's makeup with her, and her hair, to distract her. Somebody came to the door and Mr.

White answered, so I knew Ellie was gone or she would have done it. After that I went down and got the drink, and took it back upstairs."

"Nobody was in the pantry by then. Nothing seemed unusual."

"No. Well," she corrected herself, "the pantry floor had been mopped, and the trash bag was tied. That's all."

"Janet, did you see Nina anywhere around that morning? In the house? On her way in or out?" Anything, I meant, to lend credence to the idea that Nina McIlwaine could have murdered her husband.

Janet looked at me, blank-eyed. "No. I was upstairs with Hedda most of the time. I told you."

"Right, of course you did. Did you tell that to the police investigator, about the mopped floor, and the trash bag?"

None of this was going the way I'd wanted.

"Yes," Janet Fox replied, "I did. Why, is it important?"

The last time anybody asked me that, it was a widow—not, fortunately, my client—whose just-deceased husband had over a period of twenty years been secretly borrowing against his life insurance. The policy, which other than the nickels and dimes of his Social Security benefit was to have been her sole support, was by the time of his death about as valuable as used Kleenex.

"Is it," the recent widow had asked, "important?"

I didn't answer that time, either.

29

After that, things just got steadily worse:

When I got home, there was another pile of gravel bags near my driveway—those Bilco doors, I reminded myself again—and the woman I'd seen getting out of her car in front of Bob Arnold's office was waiting on my doorstep. She was an investigator from the Maine State District Attorney's office; her name was Clarissa Dow, and it was her job—she didn't say this, but I knew—to gather the information that would become the state's case against Ellie White.

I let Clarissa in while the cameras crowded around her and the reporters shouted questions, but she wasn't listening to them and neither did I. I sat her down in the kitchen, where in order to convey my feelings for the nature of her task, I created a pile of fish innards. From the look on her face, you would think she had never seen a pollack being gutted before.

She got the when-and-where details squared away first off: what time Ellie had arrived on the fatal morning, and when I found McIlwaine, and what time Ellie left. She covered Ellie's second appearance and the ice pick, and the way Ellie had phrased her confession, too.

Overall, I got the impression that Clarissa was fairly bored by the whole sordid story, and that as far as she was concerned, Ellie was merely a murderous nobody whom Clarissa would like to put away as swiftly and efficiently as possible.

Which naturally got my dander up.

"Mrs. Tiptree, how long have you known Miss White?"

"Just over a year." I finished with the scraper, and picked up the filleting knife.

Clarissa looked at me as if expecting more of an answer.

I didn't give her one.

"And do you know her parents?" she asked, a bit more crisply.

"Yes," I replied, and cut off the pollack's head. A carving knife is more appropriate for this task, but in the mood I was in, one sharp implement was plenty.

Nina, Janet Fox had assured me once more, had not been in the Whites' house the morning McIlwaine died, or anyway Janet had not seen Nina there. In fact, Janet hadn't seen anything useful, other than the mopped floor and trash bag—the remains, obviously, of the cleanup after McIlwaine's murder.

"Mrs. Tiptree," Clarissa said after a pause—possibly she was upset at my lack of enthusiasm for her goal, which was to help convict Ellie—"you do realize that this is a criminal investigation."

"The victim," I pointed out, gesturing with the bloody knife, "turned up in my storeroom."

Clarissa was thirtyish, with dark, curly hair and just enough carefully applied makeup to avoid looking mannish. Her nails were short ovals coated fastidiously with clear polish, and her eyes were the merciless blue of icebergs.

"Ellie," I added, "didn't do it."

Clarissa looked down at her hands, and when she looked up again the icebergs had splinters in them.

"Would you say you know Miss White fairly well?"

"Yes. Yes, I suppose I would."

There was another long pause, during which she apparently expected me to say more. Instead I slid the filleting knife down the pollack's spinal column. It was a tricky job and I concentrated on it, aiming the knifepoint carefully.

Clarissa sighed heavily. "Mrs. Tiptree, we're getting nowhere. I'm trying to get a sense of your relationship with Miss White."

"Friend. Ellie is my friend."

"I see." Clarissa wrote this down in her notebook. Then pointedly, "And what kind of person is Miss White, in your opinion? As I already mentioned, she has confessed to murder."

"Yes, I know that," I replied. "I heard her say it. But—"

Clarissa's expression reminded me of a securities salesman I'd known, back in the bad old days, who used to read newspaper obituaries looking for "triple crowns": recent widows who might be expected soon to receive large lump-sum distributions, with no adult children to stand in the way of a killing.

For the securities salesman, that is. "I don't believe Ellie White murdered anyone," I repeated. "She isn't capable of it, and if you'd take the time to talk with her yourself, you'd know that, instead of sitting here writing her up like she's some sort of law-school assignment."

Clarissa closed her notebook with the calm precision of a person who is deliberately not losing her temper, even though you are being as dumb as a box of rocks.

She didn't quite roll her eyes, but she might as well have. "Mrs. Tiptree, the forensic team has already fluoresced blood from the floor and woodwork of the pantry in the Whites' house, indicating that the crime most likely occurred there; we expect to find blood in the sink trap, and on a towel we recovered, which we believe was used to clean up Mr. McIlwaine's blood."

"None of that means Ellie did it. We don't lock our doors in Eastport; anyone could have walked in and killed him."

She shook her head at me, frustrated and losing her patience. This, I could see her thinking, was what happened when you tried dealing with the locals in these remote, isolated little towns. They just didn't get it. "Traces of blood are also present on clothes belonging to Ellie White. She had access to the purported weapon, which on early examination matches the wound, and she had a motive, the details of which we are in the process of uncovering. Finally," she saved her best shot for last, "Miss White says she did it."

Clarissa took a deep breath. "Now, in light of all this, are you suggesting that I go out and canvass the neighborhood, looking for some stranger who just happened to be around, wandered into the Whites' house, and killed Mr. McIlwaine for no reason? When I have evidence against someone with a motive, who's confessed?"

"No, I'm just suggesting you dig deeper than you apparently intend to. Threnody McIlwaine was a wealthy and powerful man with rumored links to organized crime. Plenty of people could have wanted him dead." Including, I added silently, his wife.

But Clarissa didn't want to consider alternatives. For one thing, if she did, that contaminated crime scene would become an issue, which it wasn't, now.

"None of whom are saying they did it, or walking around with their clothing smeared with his blood," she said firmly. "Your feelings aside, Mrs. Tiptree, there is nothing here to suggest any suspect other than Miss White. And I must say, I don't understand your uncooperative attitude."

I smacked the knife down. "My attitude, Miss Dow, is that you intend to make career points by helping to convict Ellie, put another notch in your investigator's belt, maybe get a promotion out of it. Fine. Do that if you want. But I don't have to help you without a subpoena, and I'm not. Got it?"

It was the mention of a promotion, I think, that corked it, the comment hitting a little too close to home.

She rose abruptly and snapped her briefcase shut. "I can see you and I don't have anything to talk about. Maybe you'll be less hostile when you're testifying to a grand jury."

Her comment confused me, but I didn't let that stop me. I followed her to the door. "Oh, so you're not sure you can get an indictment? And here I thought your case was already so airtight."

She spun around at me. "A grand jury is standard procedure for a crime of this type. I have no doubt an indictment will be returned."

There was a tiny spot of something on her lapel; chowder, I realized with spiteful pleasure.

"You think you can protect your friend," she said witheringly. "You think you can get away with not talking to me. But you won't when you're sitting in Federal court to testify. For," she added tightly, "the prosecution."

Then she stopped, realizing what she'd said, glancing sharply at me to see if I'd caught it.

I kept my game face on despite feeling I'd been suckerpunched.

"Prosecution," I repeated slowly, making sure that I sounded aghast at the idea. "Why, I couldn't possibly do that."

Clarissa's blue eyes narrowed in satisfaction and relief.

"Oh, you will," she promised unpleasantly. "You should have thought about it before you made an enemy out of me."

But I hadn't. She'd already been one. After she left, I went back into the kitchen, thinking about what she'd said.

The plan was obvious, now that she'd made her slip: Clean the case up, make sure it's all shipshape. Then hand it over to the Federal government, which must already have indicated its interest. Otherwise how could Clarissa already have known that Ellie was headed for a Federal court? That's what she'd meant by her talk of grand juries and indictments.

Jemmy's information, plus my experience in nurse-maiding the ill-gotten gains of a whole thieves' gallery of nervous clients, gave me a theory about why, and it was a theory that chilled my blood.

McIlwaine's mob-relatedness—and I had no reason to doubt Jemmy on this—could make him a potential witness for an organized-crime probe, one of which always seemed to be going on. He might have had good reasons for cooperating with such an investigation, the strongest—at least according to many of my ex-clients—being the promise of his own immunity.

I got on the phone to Toby Alderman. "Hey, Toby, did you see any guys who didn't belong there sniffing around Ellie's case? Having mysterious conferences in the judge's chambers, or hanging out in the municipal building, anything like that?"

If they were on it, they'd be on it from day one.

"The kind of guys I mean would all have short hair-cuts," I continued, "and they'd wearing good, dark suits but not too good, not tailored or anything. And they would give the impression that they thought all the local folks were ants, that they could step on them with their wing-tips if they wanted to. A sort of aura of controlled contempt," I went on urgently.

Toby listened intently; that's the thing about Toby. Through the telephone, you can *feel* him listening, and in person you almost have to be sitting down or the force of it would knock you over.

"You know," said Toby, "I've been wondering about that, myself."

Which, unfortunately, was my answer. For whatever reason, the Justice Department had liked McIlwaine. They'd found—and Clarissa's slip confirmed me in this— a reason to treat his murder as a Federal crime.

And while Maine courts don't hand down the death penalty, Federal ones do.

30

"Listen, George, I'm sorry I upset your applecart. About the trouble you had."

We were down in my cellar, trying to keep the house from floating away.

"Don't worry about it," George said reassuringly. "Would've come out sooner or later, anyway. I'm not mad at you about it."

He gave the pipe wrench a final twist and eyed the result.

"That ought to hold you for now. I'll be over soon to replace all this stuff, put in copper."

"Fine," I said, following him to the stairs. "Meanwhile, can we drink the water?"

Once the horrible Clarissa had departed, I had gone down to the cellar to check on the floor jacks that the men from Guptill's had put in, on the theory that one disaster follows another, and sure enough there was a pool of water under the steps. I'd touched the pool to make sure it was water and not heating oil, since the fuel tank in my house consists of old oil drums linked in series, an arrangement that has been in place since 1938.

"Oh, sure," said George. "Might want to take a

couple teaspoons of Rustoleum, though. Keep your innards clean."

My finger had come up red from the spreading pool, which was when the phrase "heavy metal poisoning" had begun flashing in my brain like a neon sign.

"Only kidding," George relented. "Put a filter on the tap, you're worried about it. I've got one out in the truck."

"Thanks." I watched gratefully as he hefted his toolbox and went up. The basement was cool and damp, its ceiling underslung with old hand-hewn beams from which most of the whitewash had long ago powdered away. There was a root cellar, its interior smelling mustily of potatoes, a room where slabs of meat had hung from iron hooks, and along the walls, numerous swatches of deer hide nailed randomly here and there, evidence of long-ago hunting seasons.

"When it happened," I began again when I got upstairs. "When McIlwaine died, where were you?"

Before answering, he positioned himself on his back with his head inside the cabinet under the sink. I thought that if an atomic bomb were to go off in Eastport, George would be poking his face up out of the shelter before the ash had finished falling, peering around to see which plumbing to fix first.

"Working on the Whites' house." His hand emerged, landed accurately on the basin wrench, and disappeared. The gritty sound of old metal turning came from under the sink.

"Yes, I know, but working where, exactly?"

"Don't know. I don't know when he got killed, so I don't know where I was at the time."

Which was reasonable but unhelpful. "Okay, so let's go on the theory that you didn't do it yourself."

A bang from under the sink. "Yeah, let's."

"You must have seen something."

George eased out of the cabinet, as he has often done before. The plumbing in the house has been jury-rigged so many times over the years that I sometimes think I ought to install a roller under there, of the kind that Gerry Porter uses to slide in and out from under automobiles.

"I saw the McIlwaines' blue Lincoln pull up."

I also sometimes think I should install dental equipment, for use in extracting answers out of George Valentine.

"What else?"

"McIlwaine got out. His wife was driving, the pretty blonde woman. Nina. Then she drove away."

"She didn't get out?"

"Not that I saw. It wasn't my job to watch her," George added, unhelpfully.

"Right. What did you see after that?"

He positioned the filter on the sink top. "That's it. I was busy fixing the vent pipe. Up on a ladder, or getting stuff from the truck."

Vent pipes insure that water exiting the plumbing system will be matched by an equal volume of air entering the system, and without going into messy detail, may I just say right here that you do not want troubled vent pipes. "Did you hear anything?"

"Alvin White and McIlwaine arguing." He tightened the nuts on the sink, and gave the faucet handle an experimental twist.

"Could you hear what they were arguing about?"

"Nope." The faucet spat wheezily twice and began to run water.

"You will have to buy cartridges for this filter."

Which was no surprise. The amount of equipment required to make a two-hundred-year-old house run properly in the twentieth century makes operating a space station look economical by comparison. In fact, I have sometimes wondered if shooting the house into space might be a viable plan, or at least an eminently more restful one.

He closed his toolbox and wrote me up a bill from the pad of printed slips he kept in his pocket, and put it on the counter as he headed for the back door.

"George, why do you suppose Alvin and McIlwaine

stayed in touch? I mean, I know they grew up together. But it doesn't seem they'd have gone on having much in common."

"Don't know," George answered thoughtfully. "My old man used to say he liked his old friends best, 'cause they remembered the same things he did."

Which to me made sense. That morning, for no particular reason, I'd woken up thinking about a night when Sam was a baby. He'd had croup, and when he tried to breathe he made a sound like a strip of wet bedsheet being ripped lengthwise, violently. I'd been so sure he was dying that I baptized him in the back seat of the car on the way to the emergency room, using a bottle of Perrier from my shoulder bag. And now the only person besides me who remembered that night was my ex-husband.

George put his hand on the door, looking woebegone. "I wish I had done it, tell you the truth. I'd go right on down and confess, get Ellie out of jail."

"I know you would. You're sure you didn't see anything else. Another car, or someone else going into the house?"

He shook his head. "Like I said, I was up on the ladder. Only other person I saw was Bobby Taylor, up on his own ladder, halfway across town up against the Heddlepenny House. The one," he added, "that those two women from Bangor are putting all that work into, trying to turn it into a bed-and-breakfast."

I knew the house he meant. It was the talk of the town, what color they would paint it and whether they would recondition the old wooden windows or go for brand-new thermopanes—more practical but less attractive and a third the cost.

I was betting on the former; from what I'd seen—the Heddlepenny House had eight chimneys, and all of them were being repointed, relined, and in one case rebuilt from the cellar up—the women from Bangor were backed by the Sultan of Brunei.

But what interested me now was what else Bobby

Taylor could see, high on his ladder against the Heddlepenny House. Nearby, the white clapboard clock tower of the Congregational Church stood tall over all the other buildings in town; so tall, in fact, that you had to crane your neck up just to see it.

Unless, of course, you happened to be perched on a ladder, in which case you could tell the time merely by turning your head, and if you didn't want to do that you could simply listen, because the clock rang the hour and once on the half and the quarter every day from six in the morning until ten at night.

"Bobby Taylor," I said slowly, "saw you."

"Yep. He waved to me," George agreed. And then he got it. "He saw me, and he knows *when* he saw me."

Then he frowned. "But the idea isn't to clear me. Nobody's saying I did it. Except," he added, "you, for a little while. I'm still not quite sure how I feel about that, Mrs. Tiptree, having you think I might be such a sneaking kind of a person."

It was typical of George that he minded less being suspected of bloody murder than he minded being thought a sneak.

"You said yourself you would confess if it got Ellie out of trouble. I was just thinking along those same lines, trying to be helpful."

"Yeah. I'd hate to be around when you weren't trying to be helpful. So now what?"

"Now I talk to Bobby Taylor, make sure he says what we think he's going to say: that you were up on a ladder in his plain sight during the time when Threnody McIlwaine was having a little unscheduled ventilation work done on his head."

He nodded enthusiastically. "And after that, we tell Ellie that I was, and she stops trying to confess to something she didn't do. And then she comes home, and we get the whole wedding thing over with."

Then he sighed. "I swear, Mrs. Tiptree, I don't care if we have to live in a tent in the backyard, if only we can get all this murder business done and finished."

"It might not be as simple as all that," I cautioned.

In fact, it definitely wouldn't. George opened his mouth to say that once Ellie withdrew her confession, and especially once she had explained the reason she had confessed—her desire to protect George—surely any right-thinking, open-minded, halfway decent prosecuting attorney worth even a modicum of his salt would believe her, and release her immediately.

Which was precisely what was not going to happen, on account of all the blood evidence and other stuff that Clarissa Dow was so excited about, and I had no idea how to get around that.

At this point, Ellie could recant her confession until the cows came home, but it wouldn't do her a bit of good.

What I needed was for her to recant *and* for me to find who really killed McIlwaine, and then to present that person to Clarissa Dow in a way she would believe.

Just at the moment that didn't feel very likely, but Bobby Taylor was a start.

"What," George asked, seeing my face and deciding not to express any optimism after all, "are you going to do, now?"

"Well, right now I'm going over to Heddlepenny House, get Bobby down off of his ladder, and make him confirm what you just said. Also, I'm going to ask him what else he saw, if anything."

Such as, for instance, whether Nina McIlwaine was doing something other than driving swiftly and harmlessly away; such as her going into the house and killing her husband.

"You know what should've happened," George said, looking grim. "Ellie should've said that old witch Hedda did it. That'd get Hedda out of everybody's hair."

He hefted his toolbox meaning to go on, but then came the sudden din from out in the street: the roar of an engine, a shriek of brakes, the sound of a car speeding off down the street very fast, and the clatter of bottles and cans.

Lots of bottles and cans.

31

"Did you see it? Did you see who it was?"

George shook his head, bent over the prostrate figure of Can Man sprawled a few feet from the gravel pile. I had already called the ambulance, and the police. A crowd was beginning to gather, including some of the reporters who were still hanging around—many of them, now that Ellie was gone and McIlwaine's body transported off the island, had begun packing up and leaving like vultures headed for the next carrion-feast—but when they discovered it was only Can Man, the reporters lost interest.

"Is he dead?" Sadie Peltier demanded. "Is there *blood*?" Her bright eyes peered avidly as she shoved herself forward between the legs of the grown-ups.

"Is there," she asked insistently, "any blood and *guts*?"

Somebody shushed her, and when she protested, seized her by the raggedy fur on her jacket collar. "You," somebody brave growled at her threateningly, "pipe down."

The child subsided, rebellious but silent for once. Behind her tangle of dark curls, her eyes were full of vengeful mischief that she clearly intended to accomplish as soon as possible, and I felt sorry for whoever had disciplined her.

"Sticks and stones," Can Man said, struggling up. "I can do it. I can do it myself." He looked around dazedly.

"Hey, buddy," George soothed him. "Take it easy."

Can Man tried standing, then sat down defeatedly again. "My cans," he mourned, seeing them rolling everywhere.

There was a moment of silence. Then people looked at each other and began collecting cans, putting them into Can Man's bag.

"Thank you," Can Man said politely, beginning to get his wits about him again. But fresh alarm crept into his eyes as the ambulance arrived, with Bob Arnold following in the squad car.

"Someone knocked Can Man off the road," George said as the ambulance fellows got out their first aid kit. Can Man's hands were scraped, and the knees torn out of his pants, but he seemed otherwise unhurt and was refusing to get into the ambulance.

"I don't think he was hit," George added. "I think somebody just gave him a scare. Took a run at him, made him jump."

"Anybody see it?" Arnold asked.

The people gathered around the scene shook their heads. It was nearly dinnertime, and the kitchens in the old houses were at the back, away from the street. Somebody propped Can Man's bag of cans up beside him.

Arnold crouched beside Can Man. "Hey, Whitfield"— that was Can Man's real name, Whitfield DeSautell—"who did this to you?"

Just then Hedda White arrived home from some errand, with Janet Fox sitting beside her in the passenger seat of the Whites' red Buick. Hedda stalked straight in the back door, her head in another piece of outlandish headgear—today it was a green paisley turban—and held disdainfully high, with Janet right behind her. Meanwhile, not seeing them, Alvin White came out the front door and across the street, to find out what was the matter.

"Whitfield, who knocked you down?" Arnold asked again. "Can you tell me?"

Can Man's eyes widened in terror. "No," he moaned, "oh, no. Cat's got my tongue."

He gazed in frightened appeal at Alvin, who had always liked Can Man and made a point of saving returnables for him, even though Hedda said cans and bottles were dirty, that they attracted vermin, and that Can Man—she had threatened him directly with this several times—ought to be locked away in an institution.

Can Man's mouth worked as he swiped tears with his wrists.

"What is it, Whitfield?" Arnold put a hand on his shoulder.

Can Man stared at Alvin. In the Whites' upstairs hall window, Hedda stood glaring furiously down at the scene, looking as if she could have fired the pearl-handled revolver quite happily if she'd had one, and if she were able to.

I saw her frown at my gravel pile. Probably she would write a letter to the editor of the *Quoddy Tides* about it, complaining about the unsightliness and squalor, dictating her missive while Janet laboriously penned the thing. Hedda, when she wasn't causing other unneeded trouble, was a great one for letters to the editor.

Can Man's gaze turned from Alvin, to Hedda up in the window, and away. His fists clenched the rolls of gauze the medical technicians had given him to staunch the bleeding. I noticed uneasily that Sadie wasn't around anymore, which for Sadie was unusual, since even when she was not provoking a crisis herself she liked to be at the center of one. I turned back to Can Man just as a word popped from his lips.

"Buh . . . buh . . . *blue!*" he said.

32

"Nina McIlwaine's Lincoln Continental is blue," I said.

Wade looked skeptically at me. The storm had not damaged his house—he'd had his hatches battened—but it had wreaked havoc on his neighbors, many of whom were also his relatives.

"So," he noted, "is the sky, sometimes."

He had spent half the day nailing shingles back onto the roof of his aunt Priscilla's cottage, and the other half chainsawing a cedar tree that had blown onto the marine supply annex run by his cousin, Lester. Now he was shaved, showered, and dressed in clean Levis and a blue plaid work shirt, looking so strong and appealing, I wanted to drape myself on him as if I were ivy and he were a trellis. But I thought this would delay dinner pretty severely, so I made a mental note to do it later.

"And everybody knows that car," he said. "Wouldn't somebody have seen it, if it ran Can Man down? Known it was Nina?"

He sat at the kitchen table where he was carving a scrap of cedar into a rose the size of a baby's fist. When he had finished a dozen of them, he would drop one into each of the small muslin bags filled with lavender blossoms that Ellie and I had grown in my back garden the previous summer.

"No one," I pointed out, "saw any car. It happened so fast. Nina was in town, though. At the Bottle Shop. Apparently all her newly arrived relatives like American whiskey."

Word around town had it that since the murder, Nina's relatives had stormed the little airfield west of town as if they were taking a beachhead, flying in on private planes they had chartered and establishing themselves in McIlwaine's mansion. Not that I begrudged her, in her grief, the comfort of her relatives' presence, but the word "opportunistic" had crossed my mind, especially since I had decided she was probably the murderer.

"And there weren't any paint chips," I went on, "or tire marks to trace to anything. Apparently Can Man was scared badly, but not actually hit."

"Well, that's good. Poor old Can Man." Wade finished a cedar rose, his blunt fingers working the jackknife to create a thorn the size of a flea on the tiny stem, and started on another.

"It really annoys me," I said, "that Nina thinks she can just do all this."

His eyebrows went up. "Do all what?"

"Put a whole peaceful little town into an uproar, that's what. Kill her husband and make it look like someone else did it, so Ellie winds up stuck in the middle."

I squeezed about a cup of basil pesto from the freezer bag I had preserved it in, into the top of the double boiler. Along with the lavender, Ellie and I had grown masses of basil in the sunny, sandy patch of soil stretching the length of Victor Sawtelle's fence, and now we were having it for dinner with angel-hair pasta.

"I mean," I went on, putting the garlic bread into the oven, "you can bet your life nobody local is behind all this. People in this part of the world aren't the kind who do murder."

As soon as the words left my mouth, I remembered the guy who had nailed his relatives into the mobile home and set it on fire.

"I wouldn't," Wade said evenly. With his knife tip, he put a dewdrop the size of a gnat's eye into a cedar rose petal.

"Wouldn't what?" I got out the tossed salad.

"Bet my life on it. You found Bobby Taylor yet?"

"No," I replied, "and it kind of worries me. It's not like him to take off without a word to anyone."

Bobby Taylor hadn't been at Heddlepenny House. His toolboxes had been stacked in his garage, at the little house that had once been a cider mill out on Prince's Cove. Bobby had put all the shingles back onto the house and installed big eight-over-eight windows, whose frames he had painted crisp, park-bench green.

The green against the grey of the cedar, and the perfectly proportioned windows, created an air of elegance. His regular work habits weren't the only reason he was steadily employed. He was handy with a hammer, all right, but he also had a great eye.

The doors and windows were all locked, and his truck wasn't there. When I got home, I'd called his mother, making it sound as if I wanted to hire him, so as not to worry her.

But she was already worried. She hadn't seen him in two days, and she was afraid he might have gone back on the bottle again.

"That girl," she confided worriedly, meaning Janet, "isn't good for him." She said it the Maine way: *guhl*.

I didn't think so, either, but then, I do not have a

stellar win-loss record in the romance department, myself, so who was I to comment? I just told her I was sure he would show up soon and got off the phone as gently as possible.

"Did you call Janet?" Wade asked. "She might know where he is."

I shook my head, stirring the pesto over the warm water. If you heat it too much, it separates.

"If I tell Janet I'm looking for him, she might tell Nina. And even though Bobby Taylor is probably a lot harder to run down with a Lincoln than Can Man, I don't think that's a good idea."

The sequence of events was clear, or at least it was to me: Nina sees Can Man coming out of my house, Nina knows Can Man saw her going into the Whites' house, and Can Man nearly gets run over by something blue, just like the car Nina happens to have driven into town that day.

Wade put the cedar roses aside, and cleaned up the wood chips. "You could," he pointed out, "just call up that Clarissa Dow woman, put her into the big picture."

"Clarissa Dow," I retorted, "has made it plain that she does not want to be put in the big picture. She likes the picture right under her nose, which is the only place she wants to look because it's uncomplicated, and it is the one that will lead her, she thinks, to a promotion."

I stirred the pesto some more. "Which," I finished irritably, "I'm sure is all she cares about. She really hated it that I'd figured that out about her, which makes me more sure that it's true."

I set the pasta water boiling, and turned from the stove just as Sam stuck his head in.

"Mom?" He sounded worried. "I was looking at my calendar."

I dripped olive oil into the pasta water. "Whatever it is, you can tell me in a minute, when we sit down. Wash your hands, please, and please do not wear your Bleeding Skulls T-shirt to the table. The mashed eyeballs spoil my appetite."

"Aw, Mom," he responded predictably, sloping off upstairs to pull a sweatshirt over the offending garment, but he didn't sound too peeved. Having a mother who could pronounce the words "mashed eyeballs" in just the right tones of lip-smacking irony took some of the sting out, I assumed.

Wade looked thoughtful. "There is something I do want you to do, though," he said. "I want you keep the Bisley out."

I'd thought about it since he'd mentioned it, that afternoon.

"You know my position on guns in the house with Sam. Locked up, or not at all. I don't think I want to make an exception."

"Sam's not a problem. I've already explained to him that if he touches it, I will take his arms and legs off and feed them to him." He smiled when he said it, but it was the smile on the face of the tiger—have I mentioned that his teeth are as white and straight as the ones in tooth-paste ads?—and I felt sure that whatever he'd really told Sam, it had been impressive.

I put the plates I was holding down onto the kitchen counter. "You're serious."

Wade held his big calloused hand up and counted on his fingers. "Fire. Note. Tires. Can Man's accident. That doesn't sound like a stretch of calm weather, to me."

"You think it's going to get worse."

He looked levelly at me. "I think the way to beat a storm is to face right into it, not wait for it to blow you over sideways."

"Yeah," I said reluctantly, "I guess you've got a point. I'll think about it some more."

Which was when the oven timer went off, the pasta kettle boiled, and the olive oil began separating out of the basil pesto, threatening imminent ruin. So it was not until we were all at the dining room table, with the candles lit and a nice fire crackling in the only one of the six fireplaces not absolutely guaranteed to burn the house down if you strike so much as a kitchen match in it, that Sam got to drop his bombshell.

"Mom," he said, forking up some angel-hair pasta with basil pesto, "you know the weekend of the boat-school tour?"

It was raining, and I noticed with satisfaction that water was not streaming down the insides of the dining room windows, seeping behind the clapboards and rotting the wood below so that you could reach in and pull it out by the crumbly handfuls. We home-repair enthusiasts take our little triumphs where we can get them.

"Yes," I told Sam, "I know the weekend, and yes, I will do your paper route."

"But Mom," Sam said, unappeased, "don't you remember what weekend that is?"

A feeling of floating, nonspecific but definitely impending doom seized me, much like the one I felt on the day I realized that all the thick, whitish stuff wrapped around all the hot-water pipes in the basement was asbestos.

And then I remembered. "Oh, no. Tell me it's not."

"It is," said Sam. "It's the same weekend Dad's coming."

"Maybe," I heard myself say in a small, hopeless voice, much like the one I used while agreeing to have, at hideous expense, all that asbestos removed, "maybe they will decide to reschedule the boat-school tour."

Sam looked pityingly at me and ate another forkful of angel-hair pasta with homemade pesto, which might just as well have been SpaghettiOs for all he noticed.

"Maybe," he said in equally hopeless tones, "Dad will have to go to an emergency."

"Right," I agreed, but I knew as well as Sam did that his father would not have to go to an emergency the weekend he was scheduled to come here. Having been married to a neurosurgeon for a good long while, I can tell you with perfect certainty that on the day that you sprain your ankle, or your son comes down with chicken pox, or the plumbing all backs up, or you go into labor, that is the day when a blood vessel in somebody's brain will pop like the bulge in an old inner tube.

But on any day when you do not want your neuro-surgeon husband hanging around, all brains within a thousand-mile radius—even ones that have not been working well for decades—will abruptly begin function-ing flawlessly. When I was married to my ex-husband, it got so I believed that even the embalmed brains down in the pathology department would all start bobbing mali-ciously around in their formaldehyde jars, vibrating with healthy vigor, just on the bare suspicion that I might need to get rid of him for eight hours or so.

I looked up to find Wade grinning at me. I had taken care not to complain, but Wade had been present on the day the ex-husband in question had sent me a dozen roses, cutting them first so that when I lifted them from the box all the fragrant, red blooms fell off like so many severed heads, and on the day when the telegram arrived demanding to know why—this was months after Sam and I departed and several years after my ex-husband and I were divorced; that was how crazy he could be—the laundry had dealt improperly with his good white shirts, and had not ironed his undershorts the way he liked them.

"So he's coming for a visit, is he?" Wade asked, taking another piece of garlic bread. There was a glint like a lightning bolt in his eye, though his tone was innocently cheery.

"Yeah, and at the exactly wrong time," Sam said. "But listen, do me a favor and don't make him crazy, okay? You're just the kind of guy who could really do it, and my dad's already crazy enough."

Wade regarded Sam with friendly interest. "Oh? And what kind of guy is that? Who can get your dad crazy?"

"The kind," Sam replied, "who can do a lot of things right. And who isn't making my mother cry all the time."

There was a moment of silence as I digested this. It

is a rock-solid maxim of modern family life that one divorced parent does not criticize the other one in front of the children. But Sam was an observant boy, and the realities of his life had put me in the position of having to run interference between himself and his father. Furthermore, for the last part of my marriage, I'd wept nonstop. And Sam, of course, remembered it.

"When we lived in New York he would show up all the time," Sam said. "Even after they got divorced, and after I went back to live with my mom—I lived with my dad for a while, I thought I wanted to—he knew how to get her going. And when they were married, he lied. It's better," he concluded, "that we live farther away from him."

"Seems like you still care about your dad, though," Wade said, homing in with precise accuracy on the crux of Sam's difficulty. "Isn't that the whole problem about where you'll go to school, what you'll do with your life? What your dad will think about your decision?"

No reply to this.

"As long as we're on that subject," I put in quietly, "you should know, Sam, that he's bringing his girlfriend."

He seemed unsurprised. "Yeah, right," he said, getting up. "I figured he would. If he had two, probably he'd bring 'em both."

He picked up his plate and fork. "And you want to know what's really scary?" he asked Wade.

Sam took a deep breath. "What's scary is, when my dad's not screwing around with women or messing with people's heads from the outside, his *job*—"

He gave the word a sad, bitter twist. "His *job* is to get, like, a really sharp buzz saw, go in the operating room and cut right *into* people's heads. Mess around with them," he finished, "on the *inside*."

Having delivered himself of that little mixture of opinion, information, and invective, he stomped off into the kitchen.

In the silence that he left behind, I looked at Wade, who appeared about as bemused as I felt.

"Where'd that come from, do you suppose?" he asked.

"No idea. I didn't realize he was so angry at his father."

"Too bad the old man can't leave out the romantic getaway portion of the program."

"Considering he hasn't seen Sam for nearly a year," I agreed. "It's so hard to tell him that, though. Half the time I want him to at least try to have a relationship with Sam."

I poured a little more wine for both of us. "Other, I mean, than bossing him around, trying his best to turn Sam into a carbon copy of himself. God forbid," I added, sighing.

"And the other half?"

"The other half, I wish he would vanish off the face of the earth. I mean, you've seen the stuff he's pulled."

"He make you cry lately?" Wade inquired acutely.

"No. For a while, when Sam was insisting on living with his father, there was lots of opportunity for . . . discord. But not now. Sam's right; it's better that we're farther apart. In fact, he's been unusually mellow, recently. Quiet, like . . ."

Like the calm before storm. "Anyway, he'll be here next Friday."

"I see," said Wade, eyeing me closely for signs of distress. "Want me to make myself scarce while he's here? Would that be easier for you?"

"Absolutely not." I got up. "If you can stand to stick around I could use your help. But Sam's right about him, so don't make him crazy. I mean, any crazier than he already is."

Wade smiled imperturbably. The candlelight made the glint in his eye seem to dance.

"Wouldn't dream of it," he said.

33

Later that night, I went down cellar and opened the lock-box containing the Bisley and cartridges. The lockbox was fastened to the wall, like a fuse box, and while I stood there I could hear the house working all around me: water trickling down from Sam's shower, the furnace rumbling steadily to heat the water, the click of the electric relay on the thermostat in the furnace.

Wade said shooting someone else's gun, as a habit, was a way of not paying the bill. He said the only way to know how deadly it was, to understand it on a gut level, was to own the weapon yourself, and keep it, and be responsible for it.

I thought Wade was correct. It was why I had gone through the background check, and bought the Bisley.

Over in the corner, the dry-well hole waited silently for George to come and finish it up. I wished I could drop the events of the last few days into it, and let him pile gravel onto them, too. Taking the Bisley out of the box, I hefted it, thinking about Sam.

Eighteen months earlier, just before I'd found this house, one of Sam's friends had been shot while examining a gun he found under a pile of his father's sweaters, on the top shelf of his father's closet. No one ever expected the boy to find the hidden weapon, or to search out the ammunition stored separately in a carton marked "Xmas decorations."

No one expected him to handle the gun, if he found it. He wasn't, everyone said even after he was dead, that kind of boy.

Musing over this, I fingered the only key to the lockbox. I wore it on a silver chain around my neck, feeling that any circumstances under which Sam might be motivated to remove the chain were also ones under which I might want him to open the lockbox.

And otherwise not. Carefully I put the Bisley away

again, and turned the key. No one ever expects to need seat belts or air bags, either, but they do. Your chances of having an accident on any given day may be infinitesimally small, but once you are having it, the likelihood rockets to a hundred percent.

It was, I still believe, the right decision, even though I came to regret it later, and to wish I had calculated the risks differently.

34

Around seven the next morning, Bobby Taylor called to say he had heard I was looking for him. He would be working that day at Heddlepenny House, so I went over there at ten, which was when he said he would be taking a break.

I brought coffee in a thermos, and sour-cream doughnuts from the American Legion bake sale. The sale was to benefit the building fund for the Legion's new hall, and the doughnuts were so heavy they could have just gone ahead and built the hall out of them. But they were also delicious, and Bobby's eyes lit up at the sight of them.

"Thanks," he said, swallowing some of the coffee gratefully. The day was grey and foggy, with a chilly breeze coming off the water, poking its shivery fingers under my collar and riffling the puddles in the packed-sand driveway of the Heddlepenny House.

Bobby looked up, measuring how much of the job remained. The house was a sprawling old gingerbread Victorian with big bay windows and a wide front porch overlooking what had been a garden. Everything was in an advanced state of decay, including the wooden gutters that Bobby was replacing, section by section.

"How do you get them up there?" I asked. He was working alone, and wooden gutters weigh much more than their equivalent in aluminum.

He pointed at the staging set up against the house. "Bring the staging platform down, put the gutter on the platform, get on it yourself, crank the staging up. It's okay unless you're afraid of heights."

"Uh-huh," I replied calmly, faking like mad. What I'd been planning had seemed perfectly reasonable while I was planning it.

The thing is, staging is a kind of scaffolding. You use it instead of a ladder when you want to work on a wide area of high stuff: for instance, when you are painting a house, repairing clapboards, or performing large-scale gutter maintenance.

And that was the problem: high stuff. The staging consists of pairs of tall posts set into the ground in a line parallel with the building's foundation. Clamped to the posts are steel supports upon which are laid pairs of two-by-twelves, so that if the post pairs were the vertical members of capital Hs, the two-by-twelves would be the crossbars.

Crucial to the arrangement is the fact that the two-by-twelves are not fastened to the supports, nor are safety harnesses issued to persons venturing onto these monstrosities. The boards simply rest there, bouncing gaily up and down when you walk on them and taunting you with the fact that a pair of two-by-twelves laid together is, count 'em, twenty-four inches wide, an amount of space that on solid ground is no problem at all to keep your balance on, but in thin air, it is.

I looked at Bobby's staging platform: three sets of two planks each, laid across the supports of the staging. The supports were attached to posts by a ratchet affair, which you operated with your foot while standing on the platform, clinging to the post to keep your weight off the platform if you were lowering it.

Clinging to the post all the rest of the time, too, if you were me. But I was only going to get one crack at getting Ellie out of trouble, and when I went at it, I had to have my ducks in a row.

And one of the ducks had been way up on that platform, while Threnody McIlwaine had been getting murdered with an ice pick.

I took another doughnut. What the hell, you only live once, and my cholesterol probably wouldn't even have time to rise much before I was dead of fright.

"So Bobby, what do you think of Nina?" Snooping into murder is really just indulging in gossip, but it is gossip with a point.

He chuckled, wiping his fingers with a blue bandanna. "I think Nina's about what she seems to be. Young, pretty, hungry. Saw the main chance and grabbed it. Hey, who can blame her?"

Just what the world needed, I thought: another sucker for a pretty face. Still, his non-judgemental attitude was refreshing; Bobby was a good egg.

He took a final swallow of coffee and screwed the cap back onto the thermos. "Jeez, a cigarette would go good about now."

Out on the water, the foghorns had begun a mournful hooting. "Sorry. I didn't bring any."

"That's okay. I don't smoke. Anymore," he added ruefully. "This clean-and-sober business is a pain in the tail, you take it halfway seriously."

He grinned, and I laughed with him, comfortably and easily. Bobby had been sober for as long as I had been in Eastport, but before that the story was that he could be seen on the waterfront any night of the week, clutching a paper-bag-wrapped bottle.

"Anyway," he went on, "Nina's a tough nut. Gets what she wants one way or another. And with the situation out there now, I just had a crawful. Patty bitching, Gerry kowtowing, all those relatives of Nina's everywhere you look. Not that they aren't nice people. They all seem fine except for that one guy, the cousin."

He shook his head. "But jeez, it's like a goddam Red Cross camp. And Janet's all screwed up. I used to think her spending most of her time trying to finding her mother was a crock, just a waste of time. But it kept her busy, traveling—she took lots of trips all over the place—and on the phone and so on. She had a lead in New York she was excited about for a while, but I guess that didn't pan out. Now, it's like she's lost her reason to live."

"Any idea why she gave it up?" The coincidence of that happening just when McIlwaine died seemed too perfectly timed.

"Nope. Unless it was just something she could do, butt heads with the old bastard. Drove her nuts, the way he made fun of her about it, but it was her way of standing up to him. Since he's gone maybe she figures, why bother? She's not talking about it."

"Yeah," I said. "Maybe."

He strolled over to the staging apparatus, leaned against the posts at either end, and apparently found them satisfactory. "So I took a ride out to Meddybemps and went fishing, get away from it all. That's where I was when you were looking for me."

"The situation makes you uncomfortable," I offered.

He looked at me. "Right. So I got out of it. And no, I don't believe Ellie killed him any more than you do. As for the rest, I guess I want to keep it simple, like the saying goes. I don't know who did it, or how, or why. And maybe I don't want to."

He stuffed the bandanna into his jeans pocket. "Tell you one thing, though. I'm not going back there until those relatives are gone. Man, do those people drink."

It was another reason he'd wanted to get away. I've known a few recovering alcoholics, and most of them didn't like hanging around people who were drinking, not because they were worried about slipping, themselves, but because it reminded them of the way they used to be—like looking at an old photograph of yourself and finding it's someone you don't even want to recognize.

"So anyway," he said, "you've been dancing around this staging for twenty minutes like it's a roller coaster and you're not sure whether to buy a ticket. You going up, or what?"

He stepped onto the platform, and reached a hand down to me. I looked up at him: a tall, lean man whose craggy face showed the effects of a little time and a lot of abuse. As he waited to see what I would do, his eyes did not flinch in the slightest from my examining gaze.

Like I say: you only live once.

35

"Steady," Bobby Taylor said to me from the other end of the platform.

I unclenched my teeth just long enough to smile at him, meanwhile thinking how pretty the rooftops were and wondering if I had remembered to send in my life-insurance policy premium.

Bobby cranked his end of the platform up with a foot ratchet. This of course made my end of the platform slant down. But Bobby had lent me leather gloves, which turned out to be handy for clinging to wooden support poles, and of course he would not crank his end up very much.

Bobby kept cranking. Apparently responding to nerve signals emanating from my brain stem, which I understand is the portion of the brain responsible for basic survival matters, my arms wrapped themselves more firmly around the support pole.

Little rootlets, I felt sure, would soon emerge from my arms, responding to some even more primitive brain segment that traced its heritage back to the vegetable kingdom, fastening me to the pole so securely that I would have to be excised from it by a tree surgeon.

"Okay," Bobby Taylor called. "Now it's your turn. Put your foot on the foot pad and press down."

"You," I muttered, "are out of your mind."

"I could come down there and do it," he called genially. "But then you'd have to get out of my way, so I could get at it."

Far off in the distance, I could see the windshields of cars glinting on their way across the Lubec Bridge. Turning slowly, I saw my very own rooftop, with the flashing on one of the chimneys peeling away like tinfoil and a patch of the shingles flapping, looking for all the world like someone riffling a wad of hundred-dollar bills, which was roughly what the roof work represented.

"You," Bobby Taylor clarified, patiently and kindly, "would have to let go."

"In that case . . ." I looked at my feet, remembering that under no circumstances did I wish to look past them to the ground below.

Near my right foot was the metal foot pad, which of course would not just unclamp and let go. Bobby Taylor had firmly assured me *no* foot pad would unclamp on its own and send the staging platform plunging to earth. To lower the staging you had to unbrake the pad, then turn a reluctant crank. He'd assured me that it was not at all an impromptu operation.

I put my foot in the foot pad and tentatively pressed down.

"Harder," Bobby called. "Put your weight on it."

Then, seeing that I was having difficulty, he made his way down the platform to stand behind me. Reaching his arms around me and out on either side, he braced his hands atop my gloved ones.

"Now, go ahead and put your foot on it."

I did as he instructed and was rewarded by the feeling of the platform rising beneath me until the two-by-twelves paralleled the earth. And with that, except for the Congregational Church steeple and Heddlepenny House itself, we were the highest thing in Eastport.

"It's beautiful," I said, all at once very glad I had come.

"Yeah. You don't miss much from up here. Look." He extended one finger without taking his hand from mine.

Down at the harbor, a couple of fellows in orange life jackets set out for Deer Island in an aluminum boat. Sitting amidships, a little boy clutched the rail with one hand and rummaged in a basket with the other. A napkin flew away from him and he grabbed at it, then clutched his handhold as the bow hit a wave, bouncing, the napkin flittering into the boat's wake, disappearing.

"And over there's the Whites' house," Bobby said. "See that orange stuff below the roofline? That's the Rustoleum George was spraying on his pipe fix."

Now that so many of the reporters had gone away, Key Street looked curiously vacant. "So you could see him." Relief hit me; part of the trick of getting Ellie off the hook was indeed making sure that George was off, too, or she wouldn't recant. It just wasn't the whole trick.

Meanwhile, it wasn't enough for me to hear Bobby Taylor say he'd seen George from up here that morning. I had to know for sure that it was possible. Otherwise, the way my luck was running, the dreadful Clarissa Dow would climb up here herself and prove that it couldn't be. Clarissa, I felt rather certain, was not afraid of staging platforms or of anything else.

"Of course I could see him." Bobby laughed. "Why would I lie about a thing like that?"

"I don't know, Bobby. I mean, I didn't mean to imply that you would. I'm just so glad, that's all, because you can see the church clock from here, and you saw George from here when you did, and that means that Ellie doesn't have to lie, anymore."

I felt giddy with happiness, and height.

"Yeah," Bobby said. "He was up there a long time. In my sight all the while, as a matter of fact. He hauls a lot of stuff up to the job with him, so he doesn't have to run up and down."

A thought struck me. "Did you see Nina? Can Man said there was a blue car, and I was just wondering . . ."

"Oh, sure. She pulled in, went around the side. I remember thinking that was funny."

He shot me a knowing look. "Nina's kind of sworn off the back doors of places, you know."

His voice grew sardonic. "Now that she's not a refugee in a war zone anymore, filling up on roots and berries while the bombs explode. She likes front doors, and she likes 'em best if there's a bunch of snooty butlers and footmen standing behind 'em, wearing their uniforms as she sashays in."

A squawk from below distracted me. Moments later, Martha Dodd rushed out the side door of her house—the one right next to Heddlepenny—into the garden, where each spring she put in more labor than the yearly output of your average chain gang.

"Oh, dahling," Bobby imitated with bull's-eye accuracy, waving his hand in a careless, Nina-like way that nearly made my heart stop, considering how high off the ground we were; but I couldn't help laughing.

George hadn't gone in, but maybe Nina had.

"Anyway, I didn't see Nina for a while, maybe five minutes, and then I did, going around to the front of the house."

Janet had said she heard a knock on the door, and that Alvin had answered.

"Couple minutes later, she drove away," Bobby added.

Nina, I exulted silently, had been out of the car and out of Bobby's sight for maybe five minutes: long enough to swing that ice pick.

Another shout from below interrupted my thoughts. "Get out of there!" Martha Dodd urged, swinging a broom before her as if driving a flock of chickens. A wicked little burbling laugh came from somewhere in the yard.

"Scat, you little pest!" Martha cried, as Sadie Peltier crawled out from the concealment of a burlap windbreak, her curls a mess of straw and compost.

Sadie beat feet for the garden gate, swung on it once very hard as she was forbidden to do, and pelted off down the street, pausing to turn and grimace defiantly at Martha, waggling her hips and wiggling her fingers in her ears before making good on her escape.

"Oh!" Martha mourned, crouching to inspect her rhubarb bed, then rising to wring her apron vexedly at the fleeing child.

"Sadie," I observed, "is an absolute menace."

"She's a caution," Bobby agreed. "Stout line might hold her down, but not much short of that."

He craned his neck around the post to watch Bill Blatchley's little blue scallop dragger *Sally* nip around stern-first in the dark green waters of the boat basin, and settle into her slip just as neatly as a hen settling onto her nest.

"You know, some people around here appreciate what you're doing for Ellie. Trying to help her, and all."

"Oh." A little bolt of happiness pierced me. "I thought maybe people would just think I was meddling."

He shook his head. "Nope. In fact I was telling Janet this morning, she could do worse than find a friend like you. Instead of aping after Nina all the time, trying to get her approval. Or sucking up to that old witch Hedda White."

I looked out again over the pointed rooftops, like sharp-edged cutouts snipped against the pale sky. "You spoke to Janet," I said, wanting not to have heard him correctly.

"Yeah, I went over early, after I called you. I figured I'd better. Takin' off the way I did. I'm not mad at her or anything, I just needed thinking room."

"You told her what I wanted," I said, hoping it wasn't true.

A tiny little ping came from the support mechanism under my feet, but I didn't pay attention. I was busy thinking about Janet telling Nina that Bobby could see what went on over at the Whites' house that morning, and Nina deciding to do something about it.

"Don't," said Bobby Taylor in tones of unnatural calm, "move an inch."

"What? What's wrong?" I turned my head slightly. Under the year-round tan he'd acquired by working out-side all the time, his face was waxily pale.

"See that bolt down there?"

I followed his gaze. In a way whose specifics I did not fully understand, the staging mechanism worked on friction; everything had to be tight. And now I could see that the bolt Bobby Taylor was indicating had a small, round hole machined through it, a hole intended for a cotter pin.

No cotter pin. That ping, I realized coldly. The platform descended about a quarter-inch.

"Just shut up," Bobby Taylor said fiercely into my ear, and seized me hard by the scruff of my collar with his left hand, and by the muscle of my upper arm with his right hand. Turning me, he wrenched my own hands from the support post and propelled me into, it seemed, empty space.

"Forward," he grated out. "Believe me, you want to do this. Go for the next support post, the next set of boards."

The platform jolted down six inches. I had a sudden, dizzying sense of the sky tilting and the earth rushing up to meet me, a zooming, wah-wah distortion of perspective that seemed to be sucking me sideways off the narrow platform. Bobby stayed behind me, motoring me forward, but I couldn't feel my feet and I didn't dare to look down; it was as if fear had dematerialized my body.

There was a moment, halfway between support posts, climbing, it seemed, a slope that got steeper by the second. In that instant there was nothing to stop my falling, and the two-by-twelves were sliding faster. It was like the dream where you are running, and the awful dreaming knowledge overcomes you that you are not going to make it.

Bobby hit me from behind with the force of a line-backer, and I lurched forward, slamming onto the next set of two-by-twelves. I felt his arms wrap tight around me, and around the support post.

A splinter stabbed my cheek. The post smelled of pine. I could feel my heart thudding, see stars against my eyelids. Blood oozed from my lip, tasting rusty like a mouthful of old nails.

Bobby's breath gusted urgently into my ear. "Is it there?"

"What?" I was trying to talk, but no sound came out.

"Look down," he insisted, "is the pin there?"

And then it hit me that cotter pins do not simply fall out. You may be able to remove one with your fingers, but often you cannot. The whole point of a cotter pin is that once you put it in, it stays in, unless of course somebody hammers the hairpin portion of the pin and breaks it, whereupon the straight section will slide through and fall out easily.

If this pin were missing, there would be no next set of two-by-twelves.

I squinted down. The cotter pin protruded in friendly fashion through the bolt holding the support mechanism to the post.

Only, not all the way through. The straight part of the pin was pushed almost into the hole, as if someone had tried to force it, deforming the end and giving up when the pin stuck.

"It's there," I told Bobby. "Now what?"

I felt him sigh. "Now I'm going to lower us down," he said. "You just stay here and hang on."

"What if the cotter pin over there turns out to be missing?" I pointed at the final support post.

"It got us up here," he replied grimly, already setting out across the two-by-twelves.

Which was not a particularly comforting thought, seeing as the other one had gotten us up there, too, before falling, but the final pin was present and intact, and Bobby lowered us without further incident.

"Sadie," he said when he got his breath back.

"Martha Dodd yelled at her yesterday, over at my house," I agreed.

He sank down, and I sat beside him, heedless of cold and damp. I'd have sat on a nuclear waste dump if it was at ground level. "Outside my house, after Can Man got hit."

I remembered my premonition that someone would suffer the consequences of scolding Sadie, who did not take even the mildest correction lightly.

"Probably," Bobby said, grimly picking up the fallen

cotter pin, "Sadie came over here to get her revenge, then. Give Martha the what-for."

The two-by-twelves had landed smack on a couple of Martha Dodd's rhododendrons, flattening them. The faint crack of their branches had been the only sound, and no cars had happened to be passing on Washington Street, so no one had even noticed us.

"Could she reach them?" I objected. "And do it?"

He nodded. "I lower 'em way down when I leave at night, so no kids will climb up on 'em. She could hit the pin with a rock."

He looked at the remaining two-by-twelves. "You know what I like about not drinking? I like it that when something bad happens, it could've happened to anyone. But somebody's got to talk to that kid's parents, before she kills someone."

He sounded certain, and I had to admit it made sense. Sadie had probably been watching from somewhere nearby when the two-by-twelves fell. She was always around for disasters.

He tossed the fallen cotter pin at me. "Here, you can keep it for a souvenir."

I caught the object with the sort of swift sure grab of which I am ordinarily incapable. Something about escaping annihilation, apparently, had sharpened my reflexes.

And my eyes. At the hairpin end of the steel cotter pin, which was darkened with age and the beginnings of corrosion, were a set of tiny, thread-thin, bright parallel lines.

Such as the lines that might be made on a metal object if you gripped it with a pair of pliers. And Sadie was a devil, all right, but I doubted that she carried tools.

The marks could have been made any time, during maintenance, or repair. But as I stared at them, the grooves on the cotter pin seemed to smirk thinly at me, as if knowing something I didn't.

36

"What," Nina inquired, tipping her smooth brunette head with sweet, ingenue brightness, "means this thing, 'cotter pin'?"

I'd had enough of sweet, ingenue brightness already, and I'd only been there about two minutes.

"This," I thrust the pin at her, "means cotter pin. It fell out of Bobby Taylor's staging platform while we were on it."

The house at Mackerel Cove seemed outwardly unchanged: same landscaped plantings of oversized nursery shrubs, still in their burlap wrappings against the harsh Maine coast winter, same bullying sense of vulgar display trampling any potential for beauty.

Inside, though, a new air of mad gaiety prevailed. Pop music pounded from the stereo set in the living room, remnants of breakfast littered the dining room table, clothes and magazines lay scattered where people had flung them.

Nina's eyes widened. "Is maybe bad accident."

"Yes, bad accident." I gave the final word a harsh twist, saw her catch and understand it without any impediment.

Somewhere upstairs, someone shouted: a sharp, angry bark, followed by a crash of furniture. On the mantel stood a half-empty bottle of vodka, a bag of Fritos, and a prescription bottle with the name of a Chicago pharmacy printed on the label.

The stereo stopped blaring Metallica and began on nine inch nails. Altogether, the atmosphere in the house was the one I imagine must prevail in the asylum for the criminally insane, after the attendants have been murdered and buried on the grounds and the inmates have taken up management of the place.

"You don't think that I had to do with?" Nina asked. Which was an interesting leap of logic, considering that I had so far suggested nothing of the sort, or at least not in so many words.

"Because," Nina added with another of her language-mangling mannerisms, all of which separately and together were beginning to make me want to strangle her, "I was in bed, asleeping."

"Uh-huh. So Janet didn't tell you I was going over there to meet Bobby Taylor. She didn't say Bobby was going to show me that George Valentine couldn't have killed your husband."

And that you could have, I thought but didn't say aloud. She got it, though. Her eyes narrowed, her delicate nostrils flared, and for a moment I saw the hungry, street-wise refugee kid she had been, peering out at me with feral purpose.

"Nina!" A young male voice barked abruptly from the stairs. Her eyes flickered calculatingly from me to its source, in the hallway behind her. "Nina, you must—"

I turned. It was the fellow from the photograph, not unshaven and frowzy with sleep in the middle of the morning as I had been imagining, but sharp and alert as if he had been up since dawn.

"Jacobia," Nina said, "this is my cousin." She said his name, but I could not have done so without some practice.

He tipped his head in acknowledgment, sizing me up with his eyes as he put a hand on Nina's shoulder, showing those white teeth that I remembered from the snapshot. In person, they were even more impressive: it was a carnivore's grin.

"I am guest in Nina's home," he said, glancing around at the luxurious rooms he now inhabited, the rich wood and expensive furnishings. His look had the proprietary air of a jungle animal surveying its newly enlarged territory.

"Welcome," I replied. "I hope you enjoy Eastport."

His nod, accompanied by a lazy lowering of his eyelids, said not only that he intended to do so, but that he hardly needed my good wishes; that he found them, in fact, rather impertinent.

"I am so sorry to interrupt, but we must go soon," he told Nina. His fingers moved briefly on her shoulder with uncousinlike intimacy.

"Goodbye, Jacobia," she murmured in the polite, practiced tones of a woman who would just as soon slit your throat. "I will give Janet your greeting."

What I wanted Janet to be given was a smack upside the head. Had she really run, like a good little sycophant, to let Nina know what I was up to?

If she had, this fellow could have tampered with the staging platform before Bobby got there. The morning would not yet have been full light, so he could have done it unnoticed, and the task might have taken only a moment.

Finally, there were the tool marks on the cotter pin, fresh and bright. At the door I turned again to the cousin, whose hands, hanging loosely but powerfully at his sides, appeared capable of wielding a pair of pliers without difficulty.

"So pleased to meet you," I lied, as I had countless other times to countless other bloody-minded thugs in good clothing, in countless other huge, tasteless houses full of knick-knacks chosen by trendy decorators. "What did you say you did in your country, again?"

He hadn't said, of course. Moving protectively in front of Nina, he smiled at me.

"I head government project in villages. Recording populations, various ethnic groups."

Yeah, recording them. And reducing them, if the prayer books abandoned in the glass-strewn, bomb-pocked churches didn't happen to be printed in the right language. Oh, this guy was slick.

I looked at Nina. "Congratulations," I said, "on finding him so fast." Then I winked.

Her pretty face wrinkled into a look of such fury, I thought she was going to spit at me, but I got out of there in a hurry before she could, wondering all the way to the car whether in the next instant the cousin was going to grab me, yank my throat back, and draw a knife blade across my throat.

I may not always know who is capable of an amateur, spur-of-the-moment homicide, but I do know a stone killer when I see one. After all, I used to work with them all the time.

37

Heading into town, I drove down Washington Street toward the Coast Guard building and the customs office. Not much happened in Eastport to vary the customs officials' routine of trooping aboard container vessels and clearing the crews en masse for the couple of days the boat would be in harbor. Checking out the so-called cousin's travel papers might, I thought, make a nice diversion for them. Who knew what would happen once he felt his well-feathered nest getting jostled by a lot of nosy immigration officials?

But as I was about to turn into the lot behind the customs building, I spotted the blue Lincoln in my rearview mirror, and there was really no sense in telegraphing my punches. So I continued to the next lot, alongside the fish pier, and went into the Eastport Gallery, where Derek Hart had already opened up for the day.

Inside, I was greeted by the aroma of fresh coffee mingled with the perfumes of paint and turpentine, the fine madness of a Beethoven string quartet exulting from the good speakers Derek had installed, and cascades of natural light pouring in through the gallery's big second-floor back windows, facing the water.

I paused on the top step. The gallery's old exposed rafters and beams had been washed in thinned white paint, as had the walls and trim. The floor was glossily coated in dark red, and the room divided into oblique cubicles by panels at eye level, on enameled support frames.

The effect, especially with the windows open and the tang of salt from the harbor breezing in, was of a large, wonderfully airy atelier with a work area in the brightest corner.

"Why didn't I become a painter?" I asked into the space and lightness.

"Because," Derek Hart said long-sufferingly in answer to my question, and without turning from the canvas he was engaged upon, "a quick martyrdom is so much more efficient. Burning at the stake or being shot through with arrows. Or eaten up by a lion."

He sighed, putting down his brush. "Oh, what I wouldn't give to be finished off by a lion right this minute."

But when he turned, he was cheerful, a ruddy-faced, jovially grinning man of fifty or so, wearing a blue-striped shirt with the collar open, the sleeves rolled up, and a tie stuffed in the pocket. Navy slacks and a belt with red sailboats embroidered on it completed his outfit, along with a pair of deck shoes.

"Good morning, Jacobia. What can I do for you today?" He waved at the works on the dividing panels, the product of a dozen industrious gallery members' busy winters.

"Something in pastel? Pen-and-ink? Possibly you're partial to oil. Or a woodcut."

Derek's tone skewered his dual role of artist and promoter. Once the owner of a small, wildly successful Manhattan ad shop, he was the gentlest of men and a canny, energetic marketer, with an eye for quality that set the gallery's offerings a sharp cut above the blurry daubs often seen in tourist destinations.

"Nothing today, Derek, sorry. I really just came in to use the phone."

His face fell comically. "Help yourself," he sighed. "Coffee, too, if you want. All I am here is a public convenience."

The phone was downstairs with the larger paintings and the sculptures. I pressed in Bob Arnold's number—a request for an immigration check might be taken more seriously, I decided on second thought, if it came from him—but his personal line was busy and I didn't think this was an emergency. So I waited, sniffing at a little whiff of woodsmoke drifting in from the street while gazing at Derek's latest finished painting: three men in a boat, on a tossing sea, in trouble, and a fantastic fourth figure.

In the painting, one man reached for the outstretched hand of a drowning mermaid. Another rowed energetically, while the third man pointed in alarm at something outside the picture frame, on the horizon.

Or risen from the sea. The maiden's hand reaches imploringly, with what is either her final, dying bit of strength or a fine imitation of it. No one seems to notice the pointing man's wide-eyed alarm, nor the fact that a great slosh of water is slopping up over the gunwale of the little boat, the wave's curved shape a watery reverse of the woman's hand; no one sees the trap.

A mermaid's heart, they say, is very cold. The tang of woodsmoke was getting stronger.

"Jacobia."

It was Derek, looking concerned. I started out of my moment's reverie and smiled at him, ready to debate yet again what was causing that strange wave; he loved to talk about his paintings.

"Jacobia, I think you'd better go home right away."

The smoke smell became a stink; I could see it now in the air outside the gallery, a faint, bluish haze acrid with the smell of old varnish.

"Why, what's wrong?"

Derek looked stricken, his pale hands unhappily clenched; he hated being the bearer of bad news. But like the men in the painting I still didn't get it.

"Jacobia," Derek said, "your house is on fire."

38

Through the smoke, the sun was a strange, pale disk hanging in the sky like a malignant omen. From the windows of the storeroom where I had found McIlwaine's body, orange bursts punched out like fists. Gouts of water poured from hoses around the spot where George Valentine was chopping a hole in the roof with an axe, while two other firemen advanced on the storeroom's back door, trying to muscle in close enough to battle the erupting flames.

"Sam," I managed, slamming my car to a halt and half-falling out of it in my fright. "Sam?"

The yard was a muddy battle zone filled with grim-faced men in yellow coats and boots, their sooty faces streaming with the choking smoke. "Sam!"

Bob Arnold heard me, turned, and jerked his arm toward Victor Sawtelle's palisade fence, now wetly plastered with charred bits of the antique newspapers I had salvaged from behind the plaster I had torn down out there, before it became obvious that the storeroom would have to be rebuilt entirely.

Then I saw Sam by the fence, his denim jacket around his defeated shoulders, a few of the neighbors trying ineffectively to comfort him.

He was alive, and for a moment that was all I needed. But then I saw how devastated he was: crying, his eyes wild with shock and misery when his brought his fists down from them.

"Mom!" At the sight of me, the last of the fight went out of him and he sobbed.

George broke through the roof and a glut of fire exploded from it, sending him scrambling. I wrapped my arm around Sam's shoulders and hugged him to me, hard.

"It's okay," I said. "Whatever happens, we will deal with it. We will get through it, and we will be fine."

He pulled away. "Monday's still in there. The fire guys were here when I got here, they wouldn't let me in. I could *hear* her."

George crawled back up to the hole in the roof, aiming a fire hose through it.

"She's *in* there," Sam insisted. "She was whining, scratching at something. I think she might be stuck in the basement."

Another boom of flame, and even though the fire had not yet broken through to the main house, smoke was beginning to drift out the back door. Pretty soon it would be a choking hell inside, and then it would all go at once in an incinerating rush.

"Stay here," I told Sam, gripping him. "I *mean* it."

He stared, nodding openmouthed as I strode away from him through the little groups of shocked, silent neighbors. One of them was little Sadie, of course, her moppet face with its halo of dark ringlets gazing up at the fire with an expression of awe and malicious glee.

Disgusted, I turned away from her toward the house, but a hand on my shoulder stopped me.

"Oh, but you mustn't going there," said a familiar voice dripping with sly feline charm. "It is too much dangerous."

It was Nina, looking on as my life burned down to the ground. A hundred feet away, the cousin lounged against the blue Lincoln, his face composed into a look of languid disinterest but with eyes alert.

Sighting me, he deliberately took a pack of Gauloises from his pocket and lit one, and tucked a gold lighter back into his shirt.

And suddenly, I'd had it with Nina and her selfish schemes, her perfect willingness to ruin lives—and even end them—in order to get her way. I put my hand in the middle of her yellow cashmere sweater and shoved, hard. She took two startled backward steps and sat down in the mud.

The cousin moved forward, seeming to uncoil from

where he lounged against the car, a frown beginning to spoil his pretty-boy appearance. But I moved in front of him, leaning down over Nina to speak to her.

"Get away from here," I gritted out through clenched teeth at her. "Get away and stay away from my house, or getting dropped in a mud puddle is going to be the least of your worries. Understand?"

I yanked her up by her shoulders, spun her, and shoved her again, propelling her in the direction of the looming cousin.

"I don't have time for you, now," I called after her. "But I know what you did. I can't prove it yet, but I will."

Tottering, Nina put her muddy hands out toward the cousin's champagne suede jacket, so new it might as well have had tags hanging from it. A look of dismay crossed his face as she staggered at him, dripping with filth. Suddenly her foot hit a slick patch and she pitched forward off-balance, uttering a mewing cry of alarm.

I didn't wait to see if he caught her.

"Jacobia," Bob Arnold said as I shoved through the knot of men clustered around the porch, and he made as if to step in front of me, to block my way. "We tried for the dog, but they couldn't find her. They went all through the house, and now it's not . . ."

Not safe, he was about to say. I just looked at him, and something in my expression must have told him that if he really meant to stop me, he would have to shoot my kneecaps off.

"Wait a minute, I'll go," Wade said, coming out of nowhere.

I hadn't seen him arrive, but now after a hasty conference with Sam he was bulling his way toward me, the men separating to let him pass.

"I am going after Monday," I told Arnold. "Step aside."

"Hey," Wade said, putting his big hand on my shoulder. "Let me do it. Fire's not in the main house, yet. I'll look for the dog again."

"We'll do it," I insisted, and he looked at me, two

separate impulses warring in his eyes: gallantry, or equal partners? If it was the former, I would have to stop making those sardine sandwiches; after all, one cannot have one's nurturing instincts mistaken for a political position.

"Okay." Wade gave in with a chuckle of resignation. "We'll do it together. Anybody ever tell you you're a tough little broad?"

Actually they had, and not in such polite terms, either, but I don't think it had ever pleased me so much. Wade cuffed me gently on the shoulder, his gloved fist lingering and his eyes bright with what I suddenly understood was love.

It felt like a cross between a shower of gold dust and a smack with a two-by-four. "Oh," I said softly, feeling floored for a dizzying instant.

And then we went in.

It wasn't like a fire scene in New York where the firemen and policemen will physically stop you from doing something stupid. In Eastport, plenty of people have made crazy decisions based on pure damn bull-headedness, and they will put on a slam-bang funeral for you, too, if yours goes wrong. Reluctantly, Arnold let us pass.

The smoke inside was so thick we were swimming in it, holding our breath and squinting against the burning in our eyes. Wade went first down the hallway ahead of me, feeling for the light switch and putting his hands on the basement door, checking for heat. At least we could breathe better, back here; the smoke was seeping from beneath the door to the spare room, so it was worse at that end of the house.

"Okay," Wade said in a tone that allowed no argument. "If I see fire, we're out of here. You got that?"

"Got it. Have I thanked you yet?"

"Later," he said, with a little laugh that made me fall in love with him all over again. Then he opened the door.

A gush of smoke black as squid ink billowed out. I had a moment to realize how nuts this was, hearing the nasty crackle of flames from down there, but then the smoke cleared a little and Wade began descending.

"Smoke alarms didn't sound," he observed. as he reached the bottom.

"So they didn't," I replied, making my way behind him. I had changed all the batteries, after the oven mishap, and the ones in the carbon monoxide units, too.

Wade pulled the chain switch; the lights in the basement went on. "Not," he observed with the excess of calm that I have learned means he is beginning to get angry, "an electrical fire."

Pausing at the foot of the stairs, I peered through the smoke, memorizing the cellar layout in case it should suddenly get too thick to see: to my right and behind me were the furnace, the old coal bin, the fuel drums, and about sixty square feet of clear floor space; the gun box was in the far corner, unthreatened—so far—by the flames. Directly ahead was a low, brick archway leading to the crawlspace under the storeroom, and to my left, a dozen or so feet from the stairs where I stood, were two closed wooden doors behind which lay another stair; it led up to the metal Bilco doors that opened onto the back yard.

I swung the flashlight I'd grabbed from the hall shelf into the coal bin, where the electric lights didn't reach. No dog.

"Monday!" No answering whimper, no click of canine nails on old concrete. All I could see, through the despairing lens of my mind's eye, was a black, motionless heap huddled against a stone foundation scarred by her scratching to get out.

"Huh," Wade said, lifting his head at a minute shift in air movement, sniffing it. Smoke ceased flowing from the crude, cavelike entry into the crawlspace under the spare room, and began flowing in the other direction; I could breathe without coughing.

A jolt of hope bolstered me, but when Wade saw my face he shook his head.

"Got a draft going through that hole George chopped

in the roof, like a chimney. They don't get enough water in, she'll go fast, now."

Something heavy crashed into the crawlspace in a shower of sparks. Flame brightened its interior: earthen floor, crumbling stonework, a broken wooden shutter somebody had shoved in there.

"We'd better get a move on," Wade said. "She flashes over, we could get cooked." He started around the cellar's perimeter.

"Maybe I should look upstairs again." I had, I realized, only Sam's report of hearing Monday in the basement. Maybe she wasn't down here at all.

"No." He said it flatly, from the corner where the coal chute used to be, and where those disastrously full fuel-oil drums stood waiting. "No fire escapes, remember. No one's going up there. If it flashes on the first floor, you'd have no way out."

He came back to the cellar steps. "I'm sorry, Jacobia, but she isn't here. If she's upstairs, she might still make it out, but I think maybe she went . . ."

He pointed at the blazing crawlspace, now an inferno nothing could survive. "In there," he finished.

Another crash, louder. Shouts from outside.

"Listen," he said, taking my arm, "we'd better get out, now. It could—"

Monday's puppy face loomed up in my merciless memory, her cold nose bumping my elbow as she pressed inconveniently in for the attention she adored. Oh, I thought at her, I'm so sorry.

And then somebody hit me with, it seemed, an enormous flaming sledgehammer as the crawlspace flashed over with a whooshing thump! and a bulging bomb of flames exploded from the entry into the cellar.

I stumbled back, feeling my nose hairs go crisp with the sudden rush of heat.

"Damn." Wade's voice. We were cut off from the stairway, backed into the corner by the fuse box and the pipe juncture, where the water was routed to the washing machine or to the hose in the backyard. A few yards away, the Bisley's lockbox hung silently on the wall where Wade had bolted it; once the heat got there, the ammunition closed inside it would begin exploding.

The water pipes a foot from my nose reminded me of something else: the hose, I realized bitterly, that I had forgotten to bring indoors last fall. If only I had it now; instead it was lying out in the yard, half-covered in slush, probably still frozen solid.

"Come on," Wade said, and his voice was so calm that it almost sounded dead. "Maybe the Bilco doors."

Flames shot from the crawlspace like orange tongues licking out from the doorway of a furnace. A half-dozen steps from the crawlspace entry, wooden steps led up to the metal Bilco doors that would let us out into the back-yard. Or—would they? Had I unlocked the Bilco doors as George had reminded me?

No. My mind had been in a hundred different places, and I had forgotten about the men who would be bringing down the gravel. We were locked in, I was hor-ribly sure of it, but I kept silent about it. Maybe I was wrong; maybe I'd unlocked them without thinking.

Or some other miracle would happen. Wade rattled the slide latch on the wooden door leading to the Bilco hatch. It moved open easily, but now the wooden door was jammed in the frame.

I'd stopped fixing things like that long ago; the house settled this way, and then it settled that way, so if you waited long enough jammed doors opened up again, saving a lot of trouble.

Except, unfortunately, for the trouble we were in now.

Wade hurled his body once, hard, against the door, and tore the splintered pieces of wood back, revealing Monday's body behind them, limp and suffocated, a soft boneless bundle of black fur as I lifted her and wept into her warm neck, while ahead of me Wade shoved against the Bilco doors.

Which opened at once. Air poured past me, sucking the flames momentarily out of the crawlspace. And even as I scrambled away from them up the hatch steps, I knew:

I had not remembered to unlock that Bilco door. It was open because someone had gone into the house, found my ring of utility keys, and opened it. Then whoever it was had gone back inside, started the fire, and gone out the Bilco doors—slamming the wooden hatchway door in haste, so that it had jammed—to avoid being seen from the street.

I knew it as clearly as if I had seen it: Monday was there because she had tried to follow. After all, when you have just committed arson, it will hardly do to have the victims' dog following you around, frisking and begging for biscuits. Poor Monday hadn't had a chance.

But I still did. "Here," I said, shoving her into Wade's arms. "I'll be right back."

"Jacobia," he began patiently, but I was beyond reason.

Those water pipes were ready to go kablooie, just as George had warned. All they needed was a little help.

The fire had retreated back into the crawlspace again, like a dragon retreating to catch its breath. I reached up and cranked off the water main valve; moments later and the handle would have been too hot to touch. Predictably, the valve began dripping as the packing inside it, compressed but too ancient to seal, failed to close. Then I cranked it on, again.

Nothing happened.

"Tell them to turn off the hoses," I yelled up the hatch.

George Valentine's face appeared in the hatchway. He looked at me, at the main valve, and at the pipes snaking all around the ceiling.

"The fire hoses are lowering the pressure," I yelled at him.

His face lit with understanding. Moments later, I heard the hoses stop.

I cranked the main valve off hard, waited, and twisted it back on again just as fast as I could.

There was a little *thunk!* from inside it, as I did it. Water began spewing merrily from half a dozen pipe joints, and then from a dozen more: soaking the cellar steps, cascading down the brickwork over the crawlspace entry, pouring in over the window wells and puddling in the concrete depression where the coal furnace used to hunker.

The dripping from the main valve slowed as the hoses went back on, but I was pretty sure that didn't matter, anymore. The first rule of amateur plumbing is that water prefers to flow along the outsides of pipes, and will do so whenever it can.

Upstairs, water trickled and dribbled and splashed, as if a team of rainmakers had gone to work inside all the plaster walls. Under other circumstances such a flood would have been a disaster, but at that moment I was delighted to know that I would have to replace every ceiling in the house.

The reason being that, as plumbing per se, old plumbing is decidedly unsatisfactory, but when handled with the proper amount of creativity—such as for instance the kind that will make it go kablooie—it makes one hell of an effective sprinkler system.

39

"Mom!" Sam sat in the back seat of Arnold's squad car. Beside him sat Monday, alive and observing the proceedings with apparent interest, albeit a little blearily.

I scrambled into the squad car on the other side of her and threw my arm around her, and she let her head fall into my lap with a low, exhausted *wuff*, sighed deeply, and closed her eyes.

"One of the guys from the ambulance gave her some oxygen and did CPR on her," Sam said. He looked worse than the dog, his eyes huge and dark-ringed, lips blood-less and his cuticles bitten raw. "And she woke up!"

Monday's tail thumped once in appreciation for the story, and she sneezed.

"Then she threw up a lot," he added, "and walked around in circles for a while. I think we'd better be pretty nice to her." He stroked her coat, which was dirty and dull with smoke, and she shifted comfortably under his hand.

"Oh, you bet we will." I put my face against her soft, smooth ear, thinking that if the house had burned flat to the ground, leaving me only what I had here with me in the squad car, I'd have been okay. "We're all going to be nice to each other for a while."

The guys had finally gotten the fire under control; now they were hosing water onto the embers. Steam rose from the hole George had chopped in the roof of the storage room.

"Mom?" Sam eyed the house. "With the pipes busted, and the smoke and all, are we going to be able to stay here tonight?"

"Tell you what," I said, "you go and stay with Tommy Daigle tonight, prize fights or no prize fights, and I'll camp out in the house. Maybe by tomorrow, George can get some of the water rigged back up, and once we get the smoke aired out of the place, it won't be so bad."

Wade came and crouched by the open car door, seeing how we were doing. The look that had been in his eyes on the porch came back to me, with a little rush of happiness. As you may have noticed, it is not always easy to know how Wade feels.

But now I did.

"Hey," he said, ruffling Sam's hair, and Sam grinned, tolerating it.

"Fire guys want to recruit you," Wade said affectionately to me. "Soon as they can get a rubber coat and some boots your size, they're gonna teach you to go up a ladder. Seeing," he added pointedly, "as you are already so familiar with high places."

"Very funny," I said, ignoring his reference to my adventure with Bobby Taylor; probably it was all over town, by now. "I can't believe it didn't burn through the kitchen wall. There wasn't a thing stopping it."

Sooty and exhausted, George heard my comment and paused. "Uh, well, I guess I know why."

He pulled his cap off, wiped his hand across his head. "All that asbestos I pulled out of your cellar, when you first moved here?"

He eyed me guiltily. "Well, I was stuck for a place to put it. And you were having that kitchen wall shored up at the time, pulling the old plaster down and all?"

I nodded. Picking centuries-old plaster dust out of the butter dish was just one of the charming mental images I retained from that project; another was George, suited up like an astronaut to remove the hazardous substance.

"Well," George said, kicking a muddy spot with the toe of his boot. "I figured, what's the harm? Even though I know it is against the rules," he added shamefacedly, "and if you tell anyone I could lose my asbestos contractor's license. The fact is, I stuck all that asbestos in the wall, sealed it in there real solid so none of the particles could get out, before the wallboard went up. And I guess it stopped the fire just long enough for you to get that water going."

He pulled his asthma inhaler out of his pocket and sucked on it, waited for it to take effect, then took out another and pulled on that one, too, before tucking them both away again.

"It's still," he added, "sealed in there; I checked. Damn, that smoke. I can't believe anybody breathes smoke on purpose."

"Thanks, George," I said, "for braving it. I appreciate it."

His lip twitched minimally, in the downeast Maine version of a broad grin. Then he tromped through the mud to where the other men were hauling the hoses up, tossing gear back onto the truck.

"Stay with me tonight?" Wade invited. "I mean, over at my place. You could pack a bag, come back and get going on all this in the morning."

On the cleanup, he meant, and the repairs. My insurance company would have to be notified, and an adjuster sent out, and after that a ton of phone calls would have to be made. I'd been hoping to pull back on the house-repair expenditures for a while, but now I thought I might as well just nail the checkbook to the back porch, and let people write their own.

And of course I would have to go and have a talk with Bob Arnold, arson investigation being another of the tasks on my to-do list, but not one that I could accomplish myself.

"Thanks. I'd better stick around here, keep an eye on things. You going out?" I hadn't missed the switch from "with me" to "at my place."

He nodded. "Boat goes in half an hour. Back late. I could get somebody else to go."

"Forget it." At a couple of thousand dollars per trip, turning work down cost Wade big money, and the ships weren't always as plentiful as they were right now.

"I'll be okay," I said. "Besides, I wouldn't be very good company."

Wade leaned into the car and put his arms around Sam and me. Monday lifted her head, smiling weakly, her tongue lolling.

"You are always good company," he said. "And you were great in there." He pressed his rough cheek to mine. "See you tomorrow."

And then he was gone.

"He never kisses you in front of me," Sam observed quietly. Monday put her head back down on my lap with an expressive sigh.

"I know," I said. "He's careful about it. I think he doesn't want to make you feel funny. About him and me, I mean."

Sam watched Wade striding off toward the harbor, a big man with a duffel bag slung over his shoulder. From a distance, he didn't look like anything special, just another downeast Maine guy going to his job, happy to have the work. A regular guy.

"I don't," Sam said thoughtfully, "feel funny."

40

It's not so bad, I told myself as I went through the house, and objectively I suppose it wasn't: lots of wet behind the wallpaper, loosening it; plenty of ceiling plaster sagging down. But the house itself remained standing, looking out through the trees over the harbor as it had for nearly two centuries. I was not the first weeping woman who had moved through its rooms, nor would I be the last.

At first I thought I would try to create a small outpost: a chair, a lamp, the coffeemaker, set up in the dining room where the fireplace still worked and the damage seemed least horrifying.

But gradually and against my own wishes I knew I couldn't stay. There were blankets in the cedar chest upstairs where the smoke had not seeped in, but no water to make coffee or bathe in, or even for Monday to drink, and the electricity was probably not safe. Nor was I sure that, as I slept, a hot spot wouldn't flare up in the storeroom.

Those smoke detectors, I remembered with another throb of pointless anger. Somebody had removed the batteries.

Thinking this, I put down some of the items I had taken from the cedar chest, including an old Teddy bear of Sam's that I had put away as a keepsake, and that Monday seized upon immediately. She glanced at me to see if I would take it away from her, but I didn't have the heart to.

"Go on, you can have it," I told her, my voice sounding small in the big old smoke-stinking house, and she trotted off under the dining room table with it, circling twice before lying down with her chin propped on the bear's red ribbon necktie.

Which left me standing there holding a blue lace-trimmed baby pillow, a crocheted rattle with a couple of jingle bells in it, and a satin-covered baby book containing newborn Sam's first footprint and a lock of his hair. Also taped into it was the blue-bead baby bracelet that the nurses had put on him at the hospital, and that he had been wearing when he and I went home in a taxi, my ex-husband being busy excising a pituitary tumor at the time.

A knock on the soot-smeared back door startled me. It was Bob Arnold, looking as if he thought I might give him an argument. "You can't stay here," he began, and I put my hand up to stop him.

"I know. It's too awful. Besides, a night at the Motel East might be just what the doctor ordered: a big, clean bed, modern plumbing, and complete silence."

"Well. I'm glad you're seeing reason. I really just stopped by to make sure you were okay." He gazed unhappily at the damage.

"Nina's new houseguest is a likely looking fellow," I said deliberately.

"Yeah, he is," Arnold replied, not missing anything.

"Think you could put a word in with the immigration fellows? Just ask them to do a quiet checkup?"

Arnold nodded. "You and Bobby Taylor had a little high-flying excitement, over to the Heddlepenny House earlier today, too."

"That's right. There's a lot more than meets the eye going on here, Arnold."

"Oh, it meets the eye," he said. "Don't worry about that."

The fire, I thought, had put us on the same page at last, the message being that someone had matters arranged just the way they liked them, with McIlwaine dead and Ellie in jail for the crime, and then I had stuck my nose in.

"And there was the note," I said. "The threatening note."

I got it from my bag and showed it to him. "Before this happened, I might have agreed it was just some prank. But this—"

He looked at a heap of sodden plaster that had fallen from the hall ceiling, directly under the upstairs bathroom.

"Right. This was no prank. None of it is. What a

mess," he said, and I knew he was longing for the days when he could jolly a couple of rowdy guys into the squad car and drive them home.

"I'm sorry, Jacobia. I wish I could do more about all this. I'm not ignoring any of it, or sittin' around on my hind end doing nothing, either. But—"

He spread his hands. "Nothing that's happened would make a rat's ass worth of difference to that Clarissa Dow woman."

"But what about this?" I waved my arms, to indicate all the fire destruction. "This didn't just happen by itself."

"I know. But if there was evidence of arson, it's probably burnt now. And arson's got to be proved—it's not enough for you to have a suspicion, or me, either. On top of which, this state's got one fire marshall, seven inspectors. For," he added meaningfully, "the whole state."

I gripped Sam's baby book. "So she's not going to draw the obvious conclusion? That someone did this to discourage me from trying to clear Ellie?"

He shook his head. "I've been spending a lot of time with Clarissa, trying to get her to see reason, but I tell you, she's about as useless as a rubber clam hoe. Stuff that happened before this, your flat tires and so on, I get the impression she thinks you might have done 'em all yourself, shift suspicion away from Ellie. And this, she'll say it was just some old wires, or something. Because for one thing, how are people getting into your house?"

On Wade's advice, I had begun locking my doors, and this question had troubled me, also. But the locks on my doors are as unreliable as most of the other fixtures. Lots of times, just rattling the knob will let you in.

Now at my look of outrage, Arnold spread his hands. "Yeah, yeah. I know. Half the time, I feel like pushing old Clarissa off the end of the dock."

And the other half? I wanted to ask. Something in his voice sounded funny to me, as if Clarissa Dow were occupying more of his thoughts than he liked. But I understood what he meant.

"I know, Arnold. It's different here, that's all," I said.

"You can't even fault her for not seeing it, really. She's used to the city."

"Yeah. Takes a while, I guess. I mean, to figure out that when something happens here, it actually means something, 'stead of just being background noise."

I felt a burst of affection for Arnold, for his being able to put it so clearly that way. In Eastport if someone shouts, odds are they are shouting at you, and wanting pretty urgently for you to do something about it. In more populous places, god forbid you should get involved, but in Eastport, you are already involved.

"Anyway," Arnold said, "couple of things. Alvin White asked me, could I try to find someone to stay in his house for a night or so. He says Hedda's all bent out of shape about the fire, scared to hell their place is going to be next. She's a handful, that Hedda. And since you're kind of stuck for tonight . . ."

And I had promised Ellie. Still, the thought made me quail.

"Oh, Arnold. Can't I just hire her a practical nurse? Or a lion tamer from a zoo somewhere?"

Arnold chuckled. "Yeah, a whip and a chair is about the right equipment. But you know how Hedda is with strangers."

"She's nicer to strangers than she is to people she knows," I retorted, thinking of Janet Fox.

"Alvin doesn't want Janet, anymore." Arnold dismissed my next suggestion before I could offer it. "Wouldn't say why, but he was firm on that. Old boy needs a hand, though, Jacobia. He looks frazzled."

"Oh, all right," I relented. After all, I'd had a house fire and nearly gotten my neck broken, and now that my evening would be occupied with Hedda, at least things couldn't get any worse.

"Thanks, Jacobia," Arnold said, heading out. "Oh, and one other thing I meant to tell you."

He paused at the door. "There was a fellow downtown, a guy from away, asking about you. What with the fire and all, it kind of slipped my mind."

"Really? What kind of a guy?"

Arnold shrugged. "Don't know. Didn't see him, myself. All I know is, he was looking for you. Pretty girl with him, and he was driving a yellow sports car."

I began to have an awful suspicion, which Arnold confirmed.

"What I heard," Arnold said over his shoulder as he went down the back steps, "this fellow, he says he's your ex-husband."

41

As I hurried into the Baywatch Cafe, I could already hear my ex-husband's voice, loud and dripping with self-importance.

"Of course, the people around her are almost all dirt-poor," he said, "so you can't expect much sophistication. Salt of the earth folks, though. Best place in the world to raise children."

Which was interesting to me, since I'd had to fight tooth and nail to get him to let me bring Sam here, and what he knew about raising children he could have fit into his martini olive.

The part about their being poor and unsophisticated was also fascinating, I could tell, to the local people who were having a drink at the bar or enjoying an early supper.

There was Watty Castleman, who had retired from a career as a special collections curator at an art museum in San Francisco, and Franklin Durang, until recently first oboe with the Boston Pops. Across the room I spotted a trio of performance artists who had rented a house on Harris Point for the winter, and the members of the musical group Border Crossing, fortifying themselves with broiled salmon and butternut ale before a sold-out concert tonight at the Eastport Arts Center.

Of course, there were also tradesmen and fishermen,

workers from the aquaculture outfit, a tableful of blue-haired ladies in subdued silk dresses, and a scattering of fellows whose employment I would classify as uncertain; several of them had helped put out my house fire.

My ex-husband took another sip of his martini. He was a commanding-looking fellow with thick, black hair now gradually acquiring some salt-and-pepper, a strong, patrician profile, and the eyes of an experienced riverboat gambler, the kind who always knew the odds, and the cards, and what he intended to do about it.

The girl sitting across from him was drinking, it looked to me, a cherry soda, but that may have been merely my perception of the drink appropriate for a child her age. I crossed the dining room to their table.

"Jake!" my ex-husband exclaimed when he saw me. "This is great, we were just about to go back out looking for you. Where are the street signs in this town, anyway? Locals been using them to patch their roofs up, again?"

People in Eastport used shingles like everyone else. The girl sat silently, waiting to be introduced.

"Tiff," my ex-husband said when he had finished being amused at his own joke, "this is my ex-wife; Jake Tiptree, this is Tiffany Emmerling. Tiffany teaches learning-disabled kids at the hospital clinic."

Tiffany smiled, and put her cool hand in mine. She was very beautiful: cornsilk hair, wide, blue eyes, and flawless skin.

"How do you do," she said. "It's kind of you to have invited us."

"You know, Tiffany," I told her, glancing at my ex-husband, "I think that if I were you, I'd go order a real drink. A double, even."

The perfect little click of comprehension that occurred in her blue eyes, accompanied by a widening smile of such radiant gorgeousness that it nearly knocked me backward, told me that this time, my ex-husband had hooked a smart one.

Although of course she had already spent eight hours in a car with him, so it wasn't all my doing. "What a good idea," Tiffany said. "I think I'll go get it, now." She rose with alacrity.

"But Tiff, you don't drink," said my ex-husband.

"You've known me one month. Don't tell me what I do and don't do, all right?" she requested sweetly, putting her hand on his shoulder briefly as she departed.

"What was that all about?" my ex-husband demanded to know when Tiffany had left the table, and he had gotten his eyes popped back into his head. She wore a green cashmere sweater and beige tailored slacks, and watching her cross a room was an education in fluid dynamics.

"She's never argued with me before." He frowned accusingly at me.

"She's road-weary," I told him, sitting down across from him unasked. "You shouldn't put so many miles on them, right off the bat. You were supposed to come," I added, "next weekend."

"No, I wasn't." Bang; his reflexive denial was as reliable as a light switch. "You must have gotten it wrong."

Edna, the afternoon cocktail waitress at the Baywatch, put a glass of cold white wine in front of me. She was a motherly-looking woman with a thick shock of short, iron-grey hair, and the warm glance she gave me as she went away did me a world of good.

My ex-husband frowned at the wine; how had that happened? He didn't like things occurring without his understanding them. Then he decided how he could twist it.

"Come here a lot, do you?" he smirked, meaning that I made a habit of hanging out in bars, leaving Sam to fend for himself, and so of course the bartenders would know what I drank.

I didn't tell him that if he came in here again next year, which I fervently hoped that he would not, Edna would bring him a martini with three olives in it without his having to ask.

"But it doesn't matter," I went on, ignoring his nastiness, "who got it wrong, because I have nowhere to put you. I had a fire at my house today, and things are a mess."

"Well, how did you do that?" he wanted to know immediately. "Jacobia had a house fire," he added in injured tones to Tiffany when she returned.

"Oh, I'm sorry," she said, putting her drink down. "Are you all right? Is your son all right?"

"We're fine. Thanks for asking. But I was just saying," I went on, "that I'm terribly sorry, but you'll have to stay at the motel, or at one of the little bed-and-breakfasts here in town."

I sipped my wine. "They're really very charming, I think you would enjoy them," I added, contemplating pleasantly the idea of my ex-husband trapped with his nubile honey in a room whose walls were about as soundproof as your average hanging bedsheet.

"You could probably," I said to Tiffany, ignoring his scowl, "still get a room at one of them for tonight."

"Oh, wouldn't that be fun!" she said, turning to him eagerly. "Or maybe," she added, catching sight of his expression, "not."

The look on her own face was one of amusement, I saw with what I identified after a moment as relief; I was getting to like Tiffany, and I didn't want her to have a bad time.

"The Motel East is comfortable," I said, taking pity on him for her sake. "And there's hardly anybody there this time of year. It's quiet here, in winter."

She looked out at the water. At five in the afternoon it was getting on for dusk; Campobello Island showed sketchily through a hanging grey fog, in minimally connected black ink-strokes.

"I think it's beautiful," she said, and I got up before my ex-husband could react to any more of her attention being stolen from him.

"I don't suppose Sam's around." He glowered at his martini. "Our plans have changed. We're leaving tomorrow, for Prince Edward Island."

"Well, he was expecting you next week." I tried to say this gently, but I could see that it roused his ire even more. Of course I did not add that next week would have been vastly more troublesome; on the order, in fact, of World War III. Nor did I bring up the notion that his sudden change of plan might inconvenience me; my ex-husband leaving earlier is always better than his leaving later.

"But maybe you could see him tonight. He's staying over with a friend on account of the fire, but you could take him out for dinner."

This more than anything had been my purpose for coming here. If Sam saw his father tonight, and if he didn't spill the beans about the boat-school trip, we might yet get through this visit without any fireworks.

"No," said my ex-husband decisively, "that's inconvenient. We have our own plans, tonight. But there's something in the trunk of my car for him. Take it and tell him I'll see him later if I can."

Tiffany appeared to be studying a painting on the wall of the Baywatch. It was one of Derek's, and she seemed intrigued by the flat planes and unexpected splashes of color that somehow captured the essence of the town, without pretending to be photographic. She was, I calculated, about seven years older than Sam.

I got up. "It was nice to meet you, Tiffany."

What in the world were you thinking, I wanted to ask her, but of course I knew; my ex-husband exudes killer charm when he wants to. It is only when he has you in his clutches—for instance, when you are stuck in a remote Maine village with only his little sports car to get you back home again, unless you are actually desperate enough to start reading bus schedules—that you begin remembering the old rhyme about the spider and the fly.

"Tell Sam I'm sorry I missed him," my ex-husband said.

For his part, all he wanted at this point was to get rid of me. I wasn't going to give him a bed, cook him a meal, or provide any of the other domestic services he'd been expecting, so my presence was superfluous, and as for Sam, well, Sam would have to take what he could get.

"Tell him," my ex-husband said, "I'll catch him next time."

"Right. If it's convenient."

He ignored this, waving for another drink, looking around in annoyance to try signaling Edna with one of the brisk, imperious gestures that worked so well for him in the operating room. Soon he would start snapping his fingers, and then he wouldn't be able to get so much as a glass of water in this place except possibly by lighting himself on fire.

I got out of there.

42

The walk home was chilly and depressing, through a thin, salt-tasting rain that haloed the streetlights and made my bones feel creaky and old. Seeing my house, forlorn and miserable-looking in the sodium glow, didn't help any, and knowing that I wouldn't be able to stay there was the worst thing of all. Promise or no, the idea of spending a night under the same roof as Hedda White made me feel like Daniel, contemplating the lions' den.

Under my arm was the package from my ex-husband's car trunk. The box said that it was a laser-beam level, a carpentry tool for which Sam had no use whatsoever. When I got into the sooty, grimy, smoke-smelling house, I opened and examined the thing.

The directions printed on the box said that when you pressed a button, the device emitted a pulse of ruby light that could be spotted over long distances, so that if you were laying out the floor of a hockey rink or putting the sewers in a new subdivision, you could get the grading exactly right.

On a boat, it would be a waste of toolbox space, and this was so like my ex-husband that I nearly threw the thing away. He had seen it, and enjoyed the idea of it—technology!—and having no use for it himself, had bought it for Sam as a sort of sop, to show how tuned-in he was to what he imagined were Sam's interests.

On top of which, the laser level was broken. I scanned

the instructions again, noting the large-print warning that on no account should the beam be directed into someone's eyes; serious injury or even blindness might result.

Oh, good, I thought; a carpentry tool that can also be used as a dangerous weapon. Just the thing for a teen-aged boy. But no pressing of buttons produced any light, injurious or otherwise, nor did putting in a fresh battery correct the problem.

Still, it was up to Sam to decide the gadget's fate, so I left it there on the counter, where Sam would see it when he got home. Monday, who had been all agog when I came in, caught my mood and sank onto her sleeping-bag bed—like almost everything else in the house, I realized with a wave of deep fatigue, it needed a thorough laundering—and curled her paws over her eyes.

I wanted to curl my paws over my own eyes, too. I had gotten precisely nowhere with all my running around: McIlwaine still dead, Ellie still in custody, Nina still cavorting with her so-called cousin out at Mackerel Cove, while my own place stood in shambles. Even the myste-rious portrait on the mantel seemed to mock me, the unknown woman still wearing her soft, inscrutable—and at the moment infuriating—smile. For an instant, I wanted to rip her to shreds.

And then sanity kicked in: this, I told myself, would not do. There was still some hot coffee in the thermos I had taken along that morning to Heddlepenny House, and two doughnuts in the bottom of the bag. As a pre-caution, George had switched off the power to the house until it could be checked, but I had the battery radio, which was playing old Dave Brubeck numbers, and a flashlight, so I could read the *Quoddy Tides*.

The Eastport Clam Board, the newspaper said, had decided to open half of Carryingplace Cove to clamming instead of only a quarter as originally planned, after the clammers had gathered to picket in protest of the tighter restrictions, outside the IGA.

The Passamaquoddy Water District announced that the pump at the treatment plant had broken down, but the fire department had lent them their old diesel pumper, so no interruption in service was expected; repairs would be complete in about a week.

Finally, the Eastport police log for the previous fourteen days—not including the murder; the *Tides* is biweekly, and went to press before that—listed seven minors possessing tobacco, two complaints of loud music, one unregistered motor vehicle, and a fistfight. In the latter, the combatants were lectured by Eastport Police Chief Bob Arnold and afterwards required to shake hands, and no arrests were deemed necessary.

And this, I have to report, did cheer me more than somewhat: ordinary life, going on in its ordinary way, a perception that doughnuts and coffee did nothing to dull. So that by the time the kennel lady came by to get Monday and take away her for a holiday—I might have to stay at the Whites' house myself, but there was no way I was going to put Monday through it—I felt better.

Monday frisked with excitement at the prospect of an outing. She was fully recovered now, rowdying around, begging for biscuits and flashing her pink-tongued, irrepressible grin, and I sent her off feeling happy that she at least would have a good time. Eastport's kennel, located on three fenced acres overlooking the cove at Kendall's Head, is the canine equivalent of Club Med. But when she was gone, discouragement washed over me again.

If Ellie were here, she would be moving around the house with crisp efficiency: vetoing my overnight-bag decisions, criticizing my toiletry choices, and generally leavening her assistance with dry, downeast commentary on everything from the weather to the organization (or lack thereof) of my underwear drawer.

I missed her dreadfully, and when I reached the Whites' house it was clear that Alvin missed her, too. He looked worn and haggard, his hand trembling as he let me in.

I pressed past him and he closed the door hurriedly as if against a rush of reporters, unaware, apparently, that they no longer swarmed outside. Too bad, I thought, that they hadn't been around to get film of Nina, sputtering in a mud puddle.

Shaking his head in dismay, Alvin turned the dead-bolt. "Thank you for coming, Jacobia," he said.

"Who's that?" Hedda demanded from upstairs. "Who's there?" she cried in a voice that sounded danger-ously on the edge of hysteria, and I saw Alvin flinch as her cane thumped insistently on the floor above.

"In fine form," I observed, putting my things down.

"Oh, yes." He managed a smile, his voice a thready quaver. "She's vigorous. As always."

He shuffled away from me into the parlor. I had never seen him shuffle before, nor his shoulders slump beneath the rumpled pullover that he wore in place of his usual crisp shirting. He seemed on the edge of exhaustion, which puzzled me—Janet Fox had been here for at least part of the day—as did the reek of burnt vegetables ema-nating from the kitchen. But a quick glance through the pantry told the tale:

In the kitchen, the sink was heaped with unwashed pots and plates, the stove crusted in spilled food, and the trash bin overflowing. Opened cans, frozen pizza wrap-pings, and an emptied bourbon bottle littered the coun-ter. Janet's duties, it seemed, consisted of helping Hedda ingest junk food and booze.

"Nurse!" Hedda yelled from upstairs. "Help, murder, police!"

"I'm so sorry," Alvin said, appearing behind me.

"Alvin, has Janet been giving Hedda drugs?" Of course she had; she'd said so in the craft shop, but this sounded much more serious than half a Valium tablet.

Alvin's eyes filled with tears. "I don't know what to do. Hedda was all right until a little while ago. Well," he amended, "she was drunk. But now she's—"

"Help! They're killing me!"

Alvin began to weep. "I'm so ashamed. I don't want anyone to see . . ."

He sobbed helplessly. "We're too old for this, Jacobia. And without Ellie to help us, we're just falling apart."

I had seen it before in elderly clients: they were fine until some big stress came along, but when it did, it ate up more than their financial reserves. An accident, an illness, or some other change in their routine suddenly gobbled up the last of their energy. Still, the change in Alvin was shocking.

"Alvin, believe me, this isn't your fault. Now, I want you to find all the prescription bottles you can, and bring them to me."

"Whenever I start to clean up," he went on, not hearing me, "Hedda needs something, but then I can't seem to do the right thing for her, either. It's awful, realizing you can't take care of yourself anymore. And I'm so worried about Ellie."

He was past being able to help me, or anyone. "Okay, Alvin," I said. "You go sit down. Everything is going to be okay."

I thought about calling an ambulance, getting Hedda out of the house and into the hospital in Calais for the night, if only to get Alvin some rest. But that would only upset Alvin further.

"Alvin, I want you to stay right there in that chair."

" 'Don't you move,' " he quoted, with the heart-breaking ghost of an Alvinish smile, " 'a goddamned inch.' "

I wanted to ask him why McIlwaine had paid him all that money. I wanted to grab him and shake him, make him tell me the whole truth. But he looked so fragile and careworn, I just didn't have the heart to, and besides, there was nothing I could do about it now, anyway.

Tomorrow, I thought. Tomorrow morning will be time enough.

That's what I thought.

Alvin's smile vanished, and when he spoke next I couldn't be sure if he was quoting or merely reporting.

"I tell you, Jacobia," he said, "my day's just been one long fizzle from beginning to end."

Mine, too.

43

"Pearl-handled revolver," Hedda muttered.

It was almost midnight, and outside Hedda's window, the fog billowed up from the waterfront in thickening waves, urged along by the foghorns in the murky night.

"I don't see why any of this is necessary," Hedda slurred.

"Because you weren't feeling well. Some of the pills you took reacted badly together, and the bourbon didn't help any, either."

Hedda's sour expression, as I adjusted her pillow and pulled the shade behind her head, showed her opinion of that diagnosis.

"Janet gave me the pills. Janet lets me drink." She glanced hopefully at her water glass, which she had kept emptying all evening and I had continued refilling.

I'd called her doctor in Machias, who suggested that I watch her carefully, and wash some of the pills out of her system with plenty of fluids. If her condition changed, he said, I should call him and he would come up right away, but so far his suggestions seemed to be working: Hedda was less crazy. Meanwhile from various caches around the house I'd collected enough little orange bottles to stock a pharmacy, for drugs prescribed for Janet by a variety of physicians in Chicago and New York.

"Janet," I said, "is a fool."

She was also something of a con artist, it seemed. I'd have bet money that all those doctors in Chicago were not aware of one another. Janet's trips hadn't only been to find her lost birth mother. They were also, apparently, to feed a narcotics habit. No wonder she was so flat and affectless; Janet was chronically sedated.

Hedda's eyes, bright and birdlike, glittered with dislike, but her pupils had shrunk to their normal size and her speech was not as slurred as it had been. I'd put Alvin to bed on the sofa in the downstairs parlor, giving him half of one of the sedatives Janet dispensed as liberally as Halloween candies.

"I'm going . . ." Hedda began, lurching up determinedly.

I stood over her. "You're going nowhere except maybe to the bathroom and back."

Fortunately, she could do that on her own, although by the third or fourth trip I'd given in and started helping her get her legs back up onto the bed, pulling the blanket up over the scars that crisscrossed her ankles and climbed up her lower legs. Even after thirty years, there was no mistaking the devastation that long-ago attack had wreaked upon her, the marks sharp and ugly as old barbed wire.

I thought again about what Jemmy had told me: that McIlwaine was behind the attack.

"Bastards," she spat when she saw me looking at the scars. "Ruined my life." Snatching the blanket, yanking it over herself, she'd winced at the pain in her arthritic hands, her fingers so swollen and misshapen with the disease that she could barely hold her water glass.

"Damn it, I need something," she'd complained.

"I know, Hedda." Her usual arthritis medicine, a mixture of aspirin and codeine, was in my pocket. "But I can't give you any pills until I'm sure the mess of stuff Janet gave you has gotten out of your system."

By that point, I really did feel sorry for her. One side effect of Janet's unorthodox medication scheme was that Hedda had been relatively pain-free for a couple of days. But her doctor had warned me against putting anything on top of the mixture she already had on board. He would come if I needed him, he'd repeated, but he expected that Hedda would probably sleep it off.

"And if I have to tie you into that bed to make sure that's what happens, that's what I'll do," I assured her sternly.

Hedda gave me a glare that could have curdled milk, then settled back at last in defeat, her eyelids lowering slowly like heavy crepe draperies. Gradually her harsh breathing subsided into the regular rhythms of sleep, and after a while I knew that it was safe to leave her.

From the top of the hall stairs I could hear Alvin snoring softly, too, the sound reassuring because I had felt nervous over giving him the sedative. But it seemed to have done no harm, and with the two old people at last safely out for the count, I went to the kitchen and put on a pot of coffee, and turned my attention to the dishes.

I had cleared away the trash, scrubbed out the crusted pots, and gotten the plates and silver stowed into the dishwasher when a tap came on the back door. My first thought was that it was some lingering reporter, but when I turned the back porch light on and peered cautiously out, it was Clarissa Dow.

I opened the door. By now it was misting steadily, the sort of thin, penetrating rain that seems to come at you from all directions. She stood there in a too-large yellow slicker, soaked shoes, and no hat, her sodden hair plastered to the sides of her face. But from her expression I could see that the weather had nothing to do with the sea-change that had come over Clarissa.

"Can I come in?"

I stepped aside. Her stockings were mud-spattered. She'd gotten a pair of green rubber chukkas from somewhere, and at the ends of her slender legs they looked as big as duck feet.

"So," she said, glancing around the Whites' kitchen, "how do you make sure you've got all the bones out of those fish you were cleaning yesterday, anyway?"

I held my hand out for her slicker and her shoulder bag, and hung them on a hook. "The test is, you cook the fish and eat it. If you choke, then you missed one."

She laughed, shivering. "Figures. Not a lot of leeway for beginners around here, is there?" She ran a cold-reddened hand through her dripping hair.

"Do you want a towel?"

A pause. "Yeah. Thanks, I do. And some of that coffee, if it isn't too much trouble."

I tossed her a towel from the linen cabinet in the back hall, then poured her a cup. "So. I guess Arnold must have told you I was going to be here. To what do I owe the honor?"

She let out a big breath. "To me screwing up," she said. "And to you being so stand-up about it."

The surprise must have showed on my face.

"Hey, what can I say, you were right to be stubborn. I saw Ellie White again, today, and if she's a killer then I am Imelda Marcos. And her story . . ."

She sighed again. "It doesn't work."

"The cleanup factor." That was the sequence-of-events thing that had kept bothering me—when had Ellie had time to clean up after the murder?—but in the craziness of the day it had fallen to the bottom of my bag of assorted miseries.

"Right." She finished rubbing the water out of her hair and pushed the damp strands away from her face.

"Everything else worked so well: great motive, all the blood evidence, her confession. And everybody else in the house can say where they were, what they were doing, vouch for one another."

"Even Alvin? Not that I think it's him, but . . ."

Alvin had only told me he was in his office at the critical time, not that anyone could swear that he was.

"We got the phone records this afternoon," Clarissa said. "He was on the phone with his insurance company, trying to cash in an old policy. They record calls from customers, and he's so deaf on the phone, the call took a long time."

"So what's the problem?" I asked. "Ellie's the one who's in custody, and if you don't think she did it . . ."

"The problem," she replied tiredly, "is that number one, it's not my call. The judge in district court decided not to accept her guilty plea."

Toby Alderman had probably tried to call me with

that news, but with the power at my house gone out, my answering machine was incommunicado, too.

"So now the whole thing goes to superior court. Or," she added, "ordinarily that's what's supposed to happen. But it's the attorney general who decides who gets prosecuted, not me."

"But don't they take your recommendations? I mean, isn't that what they send you out here for? And if you don't believe in her confession—"

"Right again. Usually. But I'm being reassigned. Tomorrow, I go up north to investigate some guy who poured gasoline on a house trailer and lit it."

She shook her head. "God, why did I become a lawyer?"

"Dog catcher jobs all taken?"

She grinned wryly. "Thanks. Anyway, the problem is this: I told my boss what I thought, that I made a mistake. It's not so rare, you know, that confessions turn out to be unreliable. They are almost as unreliable as eyewitnesses, who almost always turn out to have it wrong."

She looked down at her coffee. "So I told him I thought this was one of those times, that I thought later on we were going to get nailed through the foot, if we let her plead on this. There's something wrong with it."

"Really. And how did that go over?" By now, I thought I could guess.

"That," Clarissa replied, confirming my suspicion, "is how I got sent to Aroostook County, where I hear the gene pool contains approximately three working chromosomes."

I felt my hackles rise reflexively. "Hey. That's not a very nice thing to say about people. You don't know anything about what they're like, up there, so why don't you take your snotty attitude and go back to where you—"

"Sorry." She held one hand up in a please-stop gesture.

I stopped, but I wasn't finished, and I let her know it with the look on my face. For all I knew, she might not even be telling the truth. Maybe this was just some kind of trick to get useful information out of me.

"Sorry, sorry," she repeated. "I'm such an idiot. I didn't even mean that. Bad habits die hard, I guess. And stupid habits. Ignorant ones." She frowned, chastising herself.

I backed off a little; at least she'd apologized. But after my ex-husband's comments about my friends and neighbors, I was feeling sensitive.

"Arnold's been taking me out to every clam shack and lobster house between here and Camden," she went on, "but I guess fish isn't really brain food. Or maybe," she finished, "it's too late for me. I've been in the big city too long."

She fiddled with her coffee spoon. "He says there might still be hope for me, but maybe he's too nice a guy to tell me the truth."

Then it hit me, what she'd said and the look on Arnold's face when he'd talked about her, earlier. "Arnold's been taking you out?"

"Yeah," she admitted sheepishly. "Working on me. Trying to soften me up."

"So?" I squinted in mock-assessment at her and she laughed reluctantly.

"I guess it worked a little bit. He's the one got me to go see Ellie again, talk to her. That's when I figured out that for the time frame to work, she'd have definitely needed help, and there wasn't any. Earlier, I'd thought I could finesse it, but . . . ."

She suppressed a damp shiver, and drank hot coffee. "That's the part she got wrong, see. She's specific about the time she got to your house, and it agrees with what you said."

"She knew what I would tell you."

"Right. She couldn't lie about that. We also know what time McIlwaine's wife dropped him off here; she and Alvin White agreed independently on that. And we know what time it was when you found him. All together, that time frame covers about an hour, between when he arrived and when you found him dead."

"Sounds like a pretty big window of opportunity, to me."

"But it's not, because she didn't have all that time. He had to be killed between the time he got there, and the time you found him at your place, right? But," she went on without waiting for an answer, "within that time frame, it turns out there are only about five minutes during which McIlwaine *was* in the Whites' house and Ellie *wasn't* in yours."

"Well. That is a little better. Two problems, though."

I sat across from her. "George Valentine says wounds don't bleed much until the weapon comes out. So maybe there wasn't very much cleanup to do."

I thought a moment. "And second, what if your times are off? Five minutes one way, five minutes another, now we've got ten or fifteen minutes total."

"Whose side are you on?" She grinned briefly. "But yeah, that is exactly the way I'd have started tearing the thing apart."

She warmed her hands around the coffee mug. "So okay, let's do that. Give her fifteen minutes. To kill him, lose him—and by the way, if you'd done it, wouldn't you have followed him if he got away?—clean up, change clothes, and get over to your house, cool as a cucumber."

"She did," I agreed, "seem perfectly calm and normal until I found him. Even then . . . And no, I wouldn't have let him wander off."

Jemmy Wechsler's comment on that part came back to me; for an instant I wondered where Jemmy was now. "Because what if he didn't die? Then he could say who did it."

"Precisely. And I don't care what George says," Clarissa went on. "This wasn't your normal stab wound, because he was a bleeder, he had chronic headaches and he ate aspirin for them like candy. And because there was that preliminary scalp wound. It fluoresced all over the place. The only reason he didn't bleed at your house was, by then he didn't have much blood pressure."

I must have looked skeptical. She shivered again, and some of the feistiness seemed to go out of her.

"Okay, so maybe she's a fast cleaner-upper, she didn't

think of chasing him, and it could have happened the way she says. It's close enough so that her confession finishes her off. My point is, now that I've thought it over, I still don't buy it."

She straightened. "Because look: I can swallow the part about panicking, leaving the scene for a minute, for one reason or another. After all, he was supposed to be dead already. Then she discovers he's gone, mops up as fast as she can, changes clothes, and zooms out, making like it never happened. What I don't get, on top of all that, is taking the ice pick away and then bringing it back, hours later."

"Fingerprints?"

"Uh-uh. It came from her house, remember? There were plenty of innocent reasons for her prints to be all over the weapon."

"Which means?"

"Which means something changed between the time of the murder and the time you caught her, later, in your storeroom. Something," she repeated, "happened."

"What," I asked reluctantly, "about George Valentine?"

"That she was covering for him?" Clarissa made a dismissive face. "I wondered about that. So I asked her. She said he was up on a ladder the entire time, and if I didn't believe it, I could ask Bobby Taylor."

Then she caught my expression. "Something funny?"

"Not exactly." The information hit my tired brain with a thud. Ellie had known all along that George's whereabouts were accounted for.

"Did you tell her you didn't believe her?" I demanded. "Did you ask her why she's doing all this?"

"Yep. Whereupon she wouldn't say another syllable."

Which pretty much assured me, if I'd had any doubts, that Clarissa really had been talking to Ellie, who could be as silent as her pirate forebears when she wanted to be.

"Okay, back to square one," I said. "Let's say she knew she had to do something to be sure her confession would be taken seriously. She meant me to find her. She knew I'd hear her out there, moving on those creaky floorboards."

"And," Clarissa agreed, "last time I looked, guilty people didn't need to do that. Stand up and wave red flags."

"The blood evidence? On her clothes?"

Clarissa shrugged. "Could have been planted, I suppose, maybe by someone who didn't know she was going to confess. Or a simpler explanation: she brushed against it—at your place, or when she went home. Whoever cleaned up after the attack on him, they were in a hurry, didn't get it all."

She finished her coffee, got up and poured herself some more. "I don't have any great ideas about who did it, only who didn't. But what we're left with, I think, is somebody getting into the house, someone we haven't thought of."

"Have you considered Nina McIlwaine?" I went through the reasons why I still suspected Nina: her money motive, her marked lack of grief, and what Bobby Taylor had seen the morning of the murder, not to mention Can Man's frightened comments.

"And somebody definitely wants my interest discontinued," I finished. "She could be the reason behind all the rotten stuff that's been happening to me—the weird note, flat tires, the cotter pin on Bobby Taylor's platform, even the fire at my house. And by the way, I wasn't doing that stuff myself," I added defensively.

Clarissa's nod was grudging. "Okay, so I was wrong about that, too. But it's still the same problem: time. If what you are saying is right—and eyewitnesses have a way of misremembering things, even sober ones like Bobby Taylor—Nina wasn't on the scene long enough, any more than Ellie was. Besides, why would Ellie confess for Nina?"

Then she paused. "Although," she said, "if Nina had help, it would be another story. Someone who might also help her perpetrate the crimes against you. Someone who's always around, maybe, whose presence wouldn't really be noticed."

A clear mental picture of Sadie Peltier popped into my head. But that was ridiculous; she was a child, and however monstrous a little terror she might be, I couldn't see her cleaning up a mess of blood, or anyway not without shouting at the top of her lungs about it, all over the neighborhood.

Clarissa turned her head, stretching the kinks out of her neck, and looked out the window, which was dark and beaded with rain.

"Listen," she said, getting up, "I've got to move, clear my head, or I'm going to crash out, and I can't afford to. I get behind the wheel of a car the way I'm feeling, I'll be roadkill."

She pulled on her slicker. "Don't suppose you feel like going for a walk?"

I did, actually. A couple of hours with Hedda had made me feel trapped and smothered; I'd have welcomed the fresh air. But I didn't want to leave the Whites alone.

Just then, though, Arnold's squad car pulled into the drive. He made his way up the back steps and beamed at Clarissa as he came into the kitchen.

"Thought I'd find you here. Just leaving?"

She pulled on her slicker. "Trying to talk Jacobia into taking a stroll with me, help me get my second wind. But she's duty bound."

Arnold shrugged, eyeing the coffee pot. "I'll stick around. I doubt the old folks'll wake up, and if any calls come in—" he indicated the radio on his belt—"I'll swing downtown, let you know to come back. How's that?"

"Perfect." I grabbed my jacket.

44

There isn't much real silence left in the world, but some of it is in Eastport at night. The snow was all melted and our feet crunched softly in the sand that the trucks had spread during the storm as we headed down Key Street toward the water, past the old Victorian houses looking ghostly and untenanted in the brackish mist.

"Not," Clarissa observed, "a lot of late-night action."

I smiled at the thought, remembering Manhattan at this hour. "No. If you needed a cop right now—and you wouldn't—ordinarily, you'd have to get one out of bed."

She shook her head. "I don't know if I could get used to it. Even in Portland, there's more . . ."

"People," I finished for her. "That's the difference. More people, more chances mathematically for more of them to be doing more things, at more hours of the day and night. Interacting."

She laughed quietly. "That's a nice term for it. Shooting and stabbing and robbing and fighting."

"We've got some of that. Guys around here pretty much stick to fists, though. Statistically, I'll bet we've got one of the lowest real crime rates in the country."

"Right," Clarissa agreed wryly. "Except for the recent binge of arson and murder you've been having . . ."

"That," I replied a bit defensively, "is a statistical aberration."

She laughed as we turned onto Water Street, toward the dock. "You look at everything like that?" she asked. "In terms of numbers?"

From out on the water, the foghorns hooted steadily. "Hadn't thought of it that way, but yeah, I guess I do," I said. "That and money. I've always been interested in money, on account of growing up not having any. You might say it focused my attention."

"Uh-huh." She walked in silence for a while. Her stride was calm and unhurried, not rushed in the anxious way that the eerie silence of Eastport at night can make some people. A truly deserted, motionless late-night street scene is a thing to behold; you keep waiting for the flicker of movement in the corner of your eye, and when it doesn't come you can start imagining it.

We crossed to the seawall, and the paved walk alongside it. She was looking for a way to ask, and finally I decided to make it easy for her.

"My dad was Jake Tiptree, Jr.," I told her simply. "He went to prison when I was three, for blowing up a townhouse with eleven of his friends in it. All underground social activists, like him. I don't think he actually made the mistake with the explosives," I added, "but he was the one who survived, so he was the one who got to go to jail."

Clarissa nodded, looking down into the boat basin where all the fishing boats bobbed gently on the incoming tide. "I figured there had to be a connection. It's an unusual name. What happened to you after that?"

Just about anyone with a degree in law enforcement knows my mother was also in that townhouse, and Clarissa was no exception.

"I went to live with an aunt and uncle, in Tennessee. My uncle was an explosives guy, too, for a mining company. Interest in loud noises ran in the family, I guess. Unfortunately, he was also a big drinker."

I remembered that for a millisecond, stopped deliberately, as I always did. "I left there when I was sixteen, headed for the big city, and that's where I stayed until about a year ago."

The memory of the Port Authority bus terminal flew into my mind—the noise, the smell, my fear, the cruising hustlers on the lookout for girls like me—and I banished it forcefully.

"I did," I added with considerable understatement, "a lot of things to stay alive. But finally I got into City College, got some loans and a part-time job in the accounts department at St. Vincent's Hospital, and everything just went on from there."

"Everything including a couple of years as money advisor for the crookedest, most corrupt bastards the world has ever known."

I glanced sideways at her. "You do get your homework done, don't you? I pursued some opportunities, yeah. Is that what you got me out here to talk about?"

She shook her head as we started out onto the dock. "Curious, that's all. Wondering if there's some connection I don't see."

Then I got it. "Like maybe one of my old customers hired me to get rid of McIlwaine?" I chuckled in spite of myself.

"What's so funny? People like that don't usually let their employees retire."

"Right." The dock stretched ahead of us, a wide grey ribbon leading out into an endless expanse of black.

"And the employees don't usually know as much as I know, about as many as I know it about, while being as squeaky-clean as I am. There's no law," I added, "against giving financial advice to crooks, and I made sure never to have any material knowledge."

That I could testify about, I meant, and she understood. I'd made it a condition of my employment, right from the start, and I had been good enough to be able to demand it. Otherwise, I would still be working for the guys with the smiles on their faces and the larceny in their hearts.

Larceny and worse. We came to the end of the dock. There's no rail to keep you from going over, just a low barrier to forestall vehicle mishaps. When Clarissa walked right up to the edge and peered into the watery dark, I knew she had made her decision about me.

"So why'd you leave?" she asked, gazing at an isolated light twinkling mistily across the bay, by the fish pens near Campobello. "You must have been clearing a world-class fortune."

"All that darkness," I said, not meaning the water. "And one little light. It was here and I grabbed for it, that's all."

She nodded, her face washed pale in the glow of the dock lamps. "And that's why you're going the distance for Ellie White? Because you've got yours, and you don't really think you deserve it?"

I thought about it a second. "Yeah. You could put it that way. But she does deserve it. An ordinary, happy life—Ellie's one of the good guys. So if she gets shafted and I don't, it'll be too ... uneven. Besides, she's my friend and I promised. Or does that sound corny?"

Clarissa laughed. "Nope. Antiquated, maybe. Out of touch, and hopelessly idealistic. But no. It doesn't sound corny to me."

The rain had stopped. We turned and started walking back. "I can't shake the idea that somehow she's directing all this. Ellie, I mean. That she got herself locked up on purpose, so I'd be on my own. To do—"

"Whatever you end up doing. Like a test. Funny, that was my feeling when I talked to her."

"Right. But it's more than that. Like I'm supposed to do it because she can't. So," I went on, "to make sure I would, she made sure she couldn't. If you follow me."

"Sort of." Back on Water Street, Clarissa turned to the left and right, taking it all in: the silent storefronts and brick chimneys, columned posts and ornate cornices, the boats floating peacefully on the glittering black water under the dock lamps.

Her car was parked in front of Arnold's office. "I gotta go," she said. "I'm supposed to be in Caribou in the morning. We'll see if I make it there, but really, I just came over to apologize."

She made a wry face. "I came into this town with an attitude, and got my butt kicked. Poetic justice."

I walked her to the car. "Listen, do you know why the case is going to the Federal side? If it is, I mean. If you didn't just say that to scare me. Maybe you're a better actress than I think."

"Yeah. Well. Big mouth on my part. You made me pretty mad."

I was kidding her a little, but she took it seriously, and she didn't like remembering her slip.

"But what the hell, you earned it by sticking up for her," she went on, "and I'm too disgusted to care. You know the guy staying with McIlwaine's wife? Real smooth, but he looks like a guerrilla terrorist?"

I indicated that I did.

"He's what they call the focus of some covert inquiries."

The light bulb went on. "So I was right about him."

"Yeah, if you thought he was a slime toad. My understanding is that the FBI agreed to let some indiscretions of McIlwaine's go by, if he would help them out with information about this fellow."

She frowned. "Past six months, McIlwaine was having second thoughts about cooperating, turned out maybe he wasn't so helpful as they hoped. Unfortunately for Ellie, though, they had him sworn, and he's been useful to them on a lot of other things over the years—"

Chalk up another check-mark in the "right" column for me; too bad it wasn't doing Ellie any good—

"So now not only have the Feds got their undies in a twist," Clarissa went on, "but they're in a position to do something about it, payback-wise."

"Bottom line, their witness got himself murdered."

"Yeah, don't you just hate it when that happens?"

It explained a lot of things: why McIlwaine could tip Alvin on stocks without tripping SEC alarms, how Alvin could take three big money gifts from McIlwaine without any IRS curiosity being stimulated ... all rewards, probably, for McIlwaine's cooperation.

"Any idea why McIlwaine was backing down?"

She nodded. "Uh-huh. My source—and you do not want to let on I told you this—says McIlwaine found out about six months ago he had a brain tumor, or something, that it was going to kill him. I guess prosecution didn't look so scary, next to that."

That aneurysm my ex-husband had talked about: McIlwaine had welshed on his deal with the government at about the same time as he'd engineered the stock deal that ruined Alvin White—and at about the same time he must have found out he didn't have long to live. Bottom line: in his way, he had been getting his affairs in order, and that included screwing Alvin.

"Ellie's dad has been part of some insider stock trading," I told Clarissa, "that involved McIlwaine. But it started a long time ago. Could the government have been giving McIlwaine immunity for that long? Thirty years?"

"Oh, hell, yes," Clarissa replied. "McIlwaine's been playing both sides of the fence for so long, he ought to have an office in the Federal Building. How do you think he's gotten away with so much? Labor unions, restraint of trade, monopolies . . . law enforcement loved him, and they treated him good in the getting-away-with-stuff department."

"Damn," I said. "So they're not going to let any kinks in the timeline discourage them when it comes to prosecuting Ellie."

"You kidding? If they need to, they'll get thirty experts to swear that an hour takes ninety minutes; or that she could have been in two places at once. They'll make that case fly, one way or another, just to make an example of her. You don't," she added, "want people thinking they can knock off the government's favorite blabbermouths."

Yeah, because for one thing it would discourage other people from becoming blabbermouths: no future in it. "And even if they knew it was Nina . . ."

"Yeah. Don't want to upset the applecart with the target in it. Darn," she added, frowning at the car door, "I left my bag up at the house. Get in, I'll drive you back."

We didn't talk on the short ride to Key Street. I had the sense that Clarissa was mulling something.

"An island," she said finally as we pulled in front of the Whites' house. "Miles from anywhere."

Arnold waved as he pulled away in the squad car; apparently he had just gotten a call and had been setting out to find us.

"Yeah," I said quietly as Clarissa and I got out into the kind of silence that makes you whisper in spite of yourself. "It's great. If you like that sort of thing."

Inside, she glanced wistfully around, stalling as if she wanted to stay. Her eye lit on the portrait of the unknown woman; on a whim I'd brought it along with me from my house, along with Sam's baby book and rattle. In the Whites' place, I'd wanted the security of my own things, talismans against the pure meanness Hedda seemed to radiate twenty-four hours a day, and I'd propped the portrait on the counter to puzzle at while I scrubbed pots.

"Who's that?" Clarissa wanted to know, squinting at it.

"Oh, just another mystery. A private obsession of mine, no connection with this mess. I'm trying to find out who she is, or was. But I probably never will."

"Huh." She kept staring at it. "Funny. Anyway, it reminds me: Ellie gave me a message for you. She said to tell you she's sorry about the portrait, and if you look in the attic, you'll figure out who it is. That must be the one she meant, I guess."

Which was odd, Ellie's mentioning it twice: once to Toby Alderman, and again to Clarissa. A flicker of disquiet nudged me.

Clarissa looked at it again. "Boy, I feel like I've met that woman, somewhere. Or maybe my brain is playing tricks on me, I'm so tired." She opened the door. "Message mean anything to you?"

"No. I don't know the half of what Ellie means, lately. But thanks for passing it along."

"Thanks for the coffee," Clarissa said. "And, listen, I am sorry. I wish I could help."

"Yeah, me too."

"If you think of anything to do, my advice is, do it fast. Word is, they're transferring her soon. That's on the quiet, you understand, nothing official, but I don't think this one is going to get to superior court."

She meant the Federal hammer was going to come down, and when it did, it would be all over. Ellie's future would get sucked into a bureaucratic maelstrom of case numbers, court calendars, and big career ambitions: abandon hope, all ye et cetera.

"Call me if you want," Clarissa finished. "Arnold's got my number."

I followed her onto the back porch, stopping as she continued down the Whites' driveway. She reached the sidewalk, stepped into a patch of yellow under the street-light, and stopped, turning her face up into the rain, which had resumed.

"I must be crazy for what I'm thinking," Clarissa said.

45

Back inside, the only sound was the hollow ticking of the mantel clock in the darkened dining room. Once I thought I heard something else, but when I went into the hall to listen it was just the water running in the upstairs commode, followed by the creak of Hedda's wooden bedframe.

The night seemed endless; it was four in the morning, but there was still plenty of dark left to get through. I went around checking window and door locks and made a last tour of the downstairs, switching off lamps and turning off the coffeemaker.

Finally I checked on Alvin, left him in the parlor asleep with an afghan thrown over him, and climbed the stairs. Slow, even breathing from Hedda's room said she was asleep again, too.

Ellie's things, neatly arranged in her room, made the place feel as if she would be back any minute: her silver dresser set with mirror, brush, and comb lined up like shining soldiers, shoes in her closet perched as if waiting on a shoe tree, a chenille bedspread smoothed over a pine single bed that I imagined she had been sleeping in since childhood.

My own belongings lay in a heap where I had tossed them in my rush to get things under control downstairs. Fortunately, I'd brought a change of clothes; the jeans and sweater I was wearing felt as if I'd been in them for a year. I took a hot, soapy shower in Ellie's bathroom, listening all the while for sounds from Alvin or Hedda, and put the fresh clothes on, unwilling to relax enough to get into bed. Tomorrow I would put Sam's baby book back in the cedar chest and take the mysterious portrait back to my kitchen, exchanging these useless objects for practical items like more clean socks.

On the bed was a balsam pillow embroidered with lupines in soft tones of lavender and blue. Lying down, I pressed my cheek against it, inhaling the sweet, woodsy fragrance of the evergreens inside and thinking that I would rest my eyes for a moment.

Whatever Ellie had meant to do, it had all gone badly wrong. She couldn't possibly have meant it to come to this.

Still, it had. Maybe it was the lateness of the hour, or my fatigue, or the unpleasant strangeness of being in an unfamiliar house whose haunts, if any, were foreign to me.

But I couldn't help feeling that I had failed her.

46

When I woke, the sun was shining into my face through Ellie's white lace curtains. The smell of coffee and the sound of the Calais radio station broadcasting the weather report rose from the kitchen, along with the clink of plates and cups.

I got up and went to the window; the storm front had passed, taking the chilly rain and low sky with it. Across the bay, I could see the thunderheads vanishing behind the mounded hills of Nova Scotia.

I raised the window, and let the clean breeze rush in. Even the sight of my ex-husband's little yellow sports car parked in the street below—no doubt so that he could survey the extent of the fire, and think about how incapable I was—failed to faze me. He didn't know where I was now, or Sam either, and with any luck he would simply go away.

Standing there letting a wash of chilly sunshine pour over me, I looked upward to the windows of my own attic. In it I had found nothing helpful, and Clarissa's report of Ellie's message the night before had meant nothing to me, at the time.

But now, with the advantage of perspective and a few hours' sleep, not to mention the salutary effect of a rising barometer, what Clarissa had said took on new clarity.

Wrong attic, of course.

47.

The stairs to the Whites' attic were in better repair than mine, but I still had to step carefully to avoid creaks. At the top, a big hook held the attic door shut; I pushed it open, slipped inside, and shut it behind me. A chain switch turned the overhead light on.

At first glance, it seemed as if finding something up here would be easy; the attic's contents were neatly arranged in labeled cartons. Clothes in zippered bags hung from closet rails; golf clubs, tennis rackets, a croquet set, and some old badminton equipment stood together in their own well-organized area.

Taking care not to step on any loose floorboards, I crossed to a set of filing cabinets—tax records, bank statements, all the stuff that people tend to store up against the dreaded day when the audit notice arrives.

Next to them lay stacks of photograph albums: more pictures of Hedda in her flaming youth, each photo captioned with a note of the date and place, many of the later ones professional shots of her, costumed and dancing onstage. Like the rest of the attic's contents, they were well organized; someone had even taken care to arrange them in chronological order.

From the yellowed newspaper clippings that accompanied them it appeared as if Hedda really had been on her way to a career. A break of about six months seemed to indicate a spot of trouble; no photos or clippings from this period. But then things appeared to take off again for the budding dancer: from an anonymous location in the chorus line at something called the Hawthorne

Theatre, she had moved swiftly to a featured spot right up front.

One of the captions from this period identified a Hollywood talent scout, watching from the wings. A couple of mentions in the tabloid gossip columns—Hedda linked with gentlemen whose names appeared in bold type, to denote that they were social Somebodies—wouldn't have hurt her career, either.

And then, suddenly, it all came crashing down. The sight of those long legs high-kicking reminded me painfully of the scars I'd seen on her ankles the night before. The mugging had ended her career with the brutality of a sledgehammer. The newspaper reports gave the details: unknown assailants, motive robbery, apparent rage of the attackers, probably because Hedda resisted.

And something I hadn't known: that there had been another young dancer attacked in the same incident. The other young woman had died of her injuries.

A stray breeze rattled a window sash in the corner; getting up, I felt tired twinges in my bones, like the ache of a lingering illness. Maybe there was something else instructive in one of the cartons, or folded among the neatly stowed summer clothes, but I would have to stay up here all morning to find it.

If it was here at all. Impatience washed over me; why couldn't Ellie just tell me what she wanted me to know? Reaching for the light switch I took a clumsy half-step sideways and to the right, to avoid walking into the attic door which swung inward, the reverse of the way the door swung in my attic at home.

My foot touched a loose board outside the normal traffic pattern, alongside the wall. It was a short board, about a foot long, and it gave as I put my weight on it. Curiously, I lifted the board, and it came up as neatly as a puzzle piece.

Underneath it lay a small, towel-wrapped bundle; inside the towel was a box, the size and shape of a small safety-deposit box, but without any lock.

I carried the box to the window and opened it. Inside lay a New York birth certificate. Under that was what remained of the portrait of the woman from my kitchen, torn into small pieces—not the same photograph, but another print of it, hidden here. Finally there was another copy of the newspaper clipping detailing the attack on Hedda, and the death of her young woman companion.

Leaving the box, I carried the birth certificate, the newspaper clipping, and the pieces of the portrait down-stairs. Alvin and Hedda were still in the kitchen, having breakfast. I would confront them, I decided, and demand an explanation.

The parlor was bright with morning sun, shining on the tops of the tables and glinting off the glass-covered photographs of a youthful Hedda decked out in glamour-girl costumes, her glorious blonde hair heaped in intricate coiffures and her face a smooth, smiling com-posite of youthfulness and makeup.

If you'd known her then, you wouldn't recognize her now, I thought. Purposefully, I made for the kitchen—maybe I couldn't find out who was guilty of McIlwaine's murder, but I'd had it to the eyes with the portrait business—then stopped as a familiar voice made me want to rush back upstairs again.

Instead, I trudged dully forward. My ex-husband sat in the Whites' kitchen, making himself comfortable at their butcher-block counter, drinking a cup of coffee and regaling them with a story of one of his most amusing operating-room triumphs.

"And then," he said, his voice lingering richly, "just as I was about to incise the *dura mater* . . ."

He stopped when he saw me, holding the registration papers for Sam's boat-school trip in his left hand. "Well, hello there, Jacobia. How's my charming ex-wife and mother of my son, today?"

His voice came down hard on *"my son,"* and his hand closed on the papers, crumpling them.

"You went into my house," I said, feeling as if the

blood from the operating-room story was falling over my eyes in a thick veil of fury.

"Yes." His voice remained cordial; dangerously so. "I rattled the doorknob, and it opened. And I'm very glad I did, because what did I find there?"

In the corner of the kitchen, Tiffany perched unhappily on a wooden stool, looking as if she'd been sent there to be punished.

"This," my ex-husband said, shoving the boat-school papers at me.

"I saw you," he went on, jerking his head upwards, "at the window upstairs. So I knew you were here. And I think we'd better have a little talk, you and Sam and me. Right now."

Just outside the kitchen window, Sam sat in the right-hand front bucket seat of the yellow sports car, his shoulders slumped in an attitude of misery. "What's he doing out there?"

"Waiting for me to take him back to New York, where he should have been all along. I saw him downtown, picked him up."

"He's agreed to go?"

My ex-husband looked long-suffering. "Despite your influence, Sam still does what I say."

He got up, flashing an apologetic smile at the Whites, who were glancing at one another uncertainly. "I'm so sorry you've had to hear all this," he said. "Thanks for your time and the coffee."

Tiffany rinsed her cup at the sink and followed after him, her glance as she passed me unreadable. "Thank you," she murmured to the Whites.

"Come along, Jacobia," my ex-husband said, his voice like a whip-flick. "Let's not inflict your problems on these people."

With distant satisfaction I noticed that even Hedda didn't know what to do about a person like my ex-husband, who has a way of barging cheerfully in on you, then leaving you feeling as if you'd been sprayed with insecticide.

With anyone else, by now she'd have been ordering him out, raving about the pearl-handled revolver. But even when I slapped the clipping, the birth certificate, and the portrait pieces down in front of them, they just kept on staring after my ex-husband, looking as if they had been nerve-poisoned.

Which was precisely what would happen to Sam, if I let his father take him back to New York.

"Coming, Jacobia?" my ex-husband called with heavy patience.

I turned and followed him.

48

My ex-husband's name, appropriately, is Victor.

"I'll wait outside with Sam," Tiffany said, "while you two talk."

"No," Victor said irritably, "you come, too. I want you to understand what I go through."

Understanding what he went through was, by this time, the last thing on Tiffany's wish list. Still, she squared her shoulders and followed him in, while Sam—who knew a hornet's nest when he saw one—stayed in his father's car.

With Victor in it, the kitchen of my old house seemed to shrink back into its former cold, unlived-in incarnation—its scuffed wooden floor, chipped woodwork, and curtainless windows projecting a shabby, unfriendly version of its usual spare beauty.

The smoke smell and soot marks didn't help any, either, nor did the water stains streaking the wallpaper. Victor glanced around with obvious disapproval, tossing the boat-school papers onto the kitchen table with a little *moue* of distaste for the hominess of the checked oilcloth.

"I told you I didn't want him pursuing that nonsense," he said. "He could be using the time to study."

"Victor, he wants to go, and I don't see what harm—"

"That's just the point. You don't see. I do."

He marched around the kitchen importantly. "That's why I'm taking him back to New York, where he can get the guidance he obviously isn't getting here. With any luck, he can make up the time he's lost and still get into a decent college."

"Have you forgotten I have custody?" Which, I wanted to say, you happily gave up when Sam's problems got to be too much for you, but there was no point in antagonizing him further.

"That can change, Jacobia. And it will, if Sam says he wants it to."

He went to the window, glanced out, and turned with a wince of dislike from the quiet serenity of the view: tall green-black fir trees, white clapboard houses, puffs of woodsmoke curling from the red brick chimneys.

"Jacobia, can't you see what a dead end this place is? Sam needs somebody to set goals and limits for him, and you're just too deep in your small-town fantasy escape to understand that, but he does. I know if I ask him about it, he'll agree."

Because he'll do anything, say anything, to please you, I thought. It was a mental state I remembered sadly.

"He needs," said Victor, "some structure in his life, some discipline. Somebody to make him perform to his capabilities . . ."

While he talked, Tiffany looked through some of Sam's school papers, which he had left on the kitchen table for me to see. She paused over one, tipped her smooth, blonde head with a sharp look of enlightenment, and turned to the next.

"As you can see," Victor told her, "my son hasn't been encouraged in any intellectual pursuits whatsoever. His mother is content to let him coast on mediocrity, or worse."

He turned to me. "But when you're a parent," he lectured me virtuously, "you can't do things the easy way. You have to do what is best for the child."

I felt myself drifting into that dreamy, anything-is-possible condition, the one in which you smile and nod and meanwhile your hand, quietly and on its own account, balls itself up into a fist, getting ready to cold-cock somebody.

Tiffany glanced from the papers with a grimace of annoyance, like someone who has gotten tired of the buzzing of a mosquito. "Has he been tested for dyslexia?"

"Yes," I said. "In New York, when Victor had him."

Victor stopped talking and frowned; he was not used to being interrupted. A flicker of something else seemed to cross his face, too.

"Yes, of course," he began, "I sent him to—"

"No," said Sam, who had come in unnoticed behind us. "What's dyslexia?"

A sudden, interesting quiet settled over the room. I looked at Victor, whose face now wore a cornered expression.

And then I knew he hadn't just lied about other women. He had lied about Sam, as well.

"You told me," I said, "that you'd had him tested. A whole battery of diagnostic testing, you said: physical, mental, and emotional, all the possible things. At the university school."

"Because," Tiffany said gently, "I'm no expert, of course. But I've worked with an awful lot of dyslexic kids Sam's age, and the thing is, quite a lot of them write this way."

She held up one of the papers, speaking directly to Sam, now, not to his parents. Sam moved beside her, peering with interest at something she was pointing out to him. Together, they looked like brother and sister; I lowered my mental estimate of her age.

Victor noticed this, too. "Oh, great," he said, "now my son's getting learning advice from a member of the kindergarten set."

"If you wouldn't keep choosing your girlfriends from the kindergarten set, maybe you wouldn't have that problem," I said nastily. "The point is, you told me you'd had him tested."

He folded his arms. "There's nothing wrong with him. He needs to apply himself, that's all. I'm taking him with me."

"There's nothing wrong with having dyslexia," Tiffany began.

"Shut up," Sam said quietly. "Please," he added, with an apologetic glance at her, and she nodded minutely back at him. In that moment, I wished they really were brother and sister.

Sam looked over at his father. "We could," he said, "have found out about this. What to do about it."

"Son, you don't understand. Those tests—I didn't want you labeled your whole life as some kind of—"

"Some kind of what, Dad?" Sam's voice was almost cheerful. "A dummy? A retard? That's what kids called me in the good school you paid so much to send me to, in New York. When they weren't trying to score pot off me."

Victor, to his credit, looked appalled. "But—"

"You know what, Dad? They don't have classes in six foreign languages at the high school here, or field trips to Germany and Japan. Here, it's pretty much just your basic reading, writing, and arithmetic. But the kids here don't shoot up in the bathrooms. Most of 'em don't even smoke dope. And they don't call me names."

"He told me you'd had the tests," I said helplessly.

But I hadn't seen the results. Victor kept promising to send them, and putting me off, while I had failed to press him because the less contact I had with him, the better I liked it.

Sam's face was full of love and pity; anger, too. "And you believed him. Mom, when are you going to learn? Where do we have to go, how far away, that you won't listen to him anymore?"

Which was when I understood: all Sam's attempts to placate Victor, to do and be what his father wanted him to do and be—they weren't to get his father's approval for himself. They were to protect me.

He went over and picked up the boat-school applications from the table where I had dropped them, pausing over the laser level, which I had also left there.

"It's broken," I said.

"I'll get you another one," said Victor hastily.

"No," said Sam, examining it more closely. "I can fix it."

"Sam, you can't fix a thing like that," Victor told him impatiently. "It's not a lawn mower or a washing machine." His face expressed what he thought of the ability to fix those. "It's a very complex, high-technology device. You can't just—"

Sam put the laser level under his arm, raked his father and me with a glance that should have killed us both, and walked out.

"Tell Sam," said Tiffany as she departed with Victor a few minutes later, "he should call me if he wants. I've got some information on dyslexia that he might like to have." She pressed her card into my hand.

"I'll call you," said my ex-husband, trying and failing to get the old menace, the old you-haven't-heard-the-last-of-this threat into his voice.

But I thought I had, because I wasn't listening to him, anymore. Instead I was listening to Sam, maybe for the first time.

All Sam's troubles in New York, truancy and lying and staying out late, and the drugs—they hadn't been over his own problems at all, or that hadn't been the root of them.

They'd been over me. His mother had been crying all the time. And when I'd said I wouldn't come to Eastport without him, Sam had believed me.

Sam, who knew how to fix things.

49

After my ex-husband had gone, George Valentine came over, bringing with him an electrician, and they got the power turned on so I could make coffee and see the full extent of the fire's destruction. It wasn't as bad as I'd feared, but it was going to require new plaster, new lath, and some subfloor and framing in the storeroom, which also needed a whole new roof.

"Otherwise it's just like putting Band-Aids on cancer," said George. "You tear all this stuff out, though—"

With a wave of his hand, he indicated an area that was larger than any apartment I'd ever lived in, before I came here.

"Well, then," he finished, "that's all you'll have to do for another couple hundred years."

Which was a line I'd heard before, but one that I had never developed any capacity to resist.

"Fine," I told George. "Just fix it. As quickly as possible, please."

After that I went around taking Polaroids, so I could show the insurance company the extent of the loss. I kept telling myself that I'd meant to replace the faded wallpaper and the cracked plaster anyway, and now a lot of it would just get done sooner than I'd expected. I told myself Sam would eventually come home, too. But that didn't stop me from feeling stomach-punched about everything, and around noon Bob Arnold came by to lend further glumness to the proceedings.

"I made a few calls," he said, pulling out a kitchen chair, "to some buddies of mine, over to Customs and Immigration."

"And?" I poured him some coffee.

"Turns out this cousin of Nina's has got himself a history. And so," he added, "does Nina. Well known, as they say in the big city, to law enforcement agencies."

"Yeah, Clarissa filled me in a little, last night."

"Seems like this fellow has quite a collection of passports, none of 'em in his real name, on account of half the world wants to lock him up for gunrunning, and the other half wants to lock him up for drug smuggling, which is the revenue-producing part of his operation."

"He uses the drug money to buy the guns." It figured. And when McIlwaine found out about it, he took the information to his government buddies.

"Uh-huh," Arnold said. "And the guns find their way to the kind of people, they're not supposed to have guns. The kind who think whole countries are their personal little kingdoms, they come in and butcher whole villages, if the poor people fight back."

All of which agreed with what Clarissa had said, and what I had thought of the guy, myself.

Arnold shook his head. "Trouble is, cops over here've been told, leave him alone. I guess the Feds want to wait and see where the slime trail leads."

He got up. "I don't know, Jacobia. Usually in this town, one way or another I've always been able to get things worked around, make 'em come out the way they ought to."

His eyes narrowed with frustration. "Guy goes out clamming, just tryin' to feed his family, he gets busted for some small ones, I can see he doesn't get hit too hard for it. Guy slugs his wife, I can get him locked up. But this . . ."

I followed him to the door. "I know. Clarissa told me. It just doesn't look too hopeful. We'll have to wait, and try to get Ellie out on bail."

Arnold looked stricken. "Oh, hell. That's the other thing I meant to tell you about."

We stepped outside together. Across the street, Alvin White was getting into a car driven by one of his cronies from the Breakfast Club; he waved wanly at me as the car pulled away.

Hedda, I thought with grim pleasure, was probably too hung over to perform driving duties. Still, it seemed odd that Alvin would leave her alone in the house, and if I remembered correctly there wasn't a Breakfast Club

meeting today. Besides, it was too late in the morning
for one.

I turned back to Arnold, who had continued on out to
the curb. "What? I'm sorry, Arnold, I was just watching
Alvin for a minute. What was it you were saying?"

"Bail," he repeated, reaching for the door handle of the
squad car. His face looked like seven days of rain. "Got a
call from the state cops, courtesy thing, keep me informed."

"And?" Ten percent was what you needed in cash,
and it wasn't like attorney's fees. With bail, you can get
the money back out of the rat-hole again, so I might be
able to do something helpful.

Or so I thought, until I heard what Arnold said next.

"Hearing was early this morning," he said sorrowfully.
"No bail. Not that it was likely, but . . . heinousness of
the crime, the judge said, lot of other nonsense means
somebody—probably those Federal guys—got the fix put
in, hang onto her. She's locked up for the duration."

50

After Arnold left, I wandered around the house for a
while, picking things up and putting them down use-
lessly. Glancing across the street, I spotted Janet Fox
going into the Whites' house, which meant that soon
Hedda would be liquored up again, and the sink over
there would be heaped high with more dishes. Alvin
wouldn't like it, and I knew I'd better go over there right
away and turn off the supply of alcohol.

But I couldn't face it. My house was a shambles, my
son was estranged, and my friend was in a jail cell, and I
couldn't think of anything to do about any of it. Alvin
was right, I reflected exhaustedly, to go out and forget
about it for a few hours.

Digging into my bag, I pulled out Sam's baby book
and rattle, to put them away, then spotted the little
orange pharmacy bottle at the bottom. Cleaning up the

Whites' house the night before, I'd dropped this one in my bag, meaning to speak very firmly to Janet about it when I saw her.

Then I'd moved all the other pill bottles I found to the top shelf of the medicine cabinet in Alvin's bathroom, where Hedda couldn't reach them.

But Alvin could. Suddenly, I wondered again where he had been headed, and thought rather urgently—Janet and Hedda, I decided, could wait—that I had better find out.

51

I found Alvin's old friend in the Happy Landings, having an early lunch of a haddock sandwich and coleslaw. It looked delicious, but the twinge of anxiety in my stomach kept me from feeling hungry.

"Left him off over to Hillside Cemetery," the old man said. "He said he wanted a quiet place, to think. Jeez, it's too bad about Ellie. She's such a pretty girl, and I don't know what old Alvin is going to do without her."

"Right," I said, and raced out of there.

Hillside was peaceful and deserted, with the bare trees towering over silent stone monuments under a pale blue sky. I parked by the side of the road and got out, hearing the screams of herring gulls and the putter of a fishing boat out on the bay.

I found him in the far northeast corner, the oldest part of the graveyard, where small, bright British flags mark the places of soldiers who died of smallpox or consumption while policing the town's nineteenth-century occupation. Alvin glanced up from his seat on one of the stones.

"Jacobia," he said mildly.

"Alvin." I sat beside him.

"Children," Alvin mused. "If they're bad they'll break your heart. But if they're good . . ."

"They break it worse," I finished for him, thinking of Sam. "You think you've done what you should for them.

When you find out you didn't, by then sometimes it's too late."

"Uh-huh." He gazed out over the gravestones. "That's about the size of it."

I put my hand on his shoulder. Under his flannel shirt he felt fragile and vulnerable, like a shell made of papier-mâché. "Alvin, did you take the pills yet?"

He shook his head ruefully. "Nope. Thought I would, I felt so damned low, but when I got here, I decided not to. Don't know why. Too much of a coward, maybe."

He reached into his pants pocket and handed the small bottles to me: enough, all together, to kill a horse. I thought about the way he'd taken care of Ellie all those years, and the way he now cared for Hedda.

"No, Alvin. You're not a coward. I think maybe you made some mistakes, but we all do that."

We sat in silence for a while. "Alvin, why were you able to blackmail Threnody McIlwaine? What could you do, or not do, that he couldn't take care of, himself?"

Alvin's brow furrowed in surprise. "You know. You must have figured it out by now. The papers you found, up in the attic. You left 'em on the kitchen table, so I would see 'em. Them, and that picture. You did it so I'd know *you* know: I'm as guilty as if I'd stuck him with that ice pick, myself."

Startled, I shook my head. "I know part of it, I guess, but I still don't understand why it matters so much to you, now. Or what it has to do with his murder. I know you didn't kill him. Explain it to me, Alvin. Please."

Alvin sighed, but seemed relieved at the chance to talk about it. "I hardly know how. The thing is, you never knew Hedda back when she was young. She was so different, not like now. Prettiest thing. I loved her the minute I saw her."

"But she didn't want to get married. She went to New York." It didn't seem to have any connection to my questions, but I let him go on the way he wanted, to get to it in his own way.

He nodded again. "Just about killed me, when she

left. Like Thren McIlwaine, though, she wanted to make her way in the world, or at least give it a try before she settled down."

A distant look came into his eyes. "He and I were awful good friends, as boys. We went around and did everything together. But he was always different, we all knew it. Right from the start, everybody in Eastport knew that Thren McIlwaine was going to make something of himself."

"And she was like that, too."

He made a sound of assent. "Thren's folks gave him their blessing and a hundred dollars, to go to New York. And when she heard about it, Hedda run off, too, 'thout saying a word to anyone. She was hell-bent."

And still was. I said nothing, turning the pieces over in my mind but not getting anywhere with them.

"Somehow," he went on, "she found Thren, and for a while they were both there, him already making money in business, getting to meet the people who could do him good, her dancing on stage. He kept an eye on her, and now an' again he'd report back to me, and for a while everything was all right."

Alvin managed a smile for his own youthful innocence. "I missed her, but I figured she'd be back again once the novelty wore off." His face changed.

"And then?" I prompted him; clearly he didn't like recalling this part.

"Well," he went on reluctantly, "then she got wild. Spent her time with shady fellows, ran around and got herself in trouble."

Light dawned. "The birth certificate," I said.

"Right. She got pregnant, but Threnody took care of that, paid for everything, made all Hedda's arrangements for her, kept her name out of it. Said he'd talk her into comin' home, soon as the . . . well. Afterwards."

"But she didn't come home." The mugging had occurred a whole year after the baby's birth.

"No." He frowned. "She didn't. Soon's the baby got there, and he took care of finding a place for it, Hedda went back to her old ways. Once upon a time, she'd said I was all she ever wanted, but now it seemed like she'd forgot me. And I started in thinking . . ."

A tear leaked down his face. "I started thinking she wouldn't come home at all. I couldn't stand it. And so . . ."

Finally, I saw the connection: McIlwaine, meeting people who could help him—later, probably, they would become his henchmen, but at the time they would have been just minor wiseguys—and a mugging in which two young women were injured, one fatally.

"By then they weren't on such good terms anymore. So he sent along two fellows he knew," Alvin said. "To persuade her, to make her give it up and come home."

"But something went wrong."

Even today, McIlwaine's employees—the ones who are working off the books—are known to enjoy their labors, or so say widows and orphans of the union organizers they have labored on.

Alvin nodded. "The other girl died. And Hedda came home, but she was never the same after that. That pretty, happy girl I knew—that girl was gone. And what was left . . ."

He sighed deeply. "Still, I loved her. I do even now. It would kill me, I think, to lose her. I think Ellie knows that—it's why she has been so good to her mother, all these years. On my account. Because she promised me she would be. She was always such a good girl, Ellie."

Right; so good that now she was sitting in jail. I brushed off a surge of anger; that, and the sudden wish that Ellie had turned out to be more like Hedda: selfish and hard.

"But Alvin, how did you know? Why in the world did McIlwaine tell you what he'd done, give you something you could hold over him that way?"

Alvin's face twisted. "But he didn't tell me, don't you see? I told him. I told him to do it, to do something to her, to make her come home. And he did, on account of our friendship. And to show me, I expect, that he could do it. That he was a big man in the big city. A real up-and-comer."

The dismayed surprise I felt must have showed on my face; he winced in misery away from it.

"Nothing else would convince her," he said quietly. "Unless Thren made it so she *had* to come home, that there was nothing left for her there."

His face was as hard and pitiless as a granite ledge, unforgiving of himself. "After it happened, he wrote me in a panic, trying to ease his mind. He never meant for anybody to die."

Alvin looked up, and saw my disbelief. "Thren wasn't so tough in those days," he explained, "as he pretended. He didn't know, back then, how things can get out of hand."

Proof. McIlwaine had written it in a letter. And wouldn't someone love to get a thing like that on Threnody McIlwaine: the union organizers, for one, would have a field day with it. He'd have done anything to keep it quiet. But with something on paper, getting rid of Alvin wouldn't have been enough.

"Back then," Alvin went on, "for all his plans and his fancy ways, like he was already a big shot, Thren was just a scared kid."

"You burned the letter, of course." God forbid Hedda should ever find it.

"Uh-huh. But he didn't know that, did he? He figured I'd keep it to hold over him. Because, you know, that's what *he* would have done."

Alvin's sigh seemed to come up from his feet, his whole body awash in regret. "So he always made sure I was happy, helped me on those stock deals. I never asked him for the money, he just did it on his own hook, but I knew why. We both did, but we never talked about it. Until that last deal went wrong, and then the other day when he threw it all up in my face."

"What did he say?" Out on the water, a little boat was puttering in the sunshine, moving toward Lubec. For an instant I thought it looked familiar, then turned back to what Alvin was telling me.

"Reminded me how it was my idea to get Hedda crippled," Alvin said, "that I was as much a killer as he was when it came down to it, because of the girl who died. Said he was calling my bluff—even though I'd never threatened him, nor even asked him for money until now—and that I was a foolish old man. I'd ruined myself, he said, and he was finished paying for it."

"He knew you'd been wiped out."

"Ayuh." Alvin grimaced. "All gone, every penny of it."

"And he knew you needed the money, so you could hire nurses and household help. So Ellie could get married, and not feel she had to take care of you and Hedda all the time."

"That's right. He knew. But I was the greedy one, he said, and look what it got me." His gaze, looking out over the water, was bleakly despairing.

"Maybe so, but Alvin, that's not the point. The thing is, McIlwaine lured you into buying that stock. He knew it was going to be worthless."

McIlwaine, I remembered from the *Fortune* magazine piece, was one of the few who hadn't fallen for Charlie Finnegan. But he had put his old friend Alvin into the disastrous venture. He must have, because he hadn't only been funding Alvin's purchases, he'd also been giving him tips. It was always how Alvin, never canny with money, had decided what to buy.

"And knowing you the way he did, he figured you'd probably take a flier on it. He ruined you, Alvin, and the thing is, he did it flat-out on purpose."

The penny dropped. "Revenge," Alvin breathed. "For all the years of me having that letter. Or him thinking I did. For feeling that he was under my thumb."

Another thought struck me, worse.

Much worse. "Alvin, listen. When you were arguing with McIlwaine, did he say anything else? Not about the money, or the mugging. Did he say anything about the baby?"

"Oh, yes," Alvin said tiredly. "He dragged it all out, all that old dirty laundry. Said he'd been rubbing our noses in that mess for years now, and we were too foolish to see it. I still don't see what he meant by that, maybe nothing. Probably he just said it to hurt."

He shook his head. "Enjoyed making fools of people, he did. And hurting them. Not like when he was young."

But I thought Alvin did know; he wouldn't meet my eyes any more. He was still lying about the attack on Hedda, too; there was something he was too ashamed to tell me.

I also thought that someone else heard McIlwaine's gloating the morning of the murder, and hadn't liked being made a fool of.

Hadn't liked it at all. "Alvin, did you hear anything that you haven't mentioned, after McIlwaine left your office?"

He was weeping openly now. "I heard . . . a woman's voice. A young woman. Just one sharp cry . . . Ellie's voice. I don't see how, I thought she'd gone to your house, but . . . she did it, didn't she? And it's my fault. All, everything my fault."

He sobbed, pushing his face into his hands.

"Alvin. Listen to me, now. Your hearing's not so good, and you were on the phone at the time. So, what if the voice you heard from the other room wasn't Ellie's? What if she was with me, when you and McIlwaine were having your quarrel?"

Five minutes one way, five minutes the other: it could work the opposite of the way I'd theorized the night before, talking with Clarissa. Ellie might not have had time to kill McIlwaine at all, or even hear his outburst to Alvin, because she had already been across the street, with me.

But it was an outburst I was sure had been heard all over the house, given McIlwaine's anger and Alvin's increasing deafness.

Alvin frowned, puzzled. "But how could that be? If Ellie wasn't there, then besides Thren, there was only Hedda and—oh."

He turned to me, and for a moment the ravages of the

years fell away from his face; he was once again a clear-eyed young man with a future ahead of him. Then the illusion shattered, and the reality broke over him: all that had happened, and everywhere he had gone wrong.

Beginning, of course, with Hedda. "Alvin, what was the real reason you were so angry with Hedda that you wanted her attacked? And so angry with McIlwaine that you held his crime over his head for thirty years, and as good as blackmailed him over it, even though he'd been your best friend?"

Over our heads, a blue jay screamed monotonously. Out on the water a foghorn moaned as the mist began rolling back in, its grey tendrils slithering between the ancient graves. The little boat's shape wavered in the fog bank.

"What," I pressed him as his elderly face began crumpling, "was Hedda's mistake?"

A muffled *thump!* came from the direction of the water, out toward Lubec. The blue jay emitted a startled squawk and flapped away. Alvin's head turned suddenly as smoke, darker than the fog, began boiling from something halfway between the waterfront and Campobello.

That little boat. *Jemmy*, I thought. All those explosives . . .

A stab of sadness pierced me, but I didn't have time to think about it now. "Alvin," I urged him impatiently.

"Oh," he mourned, staring out at the smoke column, "I wish I had swallowed those pills."

Then he looked straight at me, gathering himself, ready to tell the worst thing at last.

"Hedda and Thren together . . . that baby was theirs. She didn't tell me until after, but when she did, threw it in my face and laughed at me, I was so angry. I wanted to hurt Hedda, teach her a lesson, make her come home whether she liked it or not."

"And?" I asked, but by that time of course I knew.

"I told Thren what I wanted—didn't tell him what I knew about the baby, of course, only that I'd waited long enough for Hedda to come on home—and he agreed to do it. But it wasn't enough. It ate at me all that night after I talked to him, it wasn't enough."

He took a deep breath. "For that short time, it was like all my love turned to hate. Just as strong, but somehow . . . turned the opposite. Turned to poison, and I guess it poisoned me, too, because the next day I took the train to Boston, on to New York."

I waited. It was pouring out now, and Alvin was right: it was like poison, long held back, the secret he'd kept all those years. It had made him Hedda's slave, and let him start turning Ellie into one, to stand in for him when he was gone.

"Hedda said I was a country boy," he went on, hollow-eyed at the memory of what came next, "too green for the big city, but I was crazy, didn't care what happened to me. I left the big Grand Central Station, went downtown, asked around, went into terrible places, finally found the men Thren had hired. And I paid them extra, a lot extra. Told them what else I wanted done. But the fools got it wrong."

Not a case of brutal thugs going too far, but one of mistaken identity: all those years ago, the wrong young woman had died. And McIlwaine had thought he was responsible.

"And the baby? Did McIlwaine tell you who it was, the morning he died? To get the last laugh on you?"

"Oh, yes." Alvin nodded. "It was Janet, of course."

52

I raced back across town toward Key Street, hearing the howl of sirens from down at the harborfront. Alvin had refused to come with me, still wanting to be alone, and I didn't have any time to argue with him.

As I drove, I imagined it: the quarrel, the shouting. Hedda and Janet upstairs together, hearing it all.

Hearing every bitter word: that Janet's birth mother

was Hedda White, and her natural father Threnody McIlwaine. That the truth had been under Janet's nose all along.

Hedda, meanwhile, would have learned that McIlwaine, at Alvin's request, had arranged the attack that crippled Hedda for life. The two women must have been thunderstruck, and enraged.

And then one of them, the one who was able, did something about it. That was why Hedda had lied for Janet, and said that Janet was with her all the while: she knew what Janet had done, and approved.

But now Janet was alone with Hedda, which struck me as a perfect example of one down, one to go. Why Ellie would lie to protect Janet was a question I figured could be answered later. Right now, what I needed was to get between Janet and Hedda before Janet could realize the rest of her ambition: becoming an orphan. Hedda was Janet's alibi for murder, but now no alibi was needed, and Hedda was the only witness.

I pulled up hard in front of the Whites' house. Janet's little car was in the driveway, behind the Buick. Arnold's car raced past me, but he didn't spare me a glance as more sirens rose from the harbor area, the smoke from the explosion now rising high into the sky.

I hurried up to the Whites' front door, figuring I could still stop Janet from killing Hedda, probably with booze and pills as she'd tried doing the night before. Only my arrival, plus Hedda's iron constitution and long tolerance for liquor, had made a second attempt necessary.

And right now was the ideal time for Janet to be making that attempt. I burst into the house, certain that in the next moment I would save Hedda from becoming Janet Fox's second victim—her first, of course, being her own father.

That was what I figured.

I didn't figure on the pearl-handled revolver.

53

With the small, irrelevant part of my mind that was not focused on the weapon, I thought: *Blue*.

Hedda's hair, naturally white, had been rinsed at the beauty parlor just after McIlwaine's death.

Blue, Can Man had babbled to me, two days later. Probably the first time he'd said it, he had meant Nina's Lincoln.

The second time, after he'd nearly been run over, he'd meant blue hair. He'd been so terrified of Hedda, it was all he could say.

Compared to the Bisley, her weapon was a trifle, but when it was aimed straight at me, it looked like a cannon: that damned little pearl-handled revolver.

"I kept it"—she grinned horribly, enjoying my surprise—"under my mattress. And of course, when the mattress got turned, I tucked it into my handbag."

Her grin widened. "A lady needs a way to protect herself, you know. Too bad I wasn't carrying it the night I met those bastards my husband sent. My husband," she added, "and Thren McIlwaine."

I shuddered to think who must be next on her agenda: Alvin, of course. The next time she was alone with him . . .

She got up stiffly. "Turn around. Janet, stand beside her," she ordered. "Now, we are going on a visit."

Janet clutched the papers and torn portrait I had left on the table. Hedda must have summoned her here the moment I'd gone.

"March," Hedda ordered, and we proceeded together out the front door, across the street, and onto my porch: three ordinary Eastport ladies the sight of whom would not stick in anyone's mind, should we happen to be noticed at all.

The faint reek of smoke still lingered in the otherwise empty house. Janet shut the door behind us.

"Into the parlor," said Hedda. Janet looked frightened, but she obeyed.

"Go down into the basement," Hedda told her, "and make sure everything is ready."

Hedda poked her weapon into my spine. Janet did as she was told, her feet thumping down the basement stairs.

"You sit there," Hedda told me, gesturing at the sofa. Her gnarled hand gripped the revolver competently. Janet had started medicating her again, I realized. Janet would, of course, have had more narcotic supplies, and Hedda's tolerance was well established; her mind was still clear. Her hand was steady, too, as was her hate-filled gaze, and I knew she would shoot me as soon as look at me. It was what she meant to do with the revolver.

It was, I saw now, not the lightweight little weapon I'd thought at first glance. With its two-inch barrel, the five-shot Smith & Wesson .38 Chief Special may resemble a toy, but it is the standard backup weapon of New York City undercover cops. In Maine, thirty years ago, you could buy one over the counter for a hundred bucks, no paperwork required.

I'd learned all this from Wade, proudly and diligently, as part of becoming familiar not only with the Bisley but also with handguns in general. Someday, the information would come in handy, Wade had told me.

But now all it did was terrify me further. Hedda's finger was on the trigger, the hammer pulled all the way back, and from where she was standing she could place a shot through my heart without any trouble.

Other, of course, than the trouble it would cause me.

"Janet is going to put you in the hole in the basement, and cover you with lime. Then Janet will fill the hole with the gravel George Valentine has put down there. A fine boy, George."

Her lip curled, conveying precisely what she really thought of George. Janet reappeared in the doorway.

"Then," Hedda said, "Janet will take your keys and credit cards, drive off in your car, park it in the long-term lot at the Bangor airport, and buy a ticket. After that . . ."

Her face twisted happily. "Well, everyone knows you're a financial expert. They'll think you've done something clever about money, and to cover your tracks after, you've run off somewhere. Janet will take the bus back, and no one will even look for you, not here."

"But they will. No one would believe I'd abandon Sam."

Hedda grimaced. "Oh, you stupid creature, of course they'll believe that. Haven't you done it once before? That's what your ex-husband was telling us this morning, while you were snooping in my attic. That you went off somewhere and left your son with him."

I decided not to argue with Victor's version of events. "I have no reason to run away now," I said. "No one will believe it."

"Your house burnt, your son run off, your ex-husband with a pretty young girlfriend, and your lover tragically drowned," Hedda recited pleasurably. "Oh, plenty of good reasons."

My heart seized coldly. "Wade . . ."

"There was an explosion. The *Little Dipper*. It was on the scanner, just a few minutes ago. Gone." Her eyes glittered with malicious delight.

I wanted to shriek, to fall down on the hardwood floor and weep, but I couldn't, because if I moved a muscle, Hedda was going to shoot me.

Her plan wouldn't work for very long, of course. But by the time it stopped working, I wouldn't care. I'd be dead, buried in a hole in the basement.

"So you'll let your own daughter go to prison for a murder that Janet committed," I said.

"But I didn't—" Janet began urgently.

"Quiet," Hedda snapped. In the distance, I could hear one of the town trucks coming slowly up the street. With it would be the town's small payloader, scooping up the sand that the public works department had spread during the snowstorm; in Eastport, they recycled the stuff. Together, the vehicles made a low roar that increased steadily, as the trucks approached the house.

I realized what Hedda was waiting for: enough noise to cover the gunshot.

"It had to be you, Janet," I said. "Hedda's hands are good, now, but you hadn't had enough time to get her all liquored up on the morning your father died. She wouldn't have been able to grip that ice pick. But she'll let her daughter suffer for it."

"Ellie," Hedda contradicted, "is not my daughter. Oh, she is biologically," she added quickly as I opened my mouth to protest, "but that's all. And that meant nothing. I knew it from the moment she was born. I felt nothing."

My heart broke hard for Ellie, remembering what she'd said about Hedda being an unnatural mother, the calm, forgiving way Ellie had accepted it. Then Hedda was talking again, in an angry rush to get the words out before the trucks got any nearer.

"This," Hedda said proudly, "is my real daughter."

Janet nodded, but Hedda was clearly not the birth mother the young woman had fantasized about for all those years. Watching the mix of emotions play on her face, I almost felt sorry for her.

Almost. "Why," I asked Janet, "did Ellie protect you? Why did she confess if she didn't do it, and how did she know you did?"

"But I *didn't*," Janet insisted again, beginning to look quite frantic; obviously this hadn't been a part of her scheme, but now she was trapped into doing what Hedda wanted, because Hedda had the gun.

Hedda stole an exasperated glance at Janet. "Oh, for heaven's sake, tell her if you must. You girls are all such blabbermouths."

"I heard them arguing," Janet said, the words coming out in a resentful hurry. "I heard my *father*," she spat the word, "saying that he was, and that Hedda was my mother."

She took an angry breath. "And that he'd been rubbing their noses in it, without their knowing, on account of me being around all the time but they didn't realize who I was."

She put the papers she clutched down onto the coffee table, and spread out the pieces of the portrait, putting the torn parts together like puzzle pieces.

"He knew," Janet raged, "all along."

The ripped edges of the photograph dug deep grooves of hatred and bitterness into the serene young face portrayed in it, as if the violence that had been done to the paper had been done to the woman herself, over a lifetime of disappointment and vengefulness.

And suddenly I saw, really *saw* who the woman was.

You never knew her, then, Alvin had told me. *Or you would understand.*

What she'd lost, he meant: all that radiant serenity. Or what she'd learned while two faceless thugs worked at crippling her. While she listened in an alley to a woman being beaten to death.

And when she learned that the fatal beating had been meant for her.

She saw me getting it and laughed unpleasantly at the look on my face: *all along*.

"Of course I knew. You don't think Thren was afraid *Alvin* might want revenge on him, do you? Oh, no."

Her face twisted. "After all, it was Alvin's idea in the first place. Thren just did what Alvin wanted. But I—I had friends in the city, too. Friends who *whispered*. And soon enough, they whispered things to me—who was responsible, and that I'd been the one who was supposed to end up dead. And that if I didn't go, I still might."

Forgotten in Hedda's monologue, Janet listened raptly as if to a fairy tale. Every detail was, to her, another piece of the vital puzzle of what her mother had done and been. But what she heard next did not agree with her so well.

"So I did. Left it all behind," Hedda went on. "If I couldn't dance, it was nothing to me anymore. So I turned my back on every bit of it—unless it could help me get me what I wanted. Money—I didn't even care if Alvin wouldn't spend it, as long as Thren kept having to pay. And I got," she added, "the last laugh."

The hurt on Janet's face was painful to watch. "But what," she implored, "about me? Why didn't you ever try to find me?"

"You?" Hedda sounded incredulous. "Why, what in the world would I ever need you for?" She dismissed the girl with a cruel wave.

Watching Janet's eyes, I had the distinct feeling that Hedda was making a serious tactical mistake. But Hedda was oblivious.

"Really," she added in an obvious, deliberately wounding drawl, "you youngsters do exaggerate your own importance. You gave me a drink when I wanted it, and a pill if I made myself pitiful enough. And you helped to kill him and gave me an alibi afterwards. My overdose," she added to me, "was a nice touch, didn't you think?"

Her hooded eyes lowered evilly. " 'Poor Hedda. It must have been,' " she finished with dreadful relish, " 'that awful Janet's fault.' "

"So you'd have gone on that way," I said to Hedda, "pretty much forever. Taking your pound of flesh an ounce at a time, but then it stopped working. Because Threnody McIlwaine got sick, and knew he was going to die. So nothing you could reveal about him seemed important anymore, and he stopped submitting to your blackmail."

A few feet away, Janet's face was still adjusting to the fact that she'd been nothing but Hedda's tool, all along—that she'd been used. And was being used now.

"Precisely," Hedda replied. And then, with a simpering little smile that mingled craziness with malice, "Well. I couldn't just let him get *away* with it, could I? Not just let him escape."

Janet sniffled, and burst out with more of her hard-luck story. "Without *me* knowing, when it was all I'd ever wanted and he *knew* it was, he *knew* it was and he *laughed*→ "

"Stop whining and get to the point," Hedda snapped. "I want you to tell her how stupid she was. So she'll know."

Janet flinched, looking resentfully at the older woman. But a lifetime of obedient approval-seeking conditioned her response.

"Hedda wanted a drink," she resumed more quietly. "I went down to get it, down the back stairs and into the pantry. I didn't know he was still there, but when I saw him I lost my temper."

This was her chance; she would never tell this story again. Her voice strengthened as the trucks' roar grew louder, drawing nearer.

"I screamed at him," she said. "I told him I knew the truth, and I asked him how he could do it? Hide it from me that way, when it was all I'd ever thought about, the one thing that would have made me happy. How could he do it?"

But I knew. It was part of getting back at Alvin, another part of his revenge. And as usual he hadn't thought how his actions might affect anyone else, only about what he wanted.

Only about power. About pulling the strings from behind the scenes. About being boss.

"He just stood there and laughed at me," Janet said. "Asked me why I thought he'd adopted me at all—did I think it was that he wanted me?"

She shuddered. "All along I was just a tool for him, too, a way to stay one up on Alvin. He told me so." The way you just did, her glance at Hedda said clearly, but Hedda didn't see.

She stopped, gathered her thoughts. "I had the ice pick, and I was so mad by then, I swung it. It scratched his head—"

The blood, I remembered, that Clarissa said had been there.

"— and he grabbed at me, at my throat. I swung it again. The ice pick. It stuck in his head."

"And that," Hedda interrupted, "is Janet's tale of woe."

The trucks were getting nearer. Hedda stepped forward and put the tiny barrel of that damned little pearl-handled revolver right up against my forehead. It felt like an ice-cold fingertip.

"Get up," she told me. "Walk toward the basement door."

"Janet," I said softly, "you don't have to go through with this. You can stop her . . ."

"I do have to," Janet whimpered. Reliving it all again had dissolved her scanty composure; that, and realizing how things really stood. She'd realized her dream—finding her mother—and the dream had turned out to be her worst nightmare.

"He attacked you," I said. "You defended yourself. You didn't mean to kill him. People know how he was, they'll understand."

"But—"

"Shut up," Hedda grated. "Do what I told you."

"I'm sorry," Janet pleaded; to whom, I wasn't sure. "I didn't mean to hurt him, not really. But I was so angry, and then Hedda came down, and—"

"Quiet!" Hedda stamped her hard-soled shoe on the floor, the sound on the hardwood like a rifle shot.

But Janet wouldn't be quieted; not any more. "I stabbed him, he fell, but he wasn't dead. He was just sort of shocked, bleeding, and then Hedda came downstairs. She wanted her drink, and she saw him lying there."

"Be quiet, you foolish girl," Hedda spat, "we haven't time."

Janet rushed on. "He made a sound. Looking up at her, he said something to her."

"What did he say?" I asked, stepping forward slowly.

Possibly I could push past Janet, perhaps grab the gun, but first I would have to get closer.

" 'Sorry,' " she said. "I think he said he was sorry."

Maybe he even had been, not that it mattered. "What happened then?"

I took another slow step, as Hedda frowned, turning at a small sound on the back porch.

"Hedda," Janet said, "took off her shoe. I didn't know why."

"And then?"

"She raised the shoe up. She hit the ice pick with it. Like," Janet said wonderingly, "pounding in a nail."

Yes, just like that. Two wound tracks; the second one fatal. A real monster, my ex-husband had said.

"We had to clean up, and get rid of him," Janet babbled on. "So I went to get rags, and Hedda went out to the front hall, to be sure Alvin wouldn't go into the pantry. But he must not really have been dead. And when we came back . . ."

McIlwaine had vanished, leaving only the mess of blood.

"Why didn't you go after him?"

"We didn't think he could live long. And Hedda said as long as he died somewhere away from the house, no one would suspect us. She said if we just cleaned up, everything would be all right. We killed him," she concluded hopelessly, "together."

So she still thought she was as guilty as Hedda, a misapprehension that had served Hedda's purposes very well. Once I began rooting around in the matter, it was Janet—not at Nina's direction, but at Hedda's—who had tried to discourage me.

Hedda, so swollen with her grandiose greed for revenge that she had thought she could scare me off with a bullying note. Of course, I realized belatedly, it would have to be Hedda. No one else thought the world ran purely at her whim.

"How did Ellie know?" I asked Hedda. The trucks were almost here. Their racket would cover a gunshot nicely.

She sneered, relishing her victory. "Why, I told her, of course. Told her all of it, and that she'd better keep her mouth shut."

The trucks roared. "She would do anything for Alvin, just as she always has. And that," Hedda finished, "turned out to mean protecting me. So his poor heart," she added mockingly, in an awful parody of baby talk, "wouldn't be

broken. So she wouldn't break her sweet little promise,
'cause her such a good girl."

Her face was a horror. "She actually," Hedda pronounced with scathing contempt, "confessed to murder."
Then she looked up sharply. "Enough," she snapped. "I
want it done now."

"Listen," I began as we approached the hall. The cellar
door stood open, about three feet away, tall and narrow
as the opening to a grave. Just before me, a square of
lamplight from the kitchen fell onto the hallway floor.

I didn't remember turning on that light. An awful suspicion hit me, worse than anything so far. *Not the ghost.*

"Hurry up," Hedda repeated, jabbing the gun.

As we passed the kitchen door I turned, not caring in
that moment if she shot me for it.

Sam looked up from the kitchen table, surprised. In
the din of the slow-moving trucks outside, he hadn't
known we were here.

"Mom." He was tinkering with the gift his father had
brought him, trying to repair it. That had been the sound
Hedda had heard: Sam coming in.

He didn't see the gun. "Listen, Mom, I'm sorry about
what I said."

You just don't think it can get any worse, sometimes,
but it does. "Jacobia," called my ex-husband, stomping
up the back steps.

"I want—" Victor began as he came in without invitation, spotted Sam in the kitchen, and broke off his pre-
emptory demand as he saw what Sam was doing.

"Sam, I *told* you," he said, his voice heavy with
strained patience, as if he could not believe how stupid
Sam was being, "you *can't*—"

As usual, he was well into his exasperated spiel before
he bothered to notice the facts of the situation. Then he
saw the gun, and his mouth formed a soundless O.

Only Sam seemed unfazed, still peering at the laser
level with the calm, focused attitude of the born repair-
man. He moved a switch on the gadget, smiled, and
moved it again.

"You, boy," Hedda snapped. "Get up and get over here."

She swung the gun at him, her gnarled finger tightening, and time stretched out in the awful way that it does in the instants before a head-on collision.

I saw my ex-husband registering the same thought as mine: which one of us could jump Hedda faster? In a flicker of movement that made me forgive him everything, he tensed to leap.

But he would never make it in time. Only Sam's maddening obliviousness made Hedda hesitate at all; she wanted his fear, his acknowledgment that at last, she was running things.

Then Sam looked up at us out of his own world, the one in which nothing exists but the problem to be solved.

"Look, Mom," he said happily. "It works!"

Hedda hissed a breath in and lifted the revolver minutely, as a light glowed from the end of the gadget.

I felt the thing's brilliance zip past: a cherry-red needle.

Hedda shrieked, dropping the revolver, clapping her twisted hands up over her eyes as Janet stood by stolidly, doing nothing to help her. From Hedda's mouth came a high, keening sound of anguish, like the death wail of the damned.

Which in a way I suppose it was.

54

"What the hell," Bob Arnold boomed, "is all this?"

He stood alertly on my back porch, feet planted firmly, his right hand poised over his sidearm. Behind him, her dark eyes full of recent enlightenment, stood Clarissa Dow.

"Hey," said Wade, looming suddenly behind Clarissa.

Now I thought I *was* seeing a ghost.

"What's going on?" Wade asked, looking perplexed.

"I told you," said Sam, "that I could fix it."

55

It took ten days for the Federal people to get their foolish, quacking ducks in a row. So I drove downstate to pick up Ellie on the first real day of spring, the sky gone definitively from its palette of chill, drizzly greys and razor-knife blues to the pastel shades, whitewashed aquamarine and creamy azure, which in Maine are a sure sign that winter is over.

"Oh," Ellie said at the sight of Passamaquoddy Bay, glittering at the foot of Washington Street.

Can Man looked up from his task of plucking a Coke can from the gutter at the corner of Water Street, waving at us as we made the turn into downtown. His lips moved as we went by: *No place like home.*

On Key Street, Ellie got out slowly and turned in a circle. Nothing had changed, except for the realtor's "for sale" sign in front of her house. She looked at it calmly, then turned her back on it and went up the green-painted front steps into mine.

"It's wonderful," she breathed, smiling at the clean, fresh wallpaper and smooth new plaster, the gleaming, polished hardwood floors and immaculate tin ceilings. When you do these things yourself, they take forever. But contractors—paid for by fire insurance—can accomplish them in under two weeks. And it wasn't as if there weren't plenty of tasks left for me, on the second and third floors: two lifetimes' worth, I calculated, down from the previous three.

"Better come in," I said. "Everyone is waiting. And you must be hungry."

Before I left, I had baked a batch of oatmeal-lace cookies, by rights a summer delicacy to be enjoyed with iced tea, but on the grounds that you never know what tomorrow may bring, I had decided to do it now.

George Valentine stepped from the front parlor into the hall. He held the black cap with Guptill's Excavating lettered on it in orange script tightly in both hands.

"Hi, Ellie," he said.

"Hi, George," she replied.

"Or maybe," I said, "you're not that hungry, come to think of it." I left them there.

Out in the kitchen, Sam was debating with his father the merits of the wooden sailing hull over the admittedly less work-intensive but to Sam unromantic fiberglass. Tiffany had made coffee, fed Monday, and put together a plate of ham sandwiches; now she was twiddling with the radio, trying to find NPR.

"Got it," she said, and suddenly a horn fanfare, thrilling and sweet, burst out.

Wade of course had not gone down in an explosion; that had been just another of Hedda's lies, to hurt me and break my spirit.

Jemmy hadn't gone down, either, or if he had, there were post offices in Davy Jones's locker.

On the mantel in the kitchen where the mysterious portrait used to be stood a small cardboard box; inside was one link of an anchor chain, newly inscribed with an account number and code word. "Give it to the widows and orphans," the unsigned note had read.

The body of the other drowned fellow had not been found, but one had been recovered from the incinerated wreckage of the *Hoodathunkit*. It was too burnt and blasted for identification, but because of it I had a feeling that the guys who go boom wouldn't be looking for Jemmy Wechsler anymore.

Or for the money that chain link represented. I made a mental note to find out about the drowned fellow's family, and how I might manage quietly to assist them with half of it.

The other half belonged to Ellie, though she didn't know it yet. There had been, of course, no money for Alvin in McIlwaine's estate: yet another of the pirate of Wall Street's mean-spirited manipulations. But Ellie would know, I felt sure, what to do with Jemmy's cash, so she and Alvin wouldn't have to worry anymore.

"Good party," Wade said, coming over to drop a

bearish arm around my shoulders. "That Tiffany's a smart kid. What's she still doing with Victor?"

"She's not, actually. She's with Sam. Platonically," I added, as Wade glanced at me in surprise.

"They're going with Victor back to New York on Monday—Sam's enrolled in a special school at the university. He's decided," I said, still a bit dazed by the ambitious plan Sam had formulated for himself, "to become an expert on dyslexia, starting with his own. So he can fix it, before he goes to boat school."

Wade nodded slowly. "You know, I bet he will."

I watched Sam wash down a cookie with a long swig of Pepsi, then return to the argument with his father. The two of them looked so alike—dark, curly hair; long, mulishly determined faces; thick-lashed green eyes—that I almost couldn't stand it, and I didn't know how I would get along without Sam.

Wade read my thought. "He'll be back. Harpwell's already told him he's got a place for him on the design team, once he gets his degree."

"Do you think he can do it?"

Sam laughed, and pulled a scathing, you're-so-hopeless face at his father, who had apparently said something too old-fogeyish. Since learning that there was a name for his trouble, and a strategy he might follow, it seemed the weight of the world had dropped off my son's shoulders. Gone, too, was Sam's excessive desire to please his father, whom to Victor's discomfiture and my intense amusement Sam had begun calling "Pops."

Wade squeezed my shoulder. "He'll be fine, Jacobia. And so will we. I guess if you and Sam can deal with Victor, I can, too."

I followed his gaze to where my ex-husband sat discoursing about fiberglass, a topic on which he had almost no knowledge whatsoever but of course felt obliged to pretend he did.

"Every family's got one," said Wade amusedly, which was when I realized that ours did, too.

And that we were. "I'd better go over and socialize with poor Alvin," I told Wade. "He looks like a lost lamb."

Wade went back to his conversation with Bobby Taylor, who looked little the worse for his loss of Janet Fox. She, at the moment, was fresh out of detox, languishing in the Washington County jail, simultaneously awaiting a grand jury indictment and protesting her victimhood to anyone who would listen.

"Jacobia," Alvin said, shifting over gratefully to make room for me on the sofa. He had eaten almost nothing, and except for the sip he had taken for George and Ellie's toast, his champagne glass remained untouched.

"Hi, Alvin. How's Hedda doing at BMH?"

Bangor Mental Health Institute, I meant. It was where the state cops had taken her.

"Better. They've run tests, got her pills straightened out. I went to see her, and she seems in her right mind. Eyes are okay, too; she was more scared than hurt, I think. And sharp-tongued as ever. I don't guess there's a therapy for that."

In Hedda's case, I guessed not, too. "Miss Dow says there'll probably be a trial," he went on, "but she says with a decent lawyer, it could come down to not guilty on account of mental defect."

Across the room, Clarissa Dow and Bob Arnold stood together. She'd gotten halfway to Caribou, she'd said, before she made the U-turn.

"I don't know," Clarissa had told me upon her return, "what it is about this town."

Then she'd paused, as if searching for the right words, and I'd wondered if any of us who were from away would ever find them.

"But I can't see," Alvin said now, "how I'll pay a lawyer. Looks like I'm going to lose whatever I can get on the house, if I manage to sell it. So even if I can ever bring Hedda home someday, I don't know where I'll bring her to."

I sipped my champagne, thinking.

"This place, it just captured me," Clarissa had said. "It's where I belong. Although," she'd finished, "I can't imagine how I'll get people here to ever like me or accept me, after what I nearly did to Ellie."

Now I thought I knew how. She was, after all, an attorney, and a big local case would get her firmly established in Eastport. Someday she could even defend little Sadie Peltier, whom I had managed to shoo away earlier in the day, bribing her with a handful of oatmeal-lace cookies.

But she would be back. That was Sadie: she always came back.

Arnold strolled over to me. "That fellow you knew, from the boat basin. Guess he picked a pretty spectacular way, end it all."

"Yeah, I guess he did."

Arnold gazed at me, unfooled. "No way of proving that the dynamite he used is the stuff missing out of the Quoddy boys' warehouse, though. Guess I'll have to mark that one unsolved."

"Yes," I told Arnold. "Probably you will. Too bad. But you know where it went, even though you can't prove it. That ought to count for something."

Pack it against the fuel tank, Wade had explained to me. Detonate by radio, once you're far enough away not to be killed by the underwater concussion. It would be simple, if you were up for that sort of thing, equipped for the cold water and so on.

"Yeah," Arnold conceded. "Yeah, I guess it does." He headed thoughtfully back to Clarissa's side.

"You know, Alvin," I added, turning to him again, "I've got a feeling you'll have a good lawyer for Hedda, after all."

She might even come home, someday: suitably medicated and supervised, of course, so that she was no threat to Alvin or to anyone else. He might get his wish. It was within the realm of possibility.

Stranger things had happened.

"You think so?" he asked, unconvinced. But then, as

he looked at Arnold and Clarissa, and at Ellie and George, something seemed to dawn on him: that this particular bad old nightmare was over, whatever tomorrow brought.

"Well, maybe so, at that," Alvin White said.

56

"You got those papers and the photograph Hedda had torn up, and left them in that little box in the attic for me to find. You knew it was Hedda, even before she told you, as soon as you recognized the ice pick, but you wouldn't say."

It was midnight, and everyone had gone home except Ellie, and Wade was asleep in front of the television. I washed another plate, rinsed it, and set it in the rack.

"I couldn't." Ellie dried another champagne glass. "No one would have believed me, you know that. They'd have thought I was only trying to get rid of Hedda. Besides . . ."

"I know, I know. You promised."

It was the bottom-line reason she hadn't said a word. I sighed, expressing what I thought about the sensibleness of this.

But on the earlier count, Ellie was right: Hedda's well-known abuse of her daughter would have made Ellie's accusation come out sounding like the vengefulness of an ill-treated child, especially since Ellie had possessed no proof.

"I was so sure that it was Nina," I said, wielding the soapy sponge. "And her horrible cousin." They'd lit out of town soon after my house fire, after I'd told Nina—wrongly—that I knew what she'd done. Last I'd heard, they'd been picked up in Canada, which had some very interesting, little-publicized reciprocal arrangements with U.S. authorities where war crimes were concerned.

Ellie looked at me. "Jacobia, think about it. If you knew

your husband was likely to die in six months, no matter how much you hated him, would you risk killing him?"

"That depends on the husband," I said, thinking of Victor.

But I took her point, which I had missed earlier on account of Nina being such a greedy little minx.

"Anyway," Ellie went on, "I knew if I were caught meddling with the ice pick, people would believe my confession, and then you would go on and find out what really happened, especially if I kept nudging you about the portrait."

She stopped, looking down at her hands. Ellie had recognized her mother in the old photograph, abandoned when Hedda's relatives left my house years earlier. Alvin would have, too, of course, but I hadn't ever gotten around to asking Alvin.

Not that he would have answered. His own guilt had kept him obedient, all those years.

"So," Ellie went on, "I wouldn't have to accuse her. But I didn't realize that I'd be putting you in danger by getting you involved. I didn't know she really had a gun."

Telling me about the portrait would have violated the spirit of her promise to Alvin, at first because Hedda simply didn't want anyone to see the unflattering contrast, the *before* and *after* the photograph made clear, later because Ellie realized how damning it was. From it, you saw that Hedda hadn't merely aged badly, but that something had happened to her, something devastating. And from that Ellie had trusted me to sniff out a motive, and put it together with *where there's a will, there's a way*.

Which of course there had been. All the snapshots of her long-ago dancing days—a platinum-blonde Hedda thickly made up in stage paint, swathed in a feather boa—only made the portrait that much less recognizable, an effect she would have endorsed heartily.

The girl she had been before New York, before Alvin decided that if he couldn't have her, nobody could—

—the attack and her knowledge of who was behind it ruining Hedda utterly, making her each year afterwards more capable of murder, until finally she was and the opportunity arose—

—that girl was gone, as far as Hedda was concerned, until I propped the portrait on Hedda's kitchen counter, and she found it there.

And from it, as guilty people will, she'd assumed that I knew all.

Ellie couldn't say, because she'd promised. But if I found it out myself, that would be all right.

"Remind me," I told her, "not to get into any theological debates with you. But it's okay," I added, and I meant about all of it: the parts that I understood, and the parts—the *risk* Ellie had taken, the belief in me she'd had—that I didn't. In the country of kept promises, after all, I was from away, and could not be expected to understand some things.

Or at least not all at once.

"But what if you were wrong?" I said. About, I meant, whether she could count on me.

"Oh, I knew you'd sort it out, Jacobia," Ellie replied. "Once you knew about the past, the present would be obvious."

I did not comment at this display of blithe optimism. Ellie folded the dish towel.

"And now that you have," she went on, "I believe you may be the most experienced murder investigator in Eastport."

"Maybe by default," I said, "until Clarissa Dow arrives for good."

"But Clarissa won't have time to investigate things, once she is in practice. Will she? She'll be a working attorney, too busy with that. It will be up to us," Ellie finished.

I turned from rinsing the last of the soapsuds down the sink, noticing that the door to the storeroom had sneaked open an inch and wondering what Ellie could possibly mean by this extraordinary statement.

But of course I was about to find out.

"Do you," Ellie asked, "remember that fellow who's

supposed to have nailed his aunt and uncle into the trailer home, up in one of the numbered townships?"

The town without a name. And he'd burnt it, after he nailed them into it. "Yes, I remember."

"Well," she said, pouring a cup of coffee and sitting down with it. "It turns out that this fellow, the accused, is one of George's uncles."

I wasn't surprised. Half of Washington County is one of George's uncles, and the other half is a nephew or niece. Ellie wasn't only getting married, she was acquiring a clan.

"Get to the point, please," I told her, as the storeroom door eased shut again and latched with a decisive *click!*

"Well," Ellie said. "It's true that the uncle was there that night, and it's true that there was an awful quarrel. And he was seen speeding away just before the fire broke out, so the police are certain he started it."

I waited while she sipped her coffee.

"And," she went on, "there is money involved. Quite a lot of money. Forest land, with valuable hardwood on it," she explained. "And the fire marshall says the fire was ignited by a cigarette. A lit," she emphasized, "cigarette."

"And the punch line?"

"The uncle has asthma. As bad as George's, maybe worse."

Two different kinds of inhalers, I remembered, and the pills. And George's deep hatred of cigarettes. He really despised them.

It ran, he'd said, in the family.

I took an oatmeal-lace cookie out of the stash I'd held back from the party. After a moment, Ellie took one, too.

Outside, the wind moved the sharply cut shapes of the pines against a night sky bright with a full moon, streaked with clouds streaming whitely across the scattered stars.

"Interesting," I said, and we were off.

ABOUT THE AUTHOR

SARAH GRAVES lives with her husband in Eastport, Maine, where her mystery novels featuring Jacobia Tiptree are set. She is currently working on her seventh novel, *Mallets Aforethought*.

If you enjoyed **Sarah Graves's**
THE DEAD CAT BOUNCE

you won't want to miss any of the exciting
books in her *Home Repair Is Homicide*
mystery series.

Look for **TRIPLE WITCH, WICKED FIX,
REPAIR TO HER GRAVE, WRECK THE
HALLS, and UNHINGED** at your favorite
bookseller.

And turn the page for a tantalizing preview of
the next *Home Repair Is Homicide* mystery,
MALLETS AFORETHOUGHT,
available in hardcover from Bantam Books.

MALLETS AFORETHOUGHT

A *Home Repair Is Homicide* mystery by
SARAH GRAVES

On sale in hardcover March 2004

MALLETS
AFORETHOUGHT

A
Home Repair Is Homicide
Mystery

SARAH GRAVES

AUTHOR OF *UNHINGED*

MALLETS AFORETHOUGHT
by Sarah Graves

On sale in hardcover March 2004

The body was all withered sinews and leathery skin, seated on a low wooden chair in the tiny room whose door my friend Ellie White and I had just forced open. Slumped over a table, one arm outstretched, the body wore a sequined chemise whose silver hem-fringe crossed its mummified thigh.

Masses of bangles circled the knobby wrists and rings hung loosely on the long bony fingers. From beneath black bobbed hair the hollow eye sockets peeked coyly at us, the mouth a toothy rictus of mischief.

Or malice. A candle burnt down to a puddled stub stood in an ornate holder by the body's arm. A tiaralike headpiece with a glass jewel in its bezel had fallen to the floor.

Ellie and I stood frozen for a moment, neither of us able to speak for the horridness of the surprise. Then:

"Oh," breathed Ellie, sinking heavily into the window seat of the dilapidated parlor we'd been working on. It was Saturday morning and around us the aging timbers of Eastport's most decrepit old mansion, Harlequin House, creaked uneasily.

Only the wind, I told myself. Outside it was blowing a gale. But the fact brought little comfort since after a century or so without maintenance, the old mansion's skeleton was probably less sturdy than the body we were staring at. Being sealed in the room had apparently preserved it like some denizen of King Tut's tomb.

"A woman," Ellie added, her voice still faint with shock.

"Yes," I responded, sniffing the air curiously. Thinking . . . something. I just didn't know exactly what, yet.

The parlor was lit by a couple of lamps we'd brought from home, the power in the house having been turned on only the day before. This morning was meant to be a work party but it seemed the storm had discouraged all but the two of us. Around us lay damp swathes of stripped wallpaper and the scrapers and putty knives we'd been using to pull down chunks of cracked plaster.

It was behind one of those cracks we'd first found the faint outlines of a hidden aperture, and of course a secret door had been irresistible. Who wouldn't want to learn what lay behind it, where it might lead?

But now I reentered the chamber cautiously. Its air smelled of the dust to which its occupant had partially returned, and of something else, the faint whiff I'd caught earlier: *not* dusty.

Not in the slightest. The lamplight barely reached the back of the little room. As my eyes adjusted to the gloom there, I made out the shape in the corner.

And identified it, wishing I hadn't.

"Let's get out of here," I said, exiting hurriedly.

"Don't worry, I'm fine," said Ellie, misunderstanding me. "I just felt strange for a minute."

Her speedy recovery was little more than I expected. Ellie wasn't usually much daunted by dead bodies, antique or otherwise. Her shaky reaction to this one I put down to the fact that at the moment she was as pregnant as a person could be without actually wheeling into the delivery room.

"Help me . . . oof! . . . up." Gripping my hand, she struggled to her feet. "I swear this isn't a kid, it's a Volkswagen."

"Only a little longer," I comforted her distractedly, still staring into the hidden room.

"It'd better be," she retorted. "If this baby doesn't come soon I'm going to start charging it rent."

There were two bodies in there.

"Lots," she emphasized, "of rent."

One old body. And a new one. "Ellie, have you ever heard any stories about another door into this room?"

She could have, if one existed. An ancestor on Ellie's mother's side, Chester Harlequin, had owned the house in its heyday.

"No." She peered puzzledly at me. With her red hair softly framing a heart-shaped face, green eyes above freckles the color of gold dust, and a long slim body blooming out at the middle like some enchanted flower, Ellie resembled a storybook princess and was as tough as Maine granite.

But she was in trouble now and she didn't even know it.

Yet.

"I'd never even heard of *this* one," she added. "I have seen photographs of this parlor, though, back when—"

Her gesture took in the ramshackle interior wall where the door had been concealed, its trim removed and panels smoothed over by a coat of plaster topped with the same fusty vines-and-grape-leaves pattern as the rest of the ornate old chamber.

"—the wallpaper was new," she said. "Last time this room was redone was sometime back in the twenties."

Why someone had also walled a body up in it was a question I supposed might never be answered—not after more than eighty years. Which I guessed was truly how long the woman had been dead; the state of the plaster, the wallpaper, and the body's own costume all testified to it pretty convincingly.

Yet there were no additional obvious entrances to the room, and the inner walls were all of unplastered boards. Any break in them, however well repaired, would have been clearly visible. In short, it appeared that the room had been sealed since the first body was entombed. So how'd the second one gotten in there?

"I know her," Ellie said suddenly. "I've seen old pictures of her wearing the dress and the tiara. It's Eva Thane, the woman my Uncle Chester was . . . So *that's* what happened to her."

"Ellie, wait." She'd gotten her wind back and was about to reenter the room, her shock giving way to the curiosity that was among her most prominent character traits.

"Why?" she demanded impatiently. "I want a closer look at . . ."

Then she understood, or thought she did. "But you're right of course, a flashlight will help." She drew one from her smock pocket.

The windowless room was enclosed on all sides with a center hall at its rear, kitchen to its left, the parlor plus a vestibule and coatroom to its front and right. The house was so huge that a square of missing space wouldn't be missed, especially tucked as it was to one side of an enormous black marble fireplace.

Ellie aimed the flash past me and sucked in a surprised breath. "Him," she exhaled, recognizing the dead face instantly just as I had, despite the unpleasantness of its disfigurement.

But having been unnerved once, Ellie was not about to show faintheartedness a second time. "Well," she continued briskly, "*this* certainly isn't going the way we planned."

Which was an understatement. Begun just today, the Harlequin House fix-up was supposed to be a labor of love. Assisted by a small army of local volunteers, we were to ready the old dwelling for a gala put on by the Eastport Historical Society, and in doing so perhaps up the chances that someone—anyone!—might actually take the place off the Society's impoverished hands afterwards.

And the first corpse, I thought, might even have helped. A long-dead flapper from the Roaring 20s could have been just the hook this old money-pit needed to snag the attention of a buyer with cash vastly exceeding common sense.

But the newer body was of more than historical interest.

Way more. "We have a problem, don't we?" Ellie said.

She was starting to catch on. Eva Thane's antique corpse dropped off her mental radar as a new and more unpleasant light dawned.

" 'Fraid so,' " I agreed unhappily. The dead man was Hector Gosling, Eastport's most irascible real-estate mogul as well as the current president of the historical society. His face was smudged with grime, as were his clothes, a condition that would have been unthinkable while Hector was alive. But even filthy and hideously exaggerated as it was now, that furious teeth-baring grimace was an all-too-familiar expression.

Combined with his position, however—feet and head on the floor, midsection arched tautly, agonizingly up like a drawn bow—Hector's look didn't say *fury* or anything like it.

What it said, unfortunately, was strychnine.

I am the type who goes more for structural guts than shelter-magazine glory, so if Harlequin House had been mine I'd have started renovations with the underpinnings, the wooden sills and the foundation. At the same time I'd be tearing off the roof, all the trim, and the chimneys and siding. All the windows would come out, too, as would the wiring, plumbing, and heating. Inside, I'd pull down every last bit of the cracked, ancient plaster, and fix all the lath.

Only when the house sat four-square on its footings with its mechanicals updated, its windows made weathertight, insulation layered onto it, and its new trim and clapboards coated with oil-based primer and paint would I even give a thought to wallpaper.

Whereupon I would reject it. These old houses have been smothering in garish floral patterns and gloomy scenic designs for long enough, in my opinion. They need paint in a nice light color scheme, off-white woodwork, and freshly sanded floors.

But as I say, the house didn't belong to me. So for a little while Ellie and I went on puttering and pondering, deciding what we would say when we summoned the authorities.

And what might need doing afterwards.

"I mean, George and I have a problem. But mostly George does," Ellie said. "Or he might have."

At last we gathered our tools and arranged them on some newspapers at the center of the room. I'd acquired the "clean up as you go along" habit soon after I bought my own old house and began repairing it.

"Not," she added, "that anyone will *believe* he could've . . ."

"Of course they won't," I agreed hastily.

But privately I wasn't so sure. Ellie's husband George was your go-to guy for nearly everything in Eastport. In our little town on Moose Island, seven miles off the Maine coast, George was the man you called if you had bats in the attic, a bad drain, or a pet parrot scared by Fourth of July fireworks into a copper beech tree.

But George was also Hector Gosling's worst enemy. Or next-to-worst, after whoever'd murdered the old schemer in this awful manner. Strychnine—the very idea made me shudder.

"Anyway, I guess we'd better call Bob Arnold," Ellie said. It was sinking in now what this discovery could develop into.

Although, in the call-the-authorities department at least, we were in luck. If anyone knew George's good character better than Ellie, it was Eastport's police chief Bob Arnold. So George might still catch the break I already thought he might be needing.

"I mean we can't very well just wall Hector up again. Can we?" Ellie asked, briefly hopeful.

Actually we could have. Powdered lime for Hector,

quick-set plaster for that door, fresh wallpaper, and in a few hours we could be sitting pretty in the corpse-concealment department.

And nobody would ever deliberately go looking for Hector the Objector, so-called because no matter what anyone ever wanted to do, he could be counted upon to come up with a dozen reasons why they couldn't or shouldn't.

That is, unless they wanted to unload parcels of real estate at fire-sale prices. But . . .

"No," I replied grudgingly. "We can't take the chance. If we hadn't wrecked the door getting it open, we could say we'd never *gotten* it open and never seen him. But people will know we've been working in here. So now if anyone else ever *does* find him, we'll have an awfully hard time explaining ourselves."

Oh, it would have been lovely just to walk away and forget him. Poison was too good for Hector, and as for a decent burial, any hallowed soil you tried putting him in would only spit him right back out again the way you would a bad clam.

"We had better just let Bob get the process in motion," I told Ellie. State police, medical examiner, crime lab van from Augusta: the whole, as Chief Arnold tended to call it, dog-and-pony show.

"All right." Ellie sighed. "We should find George, too, let him know what's going on."

Of course he would be cleared eventually; maybe even soon. But until then I thought he could be in for an uncertain time.

"He's at the marine tech center this morning," Ellie added, "helping drop in new pilings for the dock, and the granite slabs for the boat ramp . . . mmph!"

An odd look came over her face. "A Volkswagen," she gasped wincingly, putting her hand on the fireplace mantel and leaning against it, "that kicks like a *mule*."

As we stepped from under its portico, the windows of Harlequin House peered dourly down at us through a mess of fallen gutters and sagging trim, its mansard roof rotten and the breaks in its wooden gutters home to generations of pigeons. Hunched arm-in-arm we dashed together under wind-whipped maples, unkindly shoved along by gusts bearing rain in overflowing buckets.

For a woman who was carrying the equivalent of a compact car, Ellie was moving right along; when I was waiting for my own son, I was lucky if I could move from a chair to the couch. But she just kept putting one foot in front of the other, and much as I dislike the damage they cause I adore these storms. They're the closest I'll ever get to being on the ocean in heavy weather.

My home: the big white 1823 Federal house loomed suddenly out of the storm at us, its many-paned windows gleaming a golden welcome from between green shutters. Water gushed from its downspouts, streamed down its brick chimneys, and sheeted along its clapboard sides as if someone had opened a spillway above it. But thus far it didn't look as if the sump pump had gone on. No water, I saw with relief, poured from the pipe leading from the cellar window.

So one thing was going right, anyway. In the driveway a heap of old truck parts hunkered atop mismatched tires.

"He's here," Ellie managed breathlessly, seeing the vehicle.

George, she meant. We staggered up the porch steps and into the back hall, shedding our wet jackets and sodden hats as my black Labrador, Monday, danced and wagged her tail in joyful greeting.

"Hi, girl." I patted her silky head, then reached to bestow equal attention on our red Doberman, Prill, who demanded nothing, adored everything, and received her petting with solemn gravity.

George was at the kitchen table drinking a cup of coffee and listening to the radio's report of the storm's unexpected power. Wearing a green flannel shirt, faded overalls, and battered work boots, he got up quickly when he saw Ellie.

"Hey, hey," he said, frowning a sharp question at me as he took charge, guiding her toward a chair. "You look all in."

He was the one who appeared exhausted, his chin stubbled and his eyes deeply shadowed with fatigue. He'd been working harder than usual lately to buy things the baby needed and to pay doctor bills, and the strain was beginning to show.

With him at the table was another local guy, Will Bonnet; he and George had grown up together. Will took in Ellie's drenched condition silently, then went back to the newspaper he was reading.

"I'm fine." She leaned affectionately against George but didn't sit. "I just need to get these wet clothes changed, that's all."

Wisely, George backed off. Ellie was the oxygen in his air, the stars in his sky, his own personal moon over Miami. But he knew better than to try making her do what she didn't want to.

"Hop in a warm bath, though, why don't you?" I said, putting the kettle on. "Seriously. You're giving the kid a chill."

Which was the secret: most of the time you couldn't get her to do anything strictly for herself. For the baby, though . . .

"Dry clothes of yours are in my dresser," I called after her as she went up the stairs. Over the years I'd known her, our two houses had intermingled until they had become virtual annexes of one another. "Clean towels in the linen closet."

Then I turned to George, who was still eyeing me narrowly. He was a small man with dark hair, grease-stained knuckles, and the milky-pale skin that runs in some downeast Maine families. But his size was made up for by an alert, banty-rooster bearing and thrust-out chin; most folks didn't give him any backchat.

"George, she wouldn't let me get the car," I began before he could reproach me. "It was either stand in the cold rain arguing with her or make a dash for it. It wasn't raining when we started out earlier."

He relented. "She is hard-headed, isn't she?" *Hahd*— the downeast Maine pronunciation. The radio started in on a fiddle-and-banjo version of "Beaumont Rag," a tune that always makes me feel like dancing.

Still, I had a feeling the sensation of safety wouldn't last much longer. There was a window sash standing in the corner by the washing machine; I'd removed it earlier and now just to keep my hands busy I began tinkering with it.

"George. We found two bodies in that house." A length of metal weatherstripping lay atop the washing machine, along with a sharp chisel, a hammer, and some small nails. "And one of the bodies is Hector Gosling's."

He'd returned to his chair to wait for Ellie so he could take her home. Now he peered blankly at me, his look unreadable.

Will looked up too. By contrast he appeared delighted. "Ain't that," he pronounced succinctly, "a goddamned shame."

"We haven't told anyone," I went on. "We need to inform Bob Arnold."

I'd already nailed weatherstripping into the sash channels. Now I turned the window sash so the bottom edge faced up. "And George, the police will want to speak with you."

But George shook his head. "Bob's mom took ill last night in Kennebunk. State boys'll be covering us till he gets back."

Which was not welcome news. Something Bob Arnold might've given instantly—such as for instance an ironclad character reference for George—wouldn't be available at all from a cop whose usual task was patrolling the interstate, 200 miles away.

"Anyway, why would they want to talk to me? And who's the other one?" he inquired mildly. George had a way of not getting too exercised over anything not relevant to him.

A dead body, for example. If it wasn't his or Ellie's, and it wasn't someone from my household—my son Sam, my husband Wade Sorenson, my ex-husband Victor, who lived down the street, or any of our animals—then to George it was an item to be read in the newspaper and that was the end of it.

But Will, a big, handsome fellow with jet-black hair,

blue eyes, and a deeply cleft chin—in red plaid shirt, narrow jeans, and polished boots, he was the Hollywood version of Paul Bunyan—had begun looking even more interested. "Yeah? Whose was it?"

"The other one's too old to make any difference to us," I said. Let Ellie tell the rest of that story, I decided, sometime when we didn't need George awakened to his own personal peril.

"They'll want to speak with you," I told George, "because you are the one who hated his guts the most."

If your window locks with a top clasp that holds the bottom sash down tightly, you can make it draft-free by installing some weatherstripping on the bottom edge of the window.

"And," I added to George, "everyone knows it."

There was another more specific reason, too, but I didn't want to mention it yet. Maybe I wouldn't have to at all. I positioned the length of weatherstripping in the window well, cut it to fit by tapping the chisel on it with the hammer, and lay the cut-to-fit strip on the bottom edge of the sash.

"Join the club," George said, perusing a section of the newspaper he'd picked up. "Can't think of many who didn't hate him. Can you?"

"No." I began nailing the weatherstripping to the sash with little taps of the hammer. "But they weren't talking it around that if they could find a good way to do something to Hector, they'd do something to him."

He looked unimpressed. "So you think I should get my ducks in a row? Trump myself up a good old-fashioned alibi?"

Tap, tap. "That's just what I think you should do, but a real one, not trumped up." I didn't think he was taking this seriously enough.

"And the more wide-ranging and comprehensive the better," I went on, "because . . ."

Because we didn't know yet just when Gosling had died. But a week earlier while Ellie was at a baby shower, Will and George had gone out on the town together. They'd ended up in Duddy's Tap, drinking beer and regaling the crowd with hilarious schemes.

And what all those schemes had in common, I'd been told the next day by one of Duddy's regulars who'd been there too, was the sudden, violent, and unsolvable murder of Hector Gosling.

"I just think you ought to," I finished, lifting the sash and placing it back into the window opening. The sash trim went up in a twinkling; I hadn't even bothered taking the nails out. Now I slid the sash experimentally up and down, then locked it.

It worked, the weatherstripping pressed tight by the locked window. "Nice," Will Bonnet observed.

"Thanks." A little burst of pleasure flooded my heart. "And it will be even nicer this winter."

"Hey, there." George's face brightened as Ellie returned, a towel around her head and the rest of her swathed in an enormous hot-pink sweater. With it she wore fuchsia leggings with crimson flowers printed on them, and a lime-green crocheted vest. Purple legwarmers, plaid socks, and sandals completed her costume.

"Oh, I feel so much better," she beamed.

Will Bonnet grinned at her and I suppose I must have, also. You couldn't help it; combined with the outfit, her smile made her look like an explosion at the happiness factory.

"George, did Jake tell you what we found?"

"Ayuh. She seems to think folks'll b'lieve I did it."

"Well." The smile dimmed a few watts. "Bob Arnold is going to want to talk to you. So you'd better be ready."

"Hector was a crook," George declared. "Whoever's done for 'im should've done it sooner. Before"—he emphasized this with a shake of the sports pages—"Gosling and his quack pal Jan Jesperson got near my Aunt Paula. Rest," he added sadly, "her poor addled soul."

This was the crux of the matter and the reason for George's dislike of—black hatred for, actually—Hector the Objector.

That Hector *didn't* object to swindling town ladies out of their money. Or anyway, that was the rumor: that over the years he and his partner in crime Jan Jesperson had conspired to identify women who were alone in the world, and befriend them.

Next, people said, Jan wielded a pill-bottle and Gosling worked the social angle. Hector wooed the ladies with old-fashioned courtliness while Jan turned them into doped zombies from whom it was child's play to extract shaky power-of-attorney signatures.

"Poor old Aunt Paula," he mourned. "Witch that she was, I had a soft spot for her. Wouldn't have let those two evil knievels go to town on her if I had known."

"Not your fault," Will reminded him. "She wouldn't talk to you. How were you to know those vultures had their claws in her?"

It was the reason Will himself had come home to Eastport: his own last living relative, his elderly aunt Agnes Bonnet, was a natural next target for the predatory Hector and Jan.

"If you hadn't told me what'd happened to Paula," he added to George, "*I'd* never have known."

"How is she, Will?" Ellie inquired kindly. For it seemed Jan and Hector had gotten a start on Agnes too.

Will shrugged sadly. "Not good. I don't know what that woman might've given her, and *she* says she never gave her nothing."

Anything, I corrected him silently. Will was a charming guy, but he was a little rough around the edges.

"Doctors can't find a thing. She's so fragile, though, it could have messed her mind up even after she stopped taking it."

It occurred to me that the doctors might not be doing drug tests. So his Aunt Agnes *still* could be taking it. Whatever it might be.

"You know, you might want to look around in the house."

He was living with her now, caring for her as best he could despite her increasing dementia. "In case there is anything, she might be confused and think she should swallow it," I added.

"Yeah, huh?" Will replied thoughtfully. Before coming home to Eastport he'd been in Boston for a dozen years, and city life had made him quick to pick up on the behaviors people might be getting into. "Yeah, maybe I should," he agreed.

"That Jan Jesperson," George said, understanding also what I was suggesting, "is one tricky piece of work."

With this I had to agree, if only because nothing alleged against Gosling or Jesperson had ever been proven. On the face of it, George's aunt had simply died of old age. By the time George heard about it she'd been cremated, on instructions that Gosling and Jesperson had helped her issue shortly before she expired.

"You know anything yet about the estate?" Will asked.

George shook his head. "Don't guess I'm going to, either, at this late date. You aren't in it, they don't tell you about it."

Which we assumed must be the situation: that George's aunt had left her estate to that pair of shameless carrion-eaters.

"But it's not about the money. It's that I could've tried harder," George insisted stubbornly. "She could've had us, 'stead o' bein' alone in that big house of hers, rattlin' around amongst a lot of tarnished silver and dusty old furniture."

He looked at Will. "It was her own choice the way she shut herself off from everyone but I don't b'lieve she'd've ever been suckered by 'em if she wasn't so lonely. Aunt Paula was always smart. You, though, you're lucky. You got back before things got too bad."

Will shrugged sympathetically. "Maybe. I hope you're right, but we'll see. Agnes was in pretty sad shape when I arrived."

George got to his feet. "Anyway, I better go double-check the stuff I was using this morning. I need to make sure the rain didn't seep in and wash it anywhere I don't want it to go."

Will followed him to the door. "I should get moving too. Almost time for Agnes's lunch." He'd been a restaurant manager in Boston and hoped to start one of his own, a seafood joint, here in Eastport.

Which was another story; I had my doubts about it.

"At least she's eating well," Ellie told him approvingly.

But then George's remark struck me. "Stuff? I thought you were working out at the marine center, putting in the new dock."

"Weather's too bad." He took his slicker from its hook in the hall and draped it over Ellie's shoulders.

"So I got started on those red ants over to Cory Williams's. Christ in a handcart, but he's got a case. Never saw so many."

Decades ago some big schooner must've come in here with stowaways: European fire ants. Furiously aggressive and equipped with a fierce formic acid bite, the ants had multiplied.

"And you know," George went on, tucking Ellie's hair under the earflaps of his sou'wester, "Cory's trying to raise little pigs. Pot-bellied pigs, sell 'em as pets. Says people keep 'em in their houses like dogs. Smart as dogs, too, he says."

At this Prill and Monday got up from the dog bed where they were lying together and left the room, which was probably only a coincidence. Meanwhile, with that day-glo yellow slicker and black rainhat laid on over the rest of her outfit, Ellie appeared to be wearing an entire storewide clearance sale.

"I'll make the cop call," I told her quietly. "And you call me if anything happens." The baby, I meant, and she promised to.

"So Cory," George went on, "has to eliminate the ants."

Unlike the rest of us, who doused ourselves with bug dope in summer and with cortisone ointment on the many occasions when bug dope didn't work. Boric acid sometimes got rid of them, though, and was unlikely to have been the stuff that eliminated Hector.

For that my money was still on strychnine. The awful grin on his face was a giveaway. So I felt better.

Temporarily. "Turned out, Cory's got another problem, too, with all the feed and the straw and the refuse," George added.

"Yup," Will agreed, pulling on a windbreaker.

"Although he keeps those pigs so clean you could lie down next to 'em and sleep. He's set up such nice pens for 'em, you might not mind it."

I would mind. But it was what George had said that had my attention now. "Other problem?" I asked.

George checked his pocket for his key ring, pulled out a massive one loaded with the fifty or so labeled keys he used on a regular basis, working around the island for people. It also held a truck key as backup for the one in the vehicle's visor.

"Seems no matter how clean you are with 'em, if you keep 'em outdoors," George said, "the feed spills, coupla grains here and a coupla grains there, pretty soon you've also got—"

Ellie looked at me and I looked at her, and I could feel our hearts sinking together like anchors. Because she'd seen Gosling too, and I knew she'd have come to the same conclusion as I had.

Strychnine is controlled, now. For all practical purposes the ordinary person can't even buy it. But once upon a time many households had a tin of the stuff. People used it to kill . . .

"Rats," said George, stepping out into the storm.

My sentiments exactly.